Killer WASPs

Killer WASPs

A KILLER WASPs MYSTERY

AMY KORMAN

WITNESS
IMPULSE
An Imprint of HarperCollinsPublishers

EPub Edition SEPTEMBER 2014 ISBN: 9780062357847
Print Edition ISBN: 9780062357854

10 9 8 7 6 5 4 3

For John and my family.

Chapter 1

"YOU FOUND BARCLAY Shields after someone tried to kill him last night?"

I didn't have all that much information about what had happened to Barclay Shields, local builder of shoddy mini-mansions that are about as well constructed as your average game-show set. But I knew from long experience that Bootsie McElvoy would never leave until she had put me through a Guantanamo-style interrogation that would stop just short of waterboarding.

"I did find him." I sighed as Bootsie flung open the screen door to my antiques store, The Striped Awning, and charged toward a little French chair in front of my desk. "How did you hear?"

"More like, how would I *not* hear?" responded Bootsie, her sky-blue eyes bulging with intensity. "Let's start with the police report," she said, rummaging in her canvas tote bag, and emerging with a sheaf of papers, which she brandished triumphantly. "I have a lot of questions."

I sat down at my in-the-style-of-Chippendale desk, pushing aside a stack of paperwork—actually, a pile of unpaid bills— resigned to being grilled like a rib-eye.

What a waste of a gorgeous, sunny May morning. All around Bryn Mawr, lilacs were blooming in front yards, drivers were tooling by in convertibles, and women were happily pulling out their summer clothes—which in Bootsie's case meant a pair of flowered Talbots shorts, a Lacoste shirt, and pink sandals embroidered with whales. My dog Waffles, a freckled, drooling basset hound with an oversize belly, a permanently soulful expression, and an addiction to Beggin' Strips, wagged happily at Bootsie from his bed in the front of the store. He likes to sit up there, close to the tall front windows, where he can chew his rawhide bones and check out passing poodles.

Bootsie ignored Waffles—she doesn't believe in any dogs that aren't Labs, which are the preferred breed of her L.L. Bean–catalog family. Bootsie *defines* preppy: Even her marriage is preppy, with her two adorable toddlers, a chintz-filled brick Colonial, and tennis matches galore.

Bootsie, who graduated from high school with me fifteen years ago, is six feet tall, has chin-length blond hair and a permanent tennis tan, and is married to a former Duke lacrosse star named Will, whom she met through her equally bronzed, blond brothers. Bootsie and I don't have much in common, but we've stayed friends over the years—she works just down the street from my store, at the *Bryn Mawr Gazette*, the local newspaper in our small town outside of Philadelphia, where she covers both real estate and charity events. Basically, she writes about gossip.

Working at the newspaper is perfect for Bootsie, because she's incredibly nosy. She has a network of family members and friends placed around the suburbs of Philly who funnel her information each day. When she's not on her cell phone, she's working the aisles of the Publix, the liquor store, and the post office. She's honestly pretty talented at intelligence gathering: Bootsie once called me in the middle of the night to tell me that our friend Holly Jones was getting divorced, which Holly herself didn't even know until the next morning.

"You probably remember Will's cousin Louis from our Christmas party," Bootsie went on. "Tall? Blond? Big on golf and skiing?" This described every member of the McElvoy clan, but I nodded agreement.

"Louis is a lawyer, and he's defending Barclay in a lawsuit about those town houses Barclay built that fell into the giant sinkhole. And Louis got a call from Barclay's wife at one-thirty this morning about the attack on Barclay," said Bootsie triumphantly, pleased that her husband had such a useful person for a cousin. "Of course, the police called Barclay's wife to let her know about him being attacked, even though Barclay and his wife are in the middle of an epic divorce. So, anyway, Louis got the police report faxed over, which said that a Kristin Clark—*you*, that is"—with this, Bootsie pointed a tennis-tanned finger at me—"found Barclay after he'd been bashed in the head with something heavy. Like a hammer."

I nodded glumly, and shuddered at the memory of the inert mass of real estate developer, prone under a hydrangea. It all seemed unreal, and the memory was especially blurry given that it had been made late at night, in the dark, after three glasses of Barolo wine at a party. Waffles, sensing my discomfort, gave a sympathetic whine.

"Obviously, this is going to be big news," Bootsie continued happily, not looking upset in the least at the thought of Mr. Shields's recent head injury, "because Barclay Shields is loathed by pretty much everyone in Bryn Mawr, the entire Philadelphia area, and even as far as Wilmington, Atlantic City, and Lancaster County. Even Amish people hate Barclay! And it's not like people are whacked in the head with blunt objects around here very often."

True on both counts, I thought to myself. Thanks to his habit of cramming as many townhomes as possible onto tiny plots and his zestful overcharging of unsuspecting buyers, Barclay was one of the biggest and least popular builders around Philly. (And I do mean big: Even in the dark last night, I could see that the man weighed a good two hundred and seventy-five pounds.) In addition to the man's real estate notoriety, a violent attack in Bryn Mawr is unheard of: In downtown Philly, people get beaten to a pulp all the time, but things are pretty quiet in the suburbs. Bryn Mawr is where people live in charming old stone houses, play tennis, and break out the vodka tonics at five-thirty every night. A dog show or a restaurant opening constitutes big news. For instance, a new place called Restaurant Gianni had been front-page fodder this week for Bootsie's newspaper. Actually, Wednesday's entire front page had been devoted to the chef, the fabulous decor, the chef's girlfriend—who happened to be a decorator and had designed the place—the wine list, and his recipe for cappellini con vongole.

Bootsie and I had both been at Restaurant Gianni's opening party the night before, and it was after the party that I had found Barclay, right across the street from my house, while I'd been taking Waffles for a quick late-night stroll. Barclay had been bleeding from the head when I'd last seen him, but definitely alive when police and medics had arrived and whisked him into an ambulance headed for Bryn Mawr Hospital, if you can use the word "whisk" to describe hoisting a man the size of a vending machine.

"I called the hospital an hour ago, and as luck would have it, our old babysitter Jeannie was at the nurses' station"—Bootsie has a seemingly endless supply of nursing-student nannies—"and she told me that not only did Barclay make it through the night, he's awake. Awake and eating—he ordered in a salami-and-egg hoagie from the diner this morning.

"But none of that is important," Bootsie finished. "What matters is: Who do you think hit him?"

"You must be talking about my husband," squeaked a petite blond woman from the doorway, in an accent that rang with the unmistakable tones of South Jersey. "Can you believe the police had the nerve"—in Jersey, that's pronounced "noive"—"to ask me where I was last night? Like I have the upper-body strength to knock Barclay out!"

She had on four-inch heels, purple jeans, and a swoopy Roberto Cavalli multicolored silk blouse that retailed for seven hundred dollars. I knew this only because I'd seen the same blouse in my friend Holly's closet, with the Neiman Marcus tags still dangling from it. Behind her, a massive Cadillac Escalade was idling in the no-parking zone in front of my shop.

Clearly, this apparition was Sophie Shields, aka Mrs. Barclay Shields. Bootsie stared at her, her mouth agape and her eyes registering gossip nirvana.

"Besides, I was with my Pilates instructor all night last night—Gerda's from Austria, and she lives in our guest room—and then before that I was at Restaurant Gianni's party, so I've got an alibi," Sophie Shields chattered on. "You two were at the party, too, right?" Sophie said to us, a gleam of recognition in her puppylike brown eyes. I could only nod back at her, too stunned to speak. Her voice had the timbre of Fran Drescher mixed with the intonation of Tony Soprano, all in a package the size of your average fourth-grader.

"I thought ya looked familiar! Anyway, the police told me you found him, and then I tracked you down to this place. So I wanted to come by and thank you for finding him," she continued. "You saved me a bundle. If he dies before the divorce is finalized, I'm screwed. I need him alive! He hasn't signed anything yet, except some papers that cut me out of his will if he croaks before the divorce is done."

"That's too bad," I said weakly.

"Cute store," she said, looking around at the pieces in my shop, which range from little French sofas to English dining tables to mid-century lamps. "This is like a museum of, you know, *old stuff*!"

"Thank you," I said uncertainly, getting up to make sure Waffles didn't tackle Mrs. Shields in his overly friendly way, since he definitely outweighed her, and was already huffing over toward her happily. I took hold of his collar before he could drool on her shoes.

"My ex hates antiques," squawked Sophie. Looking around again, her small face broke out in a smile. "And you know what, since we're splitting up, I can buy as many as I want! And this junk—I mean, these things—really would add an old Philly feel to the place. I gotta bring my decorator back here. Well, when I hire a decorator, I'll bring him here."

"Thank you," I said again, hoping I could show her around the shop a little. Sophie was clearly the Holy Grail of Retail: the Revenge Shopper. Just then, though, incessant honking erupted from the Escalade waiting at the curb, and a woman with incredibly muscular shoulders in the passenger's seat gestured sternly at Mrs. Shields to hurry it up and get back in the car.

"That's Gerda," whispered Sophie, looking scared and waving at her passenger in an attempt to placate her. "But anyway, I really do like your store." She teetered indecisively on her heels for a second, while Gerda gave another thunderous blast on the Cadillac's horn.

"What the hell!" Sophie finally shrieked. "I'll take all of it. I have to meet with my lawyers in five minutes, and then I got Pilates at eleven-thirty, so I can't dick around looking through all this stuff. Just wrap up the whole store, all the tchotchkes and the furniture—the whole nine yards. Here's my Visa card. I'll have a truck pick it up tomorrow!"

AFTER I'D DULY recorded Sophie's Visa number, she, Gerda, and the SUV whooshed away, Bootsie and I high-fived each other, and I did an impromptu happy dance for a few seconds. Bootsie knows I've been struggling to make rent on The Striped Awning (and, well, pay my AmEx bill, too), since I inherited the store from my grandparents last year. The contents of the whole store—sold! I started calculating in my head how much money I'd make, and took out a notepad to start listing my inventory and totaling the bill. I turned over the sign on the door to read "Closed."

Unfortunately, though, Bootsie didn't take the hint.

"Well, now we know that Barclay Shields's wife claims she didn't attack her husband, and she has reason to want him alive. Why were you wandering around across the street at midnight, anyway?" she asked.

This was a good question, because I'm not really a midnight kind of person, and Bootsie knows it. I'm more of a pajamas-at-8:30-p.m. kind of person. "It also says here in the report that you were with someone, the guy who made the emergency call when the body turned up. Named"—she consulted her paperwork—"Mike Woodford. Who is *that*?"

"Is Woodford his last name?" I blurted out. I had never met this guy Mike before last night, and had only been in his company for about thirty minutes before we'd stumbled onto Barclay Shields. And I really didn't want to talk about said person with Bootsie, because, truth be told, I had been slightly drunk when I'd met him last night, but if memory served, he was very cute. Bootsie was tapping her foot while I considered all this; I could feel my face turning fuchsia, and I started hedging.

"Mike works across the street from my house at the Potts estate," I told Bootsie. "Waffles needed to go out, and then we bumped into this guy Mike, and then the three of us found Barclay Shields," I said, heading into the back storeroom to grab some newspaper and boxes to begin wrapping up my entire store.

"Well, I better start packing all the silver and china!" I yelled cheerfully over my shoulder. "Thanks for coming by!"

"You took the dog for a walk that late?" demanded Bootsie.

"Well, I don't think it was *that* late," I said, returning with my boxes and resisting an urge to scream.

"Yes, it was. It was 12:04 a.m. when Mike Woodford called 911 and said he'd found a body at Sanderson," she sang back at me, brandishing her fax, which I was tempted to grab and rip to shreds. "It's on the police report." Bootsie's a good person at heart, but her persistence was taking on the quality of Barbara Walters during an Oscar night interview. "And why were you walking that mutt over at Sanderson, anyway?" she prompted.

Sanderson, an estate in Bryn Mawr, is home to the blue-blooded Potts family, which has, amazingly, kept three hundred acres of valuable real estate intact as an exceptionally lush farm around their 1920s stone manor house. There's a barn, a ballroom, a greenhouse filled with rare orchids, and a library that holds thousands of rare books, and all of this happens to be across the street from my tiny, slightly creaky old cottage, which is, no doubt, a blot on the landscape in the eyes of the Potts family.

Waffles, sensing that he was part of this story, went around my desk to Bootsie and pawed at her leg, then unleashed a pint of drool on her knee. Bootsie glared at him, and rose to leave.

I love that dog.

"Why were we at Sanderson?" I repeated. "Well, Waffles really had to go. You know him—he bolts sometimes, and I can barely hang on to the leash. He took off for the bushes at Sanderson last night. Sometimes he just wants to, um, do his business there!" This was mostly true. Waffles does sprint to Sanderson sometimes, but he doesn't do his business just anywhere. He's partial to a certain bush in my backyard where he enjoys complete privacy, and if desperate during the workday, he'll make use of a grassy nook behind the store. He'd never sully the gorgeous lawns of Sanderson.

Waffles whined, then went over to his dog bed to lie down. He knew he had just been dissed.

Bootsie laughed, picked up her tote, and strode in her whale-print sandals toward the door—finally. She even acknowledged Waffles by nodding at him on the way out. "That dog's got good taste. I love that he likes to take a crap at Sanderson!"

Chapter 2

So I HADN'T told Bootsie every little detail about the night before, I thought, as I continued taking inventory of the store, working from front to back, starting with an over-the-top gilded console table in the front window that I had accessorized with an antique mirror and a pair of pretty vintage sconces. I'd been honest with the police (make that singular—Bryn Mawr only has one full-time policeman, Officer Walt) about the events of the previous evening, which was the important thing. The little bit I hadn't told Bootsie had nothing to do with Barclay Shields. It had to do with the instant crush I'd developed on Mike Woodford.

The full story was that yesterday after work, Waffles and I had gotten home feeling hungry, tired, and irrationally angry at the store for not doing better and making more money. I'd actually berated a chair (1940s slipper chair, found at a flea market in New Hope) for not selling as I'd locked up. Usually, walking into my cottage, with its ivy-covered front porch and gabled windows, felt reassuring. I loved my house, which I'd inherited upon my grandfather's death last year, but given the neighborhood's hefty real estate taxes, I wouldn't be able to afford to live there much longer if the store didn't suddenly start doing more business.

This I had found out earlier in the day in a depressing call from The Striped Awning's landlord, a normally kindly man named Mr. Webster, who'd sounded quite pissy as he reminded me that I'd been late with my rent payments for every one of the past six months . . . and that I still owed him for this month. Unfortunately, business had been dismal over the past twelve months. My grandparents, who had been married fifty-six years and died within months of each other, ran the store for decades. They'd made it seem effortless to run a small business, but I didn't seem to possess the same equanimity. Lately, I'd found myself contemplating harebrained schemes just to lure customers inside, and was currently debating placing a sandwich board on the sidewalk in front of the shop proclaiming "Free Mojito Thursdays!" Maybe, I thought hopefully, I could become an authorized Powerball ticket vendor. Then again, Powerball doesn't seem to come around more than a few times a year.

I'd spent most of my thirty-three years working at the store, helping out weekends and in the summers during high school, and the presence of my grandparents there, cheerfully presiding over a quirky inventory of everything from Indian tea tables to English buffets, had always been an anchor, especially after my parents had moved away from Bryn Mawr when I was seventeen. My father, a math professor—he possesses a rogue logical gene never before or since found in the Clark family DNA—had been offered a job as head of the math department at Central Arizona College, in Winkelman, Arizona, the same month I graduated from high school. Just like that, he and Mom had gone southwestern, moving to the desert without a backward glance. Mom had opened a small art gallery, and the two had embraced a lifestyle of adobe and 110-degree days with enthusiasm.

Winkelman had some amazing mountains surrounding it, and more than its share of hot guys, including one Joe Manganiello look-alike who worked in a local quarry and with whom I shared several steamy make-out sessions during a two-month fling. But in my opinion, Winkelman bordered on the too-rustic. Actual restaurants included Antlers, a local watering hole, and the Butcher Hook (where I met the aforementioned hot quarry guy at Rockin' Rib Night, held every Thursday).

Even the excellent margaritas at Papi Juan's, in nearby Vega, Arizona, where the management wasn't overly concerned about whether patrons were of legal drinking age, couldn't numb the pangs of homesickness. I sweltered through three months in Winkelman the summer after high school, then immediately fled back to Bryn Mawr, where I helped put myself through college working at The Striped Awning, spending holidays and vacations out in Arizona with my parents. While Bootsie embarked on her newspaper job after Duke, and my closest friend,

Holly Jones, focused on spending a hefty monthly stipend from her dad, who's loaded, I couldn't imagine a career other than running the store—despite repeated remonstrations by Holly that it was a "furniture graveyard" constituting a dusty social death. This was pretty much true. I'd found myself involved with several bescruffed carpenters and artists over the past decade, most of whom had gone through an early midlife crisis and moved to Southeast Asia a few months after I'd started dating them. "There's something about you that sends guys running to the other side of the world," Bootsie had told me recently. "No offense."

Despite my epic-fail romances, though, I sincerely enjoyed running The Striped Awning. I loved attending estate sales and auctions to unearth pieces to sell at the shop, then polishing, painting, and restoring these treasures, and watching customers fall in love with a funky chandelier or vintage mirror. In my grandparents' day, the store had been successful enough to support a quiet, low-key lifestyle, in which the biggest splurge was their membership at Bryn Mawr Country Club. Until the 1990s, the Main Line—the suburban area anchored by Bryn Mawr and named for the well-traveled commuter train lines that ferried lawyers and bankers into Center City Philadelphia—was a fairly subdued community. Everyone knew one another, and socialized with no great distinction in social strata. At any Friday night gin-and-fondue-fueled cocktail party in the 1970s, you could find members of the Potts family, who reigned over the lordly grounds of Sanderson, side by side with longtime residents such as my grandparents, who had been in Bryn Mawr forever, but had no great wealth or social status. But over the past two decades, thousands of new homes had been built on the Main Line, and its residents had gotten decidedly more glitzy (this was largely due to the fact that a sumptuous Neiman Marcus had opened in the 1990s, just a few miles away off the main highway to Philly).

Business at The Striped Awning had slowly fallen off as new houses constructed by people like Barclay Shields rose up around Bryn Mawr. The new houses were centered around vaulted "great rooms," and featured kitchens bigger than Barbados and bedrooms the size of hockey rinks. These mansions-on-steroids required giant furniture, not antiques, and consequently, my shop was foundering. Holly would happily lend me money to help pay the mortgage or help keep the store afloat—no questions asked—but I'd rather die than accept it.

Anyway, Mr. Webster had strongly suggested that I pay the rent owed on the store in a timely fashion, or eviction might ensue. I couldn't think of any way to raise funds other than taking out a mortgage on my inherited cottage, which would eventually only add to my financial woes.

Despite the warmth of the evening, I shivered as I looked around my beloved home while Waffles inhaled his dinner of kibble. While the house itself is tiny, the property is beautiful. With its location right across from Sanderson, the acre-and-a-half lot is a builder's dream, even in the current dreary economy. Someone like Barclay Shields could buy it, tear down my place, and bang out a massive new mansion in less than six months.

I felt like crying at this gloomy prospect, so I did what anyone would do under the circumstances. I went to a party and got drunk.

"This is *not* a Gap kind of event," Holly had told me when she showed up at six-thirty and announced that I was going with her to the opening of Restaurant Gianni. (I started to defend myself, but then realized I was in fact wearing a yellow sundress bought on final sale at the Gap for $17.99.) Holly was holding a pink, knee-length Trina Turk dress in a hanging bag in one hand and a pair of high-heeled sandals in the other, both of which she handed to me as she ordered me upstairs to straighten my wavy hair. Her best guy friend, Joe Delafield, the area's self-proclaimed foremost interior designer, came through my back door right behind her.

Joe had arrived at our high school in tenth grade after his family had relocated from New York City, and within a week convinced school administrators to let him repaint the student lounge a natty, Billy Baldwin–ish chocolate brown. This was the birth of a stellar design career, during which Joe attended Parsons and interned at Philly's most insultingly pricey decorating firm, owned by a trio of willowy blond socialites who have convinced many a Main Line couple that not one stick of furniture can be installed until the clients and decorators have made at least four field trips to the Clignancourt furniture market in Paris on the client's dime. Joe's currently running his own design business, with Holly as his star client. And truthfully, his sense of color is unerring: Tonight, he had on a pale green checked sport coat, a striped pink-and-green shirt, and impeccable khakis. Joe may be the only straight decorator in the tri-state area, and he's definitely the best-dressed straight guy anywhere.

"Gianni's party is going to be obscene!" announced Joe, who immediately started rearranging my furniture, which he always does whenever he comes over. "Three truckloads of illegal baby lobster arrived at the restaurant an hour ago from Maine, and they're grilling as we speak. Get dressed."

I ran upstairs, did my hair, loaded on as much extra makeup as I could, and put on my borrowed Trina Turk (two hundred and seventy-eight dollars, according to the tag that still hung from it). I felt better immediately. It's amazing what berry-colored lip gloss can do for your mood—I mean, imagine the percentage of women walloped by major depression if they'd never invented makeup, I thought, as I looked in the mirror. I knew men would slobber over Holly at the party tonight in the manner of Waffles presented with a leg of lamb. With my brown eyes, small nose, and long wavy brown hair, I'll never be able to inhabit the gorgeous-tanned-blond realm in which Holly wafts through life, but with a ton of mascara double-wanded onto my lashes and my hair free of its usual ponytail, I felt quite festive in my borrowed pink frock. I'm not as tall or model-skinny as Holly, but I'm lucky to be able to fit into most of her dresses, since I've been so broke lately that I've been living on cans of Progresso soup.

Joe pulled into the immaculate, beige-pebbled driveway at Gianni at seven-twenty, while Holly checked her makeup. She had on a short black Jason Wu dress with skinny straps that looked amazing on her, since she subsists on champagne and shrimp cocktail. "You look great!" I told her as we got out of the car.

"I know," she said blithely. "It's because of the divorce. I feel horrible, but I look amazing." I've noticed this among everyone I know who's in the middle of bitterly dividing up marital assets amid mutual recriminations: Anyone going through a divorce tends to look fantastic, thereby proving to their ex how little the split is bothering them.

"Well, at least they didn't totally ruin the place," said Joe, as he tossed the keys to a valet parker and eyed the restaurant's elegantly weathered stone façade, its doors flanked by potted lemon trees, its French windows anchored open, and a jazzy bossa nova percolating from an indoor/outdoor sound system. More accurately, Restaurant Gianni—named, of course, for its chef/owner, Gianni Brunello—looked absolutely beautiful. You'd never know that until a few months ago, it had been the old firehouse, a stone and stucco building built in the early 1900s, with eaves and a slate roof. Bryn Mawr's volunteer fire company had just moved to a new, state-of-the-art building over by the post office, and now, thanks to some artful masonry restoration and the addition of new dark green shutters flanking floor-to-ceiling windows, the old firehouse resembled an Umbrian villa. The level of manicured, obsessive-compulsive perfection in evidence was truly impressive: The circular driveway of tiny stones looked as if someone raked it every five minutes, whether it needed it or not.

"I would have gone with a cerulean blue for the front door," said Joe, gesturing dismissively at the spectacular scene before us while the ridiculously delicious scent of grilling shellfish wafted our way. Clearly, since he hadn't been awarded the job of designing Gianni's restaurant, Joe had come to the party only to catalog the nonexistent flaws in its decor. "And they should have added about seven hundred more of those dinky lemon trees and a vintage Etruscan trellis to form an arbor . . . what is that *racket*?"

Blood-chilling, horrific screams had erupted from the restaurant. The teenage valet parkers looked scared.

"That's the chef, having one of his tantrums," said Holly, tipping a valet ten bucks as she dashed up the smooth stone steps to the front door of the restaurant. "Hurry, we don't want to miss it."

We all rushed into a beautiful terra-cotta colored room lit by a huge old wooden chandelier, with a long mahogany bar and lots of white-cloth tables in a roomy dining area. Over by the bar stood the eponymous Chef Gianni, who had arrived five years ago from a verdant corner of Tuscany to conquer the Philadelphia dining scene. A slim, muscular man dressed in chef's whites above the waist and MC Hammer–style parachute pants below, he had a glistening bald dome and spoke with an accent as thick as a Parma ham.

"What the fuck is this?" screamed the chef, his crimson face nose-to-nose with two cowering, well-dressed young men, waving what appeared to be an invoice at them. As usual, Gianni wore orange Crocs in the manner of Mario Batali, his culinary idol, and had his sleeves rolled up to reveal intricate tattoos including the Italian flag, the distinctive boot-shaped map of Italy, and a lavishly rendered façade of St. Peter's Basilica along his forearms.

I'd never actually met Chef Gianni, but he'd been anointed one of America's rising-star chefs by a top food magazine just a month ago. Deeply tanned, he wears several gold earrings in each lobe, and at thirty-eight, has a proclivity for dating women in their twenties. His downtown Philadelphia restaurant, Palazzo, occupies the penthouse of a luxurious hotel in Society Hill, decorated with lacquered black walls and bright red banquettes upon which patrons enjoy forty-eight-dollar pastas. Gianni, who has the touchy temperament of a star TV chef in the making, likes to threaten to dangle the busboys over the edge of Palazzo's balcony while techno music pulsates in the dining room, which customers absolutely love. "He's so *mercurial!*" they invariably giggle.

Given that Holly happens to the only daughter of a billionaire—seriously, her father is in the chicken business, and recently out-Perdued the Perdues—she visits Palazzo frequently. Joe does a fair bit of business with clients over dinner at Palazzo, too. They were definitely on the list for tonight's party, while I filled the "And Guest" slot on their invitations.

"You know those guys he's screaming at, right?" Joe whispered to me. "They're the hot florists of the moment, Colkett and Colkett. No one knows if they're brothers, cousins, or if they're a couple. Very talented. They use lots of fruits and vegetables in their work. Remember when Holly used them for her Non-Valentine Valentine's Party last winter? Their big thing is that they're incredibly overpriced."

"I love the Colketts!" Holly sang out, giving the florists a wave.

Normally, Holly evokes rapturous greetings in all men, women, and even cats and dogs, but the Colketts didn't seem to notice her. They were cringing nervously next to two topiaries the size of Volkswagens made of artichokes, pomegranates, and lemons that they'd just wheeled in. Chef Gianni studied their bill, ranting in Italian.

Bills were a sore point at the moment with Gianni. According to the front-page stories about him in Bootsie's newspaper, he'd spent months combing the hill towns of Italy for antiques for the restaurant with his young decorator-slash-girlfriend. This had proven to be a very expensive extended vacation/buying trip, which resulted in some rather testy meetings with his investors when he'd returned home with that deep tan, a lot of Versace luggage, and crates full of overpriced furniture.

As we watched, transfixed, the chef glared at the bill, tore it in two, stuck both halves into a lit votive candle, and threw the flaming paper on the glossy restaurant floor, where it ignited a tablecloth and came perilously close to setting aflame a very pricey-looking silk curtain. As the flames leaped higher, a stunned-looking waiter ran over, snatched the burning tablecloth, and ran out the front door to the driveway as smoke billowed behind him. We watched the hapless waiter stomp out the fire, but then flames began to lick the edges of his long white apron, too, so he flung the apron onto a flagstone walk-way, where the little bonfire appeared to die down.

Crisis averted. Sort of.

"Six thousand dollars," screamed Gianni at the Colketts. "You think it is okay to charge Chef Gianni six thousand dollars for flowers?" The florists looked at each other and giggled nervously, the kind of laughter that comes from near-hysterical terror. The chef turned purple, tore off his apron, and stomped up and down on it. He ripped a piece of round red fruit from a topiary and beaned it at the florists, who ducked, but one didn't duck fast enough and screamed in pain when he took the object, which appeared to be a dried pomegranate, in the ear. "Yesterday, I got an estimate from florist who says she can do all the flowers for five hundred bucks a week. You charge Chef Gianni eight times that!"

"Actually, six thousand is twelve times that," pointed out the chef's girlfriend, who'd appeared from the back of the restaurant, and was languidly rearranging her long hair and lighting a cigarette. I had met her once before—she'd gone to design school with Joe. I couldn't under-stand how this girl put up with the perpetually angry chef. His cooking skills seemed to be his main selling point, and she didn't look like a big eater. Maybe she liked the trips to Italy.

"Not at all, Chef," ventured one of the flower guys. "These topiaries will last forever. They're really quite a bargain. They're *freeze-dried*."

"They are bullshit!" The chef's face was turning a color that could only mean an imminent stroke, but just then, a small horde of guests crowded in through the front door, and a waiter started passing glasses of Barolo, which we all grabbed and started gulping down. Suddenly, Chef Gianni snapped back to normal, noticing that the party had actually commenced, that the candles were lit, and that baby lamb chops, cheeses, and olives had been piled upon a lavish buffet. The waiters surreptitiously repositioned the topiaries so that the bald spots didn't show.

Gianni straightened his cuffs, started breathing again, and spied Holly in her teeny black dress. His mood totally changed. Very bipolar.

"Holly Jones!" said the chef. His face paled to magenta, and he ran over to kiss Holly's hand. "You are gorgeous!"

In this second, I suddenly understood Gianni's charisma. His shaved head and tattoos took on a sexy, bad-boy quality. He began lavishly greeting women ranging in age from their thirties into their eighties with an athletic swagger. When smiling attentively and doling out triple kisses, he made each woman feel like he'd love to rip off her clothes, if only they were alone together. *So that's what his girlfriend saw in him!*

Dozens of people were crowding in behind us, and a minute later, I lost Holly and Joe in the haze of Chanel No. 5 and knots of well-dressed men bragging about their golf handicaps, so I made my way to the bar, hoping that the contraband lobster tails would appear soon.

"Two vodkas," I heard a voice growl behind me. I peeked around and found that this was the not-very-feminine intonation of my neighbor, Honey Potts of Sanderson, a seventyish woman dressed in a blazer, white shirt, and khakis, her skin the leathery texture of George Hamilton's after a month in Mexico. Everyone on the Main Line knows who Honey Potts is—she's a grande dame in the old tradition, and she's always front-page in the *Bryn Mawr Gazette*, judging a local dog show or leading a garden tour. Honey, her nickname since childhood (real name: Henrietta), didn't really fit her anymore, since she's more intimidating than sweet, but then, these WASPy names never make any sense. I mean, who would name a girl Bootsie?

Next to Honey was her best friend since childhood, Mariellen Merriwether. Mariellen was slimmer, taller, blonder, and wearing a pink dress and beige heels. And pearls—always pearls. There was something about Mariellen that made you feel instantly inferior, which it seemed was the point of her existence. She lived on a smaller property than the adjoining Sanderson, but it was still huge by any standard, consisting of fifteen acres with a charming old farmhouse and a horse barn, where her prizewinning gelding Norman lived in Ritz-Carlton-like conditions. According to Bootsie, who'd attended charity functions chez Merriwether, the entire house was covered in toile, and what wasn't toile was monogrammed, including her toilet paper and ice cubes. Norman's barn was almost as cozily fitted out, and Norman himself dined on organic hay and carrots from Mariellen's personal gardens.

"Well, they've ruined the firehouse, but at least there's free-flowing Stoli," Honey groused to Mariellen as she flagged down a waiter in the candlelight, waving her already empty glass. Just then, the minuscule Maine lobsters made their appearance on the buffet on massive platters, and a small stampede ensued. It seemed that even the wealthiest Philadelphians can get themselves into a lather over free lobster.

"Look at all these vulgar *trays* of lobster they're serving—so Caligula," sniffed Mariellen to her friend, as I finally got to the front of the line and tonged three of the tiny crustacean tails onto a small cocktail plate.

"Let me finish my drink, then I'm ready to hit it. I've got to get home for *Dancing with the Stars*," growled Honey, who snagged her cocktail from the returning waiter, forked in a quick plate of lobster, and then headed for the door, Mariellen on her heels.

As for the Colketts, they were out on the patio, shakily clutching drinks and sharing a Marlboro Light before coming back into the bar for a refill. Now that the party was under way, music was pumping, and cocktails were being lavished on guests by the apron-wearing waiters; all in all, it was a pretty spectacular scene. Chef Gianni, who had clearly entered the "up" phase of his rapid-cycle manic episode, schmoozed euphorically with his guests, his bald head gleaming and earrings jingling as he did a little shimmy dance around the room. The room was so crowded that I still couldn't locate Holly and Joe in the crowd. The Colketts seemed to disappear from the patio as well, but who could blame them after the trauma they'd endured at the chef's hands?

Just as Honey and Mariellen made their exit, I saw through the restaurant's front windows that Bootsie had arrived. She threw her Range Rover keys to the valet guys and greeted Mariellen and Honey enthusiastically, which Honey ignored, and Mariellen acknowledged with an air kiss that stopped about three feet from Bootsie's cheek. I wobbled out on my borrowed high heels to the restaurant's pretty brick patio to watch Honey get in her car. Mariellen rode shotgun, while Honey took the wheel, still drinking her cocktail and munching a handful of baby lamb chops, and steered the car out of Gianni's driveway.

"Honey Potts took a roadie!" Bootsie shouted over the crowd to me, impressed.

SEVERAL HOURS AND glasses of Barolo later, Joe dropped me off at home, and I let myself in the side gate from my driveway, fumbled for the house key I keep under the flowerpot by the back door, and stumbled into the kitchen. Waffles, who'd been asleep on the couch, got up and ran over to greet me. Then he went to the door, turned around, and looked at me with an expression that said, *I gotta go.*

"One second!" I told him drunkenly, as I ran upstairs, exchanged the sky-high heels for flip-flops, came back down and searched for several minutes for his leash, which it turned out he'd buried in the couch cushions. It was dark outside, except for a half moon above, a porch light at the house next door, and a few stars. Unfortunately, instead of heading for his usual bathroom area behind a leafy laurel bush near my back fence, Waffles headed for the gate and gave me Sad Eyes.

It was really too late for a walk. I pointed at his favored shrubbery, and suggested he do what he needed to do. Sad Eyes continued. Guilt gripped me through my boozy haze as I looked at his downcast, droopy face.

"Five minutes," I said, relenting. The dog totally has my number. "Up and down the driveway, maybe a quick trip to the lilacs on the other side of the yard. That's it." More Sad Eyes—which it turned out were bullshit, because as soon as I opened it, Waffles tore out of the gate like Seabiscuit, with me hanging on to the leash and running as fast as I could in flip-flops and in my tipsy state. Waffles *looks* slow, given that he's short and portly, with huge ears and goofy, freckled legs, but he can haul ass when he wants to.

This was one of those times, and he tore down the driveway, ears flying, tail wagging, and barely slowed at the street. Luckily, since it was now closing in on 11:30 p.m., there was no one passing by, so we didn't get hit by any cars as we darted onto the grounds of Sanderson. The estate has an old and very pretty entranceway with a limestone archway over the driveway, but there are no gates barring visitors from the property. The front part of the property runs for a full half mile bordering the road, with beautiful old oaks and chestnuts providing screening and shade, and just behind these woods are cow pastures. The Potts family is very big on cows, though I couldn't see any right now—they must have lumbered inside for the night. We set off on a little path with wind gently rustling the leaves above us, the moon lighting the way, and Waffles chugging along, all excited and breathing like a little Darth Vader.

The Pottses' cow barn was a quarter mile away, in the direction of the main house, but set off by a paddock and a small wooded area. Like Norman, Mariellen Merriwether's horse, the cows lived in what I was sure were cushy, upscale accommodations—at least they had a home that wasn't about to be sold out from under them, I thought sadly. Waffles and I would have to go stay with Holly, who hates dogs, and thinks Waffles is especially useless. In the midst of my self-pity, I noticed Waffles had paused on the trail to wag at something.

"Hey, are you lost?" said a man's voice from somewhere in the darkened trail in front of me. I screamed and jumped a few feet into the air. Waffles huffed over happily to get petted by the unseen guy, who bent over and scratched the dog's velvety ears. This seemed like a good sign. Evil killers who lurk on fancy estates don't usually stop to pet dogs.

"I live across the street," I said nervously, "and I was just taking my dog for a quick walk, and he ran over here." Clearly, I was trespassing. But maybe this guy was trespassing, too, which was scary. Or would have been, if I hadn't had those three glasses of wine.

"Late walk," he said, sounding amused, and coming closer while Waffles sniffed his knees assiduously and my eyes adjusted enough to the dimness to see some of the man in front of me. While the moon didn't afford much in the way of lighting, I could see the guy was wearing jeans, a T-shirt, and old running shoes, and had dark hair and was maybe five-nine. He was kind of cute. At least, he looked like he was cute from what I could see—he had a scruffy beard, a dark tan, and seemed to be in his late thirties. He smelled very nicely of soap. And like something else. What *was* that smell? It was earthy, natural, a little funky, but pleasant. I'd smelled it on really hot July days wafting over from Sanderson . . . it smelled like a country road in the summertime . . .

It was eau de cow.

"Do you work here?" I asked, relieved. Honey Potts wouldn't hire a homicidal maniac, I was pretty sure. She probably inherited her servants, *Downton Abbey* style. This guy had doubtless been born into the Potts household, the son of the family chambermaid and head gardener.

"I take care of the herd," the guy answered. "Got a minute?" he added. "You and your dog can walk to the barn with me while I check on the cows." He smiled. Waffles wagged. I wavered. "Um, okay," I said, fueled by liquid courage.

Over the next twenty minutes, I admired roughly a hundred cute and sleepy cows in the Potts cow barn. In the brightly lit barn I saw that the guy, who introduced himself as Mike, was in fact very handsome. He proudly conducted a short tour de bovine, explaining patiently that all the Sanderson cows were of the Hereford variety, originally from the British Isles. Mike, much like the cows he tended, was not too skinny, friendly, and kind of scruffy.

This kind of unconventional guy has always been my type, which is why I haven't found anyone to marry. As my friends like to point out, the men I attract usually disappear to backpack through Thailand soon after our third date, which makes it hard to pursue a relationship.

Anyway, after we looked at the cows, Mike walked me back up the path toward the road, and we reached the Potts driveway, where I intended to turn left and head for home.

Unfortunately, Waffles was straining at the leash to turn right, sniffing and wagging in the moonlight in the general direction of a hydrangea bush. He whined and pulled me closer to said flowering shrub. A few feet from the bush, Mike grabbed my free hand and paused. I felt a little thrill down my spine, thinking he was about to ask me for my number.

Instead, he said, "There's something under that bush."

Mike walked closer to the hydrangea, Waffles and I close on his heels, and all three of us noted what appeared to be a pair of Ferragamo loafers attached to a chubby, motionless man. Mike amended his statement. "Actually, there's some*one* under that bush."

You know the rest—under the shrubbery was Barclay Shields. After a call to the police, Officer Walt arrived, followed by a teenage intern, a pair of EMTs, and at one point Honey Potts—*in her nightgown*—who drove down her quarter-mile-long driveway in response to the police's knock on her baronial front door. In all the confusion, I never got to say good-bye to Mike. I did watch the medics hook Barclay up to a drip while the policeman removed the contents of his pockets. Methodically, he carefully packed up Barclay's wallet, keys, and cell phone. He also found a note, handwritten on expensive-looking, cream-colored notepaper, addressed to Barclay. It was easy to read in the bright headlights of the ambulance, and its large block letters said: "Stop building cheap houses."

Chapter 3

THE NEXT MORNING, after Sophie Shields bought everything in The Striped Awning and after Bootsie finally left, I packed up every damn thing in the store. This tedious task took a little over seven hours, but I was happy to do it. I bubble-wrapped and carefully placed items in a dozen moving boxes; I carefully folded paper around the crystals adorning the Palm Beach chandelier, wound tarps around the legs of a maple hall table and the vanity in the front window, and polished silver candlesticks and a tea set (leaving a little patina on the tea set, since I figured if Sophie had live-in Pilates help, she had people to polish silver for her).

Luckily, I had a fair amount of furniture and accessories in the back room of The Striped Awning with which I could restock the store once I delivered Sophie's loot to her. "This is a ton of stuff!" I told Waffles, who wagged back at me.

Between all the silverware and wineglasses, pillows and prints, several pages of the yellow legal pad I was using to keep track of Sophie's purchases filled up rapidly. There were old glass decanters, a needlepoint stool, and a set of blue-and-white Chinese export dessert plates, all things that I had loved when I'd bought them at flea markets and estate sales, which is important in the antiques business: You have to believe in what you're selling. I loved them even more at the moment, since they were going to help me pay my mortgage and keep the store open. I even apologized to the chair I'd yelled at the day before.

For packing music, I turned up the country-music station on the radio, and occasionally thought about cute Mike Woodford, distracted by visions of his tan forearms and dark-stubbled jaw. I also thought about Barclay Shields, wondering how he was doing with his head injury, and shuddered at the image of his extra-wide Ferragamos under the bush last night. Then I sternly ordered myself to focus.

Occasionally, I'd pause to calculate the subtotal as I worked my way through the store, singing out, "We just made another four hundred dollars!" and "Mirror: two hundred!" until I finally reached the back of the small store and the grand total: seven thousand, five hundred, and seventy dollars. Minus rent and my AmEx bill, this meant The Striped Awning was in business for at least another few months. At three, I called Mr. Webster to tell him I'd be dropping off a check for this month as soon as Sophie's Visa payment went through, probably by Tuesday. He sounded like he thought this was bullshit, but accepted my promise of payment.

Finally, at five-thirty, I went into the store's tiny black-and-white-striped powder room, washed my dusty face and hands, put on new mascara and lipstick, pulled my hair out of its ponytail, and shook it down around my shoulders. I attempted to shake the wrinkles out of my dress (Gap outlet, black cotton, thirty-nine dollars) and spritzed on some of Grandma's YSL perfume, circa 1970, which sits on a little shelf in the bathroom and, by some miracle, still smells fantastic. I hoped the YSL drowned out some of my current scent, which was a combination of dust, old furniture, silver polish, and basset hound.

Waffles was giving me a significant look at the back door of the store, so we went outside, where he did his daily double in the grass behind the store. I pooper-scooped, went back inside, filled up his water bowl, and threw a handful of kibble into a dish. By the time I'd grabbed my keys to leave, he'd inhaled his dinner and was back on his bed, asleep. That's one of the great things about Waffles. He sleeps about twenty hours a day, the bulk of them snoring on his bed in the store. The downside of this is that the four hours he's awake, he's incredibly energetic and steals all my food. He'd grabbed the chicken salad I'd bought for lunch today, as a matter of fact, while I briefly turned my back to answer the phone. He gave me Sad Eyes and looked convincingly guilty after he ate it, though I'm not sure that was the case.

"I'll be back in twenty minutes—one quick drink!" I

promised the sleeping dog, then locked up and rushed to the club to meet Holly and Joe.

"Seven thousand, five hundred, and seventy dollars. Seven thousand, five hundred, and seventy dollars," I sang good-humoredly to the tune of "Happy Birthday to You," as I drove down Lancaster Avenue, the main drag in town, where The Striped Awning sits along with the luncheonette, a few boutiques, a bakery, and the (very popular) liquor store. Then I turned left onto shady Montgomery Lane, and after a quarter mile, into the rosebush-lined entrance of Bryn Mawr Country Club.

The cars in the parking lot were a mix that closely resembled the members—some new and glossy, some old and dusty. My own slightly dented old Subaru looked even seedier than usual, I noticed, parked next to a gleaming Jaguar convertible in a nice, cool, shady spot under a two-hundred-year-old oak.

"Uh-oh," I said aloud to myself a minute later, peering around the corner of the club's wide porch from behind a wide pillar. I could see Honey Potts and Mariellen Merriwether at the other end of the porch, seated at one of the wrought-iron dining tables and watching a tennis match on the club's grass courts. Honey was eating a plate of fried oysters and drinking her trusty Stoli. Mariellen was in her pearls, smoking a Virginia Slim. Just in front of me were Holly and Joe.

Phew—I could sneak up the side steps of the porch to Holly and Joe's table unnoticed. There were a dozen tables crowded with preppy members between us, and Honey and Mariellen would never see me. I was pretty sure Honey hadn't taken much notice of me last night in the dark while she'd been talking to the police, but on the off chance that she had, I was intent on avoiding her.

I *had* noticed her eyeing Waffles, though, last night when she'd been standing there in her white cotton nightshirt—oh, that I could erase the image of Mrs. Potts in her sleep garb from my brain—since his short legs and massive ears make him kind of hard to ignore. In her mind, I was sure, not only had Waffles and I recklessly trespassed on the hallowed grounds of Sanderson last night, we'd been instrumental in discovering a crime scene that had forever tarnished the property. Eventually someone would have found Mr. Shields, but I didn't think Honey had considered that. I breathed deep yoga breaths for a moment (I don't do yoga, but I've heard the breathing is good), and gazed around at the club grounds to calm myself.

You can't beat the club for sheer old-fashioned loveliness and stateliness, especially at this time of day, with the late-afternoon sun turning into shade and shadows lengthening around the hulking building. The century-old structure is three stories high, all gables and mullioned windows, with a charming shingled roof above brick walls and the wide wooden porches. Inside is a dining room, rarely used except in the winter, vintage locker rooms with mahogany cabinets for tennis and golf gear, and an incredible old paneled bar, which until the late 1960s had actually been men-only (women had to drink either in the locker rooms, or when seated in the dining room or on the porch, which seemed a little unfair, though there were some nice comfy couches in the locker rooms). Adjacent to the tennis courts are the golf course and putting greens. The grounds are at their best this time of year, too, with rosebushes exploding with buds, and borders of lilies and peonies in fragrant, massive bloom.

Holly and I had both been coming here since childhood—like her family, my grandparents had been members all their lives, long before younger (and richer) people had started to join in the last ten years. The club had needed new members to survive, and opening up membership had been, to my mind, a great thing. The club now attracted people in their thirties and forties, with glossy hair and adorable children, alongside all the eighty-five-year-olds who wore vintage Lilly Pulitzer not because it was chic again, but because they'd been wearing it for fifty years and their closets were filled with the flowered frocks. The place was like *Grey Gardens* meets a Tommy Hilfiger ad.

One of the rich new members, as a matter of fact, was Holly's soon-to-be ex-husband, Howard the Garbage and Trucking Mogul, whom Holly had met outside the locker rooms one afternoon three years ago. Howard's gazillion-plus trash trucks handle the refuse pickup for pretty much every house along the East Coast from Jersey to Florida, and Howard had just personally paid for the club's new racquetball courts (called, of course, the Howard Jones Racquetball Courts). He'd been standing there with Ronnie, the head bartender and manager, discussing the club's waste-removal discount, when he'd spied Holly coming out of the locker room in her tennis outfit. Bingo! They'd been married four months later. It's a fact that Holly, while she rarely plays tennis, looks awesome in her Lacoste tennis whites. She's big on wearing them to the club even when she has zero intention of picking up a racket, and accessorizes the sporty outfit with some great Van Cleef Alhambra clover necklaces and earrings.

Actually, why I was still a member of the club was something I couldn't quite understand, since someone who can't pay their mortgage definitely can't afford the club dues. I'd asked Ronnie the manager how it was possible that I was still in good standing when I hadn't paid my membership fee in months (I'd only known I *was* still a member because the club directory listed me as such when it came out in March), and he'd told me that before they died, my grandparents had paid for a family membership that was good through the end of next year. I had the distinct feeling that this was bullshit, and that Holly had paid my dues.

That was really very sweet of her, I thought warmly, as I walked up the steps and sat down at her table next to Joe, who waved over a waitress and ordered me a rum and tonic.

"Sophie Shields bought out my store!" I told Holly and Joe immediately, dispensing with the formalities. "She took my entire inventory, every single thing." Holly and I had covered the Barclay Shields incident briefly earlier, on the phone, but I hadn't had time to tell her about Sophie's shopping bonanza then, because it was at that exact moment that Waffles had stolen my lunch.

"Everyone knows about Sophie and your store," said Holly. I sighed. I'd forgotten that Bootsie had witnessed Sophie's impulsive splurge. There was no way that in the intervening eight hours since Sophie had whipped out her Visa card, Bootsie hadn't lit up iPhones and BlackBerrys throughout Bryn Mawr and Center City Philly with the news, and likely blown out cell towers as far away as the Jersey Shore and the Delaware beaches.

"Does Bootsie have anything new on Barclay since this morning?" I asked.

"The police met with Barclay this afternoon," said Joe, as my drink arrived. After all those cocktails the night before, drinking didn't seem like a great idea, but after all that packing, I reasoned, who wouldn't be thirsty?

"He'd just ordered in lunch, by the way, when the police came in to talk to him," said Joe.

"What did he get?" asked Holly, curious.

"Two cheesesteaks and an order of wings from the Hoagie Hut," said Joe. "The nurses took the wings and one of the steaks away. Anyway, Barclay told the police that the whole chain of events started when he got a note hand-delivered yesterday to his office in Haverford," Joe said, leaning in toward us, and speaking in a loud whisper.

Between the clanging silverware, the chattering older guests, and the tennis players thwacking balls around, I doubted anyone at the neighboring tables could hear him, despite the fact that his voice definitely carried. A few people were staring at us, but that was because of Holly's outfit. She's not in her tennis-whites phase at the moment; instead, she's been on a kind of retro-supermodel kick, and had on a full-length silk caftan, incredibly high-heeled Gucci sandals that kind of looked like expensive Dr. Scholl's on stilts, and had added long emerald-colored beads and an Ursula Andress–style flowing hairdo. I'm not sure what to make of her new super-glam style, but she did look pretty, even if her outfit was more appropriate for, say, Club 55 in St. Tropez.

"No one saw who dropped off the note, but it was sitting on his receptionist's desk when she came back from lunch," said Joe, forgetting that he was supposed to be whispering. He practically shouted, "And get this: The note was from Honey Potts!"

Chapter 4

AT THIS, WE got a couple of dirty looks from a table of grumpy-looking men in golf shorts. Holly and I glanced nervously in Mrs. Potts's direction, but she was nose-deep in another vodka and seemed preoccupied by her fried oysters. She and Mariellen were watching the tennis matches as they snacked (well, smoked, in Mariellen's case). They clearly hadn't heard Joe.

"The note said that Honey is planning to sell off a hundred acres of Sanderson land, and that she wanted to meet with Barclay about him building houses there," continued Joe. "It was thick off-white stationery, and written in black ink and block letters, by the way."

Just like the note in Barclay's pocket.

"And in this letter, she basically summoned Barclay to her house at 8:30 p.m., like the queen would order the Spice Girls to reunite and play the Albert Hall. It was a command performance."

"That's kind of late in the day for a business meeting, isn't it?" I asked. "And Honey Potts wasn't even home last night. She was at Gianni's opening, and it had to be after eight when she and Mariellen left."

"Mrs. Potts says she didn't write it," said Joe. "The police called her to ask her about it, and she said wasn't selling any of her property, especially to a shyster like Barclay. It was very Scarlett O'Hara, with Honey shouting that she'd personally chop down every tree on her property and tear down her mansion stone by stone before she sold off a single acre of Sanderson. She'd never written any such note, nor would she."

We all digested this for a minute, staring surreptitiously across the porch at Honey, wondering if her wrath at Barclay wanting to buy her ancestral acreage might have led her to bash the hapless developer on the head and dump him under her own hydrangea hedge.

Meanwhile, our waitress dropped off a modest plate of carrot and celery sticks. By now, the club staff knows it's pointless to serve Holly actual food, so they don't even offer a menu anymore. Actually, I was pretty hungry, given that Waffles had eaten my lunch, but I didn't want to interrupt Joe's tale to order an appetizer.

"Barclay says he got there a few minutes early, at about eight twenty-five," Joe added, crunching on a stalk of celery. "He was knocking on the door for almost a full ten minutes. He was starting to get pretty steamed about being kept waiting when, boom!—he got clobbered!"

I could just picture poor Barclay at the baronial front door of Sanderson. I'd seen it before when I'd gone there with Bootsie on a garden-club tour, and it's an absolutely enormous, double-height, mahogany carved monster, with a huge pineapple-shaped doorknocker and a beautiful limestone overhang. The blow must have leveled Barclay when he was on a real estate high, thinking he was about to savor a tumbler of Glenmorangie from the ancestral Potts cellars, and practically jumping for joy as he pondered how many houses he could stuff onto one hundred acres of Sanderson land, and how much he could sell them for (well, given his size, he probably didn't jump for joy, but he had to be pretty excited).

"Didn't Honey hear Barclay banging on her front door?" Holly asked, crossing her long legs under her caftan.

"Nope," said Joe. "Honey dropped off Mariellen at the Merriwether place at eight, and Honey herself was home a few minutes after that. She claims she was upstairs with a sandwich and her TV on full blast, watching *Dancing with the Stars*, when Barclay was outside making a racket. Honey's housekeeper leaves around 5 p.m., and Honey never heard a thing."

"It's weird that Barclay wouldn't have at least stopped by Gianni's restaurant opening on the way to Honey's, isn't it?" I puzzled, as Holly waved down the waitress for more drinks. "I mean, everyone else in Bryn Mawr was there."

"Chef Gianni and Barclay hate each other," said Holly knowledgeably. "You know they had that huge feud that started a couple of years ago over a house that Barclay built for Gianni."

"Gianni's place is down off Willow Road, squeezed into a tiny lot next to the Methodist church," added Joe, with a look of revulsion. "It's hideous, and *orange*. Plus it turned out the house Barclay did for him was as sturdy as a double-wide during hurricane season. I mean, it looked okay on the outside, but the whole place started collapsing a week after the chef moved in."

I'd heard something about this debacle, but Joe sketched in more details: The chef had been in a manic up-cycle about his new house, giving his girlfriend Jessica license to spend like a Kardashian on decorating the place, and had then signed up to show it off as part of a house tour to benefit the hospital.

The chef had arrived home from Palazzo late one night, unlocked the door, and the masonry around the front entrance suddenly crumbled like a stale macaroon. "The whole foyer avalanched down on Gianni," said Joe. "He was pinned under the rubble for two hours, because Jessica was asleep upstairs with her iPod on, and never heard the screaming until after midnight."

"The chef had to have a plastic tarp around his front entrance for six weeks until he could get the wall rebuilt," said Holly, who clearly knew this story as well as Joe did. She tried to keep a straight face, but couldn't help laughing. "Sorry." She composed herself, being careful not to smudge her eye makeup, and went on. "Since the chef was worried about getting robbed, not having a door *or* a foyer, he had to station one of his busboys at the entrance to his house around the clock. And it was too late to cancel the house tour. It was so sad. I went on it, and when you got there, there was this beautiful brand-new garden with lavender hedges and fig trees. But no door. Just a tattered tarp flapping in the breeze, and a pile of debris."

Having witnessed Chef Gianni's nutty rage the night before, I mused, "That must have really upset the chef. I mean, *really* upset him."

"He filed a lawsuit against Barclay, but it was dismissed once Barclay fixed the foyer and the door," confirmed Holly, "which made Gianni even angrier."

We were all thinking the same thing: It was easy to picture Gianni, a certified rageaholic, belting Barclay on the head with a meat mallet, and then dragging the developer under a hedge. "Could it have been the chef who hit Barclay last night?" I wondered aloud.

"Not possible," said Joe firmly. "There's no way that Gianni could have been at the party, schmoozing with his guests and cooking all those lamb chops and lobster tails, *and* bashing someone's head in at the same time."

"Barclay himself must have a suspect in mind, though," I mused. "Given his reputation, he has to have a whole line-up of enemies in addition to Chef Gianni."

"Bootsie says that not only did Barclay not hear anyone creeping up behind him before he was attacked, he has no idea who hit him. He blacked out," said Holly, "until he woke up in the ambulance. He doesn't remember how he got from standing outside Honey Potts's front door to being up by the road and under a bush. And he swears he has no serious beef with anyone other than the chef. He's already agreed to a settlement with the sinkhole victims. So he's no help at all."

"That's bullshit. From what I've heard in decorating circles," Joe said—Holly rolled her eyes at this phraseology, and I stifled a laugh—"Barclay disputes every bill, and nickel-and-dimes every vendor. Tons of people hate Barclay Shields enough to want him dead. Or at least in pain."

"Well, there's definitely somebody in Bryn Mawr who doesn't like Barclay's adventures in real estate," I said. "The note in his pocket was very clear—the person who wrote it hates his ugly houses."

"Remember when I went on that date with Barclay Shields a few years ago?" said Holly nonchalantly. Now that she mentioned it, I *did* recall her night out with the developer. This was surprising, but not shocking: It's a fact that Holly doesn't discriminate based on a man's size or his character. She only evaluates men on the basis of cash flow, because Holly is a member of one of the wealthiest families in Philly thanks to a lucky incident with a chicken breast. Back in the 1970s, her father was experimenting at the test kitchen of one of the chicken farms he owned out in the Amish countryside, when he'd had an inspired moment one wintry Wednesday. Bored of eating a sauteed boneless breast for lunch the four thousandth day in a row, he decided to chop up some white meat into bite-size pieces, bread them, and have his assistant deep-fry the little suckers.

"Darling, I just had a brainwave," he'd told Holly's mother that evening, "and I think we have a new hors d'oeuvre to serve at our party on Saturday night." Presto: The chicken nugget was born (at least according to the

Dunhams; McDonald's would likely disagree). Before long, the Dunhams had more chicken farms and nugget factories than Tiffany's has diamonds. These days, they ship frozen nuggets to gazillions of supermarkets and delis and fast-food joints, and the rest of their bird-meat business is booming, as well.

Since Holly grew up rich, she's circumspect when it comes to her own wealth. It's very big in Philadelphia to *not* talk about how rich you are, unless you're someone as blustery as Barclay Shields, who's known to drop at least four references to his own net worth into every conversation. In Philly, even if your family does something way more interesting than chicken, like owning a cruise ship line or running a glossy department store, you still take your financial status to the grave. To add to the confusion, some of the richest people drive around in junker cars and wear threadbare clothes, like Mrs. Potts. Plenty of oddball types are of unknown financial status, like my next-door neighbors Jimmy and Hugh Best, two old bachelors who live in a tumbledown manor house, but whose family helped found the Philadelphia Stock Exchange. The result is that you never know if people are living on Ritz crackers and tuna fish because they're rich and eccentric, or if they're actually poor and had a coupon for Starkist that week.

Anyway, even though you can never discuss your own finances, you can definitely talk about how rich other people are. That's totally acceptable, and is a very popular topic at the club, on the tennis court, and at the luncheonette. Also, it seems that wealth has a magnetic force field that irresistibly attracts other big fortunes in Philly—people with money must marry *more* money. This explains why Holly could only date rich guys, even if they were Barclay Shields.

"My date with Barclay was three years ago, before I met Howard. And Barclay was at least fifteen pounds thinner then." Holly shrugged off her night out with the developer. We all mused silently on the fact that dislodging fifteen pounds from Barclay was the equivalent of removing one stone from the Great Wall of China.

"We went to Palazzo, but I could tell that he was cheap," Holly added.

"Holly, even the salads at Palazzo are thirty-five dollars," Joe said. "How does that translate into cheap?"

"He took home a doggie bag," explained Holly. "And, I know he doesn't have a dog."

Waffles! I shook my head at the waitress, who was pointing questioningly at my empty glass, and started to get up. But not quite fast enough.

"Who was the guy Bootsie said you were with at Sanderson last night?" asked Joe.

"It was someone who manages the cows for Honey Potts. I, um, bumped into him just before we found Barclay," I said, gathering my handbag. I knew they'd both be able to tell immediately that I had a slight crush on Mike Woodford and his tanned forearms if I gave even a single detail about him, which would be stressful since Holly and Joe invariably disapprove of any man I'm interested in. Plus I was too tired to get into the details about Mike

Woodford just at the moment. The rum and tonic wasn't perking me up the way the Barolo had last night.

Joe's eyes had glazed over. Cows and the people who take care of them aren't on his radar.

Holly merely looked disappointed as she sipped her cocktail. As usual, I'd managed to meet a man who had a job that was definitely in the low-earning-with-no-future-prospects category.

"Well, I have to go get Waffles and head home, see you two later!" I said briskly. Just then, a slim, extremely pretty blond woman of about my age came bounding off the grass tennis courts, up the porch stairs, and slid gracefully into a chair at Mariellen and Honey's table. "Mummy, you have got to stop that horrible smoking!" she scolded Mariellen gently in a fairylike, singsong voice.

"Nice game, darling!" said Mariellen, puffing on her Virginia Slim and ignoring her daughter's anti-smoking crusade. Mariellen's normally severe patrician face broke into a molasses-sweet smile as she gazed at the younger woman, who looked exactly like a junior version of her mother, down to the elegant string of pearls she wore with her white polo shirt and spotless tennis skirt. It was Lilly Merriwether, Mariellen's only child and an avid tennis player who's frequently found on the club's courts.

I have to admit, Lilly looks almost as fantastic in her tennis outfit as Holly does.

"Ugh, Lilly," said Holly, eyeing Mariellen 2.0 distastefully. Clearly, Holly considered her something of a rival in the gorgeous-tanned-blond department. *Lilly was really beautiful*, I thought sourly, considering my own dusty afternoon of wrapping china in old copies of the *Bryn Mawr Gazette* versus Lilly's glamorous day, pursuing fitness and a great tan at the club. Her superb svelteness was obviously of the type that comes from lots of exercise, fresh fruit, and antioxidants. I, on the other hand, can only fit into Holly's borrowed clothes because I have a food-stealing dog, have nothing in my fridge, and get something of a workout schlepping antiques and benches from estate sales. In the tradition of her perfect mother, Lilly seemed to roam the earth only to make you feel inferior about your lowly financial status and not-so-magnificently tanned legs.

Suddenly, I noticed that Honey Potts had finished her oysters, and was growling good-bye to Mariellen and Lilly. She threw down her napkin, rose, and was heading our way, clearly bent on making her way down the porch steps in front of our table. Luckily, the grumpy golfers next to us waved Honey down to greet her, so I got up, whispered, "Bye!" to Holly and Joe, and dashed down the steps, around the corner, and leaped into my car.

I started up the engine and noticed the time: 6:30 p.m. I had been gone for almost an hour. When I got back to the store, Waffles gave me an accusing look. I was pretty sure he knew I was late by the way he yawned disapprovingly, but he jumped in the car happily enough to head home.

As we passed Sanderson, I noticed yellow police tape was still in place, cordoning off the area where Barclay had been bushwhacked. I gave Waffles a stern look and informed him preemptively, "No Sanderson!" as we turned into the driveway. Then, for about ten seconds, as I parked and unloaded Waffles, I wondered what Mike Woodford was doing. Maybe he was taking a walk, I mused, or putting the cows away . . .

"Hello, Kristin," said a gravelly voice from a holly bush in the yard next door, putting an end to my reverie.

My neighbor Hugh Best popped up from behind the holly, a pair of hedge clippers in hand, while Waffles, suddenly awake, wagged his tail at him and went over to sniff Hugh's hairy ankles. Hugh looks much older than his age, which I believe is in the mid-seventies, and for gardening attire wore a tattered striped dress shirt, ancient khakis cut off just above the knees, brown dress socks, and black sneakers. Thanks to his precision with pruning shears, his yard looks pretty good, despite the fact that the white Colonial house he shares with his brother is in just as dire need of paint and repairs as mine. I've known the Bests forever, but I'm not sure of their financial status—they could be broke, or have millions and simply have forgotten to repaint their house and repair their gutters for the past thirty-five years.

Mr. Best greeted me with a sweet smile and a wave of Old Spice. He's very unlike his brother Jimmy, who always smells like Scotch and cigars and is prone to making rude and lascivious comments. In my mind, I refer to Hugh as the Fussy One, and Jimmy as the Crabby One.

"Horrible business across the street, no?" the Fussy One said in slightly hushed tones. I agreed, and said quickly, "Well, I don't want to interrupt your yard work!" and then bolted inside, suddenly starving. I threw some soup on the stove and refilled Waffles's water bowl, thinking about Mike's muscular arms and intriguing beard stubble. Then, in an unsettling flash, I wondered: *Could Mike Woodford have had anything to do with whacking Barclay on the head?* Because if there's anything that ruins my appreciation of a man's tanned forearms, it's thinking that said arms might have bashed someone's brains in.

As I did some laundry and folded towels, I decided it couldn't have been Mike. For one thing, why would he have helped "find" Barclay under the bush if he'd been the one to throw him under there? Waffles (whose sniffer usually only works at close range, like if someone is eating a hamburger right next to him) hadn't actually nosed Barclay out, but was merely pulling me in the direction of the developer. Mike could have easily steered me and Waffles away from the crime scene.

And unless it was some elaborate scheme by Mike to *not* seem guilty by finding Barclay, it just didn't make sense for him to call the police about something he'd done himself. And why would Mike go after Barclay? His mind was on his herd, not on real estate developers. The attacker couldn't be Mike Woodford, I was positive. Or very close to one-hundred-percent sure.

By this time, it was past eight-thirty, so Waffles and I climbed into bed and fell instantly asleep.

Chapter 5

THE PHONE RANG at seven the next morning. Waffles and I both were startled by the early call, and I cleared my throat, trying not to sound sleepy as I picked up the phone on my bedside table. It was Saturday, so I didn't think it was a credit card company calling—but then again, maybe they'd started rousting past-due customers at the crack of dawn. I hoped it wasn't the police with new questions about Barclay, or worse, Bootsie with her own interrogation.

More likely it was Holly, on one of her early-morning exercise kicks. Her fitness obsessions are rare, but they erupt semi-annually, and consist of her forcing me to go with her to a horrible gym called Booty Camp over by the library, where pudgy lawyers and doctors and incredibly fit housewives work out at 6 a.m. under the slightly insane eyes of a tattooed former marine. The women are all in great shape and barely break a sweat (except for me and Holly, who are drenched and pleading for mercy), but the accountant types invariably throw up after the four-mile jog and hundreds of squats and pushups.

"Is this Kristin? The Striped Awning girl?" bleated a small, nasal voice. "Did I wake ya up?" Sophie Shields.

"Oh, hi, Mrs. Shields," I said as brightly as I could, sitting up in bed. Sunlight was streaming in through my linen curtains, and a breeze was stirring the leaves outside the open window. "How are you? Gosh, um, how did you get my home number?"

"Gerda got it off the computer," squeaked Sophie triumphantly. "She's good at all that stuff. She can, like, get anyone's personal information and check all your bank balances!" *This was not good news.* I pictured Gerda in a darkened corner of Sophie's house in front of an enormous Mac, gleefully reading personal e-mails, studying bank balances, and learning every embarrassing secret floating around Bryn Mawr.

"She told me it's good that we bought all your stuff." Sophie giggled. "She said you're kinda broke."

"I really appreciate it," I said, feeling resentful that Gerda knew the details of every bag of dog food and seventy-five-percent-off pair of jeans I'd ever charged. I was also terrified that Sophie had somehow changed her mind about buying out the store. *Please, please, please don't be calling to cancel the sale. . .*

"Hey, I wasn't always as obscenely rich as I am now!" said Sophie, rather kindly. "Don't worry about it. The only thing is, I was calling because I can't take delivery today on all that crap from your shop. I mean, the antiques. I gotta reschedule it for Monday."

"Oh, that's fine! No problem," I said, thrilled, jumping out of bed as Waffles hauled his big stomach off the comforter and started rolling over toward the edge of the bed. Sometimes he's too lazy to jump down, so he just rolls off the mattress.

"Yeah, it's crazy over here today," Sophie rattled on. She was sucking deafeningly on something through a straw. "Sorry, I got some fresh-squeezed orange-kale juice here that Gerda made."

How was anyone so chatty at this time of day? Maybe it was all the Pilates.

"I got a call last night from Eula Morris, the lady who runs the Symphony Women's Board." I knew of Eula, though I'd never actually met her. She was a tiny but mighty battleship of a woman in her thirties, invariably dressed in swoopy beige dresses and large necklaces, who was excellent at raising money by fear and intimidation. "And guess what, there was supposed to be a big party benefitting the symphony tomorrow at Sanderson, but the police said that the place is still a crime scene because of Old Fatass"—I guessed she was referencing her husband—"getting his head bashed in there. So they can't do the event over there."

"Oh, that's too bad," I said, wondering where this was going. I brushed my teeth as silently as I could, holding the phone away from the brushing noise, since it's definitely not good manners to talk through a mouthful of Ultra Brite, even this early.

"And guess what," said Sophie triumphantly.

I was rinsing out my mouth, so I made a "Hmm?" sound indicating interest.

"I'm gonna have the party here!" Sophie shrieked.

I was shocked. First of all, the Symphony Women's Board is one of the stuffiest old-Philadelphia organizations around, and tends to attract supporters whose average age is about ninety-seven. As a whole, the group smells of mothballs and L'Air du Temps, and they wear a lot of retro gowns not because they're stylish, like the Holly types who buy vintage Pucci dresses at overpriced boutiques, but because that's what's in their closets. Eula and her aging supporters only occasionally added younger trustees.

Sophie, with her Joisey accent and precariously high heels, would stand out like a disco ball in a chintz drawing room amid the Symphony Women's sea of classic navy St. John suits. But Eula was no dummy. She must have known that Sophie would be one of the only people around town who'd jump at the chance to host a hundred-person-plus bash on two days' notice. Plus being associated with the symphony guaranteed you a story in the *Bryn Mawr Gazette*, which Sophie would love.

I should call Bootsie about Sophie's shindig, so Bootsie could cover it for the Gazette.

Or maybe I didn't need to. She had to have heard about the party already.

As if reading my mind, Sophie piped up: "You should come tomorrow night! I'll put you down as my guest, since I know ya can't afford the two-hundred-dollar ticket. And you can bring your friend, the one from the store with the flowered shorts!"

As if I could *stop* Bootsie from coming—she likes to wave her press pass and barge into events. I headed downstairs with Waffles, who launched himself downstairs and out the back door with a clatter. He made a token run at a blue jay on a low branch back by the fence, then ambled over behind the laurel bush where he likes to conduct his morning affairs.

"Thanks so much," I told Sophie, feeling embarrassed about being a freeloader at her party, but not enough to miss out on free champagne and the chance to see Eula Morris establishing eminent domain over the Shields estate. "I'll be there." I scooped ground coffee into the coffeemaker, poured in water, and pressed on, debating whether I should ask about how Barclay was doing. Technically, the two were still married. And Sophie had told us she wanted him alive (purely for financial reasons, true, but still, alive).

But while Sophie rattled on about carved ice swans and an epic shellfish buffet she was planning for her bash, it started to seem a little cold-blooded of Sophie to throw one of the biggest parties of the summer while her husband was in the hospital with a head injury, but then again, I've never been divorced. It unleashes a tsunami of anger and vindictiveness that's basically nuclear in most people.

Take Holly—when she split from Howard six months ago and moved out of the condo she and Howard had lived in downtown, she'd taken all of his custom-made squash rackets and gazillion-dollar golf clubs over the bridge to

Jersey, and given them to a YMCA up in Newark. Then she'd donated his Porsche to the Police Athletic League auction, sending out a press release gushing about his generosity to all the Philly newspapers. Howard had been screwed, because what could he do then? He had to pose gamely with some kids at the Police Athletic League ball field for photos, and suck it up.

"How is your, er, Mr. Shields doing?" I ventured to Sophie, adding half and half to my coffee.

"He's gonna be fine," replied Sophie unenthusiastically. "I'm not going to visit him, that's for sure, but I heard from my lawyers that he's got one of those big head-wrap things on and he's got some stitches and a concussion. But he'll be okay, which is good, because we have a meeting with all our lawyers next week, and I need him there with bells on! He can't die until this divorce is worked out, because suing him after he's dead would be a real bitch." She made a little harrumph sound.

"Apparently, no one has a clue about who went after him the other night," Sophie continued. "Barclay's lawyers decided to hire a security guard for his room, since obviously somebody wants him on ice." She loudly slurped at her juice. "And my lawyers got a call from Barclay's legal guys about one other weird thing happened yesterday afternoon. Two guys showed up at Barclay's hospital room with a fruit basket the size of a Barcalounger, and told the guard they were there to visit Barclay. They said they were his cousins!"

"Uh-huh," I said politely. "Well, that was nice of them."

"Not so much!" Sophie said. "Barclay doesn't have any cousins. No family at all. Both his parents were only children. It's a sad story. His mom and dad died in a freak accident eleven years ago at the wedding of a business associate. A Swarovski chandelier that weighed half a ton fell on both a them at a catering hall up near Newark! Flattened them like two chicken cutlets. But at least they died together!"

I wasn't sure how to respond to this, so I made a sympathetic murmuring noise. Getting crushed by a homicidal light fixture is something you don't hear much about in Bryn Mawr.

"Yeah, Barclay told me that when he was younger and getting started in the construction biz, he and his parents had relatives out the wazoo. But they weren't blood relations, they were all family friends. And business associates in the construction biz. I mean, everyone was Uncle Something or Other. Uncle Skinny, Uncle No-Thumbs, Uncle Meatball. There were a lotta nicknames!"

I was getting a bad feeling about the uncles.

"So, and this is just between you and me, Barclay decided to move away from North Joisey a few years after his parents' accident, and start over! He even got a new name. His real name is Beppe Santino, but he had it legally changed. He had a nickname, too, which he told me one time when he was wasted on lemon martinis at Joe's Stone Crabs in Miami. Barclay used ta be called the Forklift. Beppe 'the Forklift' Santino!"

Sophie giggled merrily for a few moments, while I

attempted to absorb this information. The Joe Pesci bar scene from *Goodfellas* was playing in my head, but I didn't want to jump to conclusions. Maybe Barclay (formerly Beppe) had just had an exceptionally close business "family," with a fondness for nicknames.

"I guess maybe the guys with the fruit basket read in the paper about Barclay's attack. Or, as they called him, the Forklift! You get the pun, right?" Sophie asked. "He used a forklift at work, plus he's the size of a forklift. And he likes to lift a fork . . . to his mouth!"

"Oh, I understand," I said, thinking that maybe the two "cousins" had indeed read about Barclay, whose beatdown had made a few local papers in Philly.

Or maybe the two had attacked Barclay themselves on Thursday night, and had come to the hospital hoping to finish the job.

"So anyway, the party tomorrow. The best part of the whole thing is that Chef Gianni is the caterer for the party! It's the ultimate screw-you to Barclay!" finished Sophie happily. "My ex hates the symphony, but even more, he hates Chef Gianni!"

Eula must have known this, I realized. She was almost as plugged in as Bootsie, and no doubt knew all the details of Sophie's divorce and of the feud between Gianni and Barclay. Sophie wouldn't be able to resist hosting the party, which was guaranteed to enrage her husband.

"I got the Colketts coming today to work on the landscaping. They said for the right money, they can install a whole new garden by tomorrow afternoon and get, like, some great trees for the pool area. And I'm pretty sure Barclay's going to be stuck in the hospital at least through the weekend. I don't want him coming over here during my party. But he probably won't—he's afraid of Gerda." Sophie's Pilates instructor did seem a little scary.

"Speaking of Gerda, I have Pilates now and I gotta choke down the rest of this juice, so I better run," chirped Sophie. "Anyway, see you tomorrow! Party starts at five. I'll be the one in Versace!"

Chapter 6

"ROAD TRIP!" I told Waffles, after Sophie's phone call.

It was the perfect day for a drive out to Lancaster County, a gorgeous area of Amish farms an hour west of Bryn Mawr where flea markets and barn sales are plentiful on Saturdays. I had quite a few pieces of furniture and some silver pieces in the back room at The Striped Awning, but not enough to completely restock the store once everything in the front of the shop was delivered to Sophie's, so it was definitely time for an antiques-scouting expedition. This would also give me time to digest Sophie's phone call, fragments of which were still ping-ponging around in my head. Barclay's "cousins" rang some alarm bells. Despite Sophie's request for discretion, I'd have to share this info with Bootsie. Just not at this moment. A phone call to Bootsie could kill most of the morning.

Since Waffles is up for anything—he even likes going

to the vet, where they always stick a thermometer up his rump—he sat by the door and drooled happily while I jumped in the shower, got dressed (Target cotton dress, $19.99), and threw a couple of bottles of water and his water bowl in a pink L.L. Bean tote bag (Christmas present from Bootsie).

On the way out of town, I stopped at The Striped Awning and hung a sign that said "Closed for the Weekend" since anyone passing by and seeing the entire contents of the store packed into boxes and wrapped in tarps would no doubt think I was closing up for good. Of course, it's not like customers were exactly lining up around the block, but just in case one of the few people in the greater Philadelphia area who weren't spending the morning whacking balls on a golf course wandered by, I wanted to make sure they'd come back another day. Next, I stopped at the drive-through cash machine to withdraw money from my still-limping checking account, and tucked two hundred dollars in twenties into my bra. You have to pay cash at the markets, and I figure it's hard for anyone to steal a bunch of money from my chest without me noticing. Plus, since I have almost no cleavage, anything I stick in there can't hurt. Feeling a little like Kate Upton, I headed out of town for the expressway.

A long drive to a flea market is one of my favorite things to do, and in May, it's heavenly. It was seventy-two degrees and sunny, the best time of the year in Philly before humidity grips the area for all of June, July, and August.

The markets around Philly are ideal for finding stock

for The Striped Awning, even if most of them open at unholy hours like 5 a.m. and close at 2 p.m. (I think this is an Amish thing.) Occasionally, things like French chairs turn up amid all the locally made Pennsylvania Dutch blanket chests and quilts, and you can find great smaller pieces—tableware, mirrors, Audubon prints—for next to nothing.

Which is not to say that all the local flea markets are hotbeds of undiscovered chic. There's one held monthly in a dusty tomato field in South Jersey that sells creepy castoffs such as vintage knickers and fusty fox stoles on rickety folding tables. I don't know why I schlep over there once a year—I keep hoping it will get better, but it never does. The last time I went, a straggly woman in a housedress behind one of the tables had a pair of old socks hanging from a flagpole, flying in the meager breeze. She claimed they were one-hundred-fifty-year-old Civil War stockings, but, honestly, who would buy old socks, even if they'd once been worn by Robert E. Lee?

Soon, the suburbs on either side of Route 76 blurred into just-planted cornfields and hillsides laced with grazing sheep and horses. I looked over at Waffles, who was sitting bolt upright and staring bug-eyed out the window in rapture at the fields and animals all around him. Waffles was given to me two years ago, by a longtime customer of The Striped Awning who raises basset hounds, when he was a nine-pound, nine-week-old puppy. His ecstatic reaction to every person he meets is contagious—Waffles is the most joyful creature on earth. So while he'd love to chase sheep around on a farm, his good looks and schmoozing ability are perfectly suited to retail. While he can't describe the provenance of a table, he's the ultimate sales associate (and the only one I can afford). I cranked down the windows and cranked up the Doobie Brothers, feeling upbeat, zooming past beautiful old white farmhouses and classic red barns, with colorful hex signs placed high over the barn doors to ward off any evildoers. "Sanderson could use one of those," I told Waffles.

Then, when we exited the highway, we did something not very Amish: We got gas at the Sunoco near Route 100, and pulled into the McDonald's drive-through, the last sign of civilization before everything goes totally Harrison Ford in *Witness* out here (if you can call McDonald's a sign of civilization). Waffles loves Egg McMuffins, so we ordered two, and as we ate and drove, I daydreamed about Harrison in carpenter mode during the barn raising, and the scene when he almost has a romp in the hay with the gorgeous Amish Kelly McGillis. This propelled me toward thoughts of Mike Woodford, so I gunned the car to the flea market before I got too distracted by his stubble-chinned charms.

Just down Route 100 is Stoltzfus's, one of the oldest markets in the area, owned by a collection of Pennsylvania Dutch farmers–turned–weekend antiques dealers. After passing a cow field (which, conjured up Mike Woodford again, darn), I pulled into the crowded gravel parking lot, snapped on Waffles's leash, and checked my bra. All was good. Money in place, things looking a little more bodacious than usual, so we headed for the indoor-outdoor market.

Stoltzfus's covers fifteen acres in all, and on sunny days like today, fifty-plus vendors sell wares ranging from 1950s bedroom sets to dolls to Spode china from long wooden tables on a grass-covered field just inside its gates. There's an outdoor snack counter selling Amish foods like bratwurst (I've never tried it, but to be honest, it smells pretty good), and inside a massive old barn are the more established dealers who sell here all year round.

Another awesome thing about Stoltzfus's, and I really don't have the words to describe how cool this is, is that there's a beer stand in the middle of the barn that opens at 6 a.m. It comes from a fantastic micro-brewery down the road, and they sell cold, frothy pilsner in the middle of the flea market. The Stoltzfus beer is exceptionally good, but it was only 10:30 a.m., so I decided to skip it and shop.

Waffles gave me Sad Eyes as we got out of the truck, then made a crazed run for the bratwurst stand, so I took a left at the barn to divert him, and stopped at a stall where a rickety-looking guy aged about ninety was selling a pair of very pretty crystal sconces that were perfect for an entrance hallway or dining room. They were just the kind of thing that I like for The Striped Awning, but the vendor wanted two hundred and fifty dollars, and though he looked like an ancient plucked chicken, he was a tough bird when it came to negotiating.

"No fucking way," he rasped, which I thought was a little rude, when I suggested seventy-five bucks as a more reasonable price. He wouldn't come down more than twenty, so I headed toward the middle of the field, passing tables of old books (not to be negative, but I'm not really sure I believed that copy of *Gone with the Wind* belonged to Vivien Leigh), and glassware (okay, old Coke bottles can be valuable, but these looked like they came out of the soda machine inside the barn earlier today), and a dealer who purported to be selling mirror-topped café tables from the original incarnation of Studio 54. Waffles and I wandered around for another thirty minutes before heading to the back field, where my favorite dealers, Annie and Jenny, are usually stationed.

Annie and Jenny are two Californians who travel to antiques shows and sales all over the country, and purvey silver and tabletop items that always include some serious deals. I've scored silver creamers (ten dollars!) and candlesticks (four dollars each!) from them before. Once, I got a beautiful footed tea tray (twenty dollars) that I sold for two hundred dollars in the shop, which sounds like highway robbery, but was so beautiful that it really merited the huge mark-up. Today Annie and Jenny, draped in their usual flowing peasant dresses circa 1973, looked very mellow and relaxed behind a table full of pretty antique serving pieces.

"Hey, Waffles," said Annie, bending down and reaching her arms around his big belly to give him a hug as he thumped his tail happily.

Annie and Jenny spend winters in a teepee outside San Francisco, and rent a tiny cottage near Stoltzfus's in the summer, when they're not making road trips. They're incredibly sweet. They had the Grateful Dead wailing away on a boom box, and had thoughtfully provided a plate of snacks on their table for anyone passing by to enjoy. A small square of paper next to the plate announced that these were homemade carrot-quinoa-gingersnaps.

"Cookie?" asked Jenny, gesturing toward the plate.

Gosh. I didn't want to be impolite, but the cookies looked terrible. They were dry, crunchy-looking, brown disks with flecks of carrot poking out. "Cruelty-Free!" read the little sign. "Made with Love, but Without Any Flour, Sugar, or Butter."

"Thanks, I just ate," I told Jenny. "But I'm sure they're delicious."

Annie handed one to Waffles, and he chowed down happily. They were so dry, though, he had trouble swallowing. He chewed and gulped for a few minutes, then finally got the lump of carrot and quinoa down his throat. He wagged, looking relieved.

"Yum!" I said to the women, on Waffles's behalf.

While chatting with the vendors, I scooped up a dozen old silver serving spoons and forks with intricate, delicate patterns, and found another great old tray from the 1950s, all of which came to sixty dollars. Annie and Jenny had some furniture today, too, including a petite dark elm-wood bench that had a curvy Art Deco shape, which I loved and was only seventy dollars, so I told them I'd take that, too.

"Hey Kristin, you might like these bookends," said Jenny, who was over by their van, holding up a silver object. Jenny's hair—which probably hadn't been cut in twenty years—flowed down her back, with some little braids in front keeping it off her face. She wore no makeup except for some glittery lip gloss and two silver stars painted on each cheek. She once told me she does this creative kind of face painting because the stars draw in mystical powers, send them straight through her chakras, then shoot them back out to the world. Anyway, Jenny was holding what looked like a large acorn-shaped bookend, maybe eight inches high and five inches wide, with a lot of intricate detail and a light patina of age over its silver-plated surface.

"We've got three of these, which I know is kind of an odd number for bookends, but you know how it is in this business. Nothing ever makes sense," Jenny said cheerfully, as if her chakra stars *did* make sense. "They were made for a school in Bryn Mawr. Isn't that where your store is?"

"Yes, that's where I live, and where the store is! Really, they're from Bryn Mawr?" I answered, surprised, as she handed me one of the bookends.

The acorn-shaped object was much heavier than I'd have thought at first glance—it must have weighed nearly ten pounds—and ornate, with the acorn figure set on a solid square base. The wide part of the acorn was designed in a crisscross pattern, with the narrow end coming to a pointed tip. The object was fantastic, I thought, solid enough to give off a masculine vibe and to sit in a library or office, but pretty enough to appeal to a female buyer. Given the weight of the acorn, I knew that underneath the silver plate, the piece was made of cast iron, according it a pleasing heft.

"I love them! And I can sell them as a single item, so it's fine that you don't have two pairs," I said, inspecting the base, thinking that someone would surely buy a single one to put on a mantel or desk. Or all three could be used on a shelf, with various books between them.

The acorn's base was marked underneath with the stamp of Farrow & Summers, longtime Philadelphia silversmiths. Inscribed above the insignia were the words, "From this acorn grows a mighty oak: Bryn Mawr Preparatory School," in a bold, elegant typeface that matched the classic style of the bookend. This lettering was old and worn, but very legible.

"This is such a coincidence, Jenny," I exclaimed. "I went to Bryn Mawr Prep. My whole family went there, and so did my best friends Holly, Joe, and Bootsie." It's an extremely expensive, competitive school these days, but when I attended, it had been basically a collection of old buildings out in the countryside, where ancient teachers vainly tried to drill Latin into our heads, and boys played on the golf team instead of trying out for football. Nowadays, thanks to some mega-donations over the past decade, the Prep has a new gym, a high-tech science building, and a glossy Olympic-size pool, and the teenage girls there are almost as chic as Holly. Even Holly hadn't been as chic as Holly when she was in high school.

I turned the bookend around in my hands, inspecting the marks on it more closely. I wondered if the bookends were sold or given to alumni as a keepsake. They definitely weren't gifting them to graduates when Holly and I had finished school fifteen years ago.

Whatever the case, they were perfect for The Striped Awning. I could see the Sophie Shieldses of the worlds loving these tangible pieces of old Main Line history. To top it off, Farrow & Summers had gone out of business in the late 1960s, so the acorns had an even rarer pedigree than I'd imagined at first glance.

"I'd love to take them," I mused aloud, squinting in the sunlight at the acorn. Annie brought out the other two bookends, which were carefully swaddled in newspaper, and unfurled the wrapping so I could see them. They were both a bit tarnished, but in nice condition, like the first one, and had the same inscription. "Where'd you find them?" I asked.

"I can't remember," mused Jenny. "Could have been that market down on South Street in Philly?" I knew this antiques dumping ground, which was so dark and dank that even Waffles and I tend to avoid it. "Or was it a church sale somewhere around here, or the festival in Massachusetts back in April . . . I'm drawing a blank," she admitted, eyes closed above her starry cheeks, lost in thought. "Then again, I've been smoking a lot of weed lately."

"You can have them for fifteen dollars each," said Annie. "We got them for ten, so it's not much of a markup, but you're on the frequent-customer discount." She smiled at me, lighting an American Spirit cigarette and sipping what looked like a cup of wheatgrass juice. At least I think it was an American Spirit. "Great!" I said, starting to help rewrap the acorns gratefully.

Just then, Waffles, seeing that I was distracted, sprang up on his back legs and tipped over the plate of cruelty-free cookies, hoovering all of them up off the grass and into his mouth in one motion. It all happened in a brown-and-white blur of ears, paws, and freckled brown-and-white basset ass.

"No!" I screamed at him. Annie and Jenny both thought it was funny, luckily. Waffles sat there, trying to look guilty and tilting up his head to give us Sad Eyes as he worked the giant mass of quinoa in his jaws. I could tell he didn't give a crap, though. He was just happy he'd gotten the cookies, so they must have been good after all.

"I didn't know he was that hungry," I said, apologizing, as we wrapped up my purchases, and Annie helped me carry the silver items and the bench over to my car, Waffles trotting along behind happily, still chewing. "He already had an Egg McMuffin. I guess I should've gotten him a bratwurst."

"He's an animal!" agreed Annie equably. "Very in tune with his desires. Hey, that can be very Zen and honest."

Just as I popped open the trunk and stashed the bookends, a big white truck pulled up to a few spaces down from me. On its side was scrolled, elegant black lettering that read simply "Colkett."

"Bye, Annie!" I said hastily, eyeing the truck with naked curiosity as Annie ambled back to her table, waving farewell. *What were the most upscale florists/ landscape designers in Philadelphia doing schlepping it at Stoltzfus's?*

Of course, that the Colketts might find things here that were useful in their floral business was possible. There were some pretty vases and planters at one stand, and great old wrought-iron and wicker pieces at another that they could paint and restore, which might come in handy for clients, but frankly, the Colketts seemed too fancy for flea-marketing. The one time I convinced Holly to come here with me, she took one look at an toothless dealer stationed near the parking lot, said she was "scared," got back into the car, and refused to get out again until we were back in Bryn Mawr.

I watched the two florists hop nimbly out of their truck and head inside the roomy barn, then trailed after them as inconspicuously as I could, given that I was accompanied by an oversize basset hound. I wasn't sure Waffles was allowed in the indoor part of the flea market, but I decided to risk it. People in Lancaster County tend to be pretty dog-friendly.

Inside the barn, the Colketts stopped briefly at a vendor who had some lovely Limoges china, bought a teapot painted with delicate roses, and then went right to the beer stand. They each got a twenty-ounce pilsner and went to one of the benches, carefully dusting off the seat with napkins before they sat down.

Now, this was shocking. The Colketts drinking beer? I didn't see that one coming.

I wasn't sure why, but I felt compelled to talk to them, like I was possessed by the inquisitive spirit of Bootsie. Since they were now working for Sophie Shields, I might learn something of interest about Sophie or her husband. So Waffles and I made our way to the bar, and after I ordered a small Summer Ale, I looked over and smiled.

"Hi! Didn't I meet you at Gianni's opening the other night?" I asked them. "You did those beautiful topiaries and flowers." I didn't mention anything about having watched Gianni rip into them and assault them, as I didn't think this was a good topic to stimulate sparkling conversation.

"Oh, hi, doll," said one of the Colketts, who was turned out in a handsome light yellow checked sport coat. He looked ready for the paddock at Ascot, but was a bit over-dressed for Stoltzfus's. He shook my hand politely, and introduced himself as Tom Colkett. "Cute dog," he added as he noticed Waffles, though in truth he looked semi-horrified at the chubby mutt before him. "This is Tim Colkett," he added, gesturing to the man next to him, and I greeted the other Colkett, who was clearly the one Gianni had nailed with the pomegranate; his ear was still red and swollen, and there was a bandage just under his scalp. "We were just visiting our greenhouses out here, they're a few miles down Route 100," Tim explained.

"You're friends with Holly Jones, right?" he added. "We've done work for her and her ex! Remember the Yellow Non-Valentine Valentine's Day Party?"

I did remember. It had been in Holly's old penthouse downtown when Holly had decided that pink and red were "over" for Valentine's Day, and had her entire apart-ment draped in pale yellow silk for a dinner party for seventy-five people. Every table had had towering vases filled with lemons topped with towering lemon-tree branches, and there had been something like four thou-sand votive candles on the terrace and no electric lights. It had been actually a very beautiful party.

"That was fab!" I told them.

"That was us!" said Tom proudly. "And let me tell you, trying to get four hundred live lemon branches to Philadelphia in February is no cakewalk!"

"Isn't this beer delicious?" said the other Colkett, as Waffles hovered near him, sniffing his handmade suede shoes. I realized I still had no idea what the relationship was between the men. They was a resemblance between them, but were they brothers?

"Sorry!" I said, yanking Waffles back over toward me and trying to surreptitiously remove some drool from his whiskers with a beer-garden napkin. "The beer *is* great," I agreed. We chatted about Holly's new Divorce House for a few minutes—the Colketts would be landscaping it to resemble the grounds of Holly's favorite hotel in Italy. "We give divorce discounts!" said Tom Colkett. "And for Holly, we'd do anything. She's so fabulously impractical."

The Colketts were clearly in a talkative mood, so I mustered my inner Bootsie and pressed on. I'm usually a failure at producing tasty morsels of gossip, which irks Bootsie. She'd grill me mercilessly once she heard I'd run into the Colketts, so I desperately threw out what I hoped was a conversation opener. "Did you ever work out your fee with the chef?" I asked. "He, er, seemed a little mercurial the night at his party," I added lamely.

"We're dealing with Jessica, his girlfriend, on the flowers for the restaurant now," explained Tom Colkett. "She's a lot more reasonable than Gianni. Not that he's *un*reasonable," he added nervously, backtracking. "Just, um, temperamental. Talented beyond belief, though."

"A genius with pasta. And his veal chops are even better," agreed Tim, rubbing his red ear agitatedly.

"But his temper is kind of deranged, don't you think?" I felt a little buzzed from the Summer Ale so early in the day, which made me blunter than I'd usually be. I didn't want to annoy the Colketts, but maybe they knew more about Gianni and Barclay's feud, having been around the restaurant a lot. In what I hoped was a casual tone, I added, "Did you ever hear about his disagreement with Barclay Shields? I mean, a lot of people hate Barclay Shields, but he and the chef really loathe each other."

Both Colketts looked alarmed, drained their beers, and got up, dusting off their jackets. They looked at each other, and finally Tim Colkett spoke.

"Look, doll, we don't want to get involved," he said urgently. "Not that we know anything, of course," he added, turning pink and running his hands through his hair. "We're just trying to make an honest living. Look at my ear! I'm still hoping to get one hundred percent of my hearing back after the pomegranate incident the other night."

"You know how it is. Business has to come first. We're out here picking up some trees and rosebushes for Mrs. Shields's party tomorrow night," whispered Tom. "She's redoing her entire yard in one day. You gotta respect that. And our policy is, we get along with everyone. Well, everyone that can afford us, that is," he added.

"Well, cheerio," said Tim, grabbing his companion. The two drained their glasses, got up, and dashed out of the barn.

I stared after them, confused. Were they just scared that Gianni would physically attack them again—maybe with something more dangerous than dried fruit—if he heard that the Colketts talked about him behind his back, or did the guys actually know something damning about Gianni that related to Barclay's attack? And were they brothers?

I went back out to the car with Waffles, gave him water in his portable bowl, then we packed up and went to a barn sale out in Lancaster. We scored a few great items, packed up, and turned toward home.

Once up in the front seat next to me, Waffles lay down with a giant thump. He drank another bowl of water, which seemed like a good idea given his cookie binge. He looked a little green around the gills. He sighed heavily and peered at his belly, looking depressed. All that quinoa couldn't be feeling good in his stomach.

I patted his head, and looked around at the lengthening shadows of the leafy apple orchards that graced the bucolic farms we were passing. It really was so gorgeous here. Life was simple. People worked hard, and no doubt slept as soundly as boulders until they rose with the sun to thresh wheat and build barns.

Maybe I could change my life up entirely, I thought suddenly. I'd find a brawny, stoic Amish man who'd forgo the sect's no-makeup rule and allow me to wear mascara and lip gloss, and together we'd sip lemonade on Sunday afternoons while lambs grazed in our yard. Waffles and I would give up borrowing Holly's expensive shoes and struggling to pay the bills, and adopt simpler pleasures.

But then again, I don't know if I'm really the farming type.

And right now, it was almost cocktail hour, and I was really thirsty. Also, I couldn't miss Sophie's party tomorrow night. I'd have to table this Amish idea for a while. After unloading my purchases into the back room of The Striped Awning, we headed home. Waffles spent some quality time behind his bush and emerged looking relieved while I took a bath, and we both went to bed at our favorite hour: eight-thirty.

Chapter 7

BOOTSIE WAS IN my driveway honking impatiently at four twenty-five the next afternoon, thirty minutes earlier than she was supposed to pick me up for Sophie's symphony benefit, but I was dressed and ready to go. I'd had a productive day cleaning up my yard and had stopped into the store to polish the silver acorns and serving pieces I'd bought in Lancaster County. I'd even gone to the 11 a.m. church service, then splurged on a five-dollar mocha at Starbucks. This was my perfect version of a Sunday.

"This party is going to be huge!" Bootsie crowed as I climbed into her giant SUV, wearing a fantastic yellow sundress that Holly had given to me after wearing it once to the post office and deciding she was "tired of it."

"Bootsie, the event doesn't start till five," I said. "And Sophie's house is less than a mile away."

"Who cares?" shouted Bootsie, gunning her engine

and throwing the gearshift into reverse. "Everyone in Philadelphia is early for parties. Eula Morris knows that. This shindig will kick off at four-thirty, mark my words."

Bootsie roared out of the driveway on two wheels, and Mario-Andrettied the short distance to the Shields mansion.

"Sophie told me yesterday that she's worried Barclay's going to crash the party tonight," I told Bootsie, while my eyes adjusted to the mind-boggling lime-green pattern of her Lilly Pulitzer dress. "If he gets out of the hospital, he'd love to make things uncomfortable for her in front of the symphony crowd."

"Sophie doesn't need to worry about Barclay coming tonight," Bootsie replied, two-wheeling it around a corner of Dark Hollow Road. "He's still in the hospital, and won't get sprung until Friday at the earliest. He wanted to leave this afternoon, but as soon as they wheeled him out of the hospital, Barclay collapsed in the parking lot. They did an EKG in the emergency room, and immediately had to perform an angioplasty."

At this, Bootsie sniffed disapprovingly. Bootsie doesn't believe in angioplasties, or in being fat. She comes from the kind of family that thinks that no matter what the problem, a brisk jog, an aspirin, and a bracing five-mile swim around an icy lake will cure you. Whenever Bootsie's mother, Kitty Delaney, gains a pound, she eats nothing but avocadoes and grapefruit for a week, and Bootsie subscribes to the same spartan regimen.

"Jeannie, our old sitter, was just arriving for her nursing shift and saw the whole thing," Bootsie continued happily. "Now Barclay's on clear liquids, and they've given him a bunch of pamphlets about lap-band surgery," she continued, delivering this news with some relish. "He's stuck there for at least five more days. And he's scared that someone's going to try to kill him again, so he hired a security guard and stationed the guy outside his room."

"Did Jeannie the nurse fill you in about Barclay's visitors on Friday?"

"Of course," Bootsie replied. "Two guys with Jersey accents, in black jeans and leather blazers. They were pissed off about not getting in to see Barclay, and said they were relatives."

"Make that Beppe," I told her. "That's Barclay's real name: Beppe Santino. His nickname was the Forklift, before he had to leave North Jersey when his parents were killed in a suspicious catering-hall incident."

"Are you kidding me!" shrieked Bootsie. "That's fantastic. I had a feeling there was more to Barclay's past!"

"Let's just hope the cousins don't show up at Sophie's," I said. "I don't think Eula Morris was counting on anything other than tomatoes arriving from Jersey tonight."

Bootsie took a left and squealed into a long driveway flanked by arbor vitae, where she almost crashed into Holly and Joe, who'd pulled into the valet parking line before us in Joe's Range Rover. Bootsie was right—we didn't need to worry about being early. There were already a dozen cars queued up to be parked. No one could wait to inspect Sophie, or more importantly, her house. Since I'm as inquisitive as anyone else, I craned my neck out the window to try to see around the line of expensive SUVs into Sophie's property.

I'd never gotten a glimpse of the inner recesses of the Shields estate before, since it was hidden from the road by those enormous hedges. Now, though, a palatial, monstrous structure loomed ahead, evoking Cinderella's castle at Disney World in size and scope. Overhead, the letters BS were woven into the arched gate of a wrought-iron fence that soared above the driveway.

"BS!" shrieked Bootsie. "I love it. This is going to be great!"

Chapter 8

IF NOTHING ELSE, the Shields house was large. I'm no architect, but anyone could see that the house in front of us was an unholy, turreted disaster. Built of brick and faux-limestone blocks, the layout was mini-Versailles in style, with two wings shooting off from either side of a dumpy middle structure. Terraces perched precariously outside most windows, and the letter S was carved into every ornate door. But its size was its most notable attribute: The imprint of the house had to be twelve thousand square feet. Parked at the far end of the driveway were two catering trucks from Gianni, with kitchen workers scurrying to the house toting cartons of what looked like some excellent hors d'oeuvres and gorgeous platters of shellfish. Remembering the lobster of a few nights before, I had a slightly embarrassing surge of excitement. Gianni might be psychotic, but he had a way with seafood.

"Are those *shrimp*?" I whispered to Bootsie, who was still transfixed by the house. "Let's go find the raw bar!"

Bootsie handed her key to a valet just behind Joe and Holly, and we followed them down a grand walkway that led around the right side of the house to the pool. Holly had been invited tonight because her parents' chicken-nugget money had helped pay for a complete overhaul of the Symphony Hall downtown; Joe, as usual, had decided he'd tag along to reconnoiter Sophie's house. "Plus I've heard a lot about Gerda, the Pilates instructor," he whispered loudly. "She's got to be here tonight!"

Holly, of course, resembled a page torn from *Vogue*. As she says herself, her sense of style is kind of wasted on Philadelphia. She had on a short orange dress with a brown Hermès belt and cool brown sandals with lots of straps, and no jewelry at all. Since she owns a lot of spectacular jewelry, I assumed this was some kind of minimalist style statement.

"Uh-oh, there are statues," said Joe, shielding his eyes as he gazed down at the pool area, looking upset.

"And there's Gerda," pointed out Bootsie. At the bottom of the path down from the driveway was a table skirted in white linen, where a symphony intern sat nervously next to Sophie's permanent houseguest.

Gerda, manning the guest checklist, didn't emit a welcoming vibe as she stabbed at our names with a pen, crossing them off with what seemed like more violence than was necessary on such a gorgeous spring evening. Judging by her scowl and somber outfit (black stretch pants and jacket, Nike insignia), Gerda hadn't gotten into the party spirit.

"Down there by pool!" she thundered at us. "That is where party is."

We all took off for said pool, a kidney-shaped affair of vast proportions that was indeed surrounded by some goofy-looking sculptures of nude Grecian women. The yard around it, though, was absolutely beautiful. There were cheerful rosebushes in full bloom, emerald-hued laurel hedges, and beds of heavenly peonies. This had to be the insta-yard created by the Colketts, who were extremely talented, I thought. A small crowd was already mingling around the two bars that had been set up for the night at either end of the pool. Suddenly, a tiny figure in purple emerged from the group clustered around the bar at left and started teetering toward us.

"Yoo-hoo, Kristin!" said Sophie. She was hobbling in a pair of glittery heels, and her small frame was barely supporting what appeared to be most of the contents of the Harry Winston flagship store.

"These are my friends, Holly Jones and Joe Delafield," I said to Sophie. "Sophie Shields," I added unnecessarily to Holly and Joe. "And you know Bootsie."

"Good to meet you. And nice to see you, Beebee," Sophie added to Bootsie, who nodded and then rudely took off, making a beeline for the house with a determined look.

"I think she's hungry," I explained, embarrassed. I knew exactly what Bootsie was up to. It had nothing to do with the buffet, and everything to do with rummaging through Sophie's belongings.

"Your friend with the flowered outfits doesn't waste any time!" giggled Sophie good-naturedly, watching Bootsie dash past the loaded hors d'oeuvres table and up a flight of stairs into the house. "I guess she must need to use the little girls' room! 'Cause the party's outside, not inside. But that's okay!" The only thing Bootsie was interested by in the bathroom were the contents of Sophie's medicine chest, and that would be only the first stop on a full forensic snooping tour of the house. Hopefully Sophie didn't mind Bootsie rifling through her shoe cabinets and flinging open the drawers of her nightstands.

"This is so nice," I said to Sophie, gesturing to the pool, where more guests had arrived, including Honey Potts, in a Bermuda-shorts ensemble, and Mariellen Merriwether, in her usual tasteful linen dress accessorized with opera-length pearls. The Colketts were there, too, futzing around with some potted boxwoods.

"You look amazing!" I added to Sophie, not sure what else to say about her appearance. She looked attractive enough, to be sure, but amazing was the best I could muster up at the moment. Not many people in Philly have the balls to put on a red-carpet-ready lavender silk, gown with a thigh-high slit for an afternoon party.

"It's Versace!" blinked Sophie. "Elizabeth Hurley has the same dress. And Kelly Ripa got it in gold! You gotta wear some major Spanx under this one, I kid you not. Listen, I gotta go mingle, but I'm so glad you came over to my humble abode!"

"Speaking of which," said Joe smoothly, "Sophie, who's your decorator on this, um, fabulous place? Let's get a drink." He took her arm and guided her down to the pool as he started his pitch.

"Sophie's husband has mafia ties!" I hissed to Holly as soon as Sophie was out of earshot. "That is, he probably does." I gave her a quick update as we made our way along a slate walkway flanked by Colkett-installed peonies.

"I love it," said Holly happily. "This town is seriously lacking in organized crime. Just think of how great it would be to have an occasional drive-by shooting!" I was about to remind her that we weren't exactly Drea de Matteo and Edie Falco, but she'd lost interest already.

"Let's go see what gossip the Colketts have for us," suggested Holly, who was scanning the crowd in front of her carefully, though she made an effort to look extremely casual.

Howard, I thought. She's checking to see if Howard is here, which she does so intently at every party she attends that I'm beginning to wonder whether she's having second thoughts about her legal separation and imminent divorce. I'd have to ask her at a quieter moment if she'd really thought through her decision. Her split from Howard is a long story, but can be summed up in that Holly believes that Howard had a fling with a busty bartender at his favorite steakhouse, the Porterhouse, which Howard denies.

"And we can get away from that annoying music," Holly added, gesturing dismissively toward a string quartet made up of symphony members who were gamely sawing away at their instruments over by the rosebushes. I thought the quartet sounded pretty good—the symphony's always playing for the president at the White House, and getting invited to play in China and Russia, so they clearly have some skill—but what do I know about classical music?

I need a drink.

"HELLO, GORGEOUS!" SANG out Tim Colkett at the sight of Holly, who smiled up at him.

"Most beautiful girl in Philadelphia!" Tom Colkett said to Holly, kissing her hand and then greeting me with as much enthusiasm as he could muster.

"What do you think of the new rose garden?" whispered Tim. "This place was a complete dump yesterday morning. It took four truckloads of plants, and thirty yards of mulch. Now, if we can just get Sophie to lose the statues."

"This is going to be nothing, though, compared to *your* yard, doll," Tom assured Holly. "Now, that's going to be freaky-chic! That Cipriani Hotel theme you've dreamed up is totally Sophia Loren."

Just then, on a patio above us, we heard—and saw—Chef Gianni. With his parachute pants billowing and earrings glinting, he launched into a tirade of abuse at a frightened teenage waiter who was about to descend the stairs down to the pool area holding a large silver tray of Parmesan puffs. At the sound of Gianni's screaming, the Colketts froze in terror, then blurted, "Excuse me, dolls," to Holly and me, and bolted toward the far end of the pool and busied themselves rearranging some flowers on the cocktail tables.

"What's with them?" asked Joe, who'd returned from wooing Sophie as a design client, and was in line to get us drinks from the bar.

"They have post-traumatic chef disorder," Holly told him.

Who could blame them? I thought, as Joe handed me a glass of champagne. These Gianni tantrums really were too stressful for a Sunday. I'd visit the buffet, which I could see consisted of a Kilimanjaro of jumbo shrimp and stone crab claws, then convince Bootsie to drive me home.

"I've got to get to the bottom of this mystery," said Holly, tapping her toe contemplatively and sipping her own champagne.

"You mean the mystery of who attacked Barclay?" asked Joe.

"No, I don't care about that," Holly said. "I mean about whether the Colketts are brothers, or if they're boyfriend and boyfriend. This landscaping project at my house will be the perfect opportunity to find out."

I rolled my eyes and veered off from Holly and Joe toward the smaller, second bar to the right of the pool, near where the Colketts were hiding out. There were only a handful of guests over here, sitting at white-clothed little tables decorated with potted orchids.

"Could I please have a little more champagne?" I asked the bartender, a pretty, dark-haired girl who I remembered from Gianni's restaurant opening. Since I was hoping to leave shortly, I figured I'd better drink up and make my move on the shrimp. I felt like a freeloader, but I was starving after my day of household chores, and is there anything better than cold shrimp and champagne? I'm pretty sure there isn't.

I put three shrimp on a little plate, then reached for the tongs again and added another, ladled a large dollop of cocktail sauce next to them, dipped a shrimp, and stuffed it into my mouth. "Yummmm," I said to myself happily, making sure I wasn't getting sauce on Holly's yellow dress.

"The shrimp are great," said a tall man next to me, who was wielding the silver serving pieces to score himself some crab claws. "Little high in cholesterol, though."

I looked up, disconcerted at being caught mid-gulp, and annoyed by the anti-shellfish stance this guy was taking. But then I noticed that he had nice blue eyes, brown hair with some gray in it, and was smiling down at me in a friendly way. I instantly revised my position. The guy was in his late thirties, I guessed, and actually was incredibly good-looking. Plus, while he was way more well-groomed than my usual scruffy type, there was an appealing hint of five-o'clock shadow forming on his handsome jaw. This man was obviously just concerned with my health.

He squeezed half a lemon on his crab, and in a gentlemanly way offered to squeeze some on my shrimp.

"Thanks," I said, proffering my plate for the lemon spritz. "Honestly, these shrimp are so good, they're worth it."

"You're right," he said, popping some crab in his mouth. "I have a theory about buffets. You need to skip all the extraneous stuff—like bread, salad, anything that's just filler—and focus on the key items. Any kind of fish or filet mignon comes first. If it's brunch, then I do the omelet bar, the cheeses, the roast turkey, and then I go right to dessert. You can't waste stomach space on things like donuts." I had to agree, this made a lot of sense.

"I'm sorry, I shouldn't have said that about the shrimp," he added apologetically. He really had nice eyes with some great crinkly lines around them, which made him all the more appealing. "I just read a story in a medical journal about some of the health risks of shellfish, but it's not good cocktail conversation."

Was he a doctor? I love doctors. As Holly would say, they're so medical.

"You're a doctor?" I asked hopefully.

"I'm a vet," he said. "Large animals, mostly. But I read the AMA journal, too. Sometimes research on people can have implications for how we treat our animal patients. Not that the animals I treat are eating a lot of shrimp." I tried to follow along with the conversation, but was preoccupied by taking in his deep tan and the sexy lines around his blue eyes.

He also had this kind of incredibly honest look to him. That isn't my usual type, but then again, my type wasn't exactly working for me. And there was absolutely nothing about the vet that said *Going to Thailand*. If anything, his vibe was more: *Going to gas up my station wagon, then take a jog around Bryn Mawr, grill a steak, and go to sleep.* In other words, he seemed really normal.

"I have a dog," I told him. "He's a really sweet basset hound. He's a little stubborn, but he's so lovable . . ." My voice trailed off for a second as I was momentarily distracted by the sight of Honey and Mariellen lurking near the house. "It's too bad that Lilly isn't here tonight," I heard Honey growl. "Where is she, again?"

"Tennis tournament," Mariellen drawled. "Up in Greenwich. You know my daughter, she won't miss a tennis match." I did a mental eye roll. How could anyone get excited enough to drive four hours to Connecticut to swat a tennis ball?

And then I noticed that standing next to Honey was a man in a navy blazer, khakis, and what appeared to be Gucci loafers. He was youngish, handsome, and not too tall. He looked perfectly at ease among the symphony crowd. And then I almost dropped my drink, because the man was grinning at me, and the man was Mike Woodford.

His hair had been combed, his stubble had been shorn, and he looked positively symphony-ready. You could have popped him into a box at the opera hall downtown, stuck a program for Mozart's Requiem in his hand, and no one would have blinked an eye.

What was Mike doing here? And more importantly, what was he doing in Gucci loafers?

"You have a basset hound?" asked the vet. I tore myself away from staring at the cowherd.

"Great dogs," said the hot vet, leaning down to grab a

few carrot sticks from the buffet. "Prone to obesity and back problems, but really great breed."

I nodded, but I had the uncomfortable sense that Mike was watching me, and I'd lost my appetite for my shrimp. Well, almost. I ate another one, gulped my champagne, and put my plate down on one of the little tables.

As I did so, I suddenly felt Mariellen's icy blue gaze fixed on me. Surprised, I looked away, then looked back, and saw La Merriwether stub out her cigarette in a glass ashtray in a positively sinister, Joan-Crawford-in-*Mommie-Dearest* way, still eyeing me with evident disdain. What had I done to upset her? Was there cocktail sauce on my face? Or did she know that I was the trespasser who'd helped make an unfortunate discovery at her best friend's estate three nights before? Then I looked back, and noticed that her malevolent glare had been transferred to the good-looking veterinarian.

It was probably time to head home.

"Oh, hiya, Kristin, ya having fun?" squeaked Sophie suddenly, appearing at my elbow. "Like the shrimp? They're from Palm Beach! Gianni had 'em flown in!"

"They're fantastic," I told her. "Thank you so much, they're really incredible, and so, uh, big! Sophie Shields, this is . . ." I gestured toward the vet, realizing I didn't know his name.

"John Hall," he said, shaking Sophie's teeny hand, which was obscured by two giant cocktail rings. "Thank you for having me."

"Think nothing of it!" she said, looking over her shoulder nervously. "Eek, Gerda looks a little mad." She giggled. "She's my Pilates instructor," she whispered to John Hall. "The one over there with the clipboard."

Gerda glared at Sophie from her check-in station, and crunched angrily on a stalk of raw broccoli. Out of the corner of my eye, I noticed Mariellen and Honey walking swiftly toward Sophie's house. Either they needed a bathroom break, or they were succumbing to the same impulse to snoop that Bootsie had given in to.

Gerda got up from her table, and hotfooted it after Mariellen and Honey, perhaps sensing an imminent ransacking of her and Sophie's desks and closets. She pointed at Sophie's glass of champagne, shaking her head in disapproval as she disappeared inside the house.

"Gerda banned me from drinking anything alcoholic or carbonated. Champagne's a double no-no, so I gotta sneak it," Sophie told me and John, turning her back on Gerda to chug a flute of Mumm. "She won't even drink beer, which is like her national beverage. Plus she and the chef already had a big fight when he brought in a tub of veal shanks for the next course. He's making osso buco to serve after the seafood tonight, but Gerda claims to be a vegan! But I happen to know that one time last year she scarfed a whole plate of leftover sausage before my ex moved out, and boy, was he pissed!"

"That's unfortunate," said John politely. He looked confused by Sophie's monologue, and he was starting to sweat a little. He signaled to the girl at the bar for a glass of water.

"Oh fuck!" shrieked Sophie, glancing up at the house, where Gianni stood on a little patio outside the kitchen.

"There's the chef, flagging me down with that goddamn dish towel again. I gotta go."

"Sophie!" yelled the chef from his terrace, his tall form bent over the railing to shout across the pool to Sophie. "There is big problem with your stove!"

Sophie hustled toward him as quickly as her tiny frame and giant heels would take her toward the house, but just as she neared the edge of the pool near the house, Gianni erupted in Italian.

We all looked up, including Sophie, whose mouth formed an O of horror.

The chef had somehow lost his balance: He tumbled off the balcony, Crocs flying, arms flailing, and did a mid-air somersault as he thumped heavily into a bank of rosebushes below. He also managed to topple onto the quartet's cello player. His colleagues crashed to a halt in their song, while Sophie, just inches away, was unhurt. She seemed frozen on the spot, and indeed for a moment, no one spoke, or even breathed.

"*Merda!*" screamed the chef, finally breaking the silence.

"Ouch," moaned the cellist.

"Ohmigod!" exploded Sophie. "Chef Gianni's dead!"

Chapter 9

THE CHEF WASN'T dead, though. No dead man could scream that loudly. The bushes he'd landed on were newly planted in a thick, pillowy layer of mulch, which appeared to break his fall, and also, luckily, cushioned his impact on the hapless cello player—though the cello itself hadn't been as fortunate. The chef was thrashing, cursing, and struggling to get up. The cello player, meanwhile, had rolled onto his back, the wind knocked out of him, his tuxedo torn and covered with rose petals and mulch. The cellist was a robust man, but he appeared dazed as he clutched his bow and stared at the tragic remains of his once-beautiful and expensive instrument.

"Excuse me," said John Hall. "I'll go check on those two," and he walked over calmly toward the two men to assist with their medical care, insomuch as a vet can doctor two-legged creatures. I noticed that Mariellen and Honey had blithely reemerged from the house by the basement door. They cast a bemused eye at the tattooed chef and the fallen musician. The Colketts, on the other hand, looked panicked. They, too, had been inside the house during the over-the-railing incident, and their heads popped out at the top of the patio from which the chef had fallen. Their sunglasses were off, and their handsome faces looked terrified, until a millisecond later, when they disappeared back into the house.

Above me, Bootsie popped out on another balcony on the third floor, outside what I guessed was Sophie's bedroom, her eyes bulging as she took in the situation below. She turned and ran back into the house. I felt a little badly that she'd missed out on the ruckus.

"Oh, Chef, I'm so sorry!" wailed Sophie, hovering over him and helplessly trying to pluck thorny branches from his thighs while the vet examined the cellist for broken bones. "You musta slipped on some seafood! Shrimp and crab get so gooey when it gets warm. I feel terrible for ya!"

"I did not slip!" screamed the chef. "I have special treads on my Crocs—I never slip." He sat up, and gestured toward the kitchen. "I was pushed!"

Sophie looked thunderstruck by this accusation, as did most of the crowd, but Gerda, standing over him, was having none of it. "No one here would commit crime. I am like security guard as well as Pilates professional." She crossed her muscular arms and stared down at the chef. "You slipped," she said firmly.

"Fuck you!" he replied.

I noticed that Gianni's girlfriend Jessica didn't look all that worried about her boyfriend. She sauntered over to a table, sucked down the last of her mojito, and ground out her cigarette with her Louboutin before she made her way over to Gianni, who was still screaming insults at Sophie and Gerda.

Within a couple of minutes, I heard the wails of an ambulance arriving. Bad news traveled fast, apparently, and I noticed the same two medics who'd removed Barclay Shields on Thursday night galloping down Sophie's driveway with their gurney at the ready. On their heels was Officer Walt.

I figured this was the perfect time to leave, so I booked it over to Holly and Joe, who were standing at the other bar, to say good-bye.

"I should go over to the chef and act sympathetic," said Holly, sighing and topping off her own glass, since the bartenders had stopped serving and were simply standing and gaping.

"I'm going to wait until the screaming subsides," said Joe, blithely munching on crab.

Mariellen, meanwhile, was watching the cluster of people gathering around Gianni with her mouth pursed in disapproval as she pulled at her pearls distractedly. Honey gathered up her L.L. Bean tote bag—not very cocktail-party-appropriate, but then again, neither were her kelly-green blazer and shorts—and, with drink and bag in hand, made one last run at the hors d'oeuvres buffet (which, given the chef's predicament, clearly wasn't going to be restocked).

If I knew Honey—which I didn't, but I seemed to be running into her a lot lately—she was at least six minutes away from departing. There was still a good twenty pounds of crab on ice on the buffet, and no matter how much Mariellen nagged, Honey wasn't going to leave until she did some damage to that pile of shellfish. From what I'd observed, while she wasn't an eater on par with Barclay Shields, Honey was no slouch.

Since I now seemed to be on Mariellen's shit list, and was still avoiding Honey, I used her proclivity for grazing as the perfect opportunity to leave before the three of us were caught in an awkward standoff in the valet-parking line. Quickly, I scanned the crowd again, wondering where the hell Bootsie was, when a glass of champagne appeared in front of me. And the flute of bubbly in question was being held by one extremely tanned hand.

"Leaving already?" said Mike Woodford.

I turned around as my stomach did a small flip. I have to admit, Mike cleaned up well. I actually preferred his usual T-shirt and Levi's outfit, but the blue blazer and white shirt looked really good with his tan. I couldn't even smell any eau de cow, just some manly-smelling soap. Irish Spring, if I wasn't mistaken. "Don't go yet," he said in my ear. The beard stubble felt amazing against my earlobe, and I looked into his dark brown eyes, which looked friendly and a little amused.

"What did I miss?" exploded Bootsie, suddenly popping up next to me. She was so anguished about missing the chef's tumble that she didn't even notice Mike and his beard stubble invading my ear.

"Bootsie, we should go. The medics need all the cars out of the driveway," I improvised, turning away from

Mike and ignoring the champagne he'd brought me. I didn't want to be rude, but this wasn't the time to introduce him to Bootsie.

"Are you nuts?" said Bootsie. "This is the social event of the season!" I shot an embarrassed glance back at Mike, told him, "Bye!" and bolted up the path toward the driveway at a quick trot, Bootsie on my heels.

"Did someone really push Gianni?" she hissed.

"It all happened really quickly," I told her over my shoulder. "It seemed more like an accident." The chef, quieter now, was being wheeled up the pathway to the ambulance into which the medics neatly inserted him and sped away. Another ambulance wailed into the driveway to pick up the cellist.

"Can we please leave now?" I implored Bootsie.

"Of course not," she said. "I'm a *journalist*," Bootsie added. "This is big news now that the che's been injured."

I'm pretty sure writing up suburban real estate transactions doesn't make Bootsie the next Christiane Amanpour, but it was pointless to argue with her.

"Honestly, it looked like Chef Gianni just lost his footing," I told her, inwardly debating my options of ways to get home.

Bootsie brushed this aside. "Just so you know, I'm here reporting for the paper *and* doing a little research for Will's cousin Louis, the lawyer," she told me. "Louis asked me to help him come up with some theories about what might have happened to Barclay Shields on Thursday night. And right now, I'm thinking Sophie and her Pilates teacher were somehow involved with both attacks."

Bootsie nodded meaningfully at Gerda, who was helping the medics push a gurney containing the cello player up the hill. "Just look at her! Sophie probably had Gerda push Gianni over the railing just now, and I think Gerda also did the job on Barclay's head the other night."

"Maybe," I said doubtfully. "But Sophie told us she loses money if Barclay dies. And why would Sophie want to kill the chef? Sophie needed the chef alive and cooking tonight. There was another whole course to go after the shrimp—Sophie wouldn't have wanted her guests to miss out on the osso buco."

"Well, then, maybe Gerda attacked him without Sophie's approval," mused Bootsie determinedly. "Gerda could be a rogue operator. I'm positive she had something to do with this. Look at her—she's beaming!"

Gerda did have a creepy smile on her makeup-free face as she left the driveway and marched back toward the house, seemingly pleased that the party was over and that people were beginning to head up the hill from the pool area.

"Why don't you come back here with me tomorrow?" I whispered to Bootsie. "I'm sending over a truckload of stuff from the store to Sophie. You can help me unpack it. Now, will you take me home?"

Bootsie perked up at this opportunity to further nose around Sophie's. "Count me in on moving the stuff from your store!"

"Great!" I said, relieved. "Let's get your car." I waved frantically at one of the valet parkers.

Suddenly, Bootsie elbowed me in my side (which kind

of hurt), and hissed, "Look at that!" She nodded at the far end of the driveway, where Jessica the interior designer was disappearing off toward an SUV parked over with the catering trucks—presumably to rush to Gianni's side at the hospital. And Jessica was accompanied by one of the cooks who worked for Gianni.

I could see why Bootsie was staring. The cook was gorgeous. He looked to be in his mid-twenties, with ridiculously muscular arms rippling under his white T-shirt and cook's jacket, a deep tan, brownish-blond hair brushed back from his high cheekbones. He was the ultimate in cabana-boy fantasy. He was shepherding Jessica up the stairs, his arm crooked under her skinny elbow, and they were whispering to each other in a way that suggested—okay, screamed—intimacy.

"That guy is *hot*!" exploded Bootsie.

She took off to eavesdrop on Jessica and the cook, and I looked at the valet parkers, who were all about nineteen and looked like they could use an extra ten bucks to buy beer with.

I bet I could bribe one of them to give me a quick ride home in Bootsie's SUV. Or maybe I could walk. My borrowed shoes, though they had three-inch heels, weren't all that uncomfortable, and the walk would take less than fifteen minutes. Unless I got a bad blister, which happens a lot with Holly's shoes.

"Kristin?" I heard an elderly voice call from behind me.

Reluctantly, I turned around. It was my fussy neighbor, Hugh Best, in a pink sport coat. Right behind him was Mike, who was handing a numbered ticket to one of the valets.

"May I offer you a ride home, my dear?" Hugh Best wheezed gallantly. He gestured toward his ancient dark red Volvo, which was idling in Sophie's driveway, a cloud of smoke bellowing from its rusty tailpipe.

"Thank you. That would be great!" I said, ignoring Mike's raised eyebrows as Hugh scurried over to open the dusty passenger-side door and push aside a box of Kleenex, a pipe spilling tobacco, and a giant container of Metamucil.

"My brother is always leaving a mess in here," he apologized.

I climbed into the car, determined not to look back at Mike. This was better than walking home in heels—probably—so who cared what he thought. "I like your jacket," I told Hugh, trying to make conversation. "It's very cheerful."

Hugh had on old, well-pressed khakis, a white-and-blue striped shirt (slightly frayed), that pink sport coat circa 1968, and a silk ascot. He did look very gentlemanly, with his white hair combed back and his good posture. He had an appealing, courtly quality. And Hugh struck me as the type who hated to stay out past 8 p.m., just like me.

"And may I say, your dress is very attractive," said Hugh gallantly, as we pulled out onto Dark Hollow Road. "This was quite an interesting evening."

"That's for sure," I agreed.

"Actually, we don't really support the symphony financially as much as we used to," Hugh told me, looking a little embarrassed. "We, er, would, but our investments are down a little this year, so Eula Morris invited me and my brother as her guests."

"I don't support it, either!" I told him. "I'm only going because the hostess, Mrs. Shields, bought a lot of things at my store the other day, and she invited me."

"Interesting decision, moving the party to the Shields residence," Hugh said chattily, steering the old car carefully. "I'd originally planned to walk over to Sanderson for this fete, but then when all that happened"—he made a vague gesture toward the crime scene tape at Sanderson, which we were just passing—"I got a call from Eula about the change of venue. My brother had been planning to go, but when he heard at was at this Shields woman's house, he 'shit-canned' the idea, as he put it. He doesn't approve of flashy people. I, on the other hand, am open to new things and ideas."

We turned into the Bests' driveway next to mine, the car huffing and puffing up the little hill to their house, belching smoke. I noticed the last inspection sticker on the windshield was dated 1989, so I guess Hugh's interest in modernity didn't include keeping current with state car inspections.

The Best house was about as different from Sophie's as you could get, though it was nearly as big. The brothers had lived in the beautiful white stucco Georgian, half hidden by hedges and old rose gardens, their whole lives. As the years went on and family members had died off, only Hugh and his brother were left. They occasionally appeared on the lawn to pull weeds and trim shrubs, but for the most part, I heard them bickering on their back porch more often than I actually saw them these days. They also listened to a lot of big band music, and songs by Ella Fitzgerald and Louis Armstrong often floated over the fence along with cigar smoke.

After Hugh's confiding that he'd been at the party as a fellow freebie, it seemed clear that the Bests' fortunes had indeed declined over the past couple of decades. No wonder their house was looking a little more rickety every year.

They belonged to the country club, too, and I always stopped to say hello if I spied them on the club porch or in the bar. My grandparents had been friendly with the brothers at one time, until Jimmy had had too many Scotches one night at the club and groped Grandma as she passed him en route to the ladies' room, which had resulted in Grandpa temporarily banning the Bests from their house. Grandma had laughed it off—she had always been gorgeous, and continued to be so into her seventies, but Grandpa apparently hadn't found it all that funny.

Hmm. I guess I was lucky that Hugh was driving me home, and not Jimmy the groper.

I thanked Hugh as I emerged from the Volvo, went in my gate, and opened my back door to Waffles, who'd heard the car pull up and was waiting like a Thoroughbred penned in the starting gate. He trampled me, Pamplona style, and dashed out the door, ears flying. I dusted off Holly's dress, grabbed a leash, and went outside to find him. Apparently, I hadn't latched the gate properly when

I came in, because Waffles was out and tearing across the driveway toward the Bests' front door, hot on the scent of Hugh, who'd already gone inside.

Waffles galloped up the front stairs to their screen door, and started scratching the door frame with his freckled paws and howling into the Bests' dim foyer. "No!" I hissed at the dog, dashing through the holly hedge to grab his collar and drag him home.

"Back already?" I heard a voice yell from somewhere deep in the old house. "You freeloading bastard!" It was Jimmy, lambasting his brother. This was really embarrassing. Once again, Waffles had landed me exactly where I didn't want to be.

"Waffles!" I shrieked, while the dog ignored me. *I really should have sprung for that obedience class at PetSmart*, I thought, racing up the short flight of porch steps to get my wayward hound.

Just as I reached Waffles, the dog let out a series of songlike howls that could be heard in Pittsburgh. Jimmy came to the door and opened it to peer out into the dusk. Unfortunately, I could see well enough to notice that Jimmy was nude.

Waffles, wagging, took advantage of the open door, ran inside, sniffed Jimmy in places that I'd rather not remember, then disappeared into the house.

Chapter 10

"WHAT THE FUCK?" said Jimmy.

"I am so sorry," I said, looking up at the portico, down at the frayed doormat, and at my shoes, anywhere but at the region between Jimmy's knees and his belly button. Where the hell had Waffles gone? "I'll just get the dog and go. I'll wait outside, though . . . while you grab a robe?"

I looked away from the expanse of elderly man-parts. Jimmy was saggy, hairy, skinny, and—I had to get out of there. He had bushy eyebrows, a big nose, a cigar stuck into his mouth, and I'd noticed an amused grin on his face under a graying mustache. Jimmy was a pincher and a grabber, but I'd never seen him wandering around naked before. Maybe he liked to get naked when Hugh went out? Or was he *having sex* with someone? Could he possibly have a lady friend?

"Ooh, my," I heard Hugh wheeze from upstairs, and heard a thud that sounded like he'd just been knocked to the ground. "Nice doggie," I heard him mumble in a cajoling tone.

"Come on in!" growled Jimmy. "I'll just go put on some shorts, and see if I can locate that hound of yours." He gestured toward their foyer and the hallway beyond, then trudged up the stairs while I turned and buried my face into some beautiful tea roses that were climbing up the porch pillars. Gosh, these roses were really fragrant and gorgeous, which helped distract me from Jimmy's rear view, which was no prettier than the front had been.

When Jimmy got upstairs and disappeared around the corner, I came inside to their foyer, and hissed "Waffles!" up the stairs. Naturally, he didn't appear, but I could hear his paws clicking on the floor upstairs as he checked out all the bedrooms. I'd never been inside the Bests' house before. It had a lot of charm, with old hunting prints in pretty wooden frames crowding the walls of the red-painted hallway, and a dining room with a long antique table to my right. There was a big living room on the left, with formal satin drapes faded by years of sunlight and needlepoint chairs and sofas in serious need of restoration and a good dusting. But all in all, it was very tasteful, if a little tattered. You'd never know this was the house of a nudist.

I had a horrible thought: What if Jimmy and Hugh came back downstairs and they were *both* naked? It was like *Arsenic and Old Lace* over here, but with old naked guys instead of adorable killer aunties. *Darn you, Waffles.*

"Waffles!" I half shouted again.

There were some very pretty pieces of china in the

cabinets surrounding the fireplace, and lots of old leather-bound books, I noticed, as Waffles skidded down the stairs and bounded happily into the living room toward me, drool flying. Jimmy appeared behind him in a smoking jacket worn over a white T-shirt and khakis, with Hugh just behind him. I knelt next to Waffles, spouting apologies as I clipped on his leash and prepared to head for the door.

"Not at all, and I'm sorry about that earlier moment," said Jimmy, with a bawdy wink. "Just caught me coming out of my bath. Don't usually wander around naked as the day I was born."

"Oh, I understand," I said, pulling the leashed dog toward the front hallway urgently.

"Do stay for a drink!" said Hugh politely. "We've got deviled eggs on the porch, if you're hungry. My brother is very sorry about exposing himself." He glared at Jimmy and gestured down the hallway, past the staircase toward their back porch.

"Well, I'm not that sorry," Jimmy said, shrugging, as herded me and Waffles along the hall and out onto the porch, where he went to a little bar stocked with a dozen bottles and glass decanters. "I always take a bath this time of night. And how the hell was I supposed to know an overweight dog was going to come bounding in the door, with Kristin after him? I can't be fully dressed all the time, you know."

"I really should go—" I said, but Jimmy sloshed Scotch into a glass over ice cubes and handed it to me as he ushered me toward an old yellow armchair on the screened-in back porch. I didn't know what else to do, so I sat. Next to me, being uncharacteristically obedient, Waffles sat, too.

"In a way, it's good timing that you popped over," Jimmy growled, emitting a cloud of cigar smoke as he glugged more Scotch into glasses, and rudely pushed a drink at his brother, "since we're in the middle of an argument here that you can weigh in on."

"Don't drag her into this!" Hugh barked. "The fact is, we've been offered a lot of money for this house," Hugh added primly, sitting down on a yellow-cushioned wicker loveseat. "And we badly need money."

"So my brother here has come up with the most predictable, bourgeois, and God-awful idea I've ever heard in my life," Jimmy spat out.

"I have a *plan*—a practical, realistic plan," said Hugh, trembling a little with indignation. "Deviled egg, dear?" he added, handing me a tray of egg halves dusted with paprika. I wondered how long they'd been sitting out germinating botulism, but took one so I wouldn't offend him. In a flash, Waffles grabbed it out of my hand and gulped it down. Luckily neither of the Bests noticed, since they were busy arguing.

I took a sip of noxious-tasting Scotch, then gulped some more just to pass the time. I figured staying five minutes was long enough to be polite, and then I'd be out of here.

"Hugh's plan is that he wants to sell our house and move to *Florida*." Jimmy pronounced the word "Florida" like his brother had suggested that they up and move into a giant pile of garbage. Personally, I like Florida, so I wasn't sure what he was so upset about. "He's even met with a developer about selling this place off as a teardown."

"Palm Beach County is a great place to retire!" retorted Hugh. "If we sell now, we'll have enough money to buy a condo. And I might even get a job down there. I've been reading the *Palm Beach Post* online. Costco is hiring."

"Costco!" thundered Jimmy, picking up a decanter and sloshing more amber liquid into his glass. "Is that what the Best family has come to? Why not Wal-Mart?"

"This member of the Best family is tired of freezing his nuts off every winter," Hugh screamed back at his brother. "And this Best wants to enjoy the few years left he has on earth enjoying himself, not huddled under a moth-eaten old quilt in Philadelphia, eating your tuna casseroles!"

This exchange didn't really bother me, because the Scotch was sloshing through my bloodstream on top of the champagne, and I was suddenly feeling completely bombed. It was too bad that Jimmy and Hugh weren't getting along, I thought boozily, because their back porch was adorable. A ceiling fan provided a nice little breeze, and a giant old 1960s-era stereo was pumping out jazzy tunes. The porch was painted white with bright green trim, with a screened wall facing a grove of oak trees. At either end of the room were bookshelves loaded with books, old *Racing Forms*, and picture frames filled with shots of Best ancestors vacationing in WASPy places like Maine and Rhode Island.

Just then, the radio broke into "What a Wonderful World," which didn't exactly fit the mood, but the
dreamy old song appeared to calm Hugh down a little.
He sat down and added in a grannyish way to his brother,
"If you hadn't married that series of waitresses from the
club, we wouldn't be in this position," then offered me
another deviled egg.

I ate one, which was thankfully still cold, and presumably not swimming with E. coli. I knew these deviled
eggs. They were from the deli counter at the Buy-Right.
The Buy-Right was the oldest supermarket in town, and
only the oldest and least progressive families still shopped
there now that the glitzier Publix had opened. I had a
soft spot for the Buy-Right, having grown up buying our
groceries there. Plus my grandparents had often bought
these very snacks, and they were really pretty good. I was
touched by the fact that Hugh had presented the hors
d'oeuvres on a slightly battered silver tray, with some ancient linen cocktail napkins at the ready, even though he
hadn't been expecting guests. He stuck to the old, formal
ways.

"They weren't all waitresses," said Jimmy airily. "There
were some dancers, as well."

"Strippers from Atlantic City!" protested Hugh.
"With giant hooters! Er, sorry, Kristin," he added.

"There was one stripper," conceded Jimmy, puffing
cigar smoke toward the screened windows. "But your
money-management skills haven't exactly helped matters. Every stock you buy turns to absolute shit. "

"You can't keep your pants zipped!" screamed Hugh.

"Not true. I haven't tried anything on this one, and she's been next door for some time now," said Jimmy, waving his cigar at me. "Sorry, darling, you're not my type. I like a little more up top than you've got. And I'm partial to blondes."

"That's okay," I said. That's pretty much the case with all men. I figured I could leave now, so I headed toward the front door. "Well, thanks," I said to Jimmy, who gave me an affable grunt, and went back to reading his *Racing Form* as Hugh walked me out while Waffles trailed happily behind us.

"By the way," I asked Hugh, as Waffles and I exited onto his front porch. "Which developer did you meet with about selling your house?"

"Shields," said Hugh. "Fellow who got knocked on the head the other night."

He looked embarrassed. "When it came right down to it, his offer was awfully low. Couldn't find it in me to take so little for our family home."

I STUMBLED OUT of the house, clutching Waffles's leash and feeling a little woozy from the Scotch. I was also digesting the news that Barclay had tried to wrest the Bests' house out from under them. Barclay really was incredibly ambitious. No wonder people got murderously angry at him. Could Jimmy Best have gotten so mad at Barclay about the low offer that he'd attacked the developer? It seemed far-fetched, but then again, Jimmy is an unpredictable, angry old dude. Hugh had displayed a surprisingly bad temper tonight, and I'd thought of him as a passive fellow all these years, but maybe there was a geyser of rage lurking under his colorful sport coats and black socks.

I'd hate to see Hugh and Jimmy's house torn down, but I could see Hugh's argument for Florida, too. Philly in winter is dark, grim, gray, and grimy. Every January, I consider the notion of grabbing Waffles, piling into the car, and driving until we reach Key West, where I'd get find a job at a taco stand and never come back.

Still, it's hard to leave a place you love. Too bad they didn't have enough money for Hugh, at least, to go to Florida for the winter. It seemed like the brothers could use a little time apart.

Waffles and I trotted through the holly hedge and, boom!—there was Mike Woodford, who was lounging against my fence, sipping a bottle of Corona and looking at me in a friendly manner. He'd taken off his blue blazer, and his nice white shirt looked fresh and clean in the early-evening air.

"What were you doing over there?" he said, patting Waffles on his brown head, as Waffles in turn sniffed his knees happily.

"Drinking Scotch with my neighbors," I told him.

"You look kind of bombed," he said. He walked closer to me and looked at me curiously. "Do you normally drink Scotch?"

I shook my head. "It was an unusual situation. Trust me, you would have been drinking, too. One of the Bests was naked for a while. He got dressed, just not right away."

"That old guy who drove you home got naked?" he asked.

"No, it was the other one," I said wearily, too tired to explain the whole thing to him. Then I added, "And it turns out that Barclay Shields tried to buy the Bests' house, which didn't go over too well with one of them. So now I have to worry about whether one of the Best brothers tried to kill Barclay." *In addition to wondering about whether you did it,* I added to myself.

However, I was mostly focusing on Mike's beard stubble, which not two hours before had been grazing my ear.

"I wouldn't worry about the old guys trying to kill Barclay," he said. "They seem pretty harmless."

After this, Mike took Waffles's leash from me, shoved me back toward the fence, took hold of my shoulders, and kissed me senseless in the dusk under a rising moon. This up-against-a-fence twilight make-out scenario was fantastic until Waffles started pawing my leg, at which point I remembered that I had a few questions for Mike.

"What were you doing at that symphony party?" I asked him.

"What were you doing there?" he countered.

"I was invited by Sophie Shields!" I told him.

"I was invited by Honey Potts," he replied, leaning back with a grin.

I guess he'd one-upped me on that one. "Have you always been a Gucci-loafer wearer?" I asked, glancing down at his shoes.

"Birthday present from my mom," he told me. "Years

ago, when she was trying to make me into a respectable business type or a lawyer."

I tried to imagine his origins, and a mom who'd hoped he'd be a lawyer or banker, and instead raised a cow farmer. "Where are you from?" I asked him.

"Maryland," he said. "Outside D.C." He paused for a minute, and ran a hand along my spine in a shivery and awesome way. "Well, I gotta go." With that, he took off down the dark driveway.

That was it? He's "gotta go"? Apparently so, since he was already gone from sight.

"Be careful," I called after him, suddenly feeling worried that he might get bashed in the head, too.

"I don't build ugly houses, so I should be fine."

Chapter 11

THE NEXT MORNING I woke up with a head that felt like it was stuffed into a helmet that was three sizes too small. Ugh. Scotch. My face felt raw from Mike's stubble, and I was as thirsty as Chevy Chase in the desert sequence of the first *Vacation* movie.

I checked the weather from my bedroom window, which was breezy and cloud-free, and froze when I noticed movement on the Bests' porch. Jimmy poked his head out, looked both ways, then ran out and grabbed his newspaper from the front lawn. He had a towel on.

"Phew!" I said to Waffles, then shut up, because it hurt to talk. This was a hangover that only a fried-egg sandwich and a giant coffee could cure.

Then I had a sudden flash of hope, realizing it was Monday, and Visa should have deposited Sophie's funds into my checking account. I dialed the bank to get my automatic balance update over the phone. Forty-five seconds later, I sprang out of bed, let Waffles out in the backyard, and practically danced back upstairs and into the shower with the kind of joy that can only come when you've just found out that there's more than seven thousand dollars in your bank account.

I could pay down my rent and settle my credit card balance! I could buy Waffles some new rawhide bones, and right after I got dressed and out of the shower, we were going to go get the biggest, most overpriced lattes in Bryn Mawr! My hangover instantly disappeared.

Forty-five minutes later, Waffles and I pulled out of Starbucks with four venti lattes anchored in a carrier, and aimed for the U-Haul rental behind the Sunoco station. Renting a truck took just ten minutes, and soon we were headed down Lancaster Avenue to pick up Bootsie. I'd called her earlier, catching her while she was dropping her kids off at nursery school, hoping she was still up for helping me move the stuff into Sophie's house, which of course she was.

In the few minutes it took for me to drive over to Bootsie's office, I briefly reviewed the night before and planned to leave the make-out session with Mike out of my chat with Bootsie. Bootsie can be surprisingly sex-obsessed, and tries to instigate other people into wild schtupping sessions as often as possible. I knew she'd eventually find out I'd kissed Mike, but decided to postpone the embarrassing questions as long as I could.

As I pulled up to the *Gazette*, Bootsie looked like she was about to explode with gossip. Her cheeks were pink, her eyes bright, and her toes tapping in the whale sandals.

"I've got a lot of news," she said, climbing into my car. "Most of it about Gianni, some of it about Barclay, and a little bit about Sophie Shields."

Even though I was still feeling the aftereffects of Mike's stubble on my neck, I wondered if Bootsie had any information about the cute vet, John Hall. Then again, I didn't have time to have a crush on a vet. I had to focus on Sophie's delivery, and on getting the store restocked and ready for business. Also, I had to focus on not having a crush on Mike Woodford. I banished all thoughts of men from my mind and sucked down some coffee.

The *Bryn Mawr Gazette* offices, which are in an old limestone-fronted bank building, had been spruced up a bit in the past few days, I noticed. Planters on the steps to the front door had been filled with ivy and white geraniums, and the door had been painted a cheery yellow. Bootsie gratefully accepted her latte and was dumping Sugar in the Raw into it as we drove to The Striped Awning to meet Gerda and Sophie.

"I like that new front door to your office," I told Bootsie, hoping to distract her from Waffles, who was currently breathing down her neck and wagging at her from the backseat. "Very south of France!"

"Circulation's doubled with all the Barclay Shields news"—she nodded, pushing Waffles's nose away— "so we're making a few improvements. And this week's bound to be even better. We've got Sophie's party and Chef Gianni's accident on page one. By the way, the chef is having some MRIs done, but so far his only real injury seems to be a broken ankle.

"Marcus, our society photographer, got a fabulous shot of Gianni mid-fall," Bootsie added. "He actually captured the moment of impact when Gianni took out the cellist. See?"

She shoved the newspaper into my lap when I paused at a red light. Yup, that was a nice shot, I had to admit. It really did give a visceral sense of the "splat" of chef-on-cellist.

Bootsie looked really good today. As usual, she was beaming with good health and tanned muscles honed by tennis and a lifetime of eating plenty of fresh vegetables and drinking one-percent milk. Her outfit was pretty subdued for her, maybe because she figured there was no point in putting on full Lilly Pulitzer to schlep furniture. She had on khakis, a pink polo shirt, and the aforementioned sandals. She was wearing a flowered belt, but that was it in terms of floral motifs.

"And while I really shouldn't be talking about this, I can tell you," she said in a confiding tone, "that Gianni's fall definitely wasn't an accident. One of his waiters who was just about to come back up the kitchen stairs swears he saw *someone* reach out and give the chef a shove."

"What?" I said skeptically. "Those waiters couldn't have seen anything from down there."

"This one did!" Bootsie insisted. "His name's Jason. And he's an engineering student at Penn, so he's no dummy. He saw a hand emerge from the kitchen door and give Gianni a good hard push!

"And," Bootsie continued, "Jason particularly noticed that the hand that shoved Gianni was jewelry-free, and the person wasn't wearing nail polish. Other than that, he couldn't say much. It wasn't a really big hand, he did notice that. Sort of medium-size. Could have been a man's hand, if the man was on the small side, or a woman's hand."

"Where were all the cooks and people working in the kitchen? Wouldn't they have noticed someone shoving the chef? He was standing right outside the kitchen when he fell . . . or got pushed," I said mildly.

"Cigarette break!" Bootsie said. "All four cooks were outside, smoking on Sophie's front steps. And that incredibly hot guy who was leaving the party with Jessica, the one with the muscles? I asked Officer Walt about him. You know who I mean, right?" Bootsie's eyes took on a lascivious glow.

I nodded. I remembered. It's not like there are that many gorgeous twenty-something guys with incredible cheekbones, dreamy eyes, and biceps rippling through their T-shirts roaming around Bryn Mawr. It's no Miami or Malibu.

"The guy's name is Channing. And he doesn't smoke," Bootsie told me, "so he wasn't out in front with the other cooks. *But* he wasn't in the kitchen when Gianni got pushed, either."

Bootsie paused for effect. "*Apparently*, Channing was somewhere else in the front yard, with *Jessica*, while *she* was having a cigarette."

I wasn't sure what Bootsie's emphatic phrasing signified, but I assumed it conveyed suspicion about what Channing and Jessica had been doing outside. As always,

Bootsie was hinting toward sex or make-out scenarios that might not have happened. Then again, the hot muscle-y guy and Jessica had indeed looked as if they were on intimate terms when we'd seen them the night before at Sophie's house.

"But this Jason might have imagined the whole thing about Gianni being pushed," I said, getting back to the chef's fall. "I know people hate Chef Gianni, but it seems pretty reckless for someone to shove him over a railing in the middle of a crowded party. I think Sophie's right, and it was a slippery shrimp incident."

"No way!" shouted Bootsie, grabbing the *Bryn Mawr Gazette* back and waving it at me. "This was a targeted attack on Gianni."

"I guess so," I said doubtfully. "You don't think one of Barclay's Jersey relatives could have had anything to do with pushing Gianni, do you?" I added. I couldn't imagine why the Newark cousins would have it in for the chef, and no one had mentioned seeing any unexpected guests at Sophie's party, but I'd much rather blame professional criminals for the attack than pin it on someone local.

"Not a chance. Someone would have noticed two goombahs like that wandering around," Bootsie speculated. "I think it was Gerda."

Oh great, I thought, since we were about two seconds away from seeing Gerda. Hopefully she wouldn't push one of us down Sophie's stairs while we were lugging furniture into the house.

"Besides, the reason that I *know* Gianni was pushed," Bootsie continued, her blue eyes gleaming with exultation, "is that Gianni got his own cream-colored hand-written note like Barclay's!"

At this moment, we were pulling up to The Striped Awning. There was Sophie, looking minuscule at the wheel of the Escalade. Gerda was beside her, looking at her watch pointedly as we drove up. Even though I knew we weren't late, I felt anxious and guilty.

"You waited till now to tell me there was a note?" I said. Bootsie has an annoying habit of waiting until a conversation is ending before doling out the pertinent item of gossip, and this was one of those times. "What exactly did the note to Gianni say?"

"Shh!" Bootsie warned me, putting her finger to her lips, pointing through her open window to Gerda.

I rolled my eyes. Obviously, I wasn't going to talk about this in front of Gerda the Computer Hacker. "I'll tell you after we pack up," Bootsie hissed.

We hopped out of the U-Haul, me bearing extra venti lattes for Gerda and Sophie, and Waffles bolting from the back and leaping out onto the sidewalk after Bootsie.

"Hi, Sophie, and hi, er, Gerda! I got you a decaf soy latte, Gerda, since Sophie mentioned you're vegan. And Sophie, yours is nonfat."

"My fave!" said Sophie, who was clad in a pink Juicy Couture tracksuit and pink sneakers. "Gerda won't mind just this once if I down some caffeine. And you better believe I need it, after the night we had!"

Gerda's expression, however, was cloudy as she re-garded Sophie sipping her venti drink, and became even stormier as she glanced down at the giant coffee I had offered her. "It's, er, decaf. And soy," I repeated hopefully.

"Starbucks, very bad. Mass product, sugar, all bad," Gerda said, waving the drink away. This really rubbed me the wrong way. I love Starbucks, and it's a luxury I can't afford on my Dunkin' Donuts budget. "Um, okay," I said. I didn't know what to do, so I walked over a few steps and put the venti cup in the big public trash can on the corner of Lancaster Avenue.

"Gerda's such a stickler!" giggled Sophie nervously, looking embarrassed. "Hiya, doggie!" she added, patting Waffles timidly on his brown head.

"What is this?" said Gerda, gazing down at Waffles, who was panting at her feet, looking incredibly cute and friendly. His brown eyes and huge ears were irresistible! Even Gerda would have to admit that.

"This is Waffles, my dog," I said proudly.

Gerda eyed Waffles critically for a few moments.

"He is fat load," she pronounced, finally. "This animal needs more exercise. And you are causing problem by spoiling him with fatty foods."

The Egg McMuffins we'd eaten over the weekend flashed before me. And then there'd been the Havarti and crackers we'd shared last night before bed. And the breakfast sandwich I'd just gotten him from Starbucks. He'd eaten it in about five seconds, and I'd tossed the wrappers in the U-Haul office trash can so Bootsie, another health nut, wouldn't see it.

"He's just big-boned," I told her, trying to sound neutral, though I was boiling inside. I guess the truth hurts.

Waffles probably could use a few more long walks and a few less sandwiches. "Well, thank you for helping us move this stuff," I added, hoping to defuse the situation.

"Will be easy," Gerda proclaimed to us. She eyed Bootsie's tawny, muscled form with beaming approval, and then turned her gaze to me and my Old Navy flip-flops ($2.99), Target dress ($24.99), and lack of bulging biceps (obviously no time or money had been spent on them). Disappointment spread quickly across her face. What the hell, I thought, annoyed, as I unlocked the store. First she dissed Waffles, and now she was dissing me.

"No security system?" Gerda asked disapprovingly as I unlocked the door, and we walked into the store. "Is bad idea, eh?"

"Oh, it's very safe around here!" I chirped breezily. "No one's into crime in Bryn Mawr. They're more into tennis and dogs."

"I think not," Gerda intoned. "Mr. Shields was nailed pretty good the other night."

I briefly considered telling Gerda to go screw herself, but I wanted to stay on good terms with Sophie. Plus Gerda was right about my flimsy old door lock. The security at The Striped Awning isn't too impressive.

When we all got inside, I picked up the heaviest box, and almost threw out my back, so I put it down, and Gerda and Bootsie toted it out. I carried out some newspaper-wrapped serving dishes and a small box of silver to the truck, while for her part, Sophie carried out a pillow, then stood watching and making helpful suggestions while the three of us did the schlepping.

Thanks to Gerda and Bootsie, we had everything packed into the truck in ten minutes flat.

"We meet you at house in a few minutes," said Gerda, as Sophie scrambled into the driver's seat of the SUV. I nodded sourly at her, and locked up.

"She's kind of rude, but she keeps herself in good shape," said Bootsie, climbing back into my car after Waffles.

"So when did Gianni get the threatening note? And what did it say?" I asked, easing out of my parking spot in front of the store and heading for a stop at my house to drop off Waffles, so as not to subject him to any more of Gerda's verbal abuse.

"Gianni's note was left in his car. He's got an old Fiat, he's really proud of it because it's an Italian classic. Actually, it's a really cool old convertible, and last night after she left the hospital, Jessica came back to Sophie's to pick up the Fiat for Gianni. I was still there, of course."

Of course. It was a good thing I'd left the party with Hugh Best. I couldn't imagine what time Bootsie had left Sophie's. Thankfully, she and Will have a live-in nanny, because you can never predict what time Bootsie might get home if there's any kind of gossip-worthy episode.

"Anyway, the note was sitting on the driver's seat. It had Gianni's name on the front, and read, 'You are swine.'"

I digested this for a minute as we drove past the country club, and steered the U-Haul onto my road.

"Interesting," I said. "Though given what we've seen of Gianni's behavior over the past few days, calling him swine might be an insult to the pork community. But does the note really mean that Gianni was pushed over that railing?"

Bootsie nodded. "I'm positive the note was a warning that Gianni ignored!" she said. "Though, I have to admit, his food is outrageously awesome. That's why people keep hiring him to cater their parties. "

"I guess it could be an employee with a grudge who pushed him—*if* he was pushed over the balcony, that is," I mused aloud.

"But the swine comment is harsh, don't you think?" I added. "It seems so specific. Not many people would come up with that word."

"Gerda would," said Bootsie confidently. "I mean, she just called your dog a fat load."

I nodded, since I was thinking the same thing. Gerda didn't mince words.

"For now, my money's on Gerda," Bootsie concluded. "She's strong, and she knows the house inside out. Plus she *was* inside while Gianni was in the kitchen, and it would have been easy for her to sneak up and, boom!— push the chef right off that little overhang."

"I guess," I agreed doubtfully.

"I made a reservation at Gianni's restaurant for Friday night for me and Will. I can snoop around while I'm there, and see what the mood among the staff is like," Bootsie said, as we pulled up to my house. "Mummy went to dinner at Gianni on Saturday night, and you know she never eats anywhere but the club. She said she fainted for a minute when she tasted the truffled tagliatelle—that's how good it was! So it's got to be someone who's not into food—like Gerda!—writing these notes," Bootsie summarized. "Because as much as you can hate Gianni personally, his pasta is perfection."

I wasn't sure this theory made too much sense, but Bootsie did have a point about Gianni's food being awesome, I thought as I parked and attempted to get Waffles out of the rented truck and into the house. He sat wedged at Bootsie's feet, looking stubborn.

"Come on, Waffles," I wheedled, trying to sound excited and happy, which the dog could tell was bullshit. His big brown eyes stared at me from under Bootsie's knees, projecting *No way* at me. When Waffles doesn't want to move, you can't budge his basset ass without an incentive. So I ran inside, grabbed two Beggin' Strips, and waved them at him to lure him into the yard. Luckily, there's never been a time when Waffles said no to fake bacon. He jumped out happily and trotted into the gate and up to the back door into the kitchen, where I gave him the treats, locked the door, and ran back to the car.

Bootsie said nothing, but her expression was pure disapproval. Her Labs never needed bribes to get moving.

Just then, the Best brothers' ancient Volvo roared down the hill next to me, billowing its usual plumes of smoke. It went by fast, but I could see Jimmy at the wheel, fully clothed, with what appeared to be a carload of cardboard boxes and paintings. He gave me and Bootsie a friendly wave, then aimed a stiff middle finger toward his brother Hugh, who was standing by their gate, shouting something and looking frantic.

I would have stopped to see if I could help Hugh, but frankly, it looked like a situation I didn't want to get involved in. Plus I was too frightened of Gerda to make her wait, so we steered out of the driveway and took off once the smoke from the Volvo had cleared a bit.

"The Bests," I told Bootsie. "They're fighting over moving to Florida."

"Heard about that at the club." She nodded. "Word is that they met with Barclay Shields about selling their place."

"Hugh met with him," I said. "Jimmy doesn't want to sell, and Hugh's not sure, either."

"You don't think those two could have attacked Barclay, do you?"

"I don't think they could stop fighting long enough to get the job done," I told her. Truthfully, I couldn't imagine the Bests going after Barclay, but I'd have to give it more thought after we were finished with this furniture transport.

Two minutes later, we pulled into Sophie's sweeping driveway behind her SUV, and I took a moment to get another good look at Casa Shields in the full light of day. Yup, it was pretty much how it had seemed the night before: huge, and from the *Dynasty* school of architecture. I could swear that even the squirrels and birds perched in the trees and bushes were gawking at Sophie's oversize house, their bright button eyes confused.

Sophie, looking excited and a little stressed, was waiting for us in the driveway in her pink sweat suit. Gerda meanwhile, unlatched the doors of the truck bed and lifted a large, heavy desk from the back of the truck as effortlessly as if it were a loaf of bread. There was a lot of action going on in the driveway: In front of the Escalade and our U-Haul was a truck bearing Chef Gianni's navy-blue logo, and a familiar black SUV.

"Beebee, it's nice of you to help Kristin schlep this stuff!" Sophie said to Bootsie. "I'll show you girls around the place."

I had to admit that Sophie herself made her house seem a lot less daunting. Her I'm-from-Joisey! vibe was friendly and easy, and she didn't seem to take herself all that seriously. Sophie was like the Keebler Elf, done up in Cavalli outfits and sent to live in the Emerald City. She definitely didn't seem dangerous, and her anger at Barclay seemed more like the kind that she would pursue with highly paid lawyers, rather than the rage that might inspire her to send Gerda out to bludgeon her ex.

I just couldn't picture Sophie as the mastermind behind trying to kill Barclay.

"Sophie, where we put this stuff?" asked Gerda, who had put down the desk in the driveway, and was buckling on a back brace.

"You know what, I'm hiring a new interior designer, so I gotta redo the whole house," said Sophie. "But the decorator said he needs to draw up plans before we figure out what to do with this junk. So for now, we're just gonna stuff it all in the wine cellar," she explained.

"In the cellar?" barked Gerda. She cracked her knuckles. "I don't think so. Cellar is where I have my office."

"We're not gonna put the stuff anywhere near your

office," Sophie explained to her. "It's all going to go into Barclay's stupid *wine* cellar. It's on the opposite side of the basement, Gerda."

Gerda's face registered an imminent tantrum, but she finally nodded her agreement. Bootsie and I grabbed a couple of small boxes from the truck.

Sophie trotted up the entrance stairs. "Come on in!" she said, pushing open the enormous wooden door. "I have a big surprise for you girls!"

"I don't like surprises," said Gerda grimly.

Inside the foyer were blindingly white marble floors, purple walls, a massive gilded staircase, and a slim young man who had a tape measure in one hand and was gazing, horrified, at a chandelier above him that looked like a disco ball had exploded.

"Here's my new decorator . . . it's your friend Joe!" shrieked Sophie. "We're gonna use all the crap from your store, and then get even more antiques," crowed Sophie to me, "which is gonna probably give my husband another angioplasty! I mean, he's literally gonna blow a gasket. He once popped a vein in his eye when I brought home a Tiffany lamp."

"Of course, that's not the goal here, to make your husband blow a gasket," said Joe, looking harried.

"He already did blow one!" said Sophie. "That's why he needed the angioplasty!"

Chapter 12

It took a few moments to absorb the foyer and the various rooms that I could glimpse from where we stood. Jeannie's bottle on *I Dream of Jeannie* and the Borgata in Atlantic City sprang to mind as possible design influences. Purple was the dominant color, and crystal, glitter, and gold vermeil seemed to be other key components of the overall look.

This color palette and profusion of shininess definitely wasn't going to fly with Joe, who stood surrounded by fan decks of paint colors, fabric swatches, and his omnipresent measuring tape, and wore the expression that one imagines the deckhands on the *Titanic* had as they helped load the lifeboats.

"Joe is gonna work some magic here!" shrieked Sophie, gesturing to him, Vanna White style. "He thinks he can make my house a little more 'old Philadelphia.' But it's still gonna be kinda glitzy and fabulous, right, hon?"

"I don't think 'glitzy' is what we'll be trying to achieve," said Joe patiently, but with desperation in his blue eyes. Joe seemed composed, but I could tell that his mind was roiling with an inner debate that went something like, *I'm going to make a ton of money from this job, but it might not be worth it if I'm institutionalized with a nervous breakdown.*

From what I could see all around me—the giant spangled chandelier, a mauve dining room to my right, and a giant gilded console table with cherub heads and wings sprouting from it over by the stairs—a complete gut job was the only shot at bringing "old Philadelphia" into this house.

I surreptitiously peeked into Sophie's dining room, which had a smoked purple glass table and chairs upholstered in lavender silk atop gold legs. It was as if a red-carpet outfit worn by Nicki Minaj had somehow multiplied, flown to Bryn Mawr, and become a dining room.

"You know, Joe," said Sophie, tapping her small, sneakered foot, evidently continuing a debate that had started prior to our arrival, "I hear what you were saying about losing some of the purple. But I gotta tell you that I took Honey Potts and Mariellen Merriwether for a quick tour of the house last night, and they were absolutely speechless!"

"I'm sure they were," agreed Joe. I wondered why Bootsie was being surprisingly well behaved, merely listening to Joe and Sophie, rather than inspecting each room. Then I remembered she'd already snooped through the house the night before.

"Actually, the only thing those two ladies said the whole time was that they both wanted their drinks topped off," giggled Sophie. "I'll tell ya, I thought people drank a lot in Joisey, but that's nothing compared to you Bryn Mawr people!"

Just then, Channing from Restaurant Gianni emerged from a hallway into the foyer, carrying a giant plastic container filled with spoons and serving utensils, heading toward the front door to take them out to Gianni's truck. When he saw us he paused, smiled, and stood there for a minute as we took in the display of rippling muscles and movie-star bone structure.

All of our jaws dropped, even Gerda's. If anything, this guy looked even better than he had the night before.

"Hi there," he said, in an absurdly deep, testosterone-oozing voice to all of us, white teeth flashing like Chiclets in his tanned face. We all sighed. It was like an Armani model had suddenly jumped off a billboard and mistakenly wandered into Sophie's crazy purple front hall.

"Everybody, this is Channing," Sophie said, grabbing one of his glistening biceps. "He's the—the—some kind of chef—what the hell are you again, Channing?"

"I'm the sous-chef at Restaurant Gianni," said Channing, flashing us a grin. "Well, nice to meet you all," he added, climbing into the truck as we all watched his departure appreciatively. He looked almost as good going as he had coming. We all came back to reality, Bootsie almost in a full drool, as Gerda shut the door behind him.

"Isn't he hawt?" squeaked Sophie. "His tush is like two big round honeydews!"

"Let's move stuff," said Gerda, getting back to business.

"Yeah, good idea," said Joe. "I'll help."

"I lead you to basement," Gerda barked. "Stay only where I tell you."

"Is Channing a, uh, trusted employee of Chef Gianni?" wondered Bootsie, as she and I each picked up boxes to schlep down to the wine cellar. We followed Gerda's spandex backside and Sophie's tiny pink one into a lavender hallway that led toward the kitchen, turned left into a side hallway, and went down a flight of stairs to the basement.

"I guess so," said Sophie. "I mean, Channing seems like a nice guy. Then again, who knows? Or cares! He's so freakin' handsome that I've never really paid attention to his personality."

"Has he worked for the chef long?" continued Bootsie, as we trudged down the beige-carpeted steps, her head swiveling around as Gerda flicked on some overhead lights.

"You know, Beebee, I'm not sure," said Sophie, "but Channing seems to be real friendly with the chef's girlfriend, Jessica. I saw them talking together a lot last night. They were over in a corner of the yard for quite a while. Channing was supposed to be prepping the shellfish buffet. Gianni got really red in the face when he noticed that Channing hadn't finished setting up that buffet by four-fifteen. I mean, the chef could be next for an angioplasty if he doesn't watch it!"

The basement was huge, the length of the house, and carpeted in basic beige, with an ugly faux-Irish-pub-style bar directly in front of us, and an equally dumb-looking pool table with lots of ridiculous scrollwork and carving on the legs to its left. There were some light-up beer signs on the walls behind it. Joe followed us down, wincing. I guess he hadn't seen the basement yet.

The space was mostly open with French doors that led out to the swimming pool, but at each end were two smaller rooms. The door to the one on the left was closed—most likely Gerda's office, since she was aggressively pointing us to the right, and blocking off the area near the closed door to the left like a bouncer on a busy night at Studio 54 circa 1977. We followed Sophie, avoiding Gerda's glowering countenance.

"Sounds like Channing and Jessica are *close*," Bootsie said unsubtly.

"Yeah, they are! I think Channing drives Jessica home late at night when the chef is stuck at work," Sophie told us innocently, opening the door to her wine cellar.

I knew Bootsie and I were both thinking more along the lines of Channing and Jessica getting hot and sweaty nowhere near a stove.

"This wine cellar is really nice," observed Joe, sounding surprised. I looked around at the room, which did have a pleasant, ancient-French-manor vibe, with charming stone floor and wooden wine racks. There was a long wooden table and chairs with a silver tray full of wineglasses and a corkscrew, evoking a dining room somewhere deep in the lavender-covered hills of Provence.

"I thought your husband hated antiques!" I said to Sophie.

"Yeah, he does. All this stuff is brand-new. It just *looks* old, since he freaks out if stuff is actually antique," she said. "Barclay paid extra to get new stones, and then had these French guys beat the crap out of the rocks over in France to give them a weathered look."

We all refrained from pointing that rocks are, by definition, weathered.

"The table's new, too," Sophie told us. "Those Frenchies whacked the hell outta that with some tire irons to give it, like, dings and dents!"

"Well, it looks great," I said.

"It *should* be great!" Sophie shrieked. "With all the money Barclay spent on it, plus the fifty thousand he spent two years ago on all those cases of stupid French wines! It was *my* idea to have an Irish pub in the basement, too."

Joe looked upset at the mention of the bar, but didn't say anything.

"Where's all the wine?" asked Bootsie.

"My ex took it with him!" said Sophie. "Truck pulled up when he moved out all his custom suits. All he left me was three bottles of crappy merlot."

"You know my friend Holly?" I asked Sophie. "She gave away all her ex's Armani and Brioni suits to charity during their breakup."

"That's a good one!" shrieked Sophie admiringly.

"You could still donate his cars," Bootsie told her. "I'd do it while he's in the hospital. Holly gave her ex's car to the Police Athletic League. I can get you in the newspaper for that, if the cars are worth more than a hundred grand.

We always do stories with a photo when people donate more than a hundred thousand dollars to charity."

"Ooh, that might work," Sophie breathed, taking a minute to roll this over in her mind. "He's got the new convertible and then there's the Porsche Cayenne. The Cayenne might be worth a hundred grand just on its own. I can have Gerda research it."

Gerda nodded, a happy gleam appearing on her face. It was like the sun reappearing on a post-nuclear landscape, and was frankly a little disconcerting.

"Good idea. I get the dollar amounts and make the donations today," Gerda agreed.

"Anyway, girls, I gotta run. Gerda and I are due for Pilates, and then I've got my personal shopper from Saks coming to drop off some clothes, and then I have hair at noon," Sophie rattled on, looking like an expensive pink chipmunk as she marched to the door, jingling her bracelets. "So I'm kinda busy. If you can unpack the smaller stuff and put it on that table, then Joe can do his decorating thing with it later.

"Help yourselves to anything from the kitchen. We got a lot of leftover crab claws up there!" Sophie disappeared, Gerda on her heels.

"Rest of basement is off-limits." Gerda chewed out the words at us over her shoulder as she left. I guess her good mood about donating Barclay's cars had disappeared.

"I keep thinking she's going to come out dressed in lederhosen, and axe-murder us," Joe whispered to me and Bootsie.

"She could beat up any of us, even me," Bootsie agreed.

"I'll help you move a couple of boxes." Joe sighed. "Then I have to get back upstairs. You have no idea how much work I've got ahead of me. That guy who climbed Mount Everest with all his toes frozen off had it easy compared to this decorating gig. Even the books in this place are purple."

"It's going to take you all summer," agreed Bootsie gleefully.

"Sophie told me she's got Barclay's crew coming to start painting tomorrow," Joe added, "so I've got to choose paint colors pronto. Normally, I don't like to rush into color decisions, but Barclay's whole crew is temporarily out of work due to all the lawsuits against his company right now, and Sophie said we should keep them busy."

Joe, Bootsie, and I schlepped in the rest of the boxes and furniture from the U-Haul. Then Joe, looking depressed, disappeared with a fan deck of paint colors.

Per Sophie's instructions, I started carefully unpacking boxes of china and lining everything up on the big table, wondering how these old Philadelphia tchotchkes were ever going to fit into the Vegas decor.

Then again, Joe is really good at what he does. Holly's place downtown with Howard was amazing, all modern art and antiques with a Parisian–New York flair. Her new Divorce House would no doubt be just as great when Joe was done with it.

Meanwhile, after three minutes, Bootsie lost interest in unpacking. She took a seat at the table and drummed her fingers on the chic, battered oak surface. Honestly,

Bootsie's attention span is even worse than mine, and was never that great, even in high school. Field hockey and gossip were about the only things that kept her interest. Her leg started tapping, too, and her sky-blue eyes took on a telltale nosy gleam.

"The Pilates equipment is up on the third floor, as I learned last night during the party when I just happened to wander up there," she told me in a loud whisper, jumping up from the table and heading to the wine cellar door back into the basement. "So I'm going to take a little exploratory stroll around down here. Gerda will never hear me from all the way on the top floor."

"No!" I hissed at her. "I don't want Sophie to be mad at me. And what if Gerda comes down here and I'm all by myself!"

Too late. Bootsie was gone. I dashed after her, lugging a pair of silver candlesticks, as she headed for Gerda's bunker—of course.

"She's probably got the door alarmed!" I told Bootsie in a panic.

Sophie was easygoing, but if she got upset with us for breaking into a locked door in her basement, she could still return my entire inventory to The Striped Awning, and if I had to refund her seven thousand, five hundred, and seventy-dollars, I was ruined. And while I didn't necessarily buy into Bootsie's theory that Gerda had attacked both Barclay and the chef . . . it *was* possible. Bootsie and I could be next on Gerda's hit list.

"She doesn't have an alarm," said Bootsie calmly. "There aren't any sensors on the door. She might have it booby-trapped, but I can risk that." She tried the door handle. Locked.

Bootsie pulled a barrette out of her blond bob and poked it into the lock, jiggled it, and the door popped open.

"Where'd you learn to do that?" I said, impressed.

"My parents' liquor cabinet. They installed a lock when we were in high school, remember? My brothers and I learned how to pick it that same night. It's been a hobby ever since."

She disappeared inside Gerda's office. I stood outside, adrenaline pumping, clutching the candlesticks and keeping watch for Gerda. Luckily, Bootsie returned in less than three minutes.

"Everything is spic-and-span in there," she said dejectedly. "And there's a desk with a padlock that I don't know how to pick on the file drawer. Naturally, the computer's password-protected."

To my relief, she shut the door. "I'll have to research that lock and get back in there another time."

Euphoric at the prospect of getting out of here before Gerda returned, I quickly finished the unpacking while Bootsie sent some text messages to her coworkers at the paper describing Sophie's purple house, and snapped a few pics of the bar and its neon Bud Light signs to share on every social media site she could think of.

"I'm heading up to check out the kitchen," Bootsie said.

"Don't touch anything!" I told her, knowing full well she'd likely post photos of the contents of Sophie's refrigerator and cabinets on Twitter.

Five minutes later, I brought the empty boxes out to the U-Haul, then went back in the house to grab Bootsie and say good-bye to Joe. I was surprised to see Gerda in the front hallway, since I figured she'd be forcing Sophie to labor through at least an hour of Pilates. She gave me a wary glare as she bounded athletically toward the basement stairs.

Uh-oh, I thought, petrified that Gerda would be able to tell that Bootsie had infiltrated her cave.

Bootsie had chattily shared with me—while I'd finished unpacking and she texted her friends at the newspaper—that her parents had never once guessed that she and her brothers had consistently raided the locked liquor cabinet. This wasn't a reassuring piece of information, because I've known Bootsie's parents my whole life, and while they're very nice people, I'd bet that Gerda could outsmart them when it came to security any day of the week. The Delaneys, Bootsie's mom and dad, are great for knowing things like when sales are coming up at L.L. Bean, or the right amount of Tabasco to perk up a Bloody Mary, but they aren't people that, say, the CIA would hire.

Apparently, Sophie was done early today with her Pilates because she and Joe were now embroiled in a decorating discussion, and it wasn't going well. They were in Sophie's mauve dining room. Sophie was pouting, while Joe was perspiring under his crisp white shirt.

"I think a more neutral color palette will lend some, uh, gravitas to the house," Joe was explaining in strained but patient tones. He rummaged in his briefcase for some fabric swatches and opened the paint fan deck to the beige paint chips.

"What do you mean *neutral*?" Sophie was asking. She looked a little winded from the Pilates, but still perky. She bounced up and down energetically on the balls of her feet. "Make sure it isn't green. Especially army green. Not that I don't support the army, I do. Those people are heroes. I love soldiers. And they're usually hot young guys, let's be honest! But I don't want to feel like I'm *in* the army."

"I was thinking of more of an oyster color," explained Joe in the tone you use with a two-year-old who's is about to have a candy-aisle meltdown, flipping to the pale beige section of his paint chips. Bootsie appeared next to Joe, and showed no sign of leaving him and Sophie to hash out their paint differences.

"No way!" shrieked Sophie. "I hate oysters! They're disgusting, and slimy. Barclay likes oysters, he said they make him horny, which—believe you me—is not a good memory for me. One time we were in Miami, and he ordered oysters at the Fontainebleau, we had all these huge platters of them sent up to our suite, and then he wanted me to tie him to this chair on the balcony and—"

"Okay, forget oyster!" interjected Joe. "Let's go with this color, a beautiful beige. And for your bedroom, a cool ice blue." He hastily shoved some paint samples toward her.

"Isn't beige kinda boring?" whined Sophie.

"Can we get back to what happened when you tied Barclay up?" Bootsie asked.

"Beige is restful," said Joe, looking at me desperately for backup.

"Definitely," I agreed quickly. "A lot of people in Bryn Mawr love that shade of beige, and I know Eula Morris would really like it. You could probably host a dinner here in the fall for the symphony once you've redecorated."

"Really?" squeaked Sophie, interested. "You're saying beige is big around here?"

"Beige is huge," nodded Bootsie, who'd moved on from the Fontainebleau-bondage scenario. "Eula loves beige."

Just then the doorbell rang, and the front door swung open. The Colketts were on the stoop, and smiled in their charming manner to everyone.

"Choosing new paint?" said Tim Colkett cheerfully.

"Hiya, guys. Come on in," said Sophie, beckoning the Colketts inside, her small face scrunched into a frown of concentration. "Well, I guess this color's okay, because I really like that symphony crowd. And Eula, she knows a lot of people. But I'm not sure I want to get rid of *all* the color," she said, turning back to Joe. "What about keeping my bedroom pink?"

"That's not going to work," said Joe firmly. He seemed a lot more confident now that he had the specter of Eula Morris as his ally.

"Definitely, darling, you don't want pink," echoed a Colkett. "Only peonies should be pink."

I gazed at the Colketts, who were taking in the situation, amused. They couldn't have been the ones who'd pushed Gianni down the stairs last night, I was positive. Or almost positive. Even though they had reason to hate the chef, and had been uncomfortably close to him at the very moment he'd taken his tumble, the Colketts just didn't seem to have a mean bone anywhere inside their well-dressed bodies.

"There's also my bathroom, or wait, even better, my closet!" Sophie cried. "My closet could be pink!"

"The closet will be in a color related to the blue of your bedroom," said Joe, "but we could go with a slightly deeper blue, or maybe wallpaper it in a Chinese floral pattern. I'll think it over."

"What about something brighter for just one part of the shoe room?" Sophie asked hopefully. "We could do the Gucci section in a separate color—like maybe gold?"

"No gold," Joe informed her.

Sophie sulked for a moment, but appeared to be digesting Joe's insistent stance against bright colors. Then she looked at me and piped up, "Hey Kristin, who was that tall guy you were talking to at the party last night? The one you introduced me to, the guy named John? Did he ask ya out or anything?"

Bootsie's nose twitched at this question, and Joe looked up from his briefcase with interest. Just then, though, I heard a loud stomping noise coming up the basement stairs. *Gerda.*

I grabbed Bootsie's hand and yanked her toward the front door.

"Thank you, Sophie!" I called over my shoulder,

and ran. Thankfully the Colketts hadn't blocked in the U-Haul with their truck, and for once, Bootsie didn't dawdle.

"WHO'S JOHN?" ASKED Bootsie as I sped toward my house.

"He's a guy I met over by the shrimp last night at Sophie's," I told her. "John Hall. He's a veterinarian."

"And?" Bootsie prompted.

"And, nothing. He didn't ask me out, if that's what you want to know," I told her.

"Was he cute?"

"Yup, he was cute," I confirmed. "If you like tall, handsome men, he was cute." Bootsie rolled her eyes at me.

"Married?"

"He didn't seem married, but I'm not sure," I told her. Actually . . . *was* he married? That hadn't occurred to me. He'd been alone at the party and had projected a distinctly single vibe, but then again, married guys have been known to do that. Maybe his wife had been over at the cheese and fruit table.

Luckily, we were pulling into my driveway, so this conversation's sell-by date was coming fast. I'd pick up Waffles and then drop Bootsie at her office, which was less than a five-minute drive away, then go to the store and get on with my life.

"You've got to work on finding out more about the men you meet," Bootsie lectured me as I parked. "You see a tall, good-looking guy, you need to find out everything about him immediately. Where he lives, if he plays tennis, where he went to college, how he likes his steak cooked, and *definitely* whether or not he's married. Or if you can't do it yourself, you can wave me over, and I'll do it for you."

"Kristin?" I heard an old and wavering voice emanating from the holly bushes next door. "Excuse me, dear, do you have a moment?" Hugh Best popped into view, a vision of skinny legs and rumpled gray hair framing a concerned expression. "My brother stormed out this morning over a small tiff we had, and he still isn't back. And, well, I'm getting a bit worried."

I glanced at my watch—eleven-thirty in the morning. *Hardly cause for alarm*, I thought.

"Well, Jimmy's only been gone a couple of hours," I said, trying to sound reassuring. "He's probably just out doing some errands, or, um, hitting some golf balls with a friend? I'm sure he'll be back soon."

"But he never shops. And he doesn't have any friends! Jimmy sometimes goes to the liquor store and the cigar store, but that's it. He refuses to even go to the Buy-Right and do the food shopping, which is a good thing, because if it was up to him we'd be eating nothing but ham loaf and Fritos!" Hugh's anger at his brother seemed intact, even if he was worried that Jimmy was missing.

"Does he have a cell phone?" I asked, feeling fairly certain I knew the answer already.

"Heavens, no," said Hugh, horrified.

"Er, well, maybe you could call the liquor store and

see if he's been there?" I suggested. Bootsie had cranked down her window and was listening with mild curiosity. This wasn't gossip at the level she really appreciates, but if Jimmy Best was doing something dangerous or had gone off on a Scotch bender at the Bryn Mawr Pub, she'd at least need to know about it.

"Maybe he's in that back room at the cigar store," Bootsie suggested to Hugh. "The room with the leather couches and ESPN on around the clock. My dad goes there a lot. You could give them a ring."

"That's a good idea," said Hugh, brightening.

"By the way, Hugh, where were you and Jimmy last Thursday when Barclay was getting whacked in the head?" Bootsie asked bluntly.

Hugh looked startled. "Thursday?" He thought for a minute. "We went to Prime Rib Night at the club," he said. "Were there all night, from six on, actually, since Jimmy got snockered and wouldn't leave till after eleven." He looked worried. "You can ask Ronnie the bartender, or anyone at the club. We weren't anywhere near Sanderson!"

"Great!" I said, relieved. I'd hate to think of the Bests spending the rest of their days in prison, which had to be worse than the conditions in their moldering old house. "Well, I'll see you later, and I'm sure I'll see Jimmy too, back home safe and sound." Bootsie and I waved goodbye as Hugh headed back inside. I retrieved Waffles, and the three of us peeled off toward town.

"Looks like you've got a new best friend next door," observed Bootsie as we drove back to her office. "Well, anyway, I'll confirm the Bests' alibis for Thursday during the time Barclay was attacked, but I believe Hugh. And I'll look into that vet. I know I've heard of him," she said slowly, taking on the faraway look she gets when her mind is whirring with her built-in database of names and faces.

"By the way, Bootsie," I said, "you know that the Colketts popped out on the landing right after the chef was pushed—or fell—last night, don't you?"

"I didn't know that," she said, coming back briefly from her internal Google search. "Did you see them?"

"Yup." I nodded, feeling guilty about tattling on the Colketts, but not wanting to rule them out if they were cold-hearted killers just because they were charming. It was bothering me that the Colketts, who obviously hated Gianni, had gone inside Sophie's house moments before the chef's tumble, and that they'd been so close to him when he fell. "But that doesn't mean they pushed him," I added hopefully. I'd much rather Gerda turn out to be the guilty party, given her critical temperament and lack of personal skills.

"Hmm," said Bootsie, unbuckling her seat belt determinedly as we pulled up at the newspaper's yellow door. "And I was so sure it was Gerda. But I'll keep the Colketts on my mental back burner. Plus Channing coming back to Sophie's this morning is interesting," she noted. "Returning to the scene of the crime. Just like the Colketts!"

"Well, Channing had to come back to Sophie's to pick up Gianni's equipment, and the Colketts are still working on Sophie's yard, but maybe they were also able to hide evidence or something," I said doubtfully, adding, "Thanks for the help this morning. I really appreciate it." Actually, Bootsie hadn't been all that much help, but at least she'd done some of the heavy lifting at the store.

"I'll be in touch!" Bootsie promised. "I'm getting on my computer right now. As soon as find out all about that vet you met, I'll see what I can dig up on Channing and the Colketts. And we'll have to find a way back into Sophie's house. I haven't given up on snooping through Gerda's desk!"

Chapter 13

It was just before noon when Waffles and I got to the store. We'd returned the rented truck and picked up our car, and I felt optimistic as I unlocked the door. I was looking forward to getting the store organized, and, truthfully, to being free of Bootsie's company for the rest of the day.

Waffles took up residence on his dog bed, while I went in the back room to see what would be suitable for restocking the sales floor. A couple of hours later, I was feeling pretty optimistic. Somehow, what I'd managed to squirrel away in storage actually filled up the shop nicely. There was a small writing desk, some curvy Louis XV–style chairs ("in the style of," in antiques parlance, which meant that they were twentieth-century versions, not really antiques, but still attractive vintage pieces), and Limoges plates that I arranged on shelves in the front room. With the addition of some botanical prints I'd been saving and now hung in symmetrical rows over the writing desk, things quickly looked a lot better. The bench and other pieces I'd bought out at the flea markets over the weekend filled out the retail area. The Striped Awning was a functioning shop again.

The storefront space isn't very big, so I basically always put all the things I like on one side of the store—funky old Venetian mirrors, 1930s vanities, oversize crystal chandeliers are on the right side. The things that most of my customers like, which are needlepoint pillows, anything Queen Anne or Chippendale, and old silver tea sets, I usually arrange on the left. One wall is painted pale pink, the other silver, and somehow everything ends up working together. Finally, I hung a Swedish-style wooden chandelier in the center of the store, where I had the ceiling rigged for the constantly changing light fixtures that came in, were sold, and were replaced.

I was polishing up the silver acorn bookends I'd gotten from Annie and Jenny, the hippie antiques dealers at Stoltzfus's, when the phone rang.

"I'm not sure I can do this job at Sophie's," said Joe, a note of hysteria rising in his voice. "She's refused to give up the cherub table in the hall, and she's digging in on the pool statues, too. I'm out of Xanax, and I've actually thought about killing myself today. Twice."

"Sophie needs you!" I told him. "She'll come around on the cherubs."

"Yeah, that's what I keep telling myself," he said, sounding depressed. "I've never quit a job before, and I'm not sure I can afford to fire Sophie as my client. The Colketts have been here for hours, arguing with her about the Aphrodites and Dianas. They're in worse shape than I am. One of them is sitting behind their truck crying."

"Sophie seems like the kind of person who could be easily influenced by celebrities," I suggested. "Why don't you bring over a book on Hollywood homes and tell her that, um, Eva Longoria doesn't have any glitter tables?"

"Okay," sighed Joe. "That might work."

I was still having nagging thoughts about the Colketts. It seemed impossible to think of the good-natured florists as cold-blooded murderers, until I remembered the humiliation they'd suffered when the chef attacked them. Everyone has their limits, and maybe they'd been pushed to the edge.

"Joe, do you think the Colketts could have shoved the chef off the balcony last night?" I asked. "Gianni really embarrassed them at his restaurant opening, and they could have easily pushed him. They were there at Sophie's all day yesterday, getting her yard ready for the party, so they know the house and could have been lurking in a closet or something."

"I guess it's possible," said Joe doubtfully. "But I doubt it. I don't think they'd take a grudge that far. Besides, Tim Colkett got his hearing back and the swelling went down, so there's no permanent damage. Anyway, I gotta get back to Sophie, but Holly and I will be at the club at five. She's bringing me some spare anxiety meds." I promised to meet them later, and as soon as I hung up, the phone jingled again.

"Hugh Best calling," said my neighbor. "Still no sign of my brother."

"Did you try the cigar store?"

"Yup, and Jimmy was there early this morning," said Hugh. "Right after he left home, he went and bought three boxes of cigars. He sat and smoked one in the back room with the ESPN and the leather couches, then took off. But that was hours ago!"

"Three boxes? That sounds like a lot," I said. Maybe Jimmy really was setting out on a road trip.

"I know! He's probably driving to Atlantic City right now to gamble all our money away!"

"Is he a gambler?" I asked, surprised. Jimmy struck me as the type who might wager a dollar on a golf putt or a Scrabble match, but that's about it.

"Well, no, but I know he likes the cocktail waitresses there," said Hugh miserably.

"Why don't you call the casinos? See if he's registered as a hotel guest," I suggested. "I'll check in with you in a couple of hours to see how things are going."

Hugh agreed and hung up, and I greeted a few post-luncheon customers, including a young couple getting married later in the month who bought some pillows and promised to think about coming back for the small bench.

Despite the foot traffic, I was unable to squelch thoughts of Mike Woodford from suddenly popping into my mind. Did he actually enjoy putting on a blue blazer and escorting Honey Potts to parties? Did he like the symphony? Maybe he could actually tell Beethoven from, say, Wagner.

Then I had a vision of John the cute vet holding his

plate of crab claws, looking tan and wholesome. As I placed the polished acorn bookends I'd gotten at the flea market on a shelf, I realized it had been nice to engage in conversation with someone who emanated steadiness and normalcy, and who didn't seem likely to become a resident of Phuket anytime soon.

"I wish I could have seen the vet's arms," I said to Waffles, "because he had really tan wrists and hands. He probably has great forearms, too." Although, if he was married, his forearms were null and void. I don't look at married guys' arms—ever—unless they're the arms of movie stars along the lines of Daniel Craig, which doesn't count.

I may have bad taste in men, but it's not bad enough to include dating married guys. I'd choose a single man who was a flight risk to Thailand any day over a man who'd vowed to love and honor another woman. And I'd probably never see John the vet again. How likely was it that I'd go to a symphony party again anytime soon?

Then again, maybe he *was* single.

I looked at Waffles, who was gently snoring, and thought: *Bingo!* John was a vet, wasn't he? Waffles could use a checkup. There was nothing wrong with him, but it couldn't hurt to take the dog in . . . and see the vet. Plus I could double-check for a wedding ring.

I opened my laptop and looked up the number of John Hall, DVM, and found out he was part of a veterinary group called All Creatures Great and Small, in Haverford, two miles down the road. A chipper-sounding assistant answered my call, and I asked for an appointment with Dr. Hall. "It's for a basset hound," I told her. "Just a routine checkup."

"Dr. Hall has an equine/bovine practice—he treats horses and cows," she sang in an infuriatingly cheerful way. "And he's not in the office much. It's hard to bring a cow into the office, so he goes to them!"

"I see," I said, stymied. "Um, does he work in the office at all?"

"He does usually spend Thursday afternoons catching up on paperwork," she said, sounding a little less cheerful. "May I ask why?"

"I've heard he's a great vet!" I told her, then asked for an appointment with one of the vets who treated dogs. "I can only come in on a Thursday, though," I told her regretfully. "In the afternoon."

"What's wrong with your dog?" she asked.

"He eats everything," I told her.

"All dogs eat everything," she told me.

"This is beyond normal," I assured her. "I'm pretty sure he has a tapeworm." She grouchily ordered me to bring a stool sample. "With pleasure!" I said, and hung up.

This was a fantastic plan!

"Waffles, you're a good boy!" I told him. I'd reward him with a late lunch of chicken salad, I decided, and before that, we'd go for a quick walk to enjoy the gorgeous sunny day. The front door was open, a light breeze lilting in through the screen door and the windows. There were a few ladies still winding up lunches at the café, moms taking their kids for ice cream down at the little shop by the post office, and a festive, early-summer feeling that school would be out soon.

As I grabbed my keys to lock up, there was a sound you don't often hear in the center of Bryn Mawr these days: the clomping of horseshoes on cement.

I opened the screen door to peer down the street, and spied Mariellen Merriwether atop her prize horse, Norman, at the end of the block, Norman's well-groomed black tail swishing proudly as he walked along. He really was a beautiful animal: glossy, clear-eyed, and magnificent. His Ritz-Carlton lifestyle had clearly paid off.

His owner, of course, sat in perfect equestrienne posture, and wore impeccable beige riding pants, polished boots, a crisp white shirt, and a black riding hat. Naturally, she had on her pearls, too. I noticed she had a CVS bag poking out of the pocket of her jodhpurs. So the rumors were true: When Mariellen needed to pick up a prescription or some calcium supplements, Norman was her mode of transport!

Waffles took one look at Norman, and kind of lost it. I'm pretty sure he thought Norman was a very large dog. And since Waffles is incredibly friendly, every time sees another dog he has a dog-gasm. He started whining, woofing, and jumping excitedly.

This didn't go over too well with Norman. The horse reared, whinnied in terror, and took off down Lancaster Avenue with Mariellen, ever the excellent horsewoman, hanging on to the reins, still in her perfect posture, trying to calm him. She shot me and Waffles a look of icy hatred as they zoomed by the store, heading in the direction of the post office as cars halted to let them by. Despite the balmy day, I felt my entire body go cold.

"No!" I said desperately to Waffles, who was looking longingly at Norman's disappearing hooves and whining.

To deal with my embarrassment at Waffles's outburst, I worked feverishly for the rest of the day. By 4:30 p.m., there was nothing left to polish or straighten. I decided to leave Waffles at the store while I met Joe and Holly. He was peacefully racked out on his dog bed after his eventful afternoon, and there was a small chance that if I tiptoed out the back door, he might never notice I was gone.

I couldn't stay annoyed with Waffles for long. I took a look at his sleeping, portly, brown-and-white form and goofy ears as I headed out, love welling up inside me. Norman the horse had nothing on Waffles.

"Is KLONOPIN SUPPOSED to make you hungry?" asked Joe. "Is it like pot?" He sucked down half a margarita in a loud slurp through a straw.

Joe already looked bombed when I arrived, and he'd only been at the club for fifteen minutes. His hair was messy, and his polo shirt was wrinkled. He'd popped one (or maybe more) of Holly's pills, and his eyes bore the glazed look of the celebrities whose mug shots are featured on TMZ. He clutched a salt-rimmed glass with a trembling hand while Holly administered sympathetic pats on his arm.

"Sophie's like a garden gnome, the one in that commercial that keeps popping up wherever you go. Isn't there a horror movie about a garden gnome?" he said in a hoarse whisper. "And there's Gerda, too. Always Gerda."

"You'll be finished there in a couple of months!" said Holly encouragingly. "And you have my house to work on, too, which of course will be amazing."

"I need a cheeseburger," moaned Joe. "I'm really hungry."

"He's not driving, right?" I whispered to Holly, who jingled her car keys reassuringly, and made a no-way gesture toward Joe.

We flagged down the waitress, which wasn't difficult because she was already staring at us. Not only was Joe semi-slumped over his margarita, Holly was wearing a yellow strapless maxi dress, with her hair in a bouffant in the manner of Julie Christie circa 1973.

She also looked a little tired and stressed. Sometime in the next few days, I was determined to have that one-on-one about her impulsive decision to split from Howard.

I've known Holly since grade school, so her bravado doesn't fool me; she seemed miserable. I thought if I could talk to her alone, away from the chaos that seemed to follow us lately, I could convince her to give Howard another chance.

Back in February, when Bootsie had heard that Holly was getting divorced, it all sounded like a big misunderstanding. Bootsie's info was based on idle gossip at the club: Bootsie had been sitting in the bar waiting for Will, and was eavesdropping on some tipsy members, the Binghams.

The Binghams are always blitzed on white zinfandel, even when they play racquetball. Honestly, you can't listen to the Binghams, because they always get things wrong, due to the fact that they drink about five bottles of wine a day. Anyway, the Binghams had witnessed a big fight that day between Holly and Howard about the length of Holly's tennis skirt—ironically the very thing that had lured Howard to Holly in the first place—and assumed their marriage was on the rocks. They shared their observations with Bootsie, which Bootsie took to the next level: a Definite Divorce.

I thought Bootsie had to be wrong when she'd called me the next morning, but then later in the day Holly had phoned me, enraged about a supposed affair Howard was engaged in with that busty bartender at the Porterhouse. At least Holly *thought* he was having an affair with this Boobs Girl, because the steakhouse's number had come up a couple of times that week on Howard's caller ID.

Howard told Holly that the Porterhouse was calling to confirm a dinner reservation he'd made for them that weekend, but Holly, who'd become obsessed with the bartender, refused to believe it.

Somehow the whole thing had snowballed into a lot of lawyers arguing in paneled conference rooms, and into Holly spending more and more time at the club in outrageous outfits. I guess I would have been suspicious, too, but I knew Howard adored Holly, and I truly didn't believe he had cheated.

"Did you at least find out anything from Sophie today about who knocked Barclay on the head?" Holly asked Joe.

"Nope," he said tipsily. "Just found out that there are more ugly shades of purple in the world then I'd ever imagined."

With a start, I heard a New Jersey accent and clacking heels loudly heading toward our table. I didn't even need to look.

Sophie. I guess she'd somehow invited herself to join Joe and Holly.

"Hi, everyone. Sorry we're late," Sophie announced. She was dressed all in pink: pink miniskirt, pink silk blouse, pink sandals. "We got held up by the weirdest thing back at the house. We were all dressed and ready to go, and then when we opened the front door to head out to the Navigator, a big smelly package wrapped in newspaper was on the front steps. So Gerda opened it, and we found a half-dozen dead tilapia inside!"

"With a note," added Gerda, who was in her usual black tracksuit. "It said, 'Beppe: Sleep with the fishes.'" We all froze, mid-sip. Geez, this was like something out of *Casino*. Could Sophie be making this up? "Could be that somebody's going to kill Mr. Shields—for real this time," Gerda added with a smile, buoyed by the threat to her ex-employer.

"That fish was disgusting!" Sophie elaborated. "Gerda double-Hefty-bagged the whole package, and it's going out with tomorrow's trash. It stunk to high heaven."

"Aren't you going to pass along the note to your ex? Or the police?" asked Holly.

"No way!" said Sophie. "If anyone wants to talk to the Forklift, they can track him down themselves.

"And then when we finally arrived here, we got lost!" she whined. "It's kinda dark in there."

"Well, the main clubhouse was built in 1910, and there's quite a bit of oak paneling," said Joe wearily. "Why don't you both sit down," he added politely, pulling out a chair for Sophie. Joe's manners rarely fail him, even when he's impaired. Gerda hoisted her own heavy wrought-iron chair from a neighboring table, moving it as easily as if she was picking up a bag of cotton balls.

"Sophie, I have to ask you, why are you getting divorced?" Holly said as Sophie and Gerda sat down, Sophie's feet barely reaching the ground.

I noticed the Binghams, sipping their Gallo white zinfandel three tables away, agog as they eavesdropped. I could only imagine their future versions of this story. With some alarm, I also noticed a willowy older blonde on the grass tennis courts some two hundred yards away. I couldn't see her face, but was fairly sure that upright posture belonged to Mariellen.

"Well, mostly because Barclay's been cheating," Sophie told us, in a confidential tone. "That is, if you count hookers as cheating. 'Cause, some people don't."

We all nodded.

"What happened first was, Gerda was suspicious because she noticed a lot of restaurant charges and Saks purchases on Barclay's credit card statement, which she hacks into every month. I mean, obviously, the restaurant bills weren't surprising, but Saks doesn't stock the sizes Barclay wears, so that was weird. And it turned out that the Saks charges were all for *bikinis*."

Gerda inclined her head grimly.

"We asked Barclay about the charges, and he got *so mad* about us checking up on him that he actually reported Gerda to immigration, 'cause her work permit and visa are, well, expired!" Sophie giggled.

Joe's head snapped up, his tequila-tranquilizer haze suddenly gone. My eyes doubled in size as I stared at Gerda, while Holly sipped her drink loudly through a straw and looked shocked. Gerda looked absolutely enraged, and I saw a vein pop out in her neck and begin to throb. Her fists balled up, and she gave Sophie the Look of Death.

Finally, a motive for Gerda to have attacked Barclay.

"Luckily, it takes a long time to deport someone! And then Barclay went to Las Vegas for a builders' convention, so Gerda and I hired a detective that she found on the Internet to watch Barclay," Sophie rattled on, oblivious to our shock at the immigration info she'd so casually thrown out. "And this guy was *good*. He broke into Barclay's suite at the Wynn and planted a video camera, and sure enough, after Barclay went to the Wolfgang Puck place for dinner and hit a couple of the buffets, he came back to the room with two girls, and I'm pretty sure they were, you know, hired help! This detective saw the whole thing! And like ten minutes after they got back to the room, one of the girls put on a Catwoman outfit, and then"—Sophie paused here, perhaps with a glimmer that her tale wasn't club-appropriate, and gulped some water. She decided to go on. "The Catwoman girl pulled out a loaf of white bread, and, well, and . . ." She hesitated again.

"And what?" asked Holly breathlessly.

"Excuse me. Ladies' room!" I said hastily, jumping up and sprinting across the porch.

I sped inside the club, and blinked in the dim hallway as I walked toward the front door, as far away as I could get from the crowded dining porch, and from Sophie and Gerda.

I stopped short when I glanced outside and noticed a horse tethered to a dogwood tree next to the parking lot. He was happily munching grass, swishing his long black tail. Norman!

I couldn't face any more of Sophie's story, and I'd had my recommended daily allowance of Gerda, who now had a concrete motive to have attacked Barclay. And obviously, with Norman parked outside the front door, Mariellen would likely be off the tennis courts soon and heading this way.

Still, I hadn't gotten a chance to drink the margarita I'd wanted. And it was so pleasant inside the clubhouse— totally quiet, with oil portraits of former club presidents looking sternly out from the walls and air conditioning blasting. To my right was a corridor that led to the locker rooms, the dining room, and the (clearly marked) rest-rooms that Sophie had struggled to locate, but I took a left into the club's paneled, cozy bar. I decided to have a quick drink in the bar, then sneak out the front door.

Perfect. As usual in summertime, there was no one in the bar, since it has a wintry vibe with leather chairs and cozy couches, heavy chintz drapes, an enormous Orien-tal rug, and a giant fireplace. I had sat in here hundreds of times with my grandfather, and always loved it. It's the one place in the club that still allows smoking, and a faint whiff of cigar hung in the air.

"Margarita?" asked Ronnie from behind the old mahogany bar. I sat down gratefully and accepted my replacement drink. Ronnie's a guy from South Philly who's been at the club forever, even though he's only in his late forties. Ronnie can always tell if you want to talk or not, and he has an amazing ability to disappear into thin air. He goes behind the bar sometimes, and if you blink, he's gone through a door hidden at the left of the bar, then magically reappears when you need another drink. I'm pretty sure there's a secret network of corridors in the club for the staff, actually. They just pop out of nowhere sometimes.

This was great, I thought, closing my eyes for a moment and relaxing in the bone-chilling A.C. I couldn't stand another moment of Sophie's stories.

"I'll have a glass of water, please, Ronnie," said a man's voice behind me. I glanced to my right and saw John Hall next to me, smiling down at me, wearing tennis whites that were damp with healthy perspiration. He'd clearly just worked up a big sweat on the courts, and he looked kind of awesome. If you're into tall, handsome men.

He reached for his glass and I checked out his forearms. I gulped. They were thinner than Mike Woodford's, but tan and muscle-y.

And no wedding ring!

"Saw you sitting with your friends outside. Recovered yet from the party last night?"

I nodded, wondering if I had any mascara left from my quick swipe applied this morning. I was also thinking I should probably cancel my fake vet appointment for Thursday, now that I'd run into John again.

"Interesting picture of the chef in the paper today," he said, with a smile.

"It was nice of you to help him last night!" I told him.

"He's lucky he wasn't badly hurt," said John.

Ronnie was heading out to the porch with a tray of drinks in his hand.

"Ronnie," I said, "by the way, could you not mention to anyone that I'm in here?"

"Haven't seen anyone in here all night," he responded in his usual deadpan way, and disappeared.

"I'm not sure that member fraternization is permitted under club rules," said John with a smile, "but we never got a chance to really talk last night. Would you like to have dinner with me this week?"

I clutched the bar to steady myself. A guy who had a normal job, no wedding ring on, and had productive hobbies like playing tennis wanted to take me to dinner. "Yes, sure," I said, smiling. We planned to meet on the porch the next night at six-thirty. I would have rather gone somewhere else, like maybe Delaware or New York City to avoid Bootsie, and truthfully, Holly and Joe, but couldn't think of a way to tell him this, so the club porch it was.

After we exchanged phone numbers, John the vet headed for the locker room. I crept out the front, trotted past Norman, who didn't seem to remember me from his traumatic experience earlier in the afternoon, picked up Waffles, went home, brushed my teeth, and put on some lip gloss. I called and left a message canceling my fake appointment at All Creatures Great and Small, then I checked in with Hugh, who morosely informed me that Jimmy was still AWOL.

I got a voice mail from Bootsie, informing me that not only was Barclay still in the hospital, but Chef Gianni was stuck there, too, since doctors wanted to make sure he hadn't sustained anything worse than a broken ankle. They were concerned the chef might have brain swelling because of his constant screaming and irrational behavior, even though Jessica had insisted that this was his normal demeanor.

Then—while sternly telling myself it was a bad idea—I walked Waffles over to the cow barn at Sanderson and found Mike Woodford, whereupon I made out with him for an hour and a half while Waffles took a nap in the tack room. After the make-out session, I came home and fell instantly into a peaceful sleep.

Chapter 14

HOLLY'S DIVORCE HOUSE is a mile away from my place, just around the corner from the Shields residence. It sits far back from the road, down a driveway shaded by old white birches and banked with irises and hostas. A stately old stone house built in the 1920s, with French doors and high ceilings and pretty moldings, it started out as your basic beautiful, classic home. But with the help of Howard the Mogul's money and Holly's chicken-nugget royalties, she and Joe are making it even more spectacular by the day.

Trucks rumble in and out of the driveway all the time, filled with topiary boxwoods, French sofas, Lucite tables, and toilets with heated seats. I never feel jealous of Holly, though, because she's just lucky that way. Style, money, and cool things pop up around her as a matter of course. If she gasses up her car at the Sunoco station, she's the millionth customer and wins free unleaded fuel for a year. If she stops into Saks for a new bathing suit, she wanders into a Calvin Klein trunk show, and Francisco Costa pronounces her fabulous and invites her to his beach house in Brazil. I don't think she's ever paid for a glass of wine in her life, because as soon as she sits down at a bar, flutes of Moët and goblets of cabernet start arriving from men all around the room. It's just the way it is with Holly. I've learned to accept it, and even enjoy it. Anyway, the only reason she'd moved back to Bryn Mawr from downtown Philly was because of her divorce from Howard, so I hoped her house was giving her some comfort and distraction.

Joe, who owns a small apartment in downtown Philly, is living in one of Holly's guest rooms for the spring while he helps her decorate the house, so she won't get too lonely during her divorce negotiations. (The sunny guest room overlooking the pool, the free meals and cocktails, plus having all his laundry done by Martha, Holly's housekeeper, were added perks.) Plus Joe is currently single. Being straight and a decorator, he meets a lot of women, but they're mostly married to wealthy men. He also meets a lot of gay fabric reps. The upshot of this is that he doesn't date much.

I admired the property as I parked in the circular drive: The house called to mind the set of an old Cary Grant movie, with its crisp, elegant white façade in classic Main Line style. An American flag flapped in the breeze from the pediment above her front door, which was flanked by enormous potted rosebushes in full bloom.

Since I had run out on Holly and Joe last night, I offered to bring over coffee this morning. I'd decided not to mention my barn make out, since I knew Mike Woodford was another bad relationship prospect. Plus I had the date with John the vet set up for tonight. This was progress! Waffles and I trotted around the side of the house to Holly's new outdoor living room, where even though it was barely nine in the morning, a festive, partylike atmosphere ruled the day. Reggae percolated from her new outdoor speakers, and about forty new rosebushes had been installed in a hedge along Holly's patio/outdoor lounge. Holly was lying flat on her back on a chaise longue, clad in black workout garb, with a tasteful sheen of sweat on her forehead.

"I just got back from Booty Camp," Holly told me, smoothing her running shorts and tank top. "I have to finish four hundred sit-ups by noon. They make you sign a contract."

Joe groaned from the sofa, looking hung over. He had on a bathrobe, sunglasses, and a straw hat, resembling a more youthful Thurston Howell III as he lay back on white cushions, sipping what I hoped was vodka-free tomato juice. The hat, at least, added a jaunty note—very Dean Martin meets Justin Timberlake. Since Joe moved in with Holly, he's been dressing in what he calls "cruise wear," and it really suits him.

And this outdoor living room concept Holly and Joe came up with is honestly genius. It's located just off her *indoor* living room, and is perfectly positioned for privacy, but the rose hedges are clipped low enough so Holly can stand up and see who's coming down the driveway.

It's perfect for all the trucks that arrive with deliveries of sandals handmade in Capri, antique beds from Sweden, and Jean-Michel Frank tables from France.

To create the space, Holly and Joe had expanded a brick terrace adjacent to the long rectangular pool, tented it in white canvas, and had modeled the decor on the pool area of the Cipriani Hotel in Venice. Since the Cipriani is on a lush little island a few thousand yards from St. Mark's Square in Venice, rather than set in a backyard in suburban Philly, the effect wasn't exactly the same, but Joe had still done an amazing job, with lots of white lounges and sofas with crisp chocolate-brown piping and potted boxwoods giving it a unique Mediterranean-meets-English-country-house vibe. This was especially impressive considering the fact that the house had previously belonged to the mother of Mr. Bingham, one half of the gossipy, white zinfandel–drinking couple from the club.

Old Mrs. Bingham been a dog-loving, embroidery-happy lady who'd sheathed the house in flowered wallpaper that had taken contractors a month to steam off, but the rooms were now resplendent in shades of creamy white. Since Joe's not finished decorating yet, much of the house and its furniture are draped under tarps, but Holly's bedroom is already done. Joe installed a Lucite bed and little Lucite tables and glass lamps, with white linens and silk curtains, an antique Swedish daybed over by the window, and an enormous modern painting in shades of pink by Elliott Puckette over the bed. Other than one antique mirror and Swedish chest of drawers, it's totally minimalist. Holly's clothes are stashed in a ginormous closet/room with racks and drawers that are also fashioned of Lucite, reminiscent of a Prada boutique.

Martha, the housekeeper of any mere mortal's dreams, had set up a silver tray with juice, a bowl of glossy grapes, and a plate of sliced mango dressed with lime on the tented porch. There weren't any muffins or anything, of course, since Holly hasn't eaten much since she got legally separated, but it was still a great breakfast spread.

"I can't believe you left last night. That Vegas story was Marquis de Sade meets *Fifty Shades*!" Holly told me happily, as I handed out the Starbucks coffees. "The girl with Barclay took the Wonder Bread and put it all over—"

"I'm not up for hearing that story!" I interrupted her, alarmed.

"*I* want to hear that story," said Bootsie, who'd suddenly appeared from the rose thicket and was listening eagerly while taking in the new and improved patio. She took off her Wayfarers, plopped down on an upholstered pouf, and pulled her iPhone out of a Nantucket basket handbag.

"Forget the Vegas incident!" I told Bootsie. "Sophie got a package of tilapia delivered to her house, and a warning that Barclay would soon be sleeping with the fishes. Even I know what that means."

"I heard about that," Bootsie said. "But I guess the Forklift is safe at the hospital. Speaking of which, I just stopped in there to talk to Jeannie the nurse. The chef's still there for observation after his fall."

Bootsie explained that because the hospital is quite small, Barclay and the chef had been installed in rooms right next door to each other. While Barclay was still barred from ingesting anything other than chicken broth and his vitamin drip, the chef was allowed to eat whatever he wanted. So to torture Barclay, Gianni had spent most of the previous day having his waiters and sous-chefs delivering incredibly fragrant dishes, making sure that Barclay saw each gorgeous plate of food as it passed by his open door.

The chef's minions had actually prepared a couple of pasta dishes at Gianni's bedside using a plug-in stove, including one with a particularly heavenly smelling tomato-and-sausage sauce, then seared a tenderloin in an iron pan with lots of rosemary and garlic until the entire hospital smelled like a Tuscan village. Nurses and orderlies had been given plates of pasta to enjoy, and had happily wandered the halls past Barclay's room.

"However, I don't think the chef is the one who knocked Barclay out last week," continued Bootsie, munching some grapes. "I've thought this over, and I don't think he could have left the restaurant that night and gotten over to Sanderson to hit Barclay, then gotten back in time without anyone noticing he wasn't at the party. I'm still convinced Gerda hit Barclay that night. And she could have pushed the chef, too."

"Are you telling me that you haven't heard about Gerda's motive for taking out Barclay?" prompted Joe, propping himself up a bit on his settee as a heavenly breeze wafted by, ruffling a clematis arbor.

"I thought you would tell her," said Holly to me, sipping water and doing stomach crunches simultaneously.

"Apparently, Barclay tried to get Gerda deported," I relayed to Bootsie. "Sophie told us at the club last night, and Gerda was none too happy about Sophie sharing this tidbit."

"That's huge!" Bootsie shrieked. "Now it all makes sense! And Gerda probably went after the chef, too."

"And that would be why?" asked Joe languidly, sipping his drink.

"Partly because she's a vegan and a health freak, and the chef is such a bad influence on the whole Main Line, serving all those really fattening pastas and cheeses," Bootsie said, as if this was obvious. "And pork! I mean, the note that was left for the chef mentioned swine, and there are at least four different dishes that feature prosciutto at Restaurant Gianni. Which is the ultimate pork product!"

I wasn't sure how prosciutto rated on the scale of pig-related delicacies, but that's not surprising given that my main source of nutrition is canned soup.

"But really I think Gerda hates the chef because he's Italian, and Italian and German people hate each other!"

"They do?" said Holly, puzzled. Honestly, this sounded like bullshit to me.

"Also, I was wondering why Gerda would keep all her desk drawers locked," Bootsie told us, "and I realized she could be the one leaving those threatening notes for the chef and Mr. Shields. So I went to the stationery store in Haverford yesterday afternoon, which is the *only* place people buy notepaper around here, and asked if anyone had bought any cream-colored stationery recently.

"Well, actually I asked at the shop if Gerda, Sophie Shields, or Honey Potts had bought any cards in that off-white shade recently," Bootsie clarified, "and Eric's not sure about Sophie, but he's pretty positive Gerda bought some note cards, and he thinks they were off-white! Or at least, they might have been!"

"Bootsie, that's the stupidest thing I've ever heard in my life. And it doesn't prove anything. Tons of people buy white note cards," Joe said, pushing his hat back and rubbing his temples. "You can get them online, or pretty much anywhere."

"Cream-colored cards," corrected Bootsie. Joe put on his sunglasses, sighed, and appeared to fall asleep.

"I'm going over to the police station right after I leave here to talk to Officer Walt," mused Bootsie. "He needs to know that Barclay wanted to deport Gerda. And he obviously should hear about the tilapia incident."

"You'd think Walt would have found that out," said Joe.

"He's overwhelmed," explained Bootsie, adding importantly, "which is why I'm helping him out.

"I can't believe Gianni serves all those dishes made with ham," complained Holly, toweling off her angular shoulders. "No one I know eats anything in the pig family."

"I do," said Joe.

"I would, if I could afford to go there," I said.

"Oh, please, everyone loves the pork dishes at Gianni!" said Bootsie. "And the other meats are amazing there, too. I mean, who doesn't like shaved Parma ham, and then there's the short-rib ravioli, the pounded veal, the Bolognese . . . you know what, I'm starving just thinking about it," she finished. "I think I'll go to the Hoagie Hut and get an egg sandwich on my way to see Walt."

With this, Bootsie got up and left. Thankfully, her attention-span problem had kicked in.

"I never got to tell her the story about Sophie and Barclay and the hookers in Las Vegas," said Holly, eating a grape. I decided I could tell them about my upcoming date with the vet later. If I stayed here too long, I feared I'd get sucked into a sofa and a vortex of island music, champagne at noon, and maybe miss meeting John at the club.

"I've got to get to work," I said. "Aren't you on decorating detail at Sophie's today?" I asked Joe.

"I told her I'd be there at ten."

"Yoo-hoo!" came a yodel from around the front of the house. "Holly, are you here? I can't see very well with all these new bushes you planted!"

There was rustling of shrubbery, and footsteps in the not-so-distant distance.

"Shit," said Holly desperately, sitting up. "That's the Binghams. And I have a horrible cramp in my stomach from all those fucking sit-ups."

"I can't *believe* what you've done with Mother's house!" said Mrs. Bingham, popping around the corner, followed by her husband. La Bingham eyeballed the scene around her, clearly appalled, yet fascinated. "What are you all doing over here, having a party? At nine-thirty in the morning?"

Joe got up, muttered, "Late to work!" and disappeared inside, his bathrobe sash trailing behind him in the sunshine.

"When am I going to get that tour inside the house, dear?" Mrs. Bingham sang out hopefully to Holly.

"Soon," promised Holly politely. "But I can't let you see inside today, because it's not perfect yet. Let me get you something to drink!"

She grabbed my sleeve and we went inside, Waffles trotting along behind us. Holly shut the door firmly behind us, while the Binghams peered unabashedly through the windows, their noses flat against the glass.

"What can I give them? All they drink is that fucking zinfandel," Holly hissed tragically. "They're here every other day, hounding me to get a look around the house. I had a bottle of pink wine for them, but it's all gone. Usually if I give them a drink, they leave and go to the club."

"They want wine this early?" I said, checking the time on the clock on her glossy new stainless range. It was 9:40 a.m. I needed to get to work.

"Of course," Holly said, looking at me as if I was nuts. "It's the *Binghams*."

"Just slosh together some red wine and chardonnay," I suggested. "They'll never know the difference."

"That's totally going to work!" Holly said happily.

TEN MINUTES LATER, Waffles and I were at The Striped Awning, where we opened up the store and listened to a message from Hugh Best. He'd called the police, who told him they couldn't do anything until Jimmy had been missing for at least seventy-two hours, unless he had dementia, which Jimmy didn't.

I was getting worried myself now. Where could Jimmy be? I called Hugh back and suggested that he go ahead with his only idea, which was calling Hugh's fraternity brothers from more than fifty years ago at Princeton. I promised to check back in with him later.

By noon, I'd had a few customers, had vacuumed the store, and was thinking about which of my borrowed Holly dresses I could wear on my date with John Hall. I was debating the merits of a white linen sheath with a pretty ruffled neckline (Max Mara, and definitely priced well above my monthly rent on the store) vs. a little black cotton dress (deceptively simple, but made by Prada—which meant I couldn't even fathom what it had cost), when Bootsie suddenly appeared and plopped down in her usual seat in front of my desk.

"Bad news. Walt said the goons from Jersey haven't been seen since they stopped by the hospital three days ago, and seafood left on someone's doorstep isn't something he has time to investigate. Plus he'd need more information to interview Gerda about being Barclay's attacker," she said. She wore a terrierlike expression, and I could only imagine her relentless hounding of poor, part-time Officer Walt. "He said he'd look into her immigration status, but if she has a valid work visa, Barclay was probably just making idle threats to try to get Gerda to leave." Bootsie sighed, then went on.

"So, after I met with Officer Walt, I went to my office and Googled John Hall, your veterinarian," Bootsie said.

I was annoyed by this, yet racked with curiosity and kind of grateful. I'd thought of doing the same thing, but had decided Googling was a horrible way to approach a date. Google always brings up weird stuff. There's a picture of me and Holly from Bootsie's paper at a charity event that's very high on the Google search links, and while Holly looks like Alessandra Ambrosio in it, I look like I'd forgotten to put on mascara (I had put on makeup that night, too, but not enough, apparently). After that, I started to listen to Joe more about wearing makeup and flat-ironing my mop of long waves. It turns out the "natural look" isn't so great after age thirty.

"And . . . John Hall got married three years ago!" Bootsie said with her usual glee at unearthing information, while my heart skipped a beat in horror. How could I have missed the clues . . . He wasn't wearing a ring, and he seemed so honest . . .

"But, don't worry, I asked around at the office, and he's divorced!" Bootsie finished.

I started breathing again. Lots of people get divorced, and while it's always really sad, it does happen. Actually, most men approaching forty, which was what I guessed John Hall's age to be, had been married at least once.

"Well, almost divorced," Bootsie amended. "He's legally separated."

My stomach did a swan dive. I didn't like the sound of "almost divorced."

"But here's the really interesting part," warbled Bootsie. "The woman he's married to is . . . you won't believe this . . . it's someone you know . . . or at least, someone you've seen around town!" She looked at me with a merry expression, while I felt a sudden urge to kick her.

"Bootsie, please," I said. "Don't do this to me."

"Okay, okay," said Bootsie. "It's Lilly Merriwether! You know, Mariellen's daughter. The one who wins all the tennis trophies at the club!"

My ears started clanging, and my heart plummeted ankle-ward. Had Bootsie really just said *Lilly Merriwether*? I clutched my desk so as to not topple off my chair. Luckily, a light breeze blew in the open door, which cooled off my clammy forehead as I gulped some water from the glass I keep on my desk. I'd heard, as had everyone in Bryn Mawr, about Lilly's epic nuptials a few summers before. But I'd never known the name of the groom, since I hadn't read the announcement in Bootsie's newspaper.

Had Bootsie really just told me that the beautiful daughter of Mrs. Perfect Pearls was the former Mrs. Cute Vet?

WHEN I REGAINED my composure, I realized I could easily picture John and Lilly zinging tennis balls around with matching golden tans and pristine white outfits, Lilly no doubt wearing a strand identical to her mother's South Seas pearls around her slim neck. "Good game, darling!" Lilly would coo to John Hall in her Grace Kelly lockjaw accent, as they clinked frosty vodka tonics at the end of a match, sitting on chaise longues with monogrammed cushions. Mariellen would look on proudly, clad in a cool linen sheath, nodding as she took a puff of her Virginia Slim and blew a smoke ring.

"When you say 'almost divorced,'" I asked Bootsie in my best effort at a neutral tone, "do you mean that the vet and Lilly are *definitely* headed for divorce?"

"I'm working on confirming that," Bootsie told me. "I know they've been separated for about a year, but I'm not sure where the divorce stands. I'm sure you heard Lilly had a huge and fabulous wedding at Mariellen's house with two tents and an orchestra. I looked up the wedding announcement in our archive, and Lilly rode into the ceremony on Norman the horse, and at midnight there were forty minutes of fireworks, and then the next day there was a tennis brunch at the club . . ."

I stopped listening at this point. How could I, with my Gap and J. Crew outlet wardrobe, long wavy brown hair, sorry-ass forehand, and weird devotion to a basset hound, ever compete with Lilly Merriwether? John must have been desperate for dinner companionship to ask me out. He was used to utter blond perfection, round-the-clock tennis, and the manicured grounds of the Merriwether house.

I looked around my slightly battered shop, which until I'd heard this, I'd considered charming, and my gaze paused at Waffles, who was sprawled on his bed, drooling, looking incredibly portly. One ear was stuck to the floor, encrusted with remnants of his rawhide bone. And there was a distinctly funky smell floating from over his way—he'd just farted. This was the final indignity.

I'd go ahead and meet John as planned tonight, since

it was too late to cancel. And then after that, I'd forget about him, and move on.

"Anyway, I think the vet would be a good person to date, if you can be sure that Lilly's out of the picture," Bootsie said.

"Um-hmm," I answered listlessly.

"Anyway, after the Googling, I stopped by Louis the lawyer's office to see if any news had come in," Bootsie continued, changing subjects. "And it had. Including one *huge* lie Sophie Shields told us!"

I listened with mild interest, too depressed about the vet and Lilly Merriwether to get excited about this development vis-à-vis Sophie.

"Remember when Sophie said that she needed Barclay alive to get her divorce settlement?" Bootsie asked. I nodded. Sophie had told us that within five minutes of meeting us, actually. And in the days since the attack, it had served to rule her out as a possible attempted murderess.

"Well, it's bullshit!" Bootsie crowed happily. "If Barclay dies, Sophie gets seven million in a life insurance policy that Barclay can't cancel until they're one-hundred-percent divorced. Louis explained the whole thing to me. He and Sophie's lawyers agreed to the insurance policy staying in place until they work out the divorce agreement. Apparently, it's pretty common to have a deal like this when a couple is splitting up and there's significant wealth at stake."

I tore my mind away from Lilly and John, and thought about what Bootsie was telling me. Sophie had a motive to kill Barclay, after all.

"But how much is Sophie likely to get in her divorce settlement from Barclay if he *doesn't* die?" I wondered aloud, secretly hoping there was so much money at stake that Sophie couldn't logically be the attacker of her ex. Sophie was starting to grow on me. "More than seven million?"

"Undetermined!" Bootsie said. "She'll get a lot, of course, since I doubt she'd marry a refrigerator like Barclay if there wasn't some major cash in the offing. Louis can't comment, of course, since he's Barclay's attorney, and it's privileged information."

I rolled my eyes. Louis had obviously breached a ton of legal ethics already by telling Bootsie about the insurance policy, and numerous other details. Why stop now?

"But I got the distinct feeling that the Shieldses' pre-nup would give Sophie less than the insurance policy," said Bootsie, with an air of knowledgeable self-satisfaction. "Louis *hinted* that Sophie would get more out of Barclay being dead than if he lived to sign the divorce agreement."

This was bad news, because along with Sophie's passion for statues, she had an upbeat, hopeful personality and an appealing, up-for-anything attitude. Hopefully her go-getter attitude didn't include trying to kill her Sub-Zero-size husband.

Bootsie rattled on about how Sophie and Gerda could have carried out the attack on Barclay in tandem, but I had stopped listening.

"Bootsie," I asked her suddenly, "do you think you could give me some tennis lessons?"

Chapter 15

BOOTSIE AND I made a date for a lesson the following morning at her parents' court, since there was no way I was displaying my crappy forehand at the club for all the Merriwethers to see. Maybe I really did have some talent with a racket, I thought hopefully, despite about thirty years of evidence to the contrary, as Bootsie left and headed back to her office.

At four, I decided no one was buying any more antiques today. I took Waffles home, showered, did a quick makeup and hair blitz, and put on the white dress. I checked in with Hugh Best, who hadn't heard from Jimmy; I encouraged Hugh to keep calling friends in the Princeton alumni directory, and promised to spend the next morning driving around town hunting for Jimmy. I decided to head over to the club early, leaving Waffles on his bed in the kitchen, snoring.

Five minutes later, I parked under my usual tree at the

club, but the familiar, charming old building didn't do much to quell my anxiety. I was an hour and half early for a date with a guy who was married to—okay, separated from, but legally married to—the Perfect Woman, and would probably reconcile with her any day now. I looked down at my outfit, smoothing the skirt of Holly's Max Mara dress.

I went inside to have a soda at the bar with Ronnie—that might calm my nerves. I was determined not to have any wine at all before my date. I went in the club's front door, crossed the hallway to the bar, peeked into the room, and saw the Binghams had invaded Ronnie's bar, and were currently working their way through a fresh bottle of white zinfandel. Darn! I did a U-turn and trotted back out the front door.

The only option left was the 19th Hole, the club's snack shed by the driving range, which dispensed beer, wine, and hot dogs. I shouldn't get that worked up about meeting the vet, I told myself, since it was the first and last date ever with him. I ordered myself to buck up as I passed banks of lilies along the clubhouse exterior. The Hole, as it's known, with its cold Heineken and free-flowing pinot grigio, was a cheerful spot, perfect for golfers during the summer. I could really go for a pinot grigio. I revised my self-imposed rule about no wine before the date. Wine was a *good* idea, I decided.

It was a perfect afternoon, breezy, quiet, and peaceful, with the metallic whump of golf clubs in the distance. What was the use of torturing myself over one more going-nowhere date? I tried to convince myself. I'd had plenty of those before!

I still had a few good years left in me, *and* I was about to learn tennis! Who needed a cute vet, anyway?

Just then, as I passed the golf cart shed, I saw a flash of red through a window that caught my eye as out of place within the shed's freshly painted, dark green clapboard exterior and orderly rows of golf cars within. Dusty, rusty red, with a metallic, gritty quality that stuck out amid the white carts, it caught my eye as something familiar, a flash of shape and color that I'd seen many times before. I paused and backtracked, sliding open the garage door that led into the roomy shed, which at night accommodated some three dozen carts, and peered deeper into the dim expanse. There was no mistaking it: The Bests' Volvo was in the back corner, a large cloth tarp partly concealing its dinged-up, late-seventies glory.

I walked over to the car and gingerly lifted one side of the tarp: There was the familiar giant dent in the driver's side door, and the inspection sticker dated July 1989. The Metamucil and Kleenex were intact on the front seat, but the backseat of the car was now stuffed with what looked like most of the contents of the Bests' attic. Silverware and napkin rings in ancient plastic baggies and old books littered the seats, and on the floor were cardboard boxes and a moth-eaten deer head mounted on a wooden plaque.

I let the tarp fall back into place and tiptoed out of the shed into the late-afternoon sun, closed the sliding door behind me, then walked back into the clubhouse and down the air-conditioned hallway toward the locker rooms. There, I sat on a chintz-upholstered bench for a minute to digest the presence of the Volvo at the club. A portrait of a 1950s-era club president in a gray flannel suit stared down at me sternly from across the hallway, which didn't help me process my next step, now that I'd tracked down my missing neighbor's car.

Had Jimmy asked Ronnie if he could park the Volvo here while he holed up somewhere local—maybe the Marriott in Villanova? It seemed unlikely. Jimmy was way too cheap to pay one hundred thirty-nine dollars a night for the Marriott, even if it did include a breakfast buffet and a free glass of wine each evening. He didn't seem to have many friends, but was Hugh right—could an old fraternity brother have taken Jimmy in?

One of the ancient members of the club, Mr. Conwell, heir to a soup fortune, walked by on his way to play tennis, and we smiled at each other. He was a very inspiring old guy, lean and fit in his eighties, much like my grandfather had been until the year before he got sick and passed away.

Too bad Jimmy Best wasn't more like the friendly Mr. Conwell, I thought. But then again, Mr. Conwell is in possession of approximately seven hundred million dollars' worth of stock in his family's food company, so you'd expect him to be in a good mood.

Then I remembered a winter night in the club bar a few years ago, when my grandfather had regaled me with stories of the club's glory days in the years just after World War II. Apparently, the club had been a crazy party palace in the late forties, with black-tie dinner dances on the lawn, rollicking nights in the basement bowling alley, martinis being drunk around the clock, and a teenage Grace Kelly dropping by. "Prettiest girl I'd ever seen," Grandpa had said, sitting on the Chesterfield sofa and sipping his vodka tonic, "including your grandmother, but I hadn't met her yet."

The club had been Grandpa's second home back then. He'd spent all his spare time there, because his parents had figured he couldn't get into too much trouble at a country club. Actually, the activities that went on in the basement bowling alley weren't *all* bowling, he'd hinted, but he clarified that he never got to "bowl" with Grace Kelly. There had been drinking, dancing, and other fun distractions for everyone back then, and members had always been dressed in great-looking suits and tuxedoes, or pretty silk gowns, or tennis whites. Old photos of parties and tennis matches hung on the locker room walls, which attested to the glamour of the forties and fifties.

"Upstairs on the third floor was where the real action was in those days," Grandpa had told me, swirling his Scotch and smiling.

"The third floor?" I'd never been in that part of the club. In fact, I'd never realized there was anything other than an attic on the third floor of the clubhouse, with its turrets and eaves under a shingled roof.

"Rowdy bunch up there," Grandpa had told me, and explained that in the first half of the twentieth century, there had been small apartments on the top floor—suites of rooms that served as a kind of upscale retirement home for members whose wives had passed away. The old guys who lived up there had wandered the halls in their bathrobes and held a poker game that began every morning at eleven, continued through dinner, and raged on until midnight, when the busboys would make everyone go to bed. Apparently, the guys were a cigar-smoking, waitress-pinching, whiskey-chugging bunch who spent their golden years in pure glee. "Good system, actually," Grandpa said.

"Very Walter Matthau and Jack Lemmon," I had agreed.

Remembering this conversation, I suddenly got up and, on a hunch, walked to the end of the hallway past the locker rooms and up a small flight of stairs that led to the second floor of the club. Here, a lofty, maple-paneled ballroom took up most of the floor—silent at this time of day, of course, with bits of dust floating peacefully in the sunlight. Just down from the ballroom, a warren of small administrative offices occupied the space directly above the locker rooms. The little stairway I had ascended landed right between the ballroom's open double doors and a warren of offices at the other end of the hallway, where, it appeared, no one was working at this time of day.

I knew that there had to be stairs somewhere that led up to the third floor. As I passed office doors marked "Food and Beverage" and "Club Manager," I came to an old wooden door painted dark green. It was unmarked, and a bit larger than the office doors.

I tried the handle to the unmarked green door. Locked.

As I yanked on the doorknob one more time, something caught my eye on the old millwork around the door frame. It was to the right, and just above my head. Something shiny. I peeked up, and hanging from a tiny nail in the side of the millwork was a very old key. And when I slipped it into the lock in the door handle and turned, the old door creaked open loudly, but easily, and revealed a set of wooden stairs. I put the key on the bottom stair (the last thing I needed was to get locked in the club attic), closed the door behind me, and started to climb.

"OH, FUCK," SAID Jimmy Best. "It's you."

I didn't take it personally.

Once upstairs, it hadn't taken much work to find him. The flight of stairs ended in a long hallway that was frayed by age. The walls were covered with red-and-yellow-striped wallpaper—faded, but as chic as the day it had been installed. There were bronze light sconces, prints of hunting scenes, and wide, beautifully aged, polished plank floors. At each end of the hallway was a round, lounge-like room with pretty, if slightly dusty, mullioned windows overlooking the club lawns. These round rooms must be the interiors of the shingled turrets that flanked each end of the club, I realized, and they were just as appealing here as they were on the building's exterior. There were two ancient poker tables in the room to my left, complete with chips and yellowed playing cards, and what I recognized as the door to a dumbwaiter directly in front of me. At the other end of the hall, I could see a billiard table and a small wooden bar. It was hot up here, of course, being late May at the top of a stuffy old shingle-and-brick building, but there was something frankly awesome about this secret part of the club.

I'd turned right when I heard jazz floating quietly from that end of the hallway. The music appeared to be coming from under a door marked the "Conwell Suite"—named for the family of the handsome old man I'd just seen downstairs. This had to be a good suite, I thought to myself, with all that soup money.

I'd knocked lightly, then gingerly opened the door to Jimmy's sour greeting. He sounded as grouchy as ever, but underneath his mustache and frown, he actually looked relieved to be found. For my part, I was thrilled that he was fully dressed in a pair of old khaki shorts and a white shirt with the sleeves rolled up.

"I'm so glad you're okay!" I told him, truthfully.

"Oh, I'm more than okay, darling," he said with a grin, and lit up a cigar. "I'm fantastic. I can't tell you how good it is to be finally free of that nagging hen of a brother. I'm smoking, drinking, and eating red meat around the clock. Should have moved up here in 1976, when I divorced my fourth wife."

Jimmy was happily ensconced on a leather sofa. White cotton curtains fluttered in the late-afternoon air by a set of double windows that had been cracked open for fresh air, and a small air conditioner hummed. Not the most energy-efficient setup, but it definitely provided comfort.

"This *is* nice," I admitted, "but what about your brother? He's terrified that something's happened to you."

"That old woman!" hooted Jimmy, puffing on his stogie contentedly. "He reminds me of Angela Lansbury."

I sighed. I'd have to somehow convince Jimmy to go home, or at least to call Hugh and tell him he was okay. In the meantime, it was hard to deny the appeal of his attic lair. For one thing, the view of the club grounds was gorgeous from up here. There was a cute window seat, and I perched there for a few moments to look out at the lawn, which unfurled in front of me in its emerald lushness. A few tennis players were still out swatting balls, and I squinted to see if any of them were John Hall or, horrors, Lilly Merriwether (which they weren't—none of the women playing was as annoyingly slim and tan as the reedlike Lilly). A trumpet vine had grown up from the porch roof and curled around the window frame, its orange bell-shaped flowers framing the sill perfectly. There was a pleasant clinking of glasses and murmur of people chatting below on the porch.

What with the relaxing music, and it now being past five, I thought to myself, well, now that I'm here, I could really go for a glass of wine.

"Your Scotch, Mr. B.," said Ronnie the bartender just at that moment, entering discreetly with a silver tray bearing a glass of Dewars, a chilled glass of chardonnay, and a dish of peanuts. "Kristin." He nodded at me, handing me the glass of wine and a cocktail napkin as nonchalantly as if I was sitting on the porch with Joe and Holly, rather than sitting in an attic with a seventy-five-year-old man who'd run away from home.

"Gosh, you're good!" I told Ronnie admiringly. Clearly,

the network of secret passageways and staff gossip in the club is extensive enough that everyone who knew Jimmy was stashed away up here also already knew that I was upstairs visiting him. Were there cameras throughout the club, or did Ronnie and his staff have some kind of sixth sense for what the members were up to? I'd have to ask Ronnie when I got a minute alone with him in the bar. In any case, some of the club staff had clearly decided to take Jimmy under their wing, and were taking exceptionally good care of him. There was an open door behind Jimmy's leather couch that led to a bedroom, where I could see that a bed was made up with crisp white linens. A thick white terry bathrobe borrowed from the men's locker room hung on a peg beside the bedroom window, and on a chest of drawers to my right, a tray held a pitcher of water, some glasses, and a bottle of Amaretto.

"Roast beef tonight, Mr. Best?" asked Ronnie. Jimmy nodded happily, rubbing his hands together with glee. I loved the fact that Jimmy, who had almost no money, was being so well taken care of in a club where ninety percent of the members were enviably rich. Jimmy's long-standing membership and no-bullshit style had clearly made him a staff favorite of the waiters and barmen, and of course he'd always flirted relentlessly with the sixty-year-old waitresses, to their delight. Most of the *members* hated Jimmy, but he didn't give a fig about that.

"Are you staying for dinner, Kristin?" Ronnie asked politely.

"No, thanks," I told him. "I have an, um, appointment tonight." I looked at my watch surreptitiously. I still had thirty-five minutes before my rendezvous with John. That should be enough time to convince Jimmy to forgive Hugh and go home.

On second thought, maybe not. Jimmy was as cozily settled in here as Hugh Hefner on movie night at the Playboy Mansion. He clinked my glass from his perch on the sofa as I sat down on the red chintz chair. "He's a reliable bastard," he said fondly about Ronnie, as the barman silently disappeared. "Good bartender, too."

"He does always seem to know just when you need a drink," I agreed.

"Now that you've found me," said Jimmy, waggling his bushy gray eyebrows at me, "what do you plan to do with me?"

"I'm not sure," I admitted. "Maybe have another cocktail?"

"I'D LOVE TO look through these boxes with you, Jimmy," I said, sipping chardonnay and feeling the delightful California grapes surging through my bloodstream. Jimmy's good mood was contagious, and Ronnie had delivered another round without being asked. I pushed the glass of wine away and focused on the stuff from the Bests' house that Jimmy wanted me to look through. "I only have ten minutes before I have to leave, so I'll have to make it quick," I told him.

Jimmy had transported several incredibly dusty boxes and an old leather suitcase to the club from his house, which he told me he planned to have me sell at The Striped

Awning or take out to Stoltzfus's flea market, and the stuff was currently shoved into a corner of the Conwell Suite. My white dress (well, Holly's white dress) would be ruined if I unpacked these musty old boxes without some kind of protection, so I asked Jimmy if I could put his on his bathrobe over my dress to protect it from smudges. He agreed affably.

"Might give old Ronnie fodder for the club rumor mill if he sees you in my robe," he said with some interest as I shrugged it on and rolled up the long sleeves.

Borrowing a pad and paper I'd noticed on the sideboard where the Amaretto bottle was perched, I sat down cross-legged on the floor, and began to open one of the old cardboard moving boxes. I didn't feel comfortable selling any of the Best heirlooms without first asking Hugh, but I could at least look through the stuff while I was here.

"You'll probably really miss Hugh by tomorrow," I told Jimmy without much conviction, as I pulled out old newspaper that was stuffed into the box to protect its contents.

Jimmy stared at me with utter contempt. "I don't think so, darling," he finally said from the sofa, swirling his Dewars disdainfully. "Been living with him for most of the last seventy-plus years, except when I was married, and haven't missed him once." Inwardly, I agreed with Jimmy. It seemed like they could really use a trial separation. But Hugh was so worried about his brother, it would be cruel to keep him in the dark about Jimmy being found safe.

"You have to at least let him know that you're safe," I pleaded. "And you two have to figure out *together* what to do about your house and moving to Florida. And what your plans are for all this stuff you brought here." I wasn't sure how Jimmy had ever gotten all this stuff out of the house by himself, but there I sat, making a quick mini-inventory of the silver and china in the box in the short time before my cute-vet date. It was your basic WASP hodgepodge: There were mismatched Limoges plates, and two ancient leather-bound Nathaniel Hawthorne books coated in pale dust. There was most of a silver tea service in urgent need of polishing, and old leather photo albums, a beautiful but tattered family Bible, and a set of gilded salt cellars. I was touched by seeing it all spread out around us, elegant reminders of when the Best family had been more prosperous, gathering for black-tie dinners and roast pheasant suppers in the proper old Philadelphia way. It was familiar, and oddly reassuring, to see the remnants of this charmed and long-gone style of living.

While I made notes, Jimmy munched his way through the bowl of nuts and told me about the last two days, which had been spent watching porn and baseball (Ronnie had wired the old TV in the bedroom into the club's satellite dish), gulping cocktails, and inhaling fatty foods.

"I check out the tennis on the lawn in the afternoon," he added gesturing toward the window seat, with its view of the grass courts, "though I must say the players here aren't exactly Maria Sharapova in the looks department.

And last night at eleven, I snuck down and bowled a few frames in the basement. Easy to wander around here at night, since the old bastards who belong here all have dinner at six. Boring fuckers, really."

There was no way Jimmy could stay for too much longer, because even if the club still allowed members to move in—which it didn't—he'd never be able to afford it. And why would the staff hide him for more than a day or two? It's not like Jimmy was Anne Frank. And he had to tell his panicked brother where he was. Or at the least, he had to tell him he was alive.

"Jimmy, you have to get in touch with Hugh," I told him. "If you want, I'll tell him that you're fine, but aren't ready to come home yet, and that you'll get in touch with him in a couple of days, okay?"

"Fine, fine," he muttered, picking up a *Racing Form* and rolling his eyes.

I kept unpacking his stuff, but I didn't have the heart to tell him that the things I'd uncovered so far, while loaded with sentiment and charm, wouldn't bring more than a hundred bucks all told at The Striped Awning. Maybe I'd have better luck with the contents of the battered old leather suitcase. The top layer of old newspaper contained some ancient and not very clean fish forks held together by a rubber band. Next was a bunch of embroidered linen napkins, and underneath those, a faded black leather box about the size of a box of animal crackers.

The leather was fraying at the edges, peeling away from the parchment and wood that formed the box, but the S-shaped catch opened easily. Inside, the interior was lined in velvet that had once been black, and was now faded by the years. There was a ring nestled in the velvet, and I lifted it out of its snug place and held it up in the light still flooding in through the windows. The ring was set with a huge dark red stone surrounded by tiny white diamonds set in white gold or platinum. While the jewel was darkened by age, it was still stunning. I don't know much about jewelry, but this elegant knuckle-grazer seemed like it must be of some real value.

"Jimmy, this ring is gorgeous," I raved. "Was it your mother's? I love it!"

"Cocktail ring," said Jimmy, looking over his newspaper with his reading glasses halfway down his nose. "Looks pretty snazzy, I agree, but not worth much. Came down through Mother's side of the family. She had it looked at some years ago—well, quite a few years ago—back in the sixties, as I recall. Took it to an antiques market in the city and they said it was basically worthless. Semi-precious stone, apparently."

"It's really beautiful," I told him, disappointed for the Bests' sake that it wasn't worth more. I slipped it on my right hand ring finger and admired it. Then I caught sight of my Timex, which looked seriously outclassed by the dramatic ring, and noticed it was 6:24 p.m.

"Shit!" I said to Jimmy. "I've gotta go." I looked down at the other unopened cardboard box in front of me and had a brainstorm. "Can I take this box with me? It might make Hugh feel better if I bring a few things home. Then

I'll come back here tomorrow, and we can look through the rest of this stuff, and figure out when you're going home."

"Suit yourself," said Jimmy. Then he gave me a grin. "Why don't you wear the ring tonight, darling? It hasn't seen the light of day in forty years. It might be fun for you. You can always give it back to me tomorrow."

"I'd love to!" I said. I hung up his bathrobe, washed my hands in his ancient white porcelain bathroom sink in the bathroom off the Conwell apartment's bedroom, taking care not to ding the cocktail ring, grabbed the box, and waved good-bye as Ronnie opened the door bearing a tray with Jimmy's dinner, which was being kept warm under a silver dome.

I DASHED DOWN the steps and was trotting down the first-floor hallway of the club, when I nearly ran smack into Bootsie.

She stared at the cardboard box tucked under my arm.

"What's in the box?" she demanded.

I ransacked my mind briefly.

"Some old silver the club wants to sell off," I lied. "They never use it, so I'm going to sell it at the store to raise money for the, er, club maintenance fund."

"Oh," she said. Luckily, Bootsie was totally bored by this misinformation, and turned to scan the scene on the porch through a south-facing window, missing the cocktail ring on my finger, which was mostly blocked by the dusty old box. "Want to have a quick drink?" she asked, adding, "I've got some time, my doubles match was canceled."

"Oh, sorry, I have to take care of these boxes," I said. "But I can't wait for our tennis lesson tomorrow!"

"Okay," she said. "Remember, 7:30 a.m. sharp. Early tennis is always fabulous!"

"Great!" I yelled over my shoulder as I headed out the front door toward my car, where I quickly stashed the box in the trunk of my car. It was 6:29 p.m., so I dialed Hugh Best as quickly as I could on my cell phone.

"Your brother is fine," I told him.

"Oh, thank heaven," bleated Hugh.

"He's safe and he has all your family heirlooms, but he refuses to come home right now, and I promised him I wouldn't tell you where he is for at least a couple more days. I think I can talk him into it very soon. Are you okay with that?" I asked Hugh hastily.

"I suppose I have to be," he sighed fussily. I could hear him uncorking a decanter and sloshing Scotch into a glass. "Stubborn bastard," he added.

"I'll stop by your house first thing tomorrow morning," I promised. I hung up, did a lip gloss and hair check, and inspected the white dress, which was blissfully smudge-free.

My Timex read 6:31 p.m., so I took a deep breath and got out of the car, wondering how I could somehow convince John that we should eat inside the club, hidden in a dark corner of the empty dining room, when everyone else was having a fabulous time outside on the porch on this beautiful night. I just couldn't conduct a date with the vet under the watchful eye of Bootsie. And even worse, what if Honey Potts, or the dreaded Mariellen—the vet's *mother-in-law*—were here tonight, Mariellen sitting and angrily smoking her Virginia Slims on the porch? She seemed to be here every other night of the year.

I looked up and there in front of me in the parking lot was John, in a sport coat and khakis, looking tanned and lean.

"Hey, there. I had an idea," he said with a smile. "Would you like to go to that new place, Gianni? I get a little tired of eating at the club sometimes."

Chapter 16

JOHN DROVE TO the old firehouse, where I was reasonably sure I wouldn't run into Holly, Joe, or Bootsie. I knew Holly wouldn't eat anything on Gianni's carb-and-meat-laden menu, and Joe was likely too weary to go out after his day of redesigning with Sophie. I was fairly sure that Bootsie was still trolling the club for someone to drink with.

However, everyone else in Bryn Mawr seemed to be at Gianni tonight: The bar was packed, and nearly every table was full, too. Wow, *this* was the suburbs on a Tuesday night?

There restaurant buzzed with a Tuscany-meets-Beverly-Hills vibe. The place smelled heavenly, and a well-dressed crowd was eating pasta with the gusto of dockhands, happily sucking down red wine and pinot grigio. I had to hand it to Chef Gianni: Even though he was still stuck in the hospital, his restaurant was doing really well.

As the hostess walked us through the crowded restaurant to a table on the shaded patio, I noticed that she was about twenty-four years old and had an enviable Olivia Munn–style body in her tight all-black outfit that would leave most forty-year-old men with their tongues unfurling from their mouths. But John, I noted approvingly, merely followed her through the dining area. Okay, he shot her one quick glance, but honestly, what guy wouldn't? He looked great, I thought, in his sport-coat-over-a-polo-shirt outfit, and the light-colored jacket in a subtle check set off his great tan and his blue eyes. He turned to smile at me as we walked along behind the Olivia Munn look-alike.

Just then, a woman at a table in the center of the restaurant clutched my arm with a coral-manicured paw. "Kristin," she sang out. "How are you, dear?"

Uh-oh. It was Bootsie's mom, Kitty Delaney, who was wearing a shocking-lime-green shift dress with pink ribbon trim, and a pink headband on her graying bob. Kitty is a nice woman, but it's from her side of the family that Bootsie inherited her insatiable taste for gossip. Kitty's base of gossip-erations is the porch off their house, over near their tennis court. She has an old green telephone out there, set up on a table with the vodka and mixers, and spends all day chatting and sharing information with her extensive network of bridge-playing friends, before they all meet up for cocktail hour at the club.

Bootsie's dad, Henry, who doesn't talk much, gave me a friendly grunt while he continued to eat what looked like delicious gnocchi.

"And who's your charming friend?" Kitty pressed on, her eyes gleaming with unbridled curiosity and a slight Stoli haze at John. I made some hasty introductions, and we continued loping after the hostess to our table.

Well, that was that, I thought, smiling in what I hoped was a relaxed and carefree way at John as we walked out onto the patio and reached our white-clothed table. As we sat down, my mind raced through the ramifications of a Kitty Delaney run-in. Bootsie had known I was interested in the vet, but I hadn't told her we had an actual date tonight. I was going to have to tell Bootsie everything about my date in painful detail tomorrow (or tonight, if Bootsie could reach me on my cell phone, which was currently on silent).

I glanced back over my shoulder at Kitty, who had produced her own cell phone and was furiously punching buttons on it. Was she *texting*? Bootsie must have finally convinced her mom that she needed to be able to receive and dispense information wherever she went. In fact, I'd be lucky if Bootsie didn't show up in the next fifteen minutes, and bribe the waitress into giving her and her husband, Will, the table next to ours.

"I hear the tagliatelle is great here. Even though the chef's not here tonight, he's got a couple of guys who trained in Italy who make it by hand," John was saying amiably as he took off his sport coat and hung it over the back of his chair. *Wow!* I screamed inwardly, checking out his arms under his white polo shirt.

While we unfolded our starched white napkins, I noticed two people lurking at the end of the large terrace. The pair was behind some potted ficus trees that the Colketts had banked at the end of the patio to camouflage a kitchen door. I caught a whiff of cigarette smoke coming from that direction.

I realized the smoker was a petite blonde in towering heels, who was huddled in close conversation with a tall guy in chef's whites: Jessica, the young and gorgeous girlfriend of Gianni, and Channing, the muscular cook, I realized. Were they *kissing* between puffs of her cigarette?

Flustered and having flashbacks to my high school days watching *The Young and the Restless*, I nodded when John asked me if I liked Italian wine. As he ordered a Montepulciano, a collective murmur came from inside the restaurant. All of us on the patio turned to stare through the screened doors toward the hostess desk, where a tattooed, muscular man in a hospital gown and Crocs had just limped in.

"I am back!" announced Chef Gianni, brandishing his crutch triumphantly. "Gianni's enemies cannot keep Gianni away from his restaurant!"

As the dining room broke out in admiring applause, the ficus trees parted, and Jessica rocketed from behind the hedge and back into the restaurant, where she silently appeared next to Gianni, taking his arm supportively while grinding out her Marlboro Light on a passing waiter's tray.

Meanwhile, Channing hotfooted it around the side of the building toward the side entrance to the kitchen. I wondered if John noticed any of this, but his back had been to them and he seemed oblivious. He good-naturedly joined in the applause, then asked me in an upbeat way, "So, how do you feel about gnocchi?"

FORTY MINUTES LATER, I took a bite of homemade spaghetti pomodoro. I'm pretty sure it was the best thing I've ever tasted. This isn't saying all that much because I don't cook, and the menu at the club, where I usually dine out, hasn't varied in the last thirty years. It's basically limited to Reubens, prime rib, and crab salads. But this pasta was a revelation.

And, actually, so was the hot vet. It turned out that he asked about the gnocchi because he wanted to order something that *I* liked, so he could share it with me. He put a generous little pile of gnocchi on my bread plate before he even tasted his dinner (light, buttery sauce with herbs and feather-light pasta), and was telling me about his job as a vet. It turned out that most of his work these days was out in Lancaster County, with all its farms, since Bryn Mawr was getting too crowded with people and houses to leave much room for cows.

"There's still a herd at Sanderson, of course," John said. "You know the property, right?"

"I live right across the street." I nodded, hoping against hope that he wouldn't bring up the Barclay Shields incident. He didn't, but what came next was even worse.

"Honey Potts is lucky. She has a great guy who manages her place, and it's hard to find that these days," John continued. "Mike Woodford. Have you ever met him?"

I choked on a gnocchi, gulped water, and while John

patted my back, I croaked, "I'm okay!" and took a gulp of Montepulciano.

"Is there any, um, pepper on the table?" I added in a desperate non sequitur. John hailed a passing waiter, who ground pepper industriously over my plate for a moment and then disappeared. "So yeah," John said, "Mike Woodford is Honey's—"

A pair of muscular shoulders and beautifully gleaming teeth flashed in front of us. "Hey, Doc Hall! It's me, Channing," said the sous-chef, smiling at us in all his tanned Armani-model gorgeousness. "I thought I saw you out here. How's your pasta, dude?" he said to John, and then noticed me.

"Hey, I know you!" he said to me, recognition dawning in his dimwitted but dreamy navy-blue eyes. "Met you at Mrs. Shields's place!"

"Nice to see you," I said, which was true.

"Great pasta," John told him.

"Dude, thanks," Channing said. "The secret is to make the gnocchi fresh throughout the night. Can't be more than ten minutes from rolling pin to boiling water.

"Anyway," concluded Channing cheerfully, "I gotta get back in the kitchen. The chef's got that bum ankle, so he can't stay on his feet all night. See ya." He made his way inside toward the kitchen door, women in the restaurant suddenly abandoning their forks and craning their necks to watch his broad-shouldered handsomeness as he passed.

"Channing used to work for Honey Potts, too," John explained to me. "While he was attending culinary school, he helped out part-time at Sanderson."

Was there anyone in Bryn Mawr *not* connected to Sanderson? I wondered. Everyone either lived near it or wanted to visit it. And those who didn't wanted to buy up some of Sanderson.

And I couldn't help thinking that if Channing was a former Sanderson employee, he'd definitely know his way around the place, and was certainly strong enough to have dragged Barclay under the hydrangea bush.

But then, what would Channing gain by attacking Barclay Shields? I turned my attention back to the vet and his chiseled features and friendly eyes. Let the police figure out what happened to Barclay—I was on a date.

Over the wine, John told me about his love of traveling to Italy, his summer weekends spent fishing in the Chesapeake Bay, his herb garden, and his new hobby of cooking. He didn't take himself too seriously, admitting that he'd recently made a lasagna so bad that he'd offered it to his dogs, but they had steered clear of it.

"None of them would eat it," John was saying after he'd paid the check and we walked to the car. "I've seen them eat deer shit, so I was a little insulted."

As we were about to get into John's car, I saw a huge SUV pull in, and a tall girl with a blond bob launch herself athletically out of the driver's seat. *Bootsie.* It was dark out, of course, since it was close to nine o'clock, but there were several lanterns illuminating the restaurant's gravel parking area, and my date and I were directly in front of one of them. Luckily, Bootsie's gaze was fixed for the moment on the entrance, but I knew she'd scan the parking area before she went in.

As John beeped open his car door, I rushed over, yanked the passenger door open, and jumped in before Bootsie could spot me. Looking quizzical, John quickly slid into the car and shot me a glance. "Are you okay?" he asked. "Anything wrong?"

"No—just tired!" I said, crouching down a little in the front seat. He smiled at me, with an expression that I interpreted as his thinking I'd had too much Montepulciano.

"I'll drive you home," he said. "Do you want me to pick you up tomorrow morning and drive you to the club to pick up your car?"

"I can walk to the club to get my car tomorrow, but thanks. It's only half a mile," I assured him.

Several minutes later, the vet dropped me off at home, where he walked me to the backyard gate, leaned down, and gave me a sweet, avuncular peck on the cheek. Luckily, the bulb on my porch light had burned out, so at least John couldn't see how badly the house needed painting, I thought, as I considered this ill-fated farewell. There's nothing worse than a cheek kiss at the end of a first date. It's literally the kiss of death for future dates. Obviously, the vet would never call again, which I told myself was okay. I didn't need any more toxic stares from Mariellen Merriwether. Feeling downcast, I jumped into bed, where I found some comfort in the presence of a snoring Waffles at the foot of the mattress. Before my head hit the pillow, I removed the huge cocktail ring and dropped it on a tray on my dresser.

The ring was too glamorous for me, and so was John.

Clearly he was destined for Merriwethers, not girls who sold antiques and were obsessed with a basset hound.

THE TENNIS LESSON was horrible.

At seven the next morning, Waffles and I trotted the short distance to the club to pick up my car. In khaki shorts and sneakers, I zoomed over to Bootsie's parents' house, with its roomy yard and clay court, where Bootsie was waiting in full tennis regalia.

"I thought you said you were going back to The Striped Awning last night," she said, glaring at me. "Then Mummy texted that you were at Gianni with that vet! But when I went to join Mummy and Dad for dessert you were gone."

"I'm sorry. I'll tell you all about it while we play," I told her. I figured I'd combine the misery of the tennis and her interrogation. Faster that way.

For the next forty-five minutes, Bootsie ran me like Louis Gossett Jr. in *An Officer and a Gentleman*. While we did drills, sprints, and rallies, she grilled me mercilessly about my date, lobbing Wilson balls and questions at me with equal vigor. I told her the truth—that once I'd learned about John's first marriage, the date seemed like an exercise in futility, which is why I hadn't mentioned it to her.

Bootsie, undeterred, continued to question me about what we'd eaten, about Gianni's dramatic mid-meal arrival, and whether John had brought up the fact that he was still legally married to Lilly.

"No, he didn't," I admitted ruefully. "It just didn't come up, and it seemed too awkward to ask him."

"At least you did something right," Bootsie informed me. "Don't ask him about his divorce. I'll find out for you. And look out, here comes my backhand."

Thwack! A Serena Williams–esque shot from Bootsie narrowly missed knocking my right shoulder out of its socket, and crashed into the wire fence behind me.

"Why shouldn't I ask him?" I said, running for the next ball and actually making contact with my racket. It sailed over the net to Bootsie, who hammered it back at me.

"Because men hate those kind of questions," she said sagely. "You just work on your tennis."

"Okay," I agreed doubtfully. I wasn't sure this was good advice, but I was running so hard to return Bootsie's slams that I couldn't focus on anything else at the moment. "I really don't think we're ever going to go out again, though," I told her.

The sun had barely been up for an hour, but it seemed to be beating down on me as if we lived in the sub-Sahara. What with the heat and a slight wine hangover, I felt like Ralph Fiennes wandering the desert in *The English Patient*.

"I called Walt last night to talk over a few things about last Thursday," said Bootsie, who wasn't even breathing hard.

"They haven't totally ruled out Mike Woodford, by the way, as the guy who hit Barclay. Did he seem dangerous to you?"

"In what sense?" I asked, trying in vain to serve, and instead sending a ball into the net.

"In the sense of someone who would hit Barclay Shields on the head!" said Bootsie, exasperated.

"Definitely not," I told her, with more conviction than I actually felt. I mean, what did I really know about Mike other than that he had great arms and was an excellent kisser?

"Well, he's one of many on the list, because they haven't narrowed down the suspects much at all," conceded Bootsie.

True to form, my aim and ball control were dreadful, so much so that at one point Waffles, after dodging a ball I lobbed dangerously close to his head, whimpered and disappeared under a nice cool azalea bush with just the end of his white tail sticking out.

Thankfully, the lesson ended at eight-thirty. Bootsie had to admit that I was nearly hopeless, but we made another date for tennis the following week.

"How about some orange juice, girls?" shrieked Kitty, Bootsie's mom, from her perch on the porch, flagging us down as we headed toward our cars. "Or something stronger?" she said, holding up a bottle of Bloody Mary mix.

"Gosh, that's so nice of you, I have to get to the store!" I said, grabbing Waffles's leash from the bench and picking up his portable water bowl. He emerged, wagging, from under the bush and trotted after me as I dashed toward the car.

"Did you enjoy your dinner last night with that handsome man, dear?" Kitty shouted loudly enough to be heard in Trenton, forty miles away.

"It was very nice," I told her. "Thank you!" I slammed my car door shut, but Bootsie tapped on my window and leaned in.

"Sorry about Mummy," Bootsie whispered. Then she added, with all seriousness, "Sometimes she can be a little nosy."

AT HOME, I showered, gulped some cold water, put on a pair of linen shorts and wedge sandals, picked up the cardboard box I'd brought back from Jimmy's rooms at the club, grabbed the Bests' cocktail ring from my bedside table, and lugged it all over to their house. When I rang his doorbell, Hugh gratefully accepted the large box with the fish forks and other old bric-a-brac. "I know you promised Jimmy not to tell me where he is," he said. "But do you think he'll come back tonight?"

"I'm guessing more like tomorrow or Friday," I told him.

I also handed Hugh his mother's ring, which I'd put safely back in its black leather box, but he encouraged me to keep it for a few days. "Wear it around for a bit," he told me. "Lord knows, my brother and I haven't even looked at it in years. It'll be nice to see it out and about again. Mother used to wear it to all the parties at the club."

"Are you sure?" I said. The ring looked just as good this morning as it had the night before, well-aged but still glittery and fabulous. I'd have to show it to Holly, who would love it.

"Absolutely," said Hugh. He hesitated. "Tell Jimmy I miss him."

Chapter 17

I LEFT HUGH, headed toward town, and parked under my favorite shady tree at the club, where I planned to do a quick check on Jimmy.

I entered the building by the grand, double-wide front door, where I intended to turn left and dash up the stairs unseen. Golfers and tennis players were visible outside, but the club doesn't serve food until eleven-thirty and the building is usually empty except for a few housekeeping staff midmorning. I saw no one, but was surprised to hear a testy exchange coming from the dining room; I could hear, but not see, the two people speaking. Realizing with a slight chill that I recognized the voices, I stopped in the foyer, seized by an irresistible urge to eavesdrop.

"It's too risky," said a male voice. "If he finds out that we noticed he was missing, he'll spiral-slice us like a honey-baked ham."

"I don't think we're in danger—that is, if you will just

shut the fuck up!" said a second man's voice, rising in anger.

"It's even riskier to stay quiet," the first voice retorted. "We can't just hope this all goes away. People are getting seriously hurt. Who knows where this is heading?"

I was certain that the voices belonged to the Colketts. But what and who, exactly, were they discussing? I desperately wanted to know—but more than that, I wanted to sneak upstairs before they saw me. It was one thing to theorize with Bootsie about the spate of local crimes, but this conversation had a far more serious, and scary tone. On tiptoe, I turned toward the locker rooms, but a floorboard squeaked and betrayed me.

"Who's there?" called out Tom Colkett nervously, poking his head around the doorway and looking relieved when he saw me. "Oh, hi, doll!" he said, beckoning me toward him. "Great to see you. Come say hello!" The florists had set up shop with huge buckets of lilies, roses, and ranunculus, which they were plucking out and skillfully arranging in the club's collection of Chinese vases.

"We're doing the flowers here now," Tim Colkett informed me of the obvious, an apron protecting his well-tailored khakis and polo shirt. "Holly set it up. Love all this paneling and portraits and the old Philly vibe, don't you? And these ladies who lunch in their vintage Lilly Pulitzer."

"It's definitely old world." I nodded, admiring a profusion of roses they'd just placed on a console table in the hallway. I also noticed a pitcher of Bloody Marys on a silver tray next to the flowers, and two half-full glasses next to it. I guess the Colketts adhere to the same early cocktail schedule as the Binghams and Mrs. Delaney, who, predictably, has a needlepoint pillow embroidered with the words "It's five o'clock somewhere!" in her living room.

The Colketts looked as uncomfortable as I did, so I turned to leave. I'd overheard enough to know that the Colketts were involved with something unpleasant and potentially dangerous.

"Well, I should go!" I said, aiming for a breezy tone. "I just was stopping in for a quick second. Better get to the store!"

"Want a drink, Kristin?" asked Tom Colkett, who seemed as eager to project nonchalance as I was. "We always find a quick Bloody in the morning gets our creative juices flowing. You can imagine how many cocktails we need now that we're working for Sophie Shields, too. She's got more statues than the Parthenon." He groaned, and I mustered a sympathetic expression.

"Oh, no, thanks," I told him as he held up the pitcher of drinks and tinkled the ice cubes in it in my direction. "I was at Gianni last night and had a few glasses of wine, but thanks so much. Well, good luck with the flowers!"

I was about to make a break for the door when I turned, and surprising myself, said, "I couldn't help overhearing you guys a few minutes ago. Do you know something about the chef being pushed down the stairs, or have information about Barclay Shields? Because if you do, you should go talk to Officer Walt. The situation could be pretty dangerous." I wasn't sure where my sudden burst of courage had come from, but I was worried about the Colketts. Whether they'd done something illegal themselves, or had witnessed a crime, it would be better for them to own up to it before anything more happened.

The Colketts exchanged glances. And then Tim Colkett wiped his hands on his white apron, and spoke up.

"Listen, Kristin, this isn't easy. We're completely baffled about who we can talk to, and we're honestly scared to tell what we know. But you're right, it might be worse *not* to say anything."

"I think the police are your best bet," I said. And then, against my better judgment, "But what is it that you know?"

Tim gestured silently toward the door to the lounge, and the three of us walked into the empty room and closed the door behind us. I seated myself on the leather Chesterfield sofa and the Colketts perched on either side of me.

"We sort of lied to you when you asked us about the chef and Barclay when we ran into you at the flea market," said Tim regretfully. "Sorry about that. The truth is that, as you know, Barclay was attacked on the same night of the restaurant opening, and of course, we were recovering from that incident over the topiaries. After I got hit with the pomegranate that night, we abandoned the flowers and snuck outside to the patio to have a couple of cocktails while the party got into full swing."

"Needless to say, we'll never work with pomegranates again," added Tom.

"So, while we were hiding from the chef on the patio, we came up with a plan where we could give the chef a big discount on his flowers, and we'd halve the cost of the topiaries if he'd put our 'Flowers by Colkett' insignia somewhere prominent on his menu. It would be tasteful, of course, a small and elegant logo, maybe right under the Gianni logo. And we'd probably get a ton of new customers from being associated with the hottest restaurant in town.

"Well, at about eight, with the party in full swing, we got up the courage to go talk to the chef about it. We figured by then he'd be in a great mood, with everyone raving about his new place. I mean, all the major socialites in town were there," said Tim. "So we searched the entire restaurant for Gianni, and we couldn't find him.

"So then we looked for Jessica to talk to her about our idea. But"—Tim paused for effect—"neither Gianni nor Jessica was there."

"What do you mean?" I asked. "Of course they were there. I saw them."

"Not after eight-fifteen you didn't," Tim said definitively. "Because, trust me, we cased the restaurant. No chef, no Jessica."

Tom, who clearly wanted Tim to shut up, wore a dismayed expression. "Kristin doesn't want to hear this," he told Tim. "You're going to get us *into trouble*."

I tried to make sense of what Tim had said about the missing restaurateur and his girlfriend.

"Maybe you just couldn't find Gianni and Jessica," I suggested. "It's a big restaurant, and between the kitchen and the dining room, they could have been anywhere. I mean, why would Gianni leave his own opening party?"

"Listen, we know it's weird," insisted Tim urgently. "But we hunted for Gianni for at least half an hour, and we looked *everywhere.* Jessica gave us a full tour during construction when we first met with Jessica to discuss flowers. We literally cased the joint—went through the wine cellar, the restaurant, the kitchen, patio, and the office upstairs. They weren't there."

"Other than the guests and all the waiters, the only staff we could find were a bunch of guys in the kitchen who didn't know where the chef was," added Tom, who had evidently decided to jettison his fears and join in the conversation.

"Those kitchen guys are incredibly efficient," said Tim. "They were in there searing baby lamb chops like nobody's business, because people were eating them as fast as they could get those hors d'oeuvres out on the platters. But the sous-chef Channing, the one with the muscles—*he* was missing, too."

"Also, the chef's car was gone," Tom told me. "The Fiat had been parked front and center outside the restaurant, but it wasn't there when we looked outside."

I thought back to the night of Gianni's event. Come to think of it, I hadn't seen much of the chef after the first hour or so of the opening party. If his car had been gone, he must have left the restaurant during the period that the Colketts were describing.

Which was around the time that Barclay Shields was getting his head bashed in.

So Chef Gianni, a certified rageaholic—one who hated Barclay Shields, because Barclay had built him a house so shoddy that it made Barbie's Dreamhouse look like fine craftsmanship—was not at his own soiree during Barclay's head-bashing.

"We finally sat down at the bar at about eight-thirty, got Bellinis, and then we noticed Jessica and Channing were back. Channing was carrying more lobster out to the dining room, while Jessica was on the patio, smoking," said Tim. "We went out to talk to her, and then we saw that the chef's red Fiat was back, too. You know the car. You can't miss it. Bright red convertible, license plate reads GR8CHEF."

"Tacky," pointed out Tom.

"Jessica, by the way, looked a little, well, *rumpled*," Tim told me, sipping his Bloody Mary and waggling his eyebrows suggestively. "Plus she had a big smile on her face, and you know she never smiles. And I thought I saw *grass* in her hair. I asked her if she knew where the chef was, and she said she had no idea.

"A minute later, we spied the chef back in the crowd of customers, mingling and looking positively cheerful," Tim continued. "He acted like nothing was wrong, he didn't have a care in the world.

"And then the next day, we read about Barclay Shields getting his nut cracked, and, well, what are we supposed to do?" Tim's face registered fear, consternation, and tipsiness.

"Maybe the chef needed more, um, crème fraîche or something, and ran to the gourmet store in Haverford?"

I hazarded. "And brought Jessica and Channing with him."

The Colketts rolled their eyes. "Come on, Kristin, you have to admit that it's beyond weird that the chef was missing while Barclay was getting attacked. Anyone on his kitchen staff could have gone to the store if he needed something. Maybe Jessica and Channing were in on the Barclay attack with the chef! The three of them could have put Barclay Shields under the bush where you found him."

While I could easily envision the chef attacking Barclay, and maybe even picture Channing helping if he had some motive, I struggled to picture Jessica helping drag Barclay Shields across the fields of Sanderson in heels with her cigarette dangling elegantly from her fingers. Didn't really compute—the only thing I could imagine Jessica dragging was on a Marlboro Light. But the Colketts needed to tell the police what they knew, that much was clear.

"I really think you should call Officer Walt," I told them. "This sounds pretty important."

Tom Colkett shook his head. "We're florists, not crime busters, doll," he said firmly. "We're not going to risk getting in trouble with the chef and losing customers over this. Customers don't like scandal, and if we're talking to the police, then that puts us right in the middle of a public mess. Plus, if Gianni's going around trying to kill people, we could end up as veal piccata."

"Did you notice anything the night that the chef fell over the railing at Sophie's?" I asked them. "Because he's convinced he was pushed. Was anyone near him around the time of his fall?" Other than you two, I thought to myself, remembering how quickly they had appeared at the top of the stairs after Gianni's tumble.

"We didn't see anything!" Tim insisted.

Tom nodded. "It's true. We were out front downing a quick vodka, and had just come back into the house when we heard all the ruckus, and then saw him flying off that balcony. We didn't see anyone else in the kitchen, so he must have just slipped."

"Anyway, we'd better get back to work," said Tim. "But please be careful about who you mention this to—we're honestly scared." The two gathered up their drinks, and headed back out to work their flower magic. I followed, wondering whether their story was invented to throw suspicion away from themselves, and onto the chef, Channing, and Jessica. Then again, the more I knew of the Colketts, the less I thought they were involved in any of the attacks. I also doubted they would have appeared on the landing if they had pushed the chef off Sophie's terrace. More likely, they wouldn't have shown their faces anywhere near the crime scene. I sighed, and made a left into the hallway.

"By the way, Kristin," said Tim, gazing at my borrowed bauble, "great ring! Love that mega-rock!"

I FOUND JIMMY midway through the Philadelphia newspapers and watching a tennis match from the window seat, drinking coffee in his bathrobe. Again, the jazz was playing and the A.C. blowing, and he looked like he didn't have a care in the world. The remains of a breakfast sandwich sat on the coffee table, along with a lit cigar in a silver ashtray. Jimmy greeted me in a matter-of-fact manner, and informed me pleasantly enough that there was no fucking way he was going home. So I drove to The Striped Awning and called Bootsie.

"THIS IS GOING to require a surprise attack," Bootsie said when I reached her at the newspaper and gave her the short version of the Colketts' confounding tale. "We need to go talk to Jessica right now, and see if she knows whether the chef had anything to do with Barclay's attack. I'm going to call Joe, too. He's friendly with Jessica, so he can come with us and convince her to spill the details. And after we talk to Jessica, I'm going to call Louis, Barclay's lawyer . . ."

Sometimes it's good to have Bootsie take over. Her plans don't always make sense, and they often backfire, but at least she always has an idea.

"In the meantime, we just have to hope the chef's not at the restaurant," said Bootsie. "We need Jessica alone, and willing to blab."

We tracked down Joe at Sophie's house, where he had effected a breakthrough of sorts: He'd finally convinced Sophie to go with a tasteful shade of biscuit in her main rooms, and the painters were priming the walls, so he agreed to take a break. Bootsie swung by the shop, and she and I then zoomed over to Sophie's to get Joe. He leaped into the backseat of her Range Rover, with Sophie hot on his heels. Joe slammed the car door behind him, but Sophie, today clad in hot-pink spandex leggings and a minuscule pink sports bra, rapped on the car window, which Joe glumly rolled down.

"Hi, Beebee and Kristin!" Sophie said. "Can you bring Joe back ASAP? We got a lotta work to do here. Plus Gerda's on the warpath. She's got a major bug up her butt, and I don't want to be stuck here with her all by myself."

"It's true," confirmed Joe. "Gerda thinks someone's been fiddling around with the lock to her office, trying to infiltrate her computer. She's completely paranoid."

Bootsie and I exchanged glances. "She's nuts!" said Bootsie, who happens to be an excellent liar.

"Sometimes she really drives me crazy!" said Sophie, nodding. "But anyway, Joe said you have important business and that it might help figure out who clobbered my ex. Trust me, I want whoever did it found—so I can thank them personally!" She giggled for a second. "But seriously," she added, "I know some people might even think *I* had something to do with it."

"Oh no," we all said at once, in a rush of words.

"No one thinks that!" added Bootsie, in a patently false tone.

"Well, I didn't," said Sophie sourly, her mouth smooshed into a sad little moue. "I don't believe in violence. I believe in big divorce settlements!" She giggled again. "Well, anyway, great to see you, girls. Come over for some champagne when the house is done!"

Joe hit the up button on the window quickly as Bootsie

two-wheeled it out of Sophie's place, and I filled Joe in on what the Colketts had told me about the chef and Jessica.

"Unbelievable," Joe said. "But, yeah, I could totally see the chef attacking Barclay."

"And somehow the chef got Channing and Jessica to help him! Probably, anyway," said Bootsie.

"Did you get any more info about the Colketts' relationship? Brothers, married couple, cousins?" asked Joe.

I shook my head regretfully. "Nope. I'm starting to think the Colketts' status is one of life's mysteries, like Stonehenge," I told him. "I'm not even sure I want to know."

Bootsie steered us into the gravel driveway at Gianni, and we all trooped inside to look for Jessica. A hostess stood at her station up front, organizing the menus for the lunch crowd and adjusting her glossy dark hair.

"Is Gianni here?" I asked her, sotto voce, hoping against hope that he wasn't.

"Chef Gianni's at physical therapy for his broken ankle," said the hostess nonchalantly. "He has it for two hours a day for the next four months. And boy, is he pissed about it." She snickered to herself at that, proving again that the chef was not a beloved boss. It seems that threatening your busboys and regularly excoriating the staff as hopeless losers doesn't do a lot for employee morale.

"And *Jessssicaaa*, is she here?" Bootsie hissed in a loud whisper.

"Outside," said the hostess, looking bored and pointing to the patio.

Jessica was sitting at one of the small outdoor tables, sketching what appeared to be a furniture layout for a residential client, in the shade of a big sycamore tree. She had on jeans and sandals, and no makeup. Actually, she looked even prettier than usual without her usual Manolos and glossy façade of makeup. She had a slight tan, and, something I'd never realized before, a few adorable freckles on her elegant nose. She greeted Joe in a friendly manner, and was amiable enough to me and Bootsie when he introduced us.

"We heard something that we wanted to ask you about, Jessica," said Joe hesitantly. "It's kind of awkward—but did you know the chef was missing for something like thirty minutes during the opening party last week? Friends of ours noticed he was gone, and they tried to find him all over the restaurant, but then they noticed his Fiat wasn't parked behind the restaurant."

Jessica sat up straighter and looked at us, but appeared unconcerned. "You know what, I didn't know he left the party," she admitted. "But I had to go run an errand myself that night, so I didn't really keep track of Gianni after the first fifteen minutes or so of the party."

"An *errand*?" asked Joe, pulling up a chair and sitting down at Jessica's table. "What kind of errand are we talking about?"

Jessica, a girl not easily fazed, turned pink, and a small, goofy smile came over her face.

"Were you off schtupping that hot guy Channing that night?" blurted out Bootsie. "Because we heard you were both missing during the party, and that you had grass in your hair after you got back!"

There was a moment of shocked silence as we all stared at Bootsie, and then at Jessica.

"Um-hmm," Jessica confirmed. "You know what, I'm not gonna lie to you. I *was* with Channing that night."

"I knew it!" cried Bootsie. She and I both sat down at Jessica's table, too.

"We've been having a fling for about a month now," said Jessica proudly, after looking around to make sure none of the restaurant staff was listening in. "It started out as just a one-night thing, but during the opening party, somehow I found myself back in the kitchen, sneaking out the back door with Channing. There was something about that night—I guess it was the vodka, and the crowd, and the warm weather—that just put me in the mood!"

"Where'd you go?" Joe asked. "Did you do it in your car?"

"No, we took Channing's truck over to the fields at Sanderson and did it behind a haystack," confided Jessica. It seemed that once Jessica started talking about sleeping with Channing, she couldn't stop. She'd been bottling it up for weeks, and now the floodgates had opened.

"Channing is the best sex of my life!" she told us breathlessly. "I'm not usually the outdoorsy type, but since Channing used to work at Sanderson and loves trees and cows and all that crap, I'm trying to get more interested in, you know, nature."

"What time did you go?" Bootsie asked Jessica. "You never realized the chef was gone?"

"We left right around eight," said Jessica. "I checked the time, because I knew we couldn't be gone more than half an hour, or Gianni might realize we were both missing. And we were back here by eight-thirty—maybe a few minutes earlier, even."

"You went all the way over to Sanderson, did it, and got back here in less than thirty minutes?" I said, impressed.

"What do you think?" said Jessica, gesturing with her thin, tanned hand toward the firehouse-turned-restaurant behind her, where Channing had just appeared from a side door.

We all looked over. Channing was picking up a case of wine from a liquor truck that had just pulled up to carry it inside. He had on a white T-shirt, jeans, and a day's growth of beard over his male-model jaw. His muscles rippled in the sunshine, and he sizzled a grin our way.

"Yeah, that works," said Bootsie. "Drive over, find a spot behind some hay bales, boom, then drive back. It might not even take me half an hour!"

"Why does this even matter?" asked Jessica, frowning a little in the sun. She shielded her eyes as she looked over at us. "I mean, I know it wasn't very nice to cheat with Channing behind Gianni's back. But all Gianni does is work, and then go home and watch the Food Network. He's obsessed with getting his own show by the time he turns forty." She paused. I noticed Joe's eyes widen at this piece of information. Joe's ambition is to get a design show on TV, but he only admits this after he's had a lot of tequila.

"I promised myself I'd tell Gianni about Channing as soon as the restaurant was up and running, but then the timing was bad after he fell and injured himself. I'm *going* to break up with Gianni, though." Jessica looked distinctly nervous as she said this, and we all imagined the apocalyptic tantrum that her news would unleash.

"Well, I might not tell Gianni about Channing right away," Jessica amended, "but I am going to end it with him. I did have feelings for Gianni when we first got together, but I just can't take his temper anymore. Plus all I can think about is Channing."

The beefcake that is Channing reappeared from the side door to heft more pinot noir into the restaurant. Jessica smiled girlishly and shrugged.

"Did you notice whether Gianni's car was here when you and Channing left to go, uh, get your freak on the night of the opening?" Joe asked Jessica.

"I never looked," she said. "Gianni parks that stupid red Fiat right in front of the restaurant so everyone can see it, but, honestly, Channing and I took off so fast that night that I never even noticed Gianni's car. I guess it could have been gone." Jessica paused, and stared at us curiously.

"Why are you asking about Gianni? Do you think Gianni was *stalking* us that night?" she said breathlessly. "Does he know about me and Channing?"

"That's not what we're worried about," Joe reassured her. As we all got up to leave, he turned back thoughtfully toward her. "Jessica, considering the chef's temper, maybe you should wait a few more days to break up with him. Just till the end of the week, okay?"

"You don't have to spell it out for me," said Jessica, who seemed to be in the mood to let out a Hoover Dam's worth of information. "In fact, and I'm only telling you this because I'm planning on getting the hell out of town ASAP, people don't even know Gianni's real story! He tells everyone he came here from some fancy town in Tuscany just a few years ago, but that's bullshit. He originally came over to the U.S. from the not-so-scenic part of Sicily, and his first restaurant was a pizza parlor in Newark!"

"You mean, like actual greasy, cheesy, comes-delivered-in-a-box pizza?" said Bootsie.

"Oh yeah," Jessica said. "We're talking sixteen-inch sausage-and-pepperoni pies served on Formica counter-tops. Gianni knew Barclay Shields then, too! That's when their feud started. Barclay was named Beppe when they were back in Newark, and he had a stake in Gianni's first pizzeria. When Gianni decided to reinvent himself, he had to pay off a bunch of guys in Jersey before he could launch Palazzo. Some of the guys were upset that Gianni got a fancy new life."

She paused for a minute, looking frightened. "Barclay and Gianni really do hate each other. Barclay was always threatening to tell all the rich people on the Main Line about Gianni's real background, and vice versa."

"I'd keep this to yourself," Joe advised Jessica. "This sounds like dangerous information to share with anyone else."

"Okay," agreed Jessica, looking relieved. She was obviously petrified.

And honestly, I couldn't have agreed more. Maybe Gianni had whacked the giant Barclay to shut him up about Gianni's pizza-tossing past. I didn't even want to imagine what he could do to Jessica with a chef's knife and a meat mallet. She could end up as veal piccata, too.

"So, DO YOU believe her?" asked Bootsie, once we were back in the car.

"Absolutely," I said.

"Of course," said Joe. "It makes perfect sense. I can picture Gianni as mafia pizza guy. And he'd definitely want to keep his past quiet. But whether he was the one who hit Barclay, I don't know."

"Maybe *Jessica*'s lying, and she really was with Gianni that night, helping him attack Barclay instead of getting boned by Channing," suggested Bootsie.

We all thought about this for a second as Bootsie steered back toward Sophie's. Then we burst out laughing at the thought of Jessica messing up her Manolos if there wasn't an orgasm in the offing.

"Yeah, never mind," said Bootsie. "I guess we know the answer to that."

"But one thing doesn't add up," I mused aloud, after Joe had climbed out at Sophie's and Bootsie had turned back toward town. "If the chef whacked Sophie's husband, why did the chef also get one of the warning notes, just like Barclay? And, why would he fall off Sophie's balcony on purpose—since we know Barclay couldn't have been the one to push him?"

"To divert suspicion away from himself!" said Bootsie confidently. "Gianni decided to stage the whole thing, and left himself a fake note! A little tumble would be worth it to Gianni, if it meant he could get away with almost-murder. I have a sense for these things."

I refrained from pointing out that only an hour ago, Bootsie had been certain that Sophie had a hand in the attack, and had also repeatedly named Gerda as her go-to suspect. I also didn't mention that even during high school, Bootsie's so-called sixth sense has always been one-hundred-percent faulty. She was always wrongly predicting things like snow days, pop quizzes, and what time someone's parents would come home from dinner at the club, which resulted in things like all of us being caught mid–tequila shot at age sixteen, getting grounded, and failing chemistry.

"I'm going to drop by and talk to Officer Walt right now," Bootsie told me. "I'm pretty sure this will sew up the case!"

Ten minutes after I got back to The Striped Awning, my phone rang. "I can't talk long," Joe told me, "but Holly needs you to stay over at her house tonight. I didn't want to say anything in front of Bootsie, but you've been ne-glecting Holly."

What! There was no way I was doing that. I'd been out late last night, and up at dawn for Bootsie's horrible tennis drills, then dealt with Jimmy Best, the Colketts, and Jessica . . .

"I can't tonight," I moaned. "I'm exhausted."

"Holly's lonely!" said Joe sternly. "She's in the middle of a divorce, and she's trying to shop her way out of sadness. She's spent seven thousand dollars on bathing suits since April. She needs you. And what do you go and do? You have a date with some *veterinarian*"—he pronounced the word as if I'd gone out to dinner with Ted Bundy—"which we had to find out about from Bootsie, and you didn't even call Holly first about what to wear."

I felt terrible. I hadn't spent much time with Holly lately, it was true. Had she really spent seven grand on *bikinis*? That was scary. And I probably should have consulted with her about the right outfit for my date. "But aren't you living with her for the summer?" I asked him.

"That doesn't matter. Just because she's a gorgeous chicken-nugget heiress with drawers full of Chanel bikinis doesn't mean she doesn't have any problems," Joe informed me. "So you need to make time for us tonight. Holly and I already stopped by your house, got your key from under the flowerpot, and packed a bag for you."

I nodded, mentally calculating that I'd have plenty of time to sneak home for a nap after work and show up at Holly's around eight, in time for dinner. Unless I could weasel out of the whole thing.

"And you can forget sneaking home before you come over, because you'll fall asleep and never make it over," said Joe, whose powers of intuition are way better than Bootsie's. "I'm picking you up there at six. You can leave your car behind the shop tonight."

"But what about—"

Joe knew where I was headed, and cut me right off. "That mutt can come, too."

ALL DAY, I'D been determined not to wonder whether the cute vet would ever call me again, and since by 5:45 p.m. he hadn't, I decided it was a good thing that I was going to Holly's. I could hopefully discuss her relationship with Howard during a quiet moment. Truthfully, I was feeling a little discouraged about the vet being married to Lilly Merriwether, and Joe and Holly *are* my closest friends: If you can't count on a chicken-nugget heiress and her decorator to be there for you through thick and thin, who can you count on?

I never heard back from Bootsie about what Officer Walt had to say about the chef, Jessica, and Channing being AWOL during Gianni's opening party, which was just as well. I could use a night off from that whole mess.

As Waffles, Joe, and I got to Holly's, a torrential storm exploded over Bryn Mawr. Sheets of rain were drenching the tented roof of Holly's fabulous outdoor living room, and blowing sideways onto her weatherproof white furniture, so we moved the party into Holly's indoor living room.

The painters' tarps had been removed, and the result was amazing. As Martha brought out a massive platter of shrimp, I surveyed the room: There were three modern white couches, a giant gilded antique mirror, and a sleek, pale gray rug. The coffee table was a slab of beige marble, and over by the entrance to the kitchen, a simple white table was loaded with buckets of ice, bottles of wine, and a huge arrangement of calla lilies in a silver vase. It was all very simple and totally chic.

I had to admire the snacks Martha had set up: olives, shrimp, and some fragrant cheese, with beautiful little plates and linen cocktail napkins at the ready. You never just get, say, a Snapple at Holly's house.

The only eyesore was Waffles, who tromped in ecstatically, drenched in rain and gazing hopefully at one of the white sofas. Luckily, he flopped down on the floor near Joe's feet. This modern decor was amazing, but not exactly dog-friendly. The Binghams would need some extra white zinfandel when they saw this, I thought.

"This is gorgeous!" I told Holly and Joe.

"I know," said Holly, popping the cork on a bottle of champagne. "It's totally *Architectural Digest*, in a Bianca Jagger kind of way."

Despite her customary air of fabulousness, Holly did look a little down. Her outfit was on the conservative side for her—okay, the blue and purple Pucci jumpsuit she had on wasn't all that conservative, but her only jewelry was a Cartier watch, and she wasn't even wearing heels. I started to feel concerned: Holly always swans around with such bravado that sometimes even I forget that under her carefully honed exterior is a girl who was teased in high school for wealth accrued by breaded poultry. Ah, cruel youth.

"So why didn't you tell us about your date last night?" Holly asked sadly, passing around the champagne glasses and tucking her feet underneath her on a sofa. "Bootsie knew. Are you hiding something from us?"

I still hadn't told them about Mike Woodford, either, but since I was already getting scolded for not mentioning the veterinarian, this seemed like the wrong time to bring up Mike.

"Well, I didn't really tell anyone, because the date was kind of a last-minute thing," I said. "And I guess I was afraid that you'd tell me that he wasn't the right kind of guy, or that I was wearing the wrong thing . . ."

"What *did* you wear?" asked Joe, with a pained glance at my shorts and wedge sandals.

"I wore that white linen dress Holly gave me with the ruffle down the front," I told them.

"That's all wrong for a first date," Holly said, shaking her head.

"Bootsie also told us that the vet is *married* to Lilly Merriwether," added Joe ominously.

"But I didn't know that when he asked me out!" I protested. "And he's legally separated from Lilly."

"Separated is still married," Joe noted.

"One time my mother beat Mariellen Merriwether in bridge at the club. Mariellen wouldn't speak to her for two years, and then tried to get her blackballed from the Symphony Women's Board. What you did last night is basically throw down the gauntlet to one of the oldest families in Philadelphia," Holly told me in an infuriatingly wise manner, as if she were suddenly the Ruth Bader Ginsburg of local societal mores. "I mean, to go out to dinner with a Merriwether husband . . ."

"It's not like that at all!" I shrieked. "I didn't know he was a husband when I agreed to dinner!"

One thing I'm not is a gauntlet thrower. Especially not with pearl-wearing, patrician ladies I'm terrified of, like Mariellen. "You see, this is why I didn't tell you guys! Because I would never—"

"Don't get me wrong," said Joe soothingly. "If you're comfortable going out on a limb like that, more power to you. I kind of like that you've got the balls to stand up to the most prominent matriarch on the Main Line."

"I *don't* have the balls! That's not what I'm doing!"

Ding-dong chimed the front doorbell. Joe got up, peered through the window, and said, "Oh boy."

He opened the door and Sophie scrambled over the doorstep, looking like a Yorkie who'd gotten drenched in the rain. She was clutching a brown paper bag in one hand and an enormous Gucci handbag in the other. Her outfit was purple from head to toe, including a pair of purple Versace jeans and a tight purple shirt with the Chanel logo stamped all over it, and mud was sadly caked on her bejeweled shoes. She looked disheveled, drippy, and slightly frantic.

"Thanks!" she bleated to Joe. Sophie paused to wipe her shoes on a beige mat in Holly's Carrera marble front hallway, then appeared in the living room behind Joe, and shrieked, "I hope you don't mind me coming over here like this, but I just can't take it anymore."

She paused for emphasis, and then in her tiny squeak, erupted: "You know what? Fuck Gerda!"

Sophie was dripping on the newly refinished living room floor, and since Holly seemed frozen in her position on the couch—her champagne glass was halfway to her lips, and she seemed incapable of getting the glass all the way there, or of putting it down—I went into the kitchen to get a towel so Sophie could mop herself dry. I rooted around in the modern white cabinets—which was difficult because there were no handles; apparently having handles isn't chic at the moment—and came up with a couple of fancy white dish towels from a drawer in the marble kitchen island. The tags were still on them: eighty-five dollars. Each. Handmade in Italy, from Neiman Marcus. *For dish towels?*

"Here's what happened," squawked Sophie as I handed her the towels and she started mopping herself off. "I was feeling hormonal this afternoon, and I was *starving*. And I haven't eaten anything except tofu and kale in months! So when Gerda went down to her computer room, I snuck over to Chef Gianni's. I figured the coast was clear, because Gerda's usually down in her office for hours!"

We all nodded. Holly's arm had finally unfrozen, and she was gulping her drink. Joe was pouring himself a refill.

"I'll have some of that, if ya don't mind!" said Sophie, still dabbing at the hem of her purple pants and pointing at the champagne bottle. "So, anyway, Gianni wasn't open for dinner yet, but Channing was there, and he packed me up a pasta Bolognese in a take-out carton. And he gave me this little half bottle of merlot . . . which he uncorked for me, thank goodness! So I got home, and I was sitting in my car at the end of my driveway eating my pasta and drinking the wine, because Channing remembered to give me a straw, when Gerda popped up out of nowhere and started banging on the car window!

"And I got out of the car in the rain and started yelling at her, and then she started yelling back at me about toxic American meat. I just couldn't take it anymore. So I got back in the Escalade, gunned it, and here I am!"

"Did Gerda follow you here?" asked Holly. We all swiveled nervously toward the front door.

"Nope!" said Sophie triumphantly, still standing dramatically just inside the living room, dabbing at her Versace jeans with the dish towel and clutching her various bags and her purse. "She can't drive when I'm not with her, 'cause she only has a learner's permit! Plus I took the keys to the convertible, so she's screwed!"

Waffles, who had been sacked out on the floor, suddenly looked up, sniffed the air, ran over, and tackled Sophie, knocking her off her spiky sandals onto the pearl-gray rug. Somehow, since the first moment he'd seen Sophie, I'd known this was coming.

"I still have some Bolognese in this bag," said Sophie, who was unhurt and sitting up as I ran over, apologizing. She held up the brown bag, which Waffles was wagging at and nosing furiously. "I guess your dog sniffed it out. Here, doggie, go ahead and eat it. I kinda lost my appetite when Gerda screamed at me.

"By the way, Holly, I love your house!" Sophie added, scrambling up off the rug and looking around as she took a seat on the couch. "Hey, Joe, maybe we could do some of this modern crap at my place!"

In the kitchen, I put the rest of Sophie's pasta onto a plate, and Waffles hoovered it up. Meanwhile, Holly stared at Sophie with a mixture of exasperation, curiosity, and disbelief that this person was sitting on her white mohair sofa.

"Sophie, where did you come from?" Holly finally demanded.

"I told ya, I just came from my house, and before that, I was at Gianni's," said Sophie.

"No. I mean before that. Before you married Barclay," Holly clarified patiently. She rubbed her temple, as if trying to keep a migraine at bay.

"Oh! I came from Joisey," said Sophie. "Cinnaminson. It's not too far away from here, maybe forty-five minutes. Just over the bridge from Philly. I moved here after I met Barclay when I was selling cement. It's a family business. My parents started it, and me and all my brothers were the salespeople. You might not believe this, but I was really good at the cement biz. Our motto was, 'We stick with our customers!' Get it?"

We all nodded dutifully, then Holly disappeared for a moment and then returned with a bottle of aspirin, which she handed around to me and Joe. I looked at my watch, wondering if I could go to bed. Since it wasn't even seven-thirty yet, I didn't think so. Maybe Gerda would show and up and force Sophie to return to the Shields stronghold.

"It's kind of a romantic story," Sophie rattled on, "because Barclay liked me right away. He took one look at me, and told me something was getting hard, and it wasn't the cement, if you know what I mean. So we had a whirlwind romance. And you know, Barclay was a lot thinner then. He was under two-fifty, which is pretty good, considering he's big-boned."

"Did you know Chef Gianni back in his pepperoni days?" Joe asked Sophie.

"You know about Gianni's pizza parlor?" she shrieked admiringly. "Barclay always told me to keep that quiet. That way, he had some power over Gianni. But really, who cares if Gianni used to run a pizza joint? I'm all for people making something of themselves!"

"And Gerda?" Joe asked. "Why, uh, exactly is she living with you?"

"Gerda saved my life!" said Sophie. "We were on our honeymoon and we went all over Italy—that's Barclay's favorite country, for obvious reasons. They have something like three hundred different kinds of pasta there. And that's where I discovered Versace, my favorite designer, in Rome and Milan.

"So at the end of our trip, we went to Venice, and I was leaning out over one of those canals, because I thought I saw a Versace boutique just across the water, when, boom!—my heel slipped, and I almost went into that really slimy water. It was Gerda who caught me! She was on a vacation with her twin sister, who looks just like her. Honestly, they're identical! Her name's Gunilla, the twin."

We all swigged more champagne, except Holly, who was frozen again at the mention of another Gerda somewhere out in the world, possibly sailing the canals of Venice.

"So we took Gerda and Gunilla out for coffee afterward to thank them, and then Gerda came and gave me a Pilates lesson the next day at the Gritti Palace. Two weeks later, we were home and moving into our house when Gerda showed up in Bryn Mawr! She said her sister was getting married and her parents had both died, and she was alone in the world, so she tracked down our address on the Internet. She took a cab from the airport. I didn't have the heart to tell her to leave, so she's been here almost three years," Sophie finished.

"Why don't you give her some money and send her back to Austria?" suggested Joe. "Isn't there some problem with her green card that Barclay threatened her with?"

"I can't do that to her!" said Sophie. "She did save my life. Plus Barclay can't stand her, so she helps keep him away from the house. She's always nagging at him about being overweight. And, over the last year before he moved out, she kept telling him he was ruining the environment with all his housing developments."

The three of us exchanged glances. Given that Barclay's warning note had mentioned similar sentiments, *could* Gerda have been the one who'd gone after Barclay? Sure, earlier in the day, we'd all thought Chef Gianni was the new prime suspect, but now it seemed Gerda was back in the running.

If Gerda was that enraged about Barclay's environmental crimes, plus his threat to report her to immigration, maybe Gerda had snuck over to Sanderson last Thursday night and waited for him to arrive. Obviously, Gerda'd have had no problem hoisting Barclay and dragging him into the bushes. She could probably bench-press him, if need be.

Maybe Barclay had been lured to Sanderson by *Gerda*—as Bootsie had suggested all along.

Or possibly Sophie was just playing dumb . . . and had paid Gerda to attack Barclay? Sophie could have promised to share some of the seven million big ones from Barclay's life insurance with Gerda. Gerda could then buy her own basement bunker somewhere.

"Sophie, are you sure you get nothing if Barclay dies before the divorce papers are signed?" I asked tentatively. "Isn't there, uh, insurance or something in place?"

"I'm pretty sure my lawyer tried to work that out, but got stonewalled by Barclay," Sophie said, looking disappointed. "Although sometimes I can't understand what the hell my lawyer's talking about, but I'm almost positive I don't get any money from Barclay until our divorce is done. Which better be soon, because I really don't think I can go back into the cement business. Cinnaminson is nice and all, but it's not like Bryn Mawr with all these big trees and farms around here."

Joe and I exchanged glances. It was impossible to figure out if Sophie was as clueless as she seemed. With millions at stake, could she really not know her financial situation vis-à-vis her divorce?

"Of course, Gerda says the United States is even worse than Europe these days when it comes to ruining the environment!" added Sophie. "She keeps talking about the importance of land and about people needing open space. Bores the crap outta me!"

"Oh, great," said Joe wryly. "An Austrian dictator who's looking for more open space. It's 1939 all over again."

"What?" asked Sophie, looking at us blankly. "What happened in Austria in 1939?"

AFTER JOE HAD given Sophie a basic account of Hitler's atrocities and a fundamental explanation of World War II, she looked upset. "I didn't listen much in high school. I never knew all that. That's terrible," she said. "But Gerda isn't that bad. She's just weird about things like meat and forests. I don't think she's pure evil."

Just then, my cell phone rang: Bootsie. Normally, I wouldn't pick up a Bootsie call at eight at night, because her calls tend to be lengthy and very tiring, but since Sophie showed no sign of leaving, it seemed a good time to answer. "Hi, Bootsie," I said, excusing myself and going into the kitchen to put Waffles's plate in the dishwasher. "What's up?" I asked, wiping a stray strand of linguine off Holly's perfect white marble kitchen floor.

"Gerda's up," Bootsie told me, hollering into the phone over a lot of noise in the background. "Up and on the bar at the Bryn Mawr Pub. Will and I just ran over to get a quick burger, since the boys are at my mom's for the night. And the first thing we saw when we came in was Gerda. She was chugging beer and doing shots of schnapps with the guys from the firehouse. She's completely bombed and just ordered a bucket of wings."

"I thought she didn't drink!" I said, shocked. "Or eat meat."

"Well, she's drinking now," Bootsie informed me. "Do you know how to get in touch with Sophie? She should probably come pick up Gerda. This isn't going in a good direction."

Over the din of the pub—the clatter of glasses clinking, voices chatting, Neil Diamond on the sound system—I head a deafening thud over my cell phone, the distinctive thump of a body making contact with sticky, beer-splashed tile. All bar chatter ceased for a moment.

"That wasn't . . ." I couldn't bring myself to finish the sentence.

"Yup, that was Gerda," Bootsie confirmed.

"Sophie's here," I told her. "I'll send her over." I hung up and went back into the living room.

"Gerda's on a bender," I told Sophie, Joe, and Holly. "It sounds like she's going to need a ride home."

TEN MINUTES LATER, we all piled out of the Escalade and into the pub, where at first glance things looked relatively normal for a bar on a Wednesday night: beer flowing, Van Morrison blasting, Phillies game on the flat-screen TV. Bootsie and Will were waiting for us in the front booth.

"She's back there," Bootsie said, pointing to Gerda, who was laid atop a pool table near the back of the bar, an empty shot glass clutched in her hand. A couple of men in Bryn Mawr Fire Department T-shirts stood next to her looking concerned.

"Sorry," said one. "She looked like she could handle her booze. She said she took a cab here, so we figured she wouldn't have to worry about driving home."

"I'm pissed off at Gerda for being such a hypocrite

about booze, but I feel kinda guilty!" squeaked Sophie. "Maybe she's been working too hard." She rushed back toward Gerda's supine form.

Three firefighters rolled Gerda's spandex-clad form onto a giant wooden Heineken sign borrowed from the pub's back room.

"She's just drunk," one of the firemen told us. "No harm done. We'll load her into your car."

Most of the bar was staring by now, and not just at Gerda. We didn't exactly fit in with the casual, jeans-wearing crowd. Sophie was in her purple outfit and te-etery, sparkly sandals, Joe was in seersucker, and Holly was still in her Pucci jumpsuit.

Then it got worse. Just as the firefighters passed through the bar, bearing Gerda's supine form, Mike Woodford came into the pub. He actually held the door for the Gerda cortege, then for Holly, Sophie, and Joe, and then for Bootsie and Will, who went outside to help pack Gerda into the back of the Lincoln. Then he looked at me and raised one eyebrow.

"Don't ask," I told him, and left the bar.

"I'M TAKING THE day off from Booty Camp," Holly announced, as Waffles and I emerged from her guest room the next morning. The dog and I spent the night nestled comfortably on linen sheets hand-embroidered by clois-tered nuns. Whatever they'd cost had been worth it, and I could tell Waffles felt the same by the look of pure joy on his soulful, goofy dog face. "Getting Gerda out of the car last night and into Sophie's house was a workout in itself!" Holly said.

I refrained from pointing out that Holly had done nothing more than open the car door to assist in removing Gerda from the Navigator the night before. I could smell coffee brewing, and it was a beautiful morning, with Holly's outdoor living room once again open for business. I was just heading outside with Waffles, hoping to find a private hedge behind which he could do what he needed to do when the doorbell rang. Martha opened the front door, and a courier stood there with a giant package wrapped in brown paper, a white silk bow tied around it. It was roughly four feet by six feet in size. Martha signed for the delivery, the courier left, and Holly looked at the slip.

"It's from *Howard*," Holly said bitterly, as she tore away the paper to reveal a painting sheathed in bubble wrap. Even through the plastic bubbles, we could all see that the contents were amazing: It was a huge white canvas, with a bold black swatch of paint swooping over, the black paint forming a sort of giant, abstract wing. I'd studied one very similar to this in college. In fact, was this—could it be?—

"Is that an *Ellsworth Kelly*?" I asked.

"Probably," said Holly disinterestedly. "Howard knows he's my favorite painter, and he thinks expensive gifts will make everything okay. But they don't!"

I refrained from pointing out that most of her relationship with Howard had been predicated on the belief that expensive gifts *did* fix all problems.

"Holly, Howard really seems like he wants to patch things up," I told her. "Why don't you two sit down without lawyers and try to figure things out? I know he still loves you. Don't you miss him?"

Holly shrugged, unceremoniously shoved the Ellsworth Kelly into a corner, and headed for her patio, stepping over Waffles—who'd done the bathroom thing outside, returned, and fallen asleep in a sunbeam near the dining room table. Then she noticed the Bests' ring, which I was still wearing on my right hand.

"Where did you get *that*?" asked Holly, grabbing my hand and looking at the ornate ring with a practiced eye. "How did I miss that last night?"

"There was a lot going on," I told her.

Frankly, though I'd wondered the same thing. When at the top of her game, Holly would have spotted the ring the second I'd walked in the door. "My neighbors, the Bests, lent it to me. It's their mother's old cocktail ring," I told her and Joe, who'd appeared from his room and was now toting a coffee mug.

"It's totally Jackie Kennedy, the Onassis years!" raved Holly, looking more like her old self as she plopped down outside on a huge white upholstered chaise. "It's *so* J. Lo meets the Queen of England meets Elizabeth Taylor."

"I know," I agreed. "But the Bests had it appraised, and it's not worth anything, apparently."

"Those geezers?" scoffed Holly. "They don't know anything about jewelry. I'm calling George," she said, and poured herself a glass of water.

Waffles and I followed Holly outside, and I sat back

in a comfortable lounge chair, admiring the spectacular setting as an occasional puffy cloud floated by. The rain of the previous evening had left the grass and flowers looking particularly buoyant. A magnificent yellow butterfly floated by on its way to the rosebushes, followed by a robust, furry bumblebee. It's amazing what money can do. Even the bugs at Holly's house are well-groomed and attractive. Gosh, I could lie here all day.

My reverie was broken when Holly told me to hold my hand against the white cushions on the lounge chair, so she could snap a quick photo of the Bests' ring with her iPhone to e-mail to George.

George Fogle is a friend of ours who after high school moved to New York to attend Columbia University. There, he fell in love with a girl named Danielle, then a chef and now an entrepreneur who owns several cool bistros around Manhattan. George, in the meantime, got a master's degree in art history at Yale, and became an appraiser at Sotheby's in New York. He also has the sometimes thankless job of working half the week here in Bryn Mawr as the local Sotheby's liaison.

Basically, that means George keeps in touch with Philly's wealthiest families, who might be in the market to sell, say, a Thomas Eakins painting they inherited from Granny if they find their trust funds dangerously depleted. He's also in charge of meeting and greeting newly moneyed people like Sophie and Barclay Shields. New money often decides to start collecting the expensive and beautiful things Sotheby's sells at auction—say, fine English furniture, or twentieth-century abstract art.

(Somehow this didn't seem likely with Sophie, but you never know.) The best-case scenario for George is someone who gets addicted to buying at auction—like Holly did for a two-month stint the year before she married Howard, until her father called her one day from the chicken plant, and told her that her allowance was on hold until she stopped buying twenty-seven-thousand-dollar French console tables.

So nowadays George spends two days week in Bryn Mawr, and the rest of his time in Manhattan, which is less than two hours away by train or via the Jersey Turnpike. Handsome in a slightly goofy way, with reddish hair and a dusting of preppy freckles, he's an all-around good guy who sometimes stops into The Striped Awning when he's in town to say hi and look around, because, as he says, you never know when I might have a piece that's actually "worth something." So far, that hasn't been the case, but it's always nice to see him.

"George?" sang Holly into her cell phone a minute later. "You need to get together with Kristin ASAP. She has a ring on that deserves its own reality series on Bravo. I just sent you a picture of it. It belongs to those Jurassic neighbors of hers, the Bests, and it's the size of your eyeball!"

Holly's voice was temporarily drowned out by the sound of an engine gunning into her driveway.

"George, hold on a second, someone's just pulling up," said Holly, peering from her sofa over the rose hedge.

"Chef Gianni," she announced. "He's here to talk about the menu for a party I've decided to throw in honor of myself and my new house."

"*Chef Gianni?*" I said, getting up and taking a peek. It was indeed the chef unfolding himself from the Fiat, bitching loudly in a combination of English and Italian about his heavy cast as he climbed out of the car. Jessica, who apparently had heeded the advice to hold off on dumping the chef, patiently held his crutch, rearranged her hair, and lit a Marlboro Ultra Light all in the same motion as she waited for him to get into limping position.

"*Bastardo!*" said the chef, addressing his crutch angrily.

"Why did you hire him?" I whispered to Holly. "I thought you hated Gianni."

"Of course I hate him," Holly told me. "Everyone does. But I can't have my housewarming party without Gianni cooking the dinner. I mean, how would it look if I *didn't* have Gianni? Even I love his food, and I barely eat. People wouldn't come if his gnocchi wasn't on the menu. It's going to have its own Wikipedia entry soon."

"Oh, fuck," said Joe, who'd just appeared on the patio in his pajamas. He froze for a moment when he spied the chef, Jessica, and her plume of cigarette smoke rounding the rosebushes. "It's too early to deal with those two." He took off toward his bedroom.

"My darleeng!" said the chef, hopping on his crutch to Holly, and leaning over to kiss her twice on each cheek and several times on her hand and forearm, a gesture that hasn't been seen since Errol Flynn movies went out of production. The chef's cologne, a heavy, musky cloud of fragrance, drowned out the roses' mild scent. Holly and I both coughed uncontrollably for a minute, while Waffles sniffed the air, whined, and lay down over by a planter filled with geraniums.

"Gianni, you know Kristin," said Holly, gesturing politely toward me.

"Oh, *sí*," he said by way of greeting, while Jessica nodded at me, looking nervous.

"Holly," the chef proclaimed, "I go to your kitchen now. I need to see where I work, and to plan in advance."

"The kitchen's right through there," Holly told him, pointing at the French doors.

"So anyway, George," she said, returning to her phone call as the chef limped in, Jessica sourly clicking along behind him, giving us an eye roll as she passed us, "the ring has a big oval ruby—or a stone that resembles a ruby—surrounded by tiny diamonds, and it's very old, I think. Did you get the picture I texted you yet? Okay, great! You know someone at your offices in New York who could look at it? Perfect." She listened for a minute.

"Okay, I'll tell Kristin you're coming by her store later. And by the way, George, you have to be here for my party next weekend. It's going to be all about Chef Gianni's gnocchi with boatloads of Italian wine, and I'm having the Colketts bring in about three thousand lilies!"

Just then, the chef appeared in the French doors.

"Hollleee," he shouted. "There is big problem with your kitchen. Not gonna work. I'm gonna need my catering truck for your dinner party. I need to call Channing about this. I'll get my phone from the Fiat."

The chef grabbed his crutch, and with surprising

speed, started limping around the rosebush hedge toward his car.

Just as he turned onto the walkway that led to the driveway, something tiny, invisible as it passed, whizzed through the rose hedge and, with a metallic ping, lodged itself into the stone exterior of Holly's house, right next to one of the French doors into her living room.

A millisecond afterward, there was another whizzing sound, then the crunch of man and metal crutch hitting slate walkway. A car at the end of Holly's driveway screeched into reverse, hit a three-point turn, and squealed away before any of us could get a look over the hedge at the distant vehicle.

"*Merda!*" screamed Gianni, who'd gone down like a bowling pin.

Holly and I looked at the object lodged into her stone wall, then at the chef, and then at each other with shocked realization.

"George?" said Holly into her phone. "Can I call you back? I think someone just shot the chef."

Holly, Waffles, and I rushed inside, terrified. Joe was in the shower and Martha was in the kitchen, watching the *Today Show* at top volume and ironing Holly's dish towels, oblivious to the chef screaming outside on the walkway. Jessica was also unscathed, but had seen the shooting from just inside the living room. We sat her down and called 911, which told us to stay inside until help came.

We were pretty sure the car that had sped out of the driveway had contained the person who shot at us, so probably it was safe to go outside. So, ignoring the 911 operator's advice, Holly and I crept outside and dragged the chef back into the living room in a matter of about three seconds, in case the shooter returned to finish the job.

We laid Gianni on the hardwood floor (Holly wasn't about to risk getting blood on her carpet), where he shouted obscenities and squirmed like an upside-down caterpillar while Jessica fluttered over him uselessly.

Oddly, we couldn't see any wounds or blood on the chef, but he was screaming in apparent agony. Then we noticed a little black hole in the cast on his right ankle, and a trickle of dark liquid seeping out slowly over his exposed toes at the bottom of the cast.

"Oh, good," said Holly soothingly. "Look, Chef, the bullet went right through your cast. That's really lucky!"

"I would not call it lucky!" screamed Gianni.

"Well, it's better than getting shot in the head," said Joe, who had come out of his room and was taking in the situation. "That would really hurt."

"*This* really hurts!" exploded the chef.

"Maybe a pillow will help," Holly suggested. She took a silk pillow off the sofa and gingerly put it under the chef's bald head. She stepped back and eyed him critically, like a sales manager at Pottery Barn who's just put together a window display, and sees something lacking. Holly nudged the pillow a little straighter with the toe of her sandal, and bent over to adjust his sleeves to show a bit of the tattoo of St. Peter's Basilica on his muscled arm. "There," she cooed. "That's better."

Then a police car pulled up, Officer Walt got out accompanied by a teenager wearing jeans and a T-shirt, and that's when things started heating up in the investigation of who wanted Barclay Shields and Chef Gianni maimed, dead, or, preferably, both maimed and dead.

"WALT, I CAN totally help you with this investigation," Holly told Officer Walt five minutes later. "You too, Jared."

Jared, the teenager who'd accompanied Walt to our crime scene, was a senior at Bryn Mawr Prep, winding up a six-week internship at the police department. He had an earring, no facial hair, and smelled strongly of Axe body spray. He looked more like he was fourteen.

An ambulance manned by the same EMTs from Sophie's party had arrived. Once again, Gianni was ladled onto a gurney, and the emergency workers prepared to take him out the French doors, speaking to the chef cheerfully as his vital signs were checked. "Hey, man, good to see you again!" said the youthful medic to Gianni.

"*Vaffanculo*," the chef told him.

"Looks like you took the bullet right in that same ankle—bummer. Let's cut this cast off out in the ambulance see what's what," added the other medic in an upbeat tone, ignoring the invitation to go fuck himself.

Gianni gave him the finger as he was wheeled out across the patio. They took off for Bryn Mawr Hospital, Jessica following nervously in the red Fiat. Officer Walt, in over his head, called the Philadelphia Police Department for assistance, and detectives were dispatched.

Walt then came inside to the kitchen and pulled out a little black spiral notebook to write down what we knew. Jared, the intern, meanwhile stared adoringly at Holly, his mouth hanging open.

"Jessica—that's the chef's girlfriend—was inside my house when he got shot," Holly explained as we all perched on the white bar stools around her kitchen counter. "So at least we know *she* didn't shoot him. The shot came from the front yard or driveway. But just so you know, Walt, there's a lot of gossip going on around town about the chef, and Jessica, and Barclay Shields, and I'm going to help you get it all down in that notebook of yours."

Walt dutifully poised pen over notebook. Jared, sitting on a counter stool nibbling at a plate of fruit, appeared utterly useless. He continued to stare at Holly, his mouth agape. He was wearing a retainer, I noticed.

Truthfully, I felt for Officer Walt. For three hundred years, Bryn Mawr's been one of the more peaceful places on earth, where most troubles are along the lines of a failed soufflé or a sand-trapped golf ball. How was one thirtyish policeman with a seventeen-year-old intern in late-stage puberty supposed to solve all this?

"Walt, it turns out that Gianni and Barclay both had some ties to what sounds a lot like the mafia," Holly told the officer. "I don't know much about organized crime, but apparently they both had a lot of uncles from New Jersey."

"We have all that info," Walt said, surprising me. "I'm working with teams in Philly and from Newark, and we've been able to piece together a lot about Barclay and Gianni's past. The drive-by shooting is a surprise, actually. We're told the guys in Jersey don't have any issues with Chef Gianni. Apparently, he paid off all his debts when he sold his pizza joint."

"The chef's girlfriend Jessica is having an affair with one of Gianni's assistants," Holly informed Walt.

"Right, Bootsie McElvoy told me about that." The policeman nodded. "Guy named Channing."

"So maybe you should check to see what Channing was doing twenty minutes ago when my patio was shot at!" suggested Holly.

I was having a hard time thinking of Channing in the role of homicidal maniac. When you're as gorgeous as a young Richard Gere with a little Jake Gyllenhall thrown into the awesome-genetic blender, why would you kill someone? There's nothing to be angry about, if you look like Channing.

But maybe Channing was getting impatient waiting for Jessica to break up with the chef, and figured he could get rid of Gianni via one quick shot and have Jessica all to himself?

"I could see a possible motive for Channing to shoot *Gianni*," I said, "but attacking Barclay? What would Channing possibly gain from that, if we're assuming that the same person is after both Barclay and Gianni?"

"Bootsie told me that Channing once worked at Sanderson, right?" said Walt, rifling through his notes. "Maybe he had some grudge against Barclay for wanting to buy part of the estate." He sighed.

"We also need to discuss the Colkett Florists. They hate the chef, so maybe they shot him this morning!" Holly continued to Walt. "I love the Colketts, but *they* could have pushed Gianni off Sophie Shields's balcony. They were in the house when it happened, and were right by the stairs right after he fell!"

Walt sighed. "I know Tim Colkett pretty well. He did the flowers for my wedding, and gave us a big discount, since he said he wanted to support law enforcement and knows it's not a high-paying field." He sighed again. "But I did hear about the chef making a scene and humiliating those two at his opening. So I had Jared do some Internet research on the Colketts."

Jared nodded, his earring bobbing up and down. "Yeah," he said, pleased to finally make a contribution. "Four years ago, before Tim Colkett hit it big as a florist, he lost a house to foreclosure. And the bank sold the house after that to a developer—Barclay Shields! And that Shields dude tore the place down. I pieced it all together from the legal notices in the newspaper," he said proudly. "It was some kind of historic place. Colkett tried to stop the teardown in court, but Barclay went ahead and put up three townhomes on the lot."

"So you're saying Tim Colkett might have had a motive to go after both Gianni and Barclay?" I asked.

Walt nodded. "Bootsie told me that the Colketts claim that Gianni, Jessica, and Channing were missing from Gianni's opening. But who's to say they're not lying? Maybe they snuck off themselves to go after Barclay."

"Did you find out how exactly the Colketts are related?" Holly asked Walt and Jared.

"That's out of my area of interest," Walt told her, and headed out outside to walk the crime scene. The Philly police were due any minute, and Jared was leaving, since he had to be back at school for a calculus quiz at eleven. Officer Walt told me I could go to work, and that Jared could drop me off at The Striped Awning, where I'd left my car the night before. Walt didn't seem to think I could add much to the investigation, and I was inclined to agree. Meanwhile, Joe had joined us, eating scrambled eggs.

"I can't believe I missed seeing the chef get shot," he complained.

"I've got six messages from Bootsie McElvoy telling me that Gianni is the one who attacked Barclay last Thursday," said Walt, as he, Jared, Waffles, and I headed out the front door, so as not to disturb the crime scene on the patio. "But a couple of days ago, she left me a bunch of voice mails telling me that she thought that Pilates woman who works for Sophie Shields hit Barclay in the head. She also told me she thinks Sophie could have been the mastermind behind the Barclay hit."

"Yeah, that is one of Bootsie's theories, but they change frequently," I said. "I'm sure you've met Gerda, the live-in Pilates instructor."

"Oh yeah," confirmed Walt. "I've met her. After the chef fell off Mrs. Shields's terrace. Interesting woman, Gerda."

"Maybe—and it pains me to say this—Bootsie's right,"

mused Joe, who had walked out onto the driveway with us, still forking eggs northward. "Gerda or Sophie could have shot the chef this morning. Gerda's got to have a killer hangover this morning, but she could still have come over and nailed the chef. Just as an FYI, Walt, the woman doesn't have a valid driver's license, so that's another offense right there."

Walt shrugged, closed his notebook, and hesitated over something for a moment. "I'll look into it," he promised.

Then he looked up at each of us and spoke, Jared hovering at his elbow.

"I'm going to share something with the three of you that hasn't gotten out to the papers yet," Walt said. "I'm telling you this because no matter what I do, I know Bootsie McElvoy's going to dig out the information by the end of the day, and it'll be in the paper tomorrow, so I'll just tell you now.

"Yesterday, we found the weapon that was used to hit Barclay," he told us. "We borrowed a new police dog from Philly to take over to Sanderson in the afternoon. Jared has a dog—well, his family has a dog—and he and the dog had gone through Sanderson looking for clues last weekend, but hadn't had any luck. So we finally brought in a professional sniffer, a German shepherd."

Waffles, hearing the word "dog," wagged his tail. He knows that word.

"*Your* dog inspected Sanderson for clues?" Joe asked the teenage intern, giving him a skeptical look. "Is the dog trained for that?"

"Not exactly," Jared said. "But usually he has, like, a great nose! He can find a sandwich from a mile away. I'm not shitting you!"

This was really kind of sad. Bryn Mawr, a wealthy and historic town, used household pets to conduct crime scene investigations. But then again, you wouldn't expect the Bryn Mawr police to have much in the way of a K–9 force.

"What kind of dog is it?" Joe asked.

"It's a, uh, Labradoodle," admitted Jared.

Joe and I broke out in laughter, and Jared and Walt looked uncomfortable. Even Waffles would be better than that, I thought.

"Yeah, well, I know," said Walt with a sheepish smile. "So anyway, this German shepherd from the city came out yesterday after the Labradoodle didn't find anything. Right before the rainstorm yesterday, the police dog found the weapon. It had traces of dried blood on it. We're testing to see if it's Barclay's, but we're pretty sure this is what the attacker used."

"What was the weapon?" Joe asked.

"It's a bookend," said Walt. "Shaped like an acorn. Has an inscription on it, it was given to a graduate of Bryn Mawr Prep."

Chapter 18

I BLINKED, MY stomach churning with surprise.

"I have bookends like that at my store," I told Walt. "I just bought three of them last Saturday at Stoltzfus's, the flea market out in Lancaster County. *After* Barclay was attacked," I added hastily. "Just so you know, I didn't hit Barclay. I didn't even have the bookends last Thursday."

"That's okay. I don't think you did it," said Walt. "There are a lot of these acorn bookends floating around town, since a lot of people received them as graduation gifts over the years. In fact, I'm headed over to Bryn Mawr Prep right after I leave here, to figure out how many of the things were given out, and to which graduating classes."

Walt told us that his best guess was that older Prep alumni hadn't necessarily held on to their bookends. People who'd retired to condos in Florida, or moved into smaller town houses after their children left home, could have donated them to the thrift shop over at the hospital or sold them at garage sales. It wasn't out of the question that Gerda or Sophie Shields, or the Colketts, could have gotten hold of one of the acorns.

But Honey Potts, a proud Bryn Mawr Prep alumna, had definitely gotten a pair of acorn bookends at graduation. Honey had freely admitted this when Walt had stopped by her house yesterday to tell her about the police dog finding the acorn in her field. Honey had, in fact, invited Walt into her library to show him her own pair of bookends.

But when they walked into the paneled room, the acorns weren't there in their usual place on the bookshelf.

"Mrs. Potts looked genuinely shocked that they were missing," Walt told us. "And I tend to believe her." He added that Honey said she'd cleaned out a bunch of stuff in her house the previous spring. She said she'd boxed up some items and put them in the attic at Sanderson, and gave others away to relatives and friends. "She couldn't remember whether the acorns had been donated or given away as part of her cleanout, or if she'd stashed them upstairs."

By this time, Holly had come out to the driveway, listening breathlessly to the description of the weapon used to attack Barclay.

"Mrs. Potts was going to look in her attic last night to see if she can find the bookends," Walt said. "So I have to get over there today, too. First, though, I have to tape off your driveway and your patio, Holly," Walt finished.

"Crime scene tape?" said Holly happily. "That's fantastic! Everyone's going to doubly want to come to party next week if there's crime scene tape here. You can come, too, Walt. You too, Jared."

"Okay, thanks, great," said Walt, looking happy about the invitation as he unfurled his yellow tape, the one good thing going on for him in his life at the moment. Jared looked dumbstruck.

"The detectives from the city should be here in a few minutes," Walt added.

"Perfect!" Holly sang out. "I'm picturing Daniel Craig and Hugh Jackman as the detectives. And I've decided I'm going to help you, Walt," she added. "I'm going to become Honey's new best friend. Even if she didn't hit him herself, she must know *something* about what happened to Barclay Shields; I mean, it happened at her house. And I'm going to find out everything Honey knows."

At this, Walt and Jared looked doubtfully at Holly, who didn't inspire a ton of confidence, to be honest. She didn't look like she could pull off a Miss Marple–style investigation. Currently attired in four-inch heels and a caftan, airily applying lip gloss, Holly looked more like she was headed to the beach in Mustique than a woman on a crime-solving mission.

I pictured Honey's makeup-less face, her loafers, and her leathery hide developed from years spent in the fields with her beloved cows, and then tried to imagine Holly and Honey as a seriously miscast Cagney and Lacey.

No one else looked convinced, but I knew that Holly could befriend Honey in no time. Underneath her Gucci façade, Holly's very determined.

"As soon as the detectives interview me, I'm off to

Neiman Marcus," Holly said, screwing on the cap of her lip gloss. "I can't become Honey's new best friend without the right outfit."

It was 11:15 a.m. when Jared dropped me and Waffles off at The Striped Awning—not all that late to be opening up the shop, considering that we'd already witnessed a shooting this morning. I unlocked, turned on the lights, and booted up my computer, first checking on the acorn bookends, which were just as I'd left them. All three of them sat there, looking benign. Not at all like attempted-murder weapons, really. I picked each one up again, feeling their considerable heft, and read the inscription: "From this acorn grows a mighty oak."

More like "From this acorn, a mighty head injury is inflicted," I thought to myself.

It seemed frivolous after such a scary event that morning, but as I checked my e-mail, I couldn't help wondering whether John would call me. He'd probably already reconciled with Lilly the Beautiful Tennis Player, I thought morosely. My own tennis lesson the day before seemed like it had happened a million years ago.

The rest of the morning was uneventful, and George arrived looking spiffy in a blue blazer over a Lacoste shirt after Waffles and I had shared a bagel with cream cheese for lunch. We chatted briefly about the chef getting shot, since George had listened to the incident over Holly's cell phone, and then got right down to business over the Bests' ring.

I carefully removed the bauble from my right ring finger, and laid it in its velvet-lined black leather box, which I handed across my desk to George. He donned a pair of glasses and carefully picked up the piece of jewelry. He was quiet for a few minutes as he turned it around and examined it from all angles, then looked at the little crown insignia in the box's lid. Then he quietly and gingerly put the ring back in its little slot in the velvet, where it glittered elegantly in the light from the store's front windows.

"Let me get this straight," George said finally. "Your neighbors inherited this very beautiful piece of jewelry from their mother, and they don't know where she got it. And it's been sitting in that tumbledown house next to yours for the last five decades."

"That's pretty much it," I agreed.

"And you've been wearing it around town for the past few days, including this morning, when you were at Holly's and Chef Gianni got shot."

"Yup."

"So you've had the ring on while doing errands, walking the dog, cleaning the store, picking up dog doo," he asked in a neutral tone.

I nodded. If I wasn't mistaken, I was beginning to sense a hint of negativity. "Is that wrong?" I asked, trying not to sound defensive. "I could put it in the store safe."

"*You* have a *safe*?" said George, his voice cracking.

He looked dubiously at the store's front door, which, as noted by Gerda, is flimsy and ancient. Then he glanced at the tall front windows, which I sometimes forget to close before I leave. "And where is this 'safe'?" he asked, making air quotes with his fingers as he said it.

"It's in the back room!" I told him. "Hidden away, behind the cleaning supplies."

He sighed.

"Am I correct in guessing that the safe is a vintage item?"

"It's an older safe, yes," I conceded. I could tell that George was mentally cataloging the ease of a thief breaking into the store, grabbing the safe, and hightailing it out the door lugging the old metal strongbox. It's true that the safe isn't too big, and doesn't weigh all that much, maybe forty pounds. Since some of the window locks in The Striped Awning are missing (I keep meaning to replace those), and the deadbolts date back to about 1928, I guess someone could bust in overnight if they put their mind to it. I mean, if Bootsie can break into liquor cabinets and basement bunkers, who knows what kind of people might be out looking to burgle my store? Then again, The Striped Awning doesn't usually have much worth stealing in it.

Meanwhile, George had gotten up, walked over to the front door, and was inspecting the lock in a supercilious manner (which was uncalled for, if you ask me).

"George, that ring's been sitting in the Bests' house for decades, and no one's tried to steal it," I told him airily.

"Well, the Bests haven't been going around town wearing it, now, have they?" George asked. "Kristin, I think it might be better if I take the ring out of the store.

And I don't think you should be wearing it around town without some kind of insurance."

That seemed like a good idea. George could take it back to his new, state-of-the-art safe at the Sotheby's offices over in Haverford, or straight to New York. If anything happened to the ring, I'd feel terrible, even if it wasn't worth more than the few hundred dollars that the Bests believed its value to be.

"Do you want to take it back to your office?" I asked hopefully.

"I can hold the ring for a few hours in the safe at the office in Haverford," George said, "but I'd need the owners' signature to take it to New York. Can you get your neighbors to sign a form that releases the item to Sotheby's until we can have an expert look it over and figure out what's what?"

"Sure," I told him. "I can get the brothers to sign it today, I'm almost positive. Probably by early evening."

"Great. You get the old guys to sign the release, and I'll meet you at the club at six," George said, opening his briefcase, carefully placing the ring in its black leather box inside it, and snapping the case shut. "I'll take this right over to my office."

That'd work. I could close the shop at five, take Waffles home, get Hugh's signature, then get Jimmy to sign the Sotheby's consignment document as well.

That is, if both brothers were willing to let George take the ring to New York. I couldn't see why not. It hadn't been doing them any good moldering away in their house, and they had nothing to lose.

"I'm glad you and Holly didn't get hurt today when Chef Gianni got shot," said George, getting up to leave, then turning around with a serious expression on his handsome face. He added, "Be careful. Lot of weird stuff happening around here. Bryn Mawr's starting to make New York look quiet and uneventful. This town's full of nut jobs, but who around here is nuts enough to try to kill someone in broad daylight?"

"Nuts?" asked Jimmy Best, handing me a bowl of tired-looking peanuts up in his third-floor club apartment. George wanted to head back to New York tonight, and I had only a few minutes to get Jimmy to sign the release and hand it off to George. As expected, Hugh Best had been pleased to hear of Sotheby's interest in his family jewels (so to speak), and had already signed the document.

Also, just as important, I needed to convince Jimmy to go home, because the club staff was about to evict him. I hadn't quite figured out how to pry Jimmy out of his secret hideaway, but I was thinking of going with a blunt approach.

I sighed as I gazed into the little dish of nuts. All the cashews and almonds had been picked out. Why bother?

I had been dashing toward the club's staircase with the Sotheby's papers in my purse when I bumped into Ronnie on my way upstairs. Usually, Ronnie's perfectly groomed, but today his eyes were bleary, his shoulders slumped, and his white shirt was rumpled. He looked like a man beaten down by life as he carried a rack of wineglasses down the hallway from the kitchen, headed outdoors to where a couple of staffers were setting up an outside bar by the tennis courts.

"Kristin!" Ronnie said. "Wait a second, please."

The tennis courts were packed on this sunny late afternoon. There was a tournament going on, which meant that John was probably out there somewhere, I thought with a little thrill. I couldn't see his lean form anywhere on the first four courts, closest to the porch. But wasn't that Mariellen Merriwether's ramrod-straight back I noticed on a bench outside Court 3? I could see pearls gleaming around the woman's perfectly groomed neck, so it had to be her. I'd done a mental shiver and refocused on Ronnie.

"Are you headed up to see the old man?" Ronnie had asked, pausing to balance the rack of glasses on the banister of the club's grand front stairs, jerking his thumb in the direction of the third floor. I nodded.

Ronnie, normally so solid and upbeat, reached out and grasped my elbow, with a glazed look in his brown eyes.

"Kristin, please—Jimmy's gotta go," he had whispered desperately. "He's driving us crazy. The constant calls down to the bar. The snacks. The late-night bowling and the ass pinching. Not my ass, the waitresses," he clarified. "Plus the members are starting to ask questions about weird noises coming from the third floor. I think he sings along to the radio after the Scotch kicks in."

"I'll do my best to get him out," I'd promised Ronnie.

"If he doesn't leave willingly tomorrow, we're throwing him out."

Now that I was up in Jimmy's apartment, I understood why Ronnie was at his breaking point: Things were deteriorating quickly. The apartment had taken on a distinctively depressing scent of stale smoke and Scotch. It was cocktail hour and Jimmy was still in his bathrobe, the bed was unmade, and his lunch tray hadn't been picked up yet. Clearly, the staff wasn't being quite as attentive on day four of Jimmy's stay as they'd been initially, and Jimmy's cute-old-man gimmick was wearing thin.

Jimmy himself didn't seem all that thrilled to be here anymore, either, to be honest. He wore the slightly manic, overtired look of a kid who's been sent to stay with fun, rule-free relatives while his parents are off in Europe—a kid who can't wait to get home to boring old Mom and Dad after a week of staying up too late watching TV and eating candy for dinner.

While Jimmy poured us both a drink, I explained to him that George wanted to take the ring up to New York, and that he'd need to sign a release, which Hugh had already done. "Fine, fine," Jimmy said grumpily, taking the paper and adding his signature. He sat on the window seat and looked outside. "Wouldn't mind being out there and watching the tennis matches," he groused. "Getting a little stuffy up here."

This was all way too *Flowers in the Attic*, I thought. Time for tough love.

"Jimmy, you have to go home tomorrow," I told him.

"Ronnie said the members are starting to get suspicious," I added, truthfully, "and he can't risk getting fired."

Jimmy looked simultaneously irked and relieved.

"People are too damn nosy around this club," he complained, straightening the belt on his bathrobe. "If they'd mind their own business, no one would notice anything going on up here. But I wouldn't want Ronnie to lose his job. And the staff's slacking off quite a bit, as you can see. So I guess I'll go home tomorrow."

"Great!" I told him. "Hugh will be so happy to see you."

"Rumor has it that our crack local police force finally found the weapon used to hit Barclay Shields?" Jimmy said, sipping his drink.

I tasted mine and winced. Scotch again. Still, I took another gulp. When in Rome, I told myself.

"Ronnie heard it from your friend Bootsie at lunch, and he told me when he brought up my tray," Jimmy informed me. "The weapon makes Honey Potts look guilty, of course, but I've known Honey a long time, and she ain't the violent type. I used to date her when we were teenagers."

"You did?" I said, shocked.

"Sure," he said. "Honey was very attractive, believe it or not. Tall, blond, athletic. She always had a tan, which unfortunately now has the consistency of a boot, but back when she was seventeen, it looked fantastic."

"So why didn't you and Honey end up together?" I asked Jimmy.

"We broke up during college, and she married Phil

Edwards in 1966. Boring guy. A banker from Chester County," he said. "I knew she wasn't all that crazy about him, because she never took his last name and she never moved out of Sanderson to go live with Phil. Made him move in with her and her parents. And later that year, I married Darleen, my first waitress. Darleen was an Angie Dickinson look-alike. Gorgeous girl, very sexy, and one of the first in town to wear miniskirts in the late sixties. Honey was more like Doris Day."

"What went wrong with Darleen?" I asked.

"She had an affair with Phil Edwards," Jimmy replied simply.

"She slept with Honey's husband? That's terrible," I said, shocked.

"Well, it wasn't ideal," he conceded, snipping the end from a cigar and lighting up, "but I think it was worse for Honey. Embarrassing for her, really. They split up, and she stayed on at Sanderson."

"What happened to Darleen?"

"We got divorced, after I paid her forty thousand dollars to go away," he said, then paused to blow a smoke ring. "Which was a lot of money in those days. Between my marriages and Hugh's useless business ventures, we managed to bankrupt ourselves in the most entertainingly stupid ways possible."

He glanced out his open window. "Honey was out there earlier," he said, "watching tennis with that uptight bitch Mariellen Merriwether. Now that's one woman whose husband couldn't stay put. Soon as they had their daughter, Lilly, Martin took off for South America and was never seen again. And there were some good reasons why he didn't want to come back. I've been watching Mariellen from up here over the past few days, and she is one tough gal. Overly focused on that daughter of hers."

"I better get downstairs to meet George," I said, peering over his shoulder at the grass courts.

There was John Hall!

He was in the middle of a tennis match, hitting the ball at about one hundred miles per hour to his opponent, who looked a lot younger and faster, but was still struggling to return John's hit. I admired John's great arms in his white polo shirt for a minute, feeling a pang of regret that I'd never be able to (a) check out his biceps close-up and (b) understand how, or why, people get that good at tennis.

Then I glanced at my watch, and grabbed the Sotheby's contract from Jimmy's coffee table.

"So you're going home tomorrow morning?" I prompted Jimmy.

"Guess so," he conceded. "I'll be home in time for one of Hugh's awful casseroles for lunch. If it's tuna-noodle, I'm going to hit *myself* in the head with a bookend."

Chapter 19

DOWNSTAIRS, I PEEKED into the bar, didn't see George, and went over to the window by the front porch to look for him on the patio, where I was poleaxed by the sight of a shocking duo at the front table.

Honey Potts and Holly were sitting together, chatting away, a bottle of Mumm in an ice bucket between them. What had me reeling, though, wasn't the odd pairing of Honey, the doyenne of Sanderson, and Holly, the younger heiress, but the fact that Holly was wearing khakis. They were perfectly cut, skinny beige pants that looked like jodhpurs, but were still khakis. Her shirt was a white button-down in gorgeous Egyptian cotton, cut very narrow and rather low. She had on almost no makeup, flat beige sandals, and she looked amazing. But it was unnerving to see Holly looking so toned down.

Honey, meanwhile, had on a yellow polo shirt that was boxy and none too flattering, and a pair of green Ber-

muda shorts. So, actually, Holly's outfit didn't look anything like Honey Potts's, but obviously Holly isn't going
to wear green Bermuda shorts.

I hovered there at the window for a second, gaping
at this strange pairing. It was like stumbling on Darth
Vader and Yoda sitting down for a nice cocktail together.
Suddenly, I felt a large, very strong hand grab my arm. I
looked down and saw hockey muscles, so I knew it was
Bootsie.

"What are *those* two doing together?" she whispered.

"Exchanging recipes?" I guessed.

Bootsie, keeping one eye on Holly and Honey, told me
that she'd just gotten off the tennis courts, where she'd
been beaten in the club tournament by Lilly Merriwether,
and she wasn't too happy about it. Bootsie had grumpily
packed up her stuff and was on her way to her car when
she'd just happened to stroll by the porch to see if anything was happening. Then again, Bootsie checks all the
aisles of the Publix and trolls her sons' Gymboree classes
in the pursuit of gossip. And here was something finally
worth watching.

"What's Holly wearing? She looks like Country Club
Barbie," hissed Bootsie. "Let's go out there and sit with
them."

Firmly in Bootsie's steely grip, I was dragged to Holly's table as I frantically scanned the porch for Mariellen.
Thankfully, she was nowhere to be seen. Probably she was
congratulating Lilly on her tennis triumph, and trying to
figure out a way to get her daughter back together with
John.

"Champagne?" asked Holly, waving at us to sit down, then introducing us to Honey. "Kristin lives right across the street from you!" she added to Honey, who shook my hand politely enough with her leathery paw, but appeared to take zero notice of me, or connect me with finding Barclay Shields at Sanderson.

"I've met Mrs. Potts dozens of times," Bootsie bragged. "She knows Mummy from school."

"Ungh," said Honey, who was mid–crab cake, and didn't seem too interested in this nugget of information. Meanwhile, I looked around for George so I could hand off the Sotheby's release and leave.

"You might have seen Kristin around your property with her dog," Bootsie said, as I gave her a swift kick in the shin under the table. Of course, she kept talking. "She has a drooling, disgusting basset hound that she's obsessed with. Kristin was there when your cow guy found Barclay Shields at your place!" At this, Honey looked up from her crab cake, and leveled a none-too-friendly gaze upon me, while I silently cursed Bootsie. I also realized Bootsie might have downed a post-tennis cocktail or two already. She seemed a little drunk.

"Honey and I started chatting while we were watching the tennis matches this afternoon," Holly said, ignoring Bootsie, "and she was telling me about the old days when the club used to actually be fun. Then we came up here for a drink, and on the way to our table, I innocently flirted with old Mr. Conwell over there for a minute. He's such a charming old man. He even asked me to sit in his lap, but then his wife showed up."

"Best thing to happen to old Conwell for years!" Honey hooted. She looked fondly at Holly. The look that Mrs. Conwell, an attractive eighty-year-old, was shooting at our table from across the porch was not quite as fond. She looked like she'd like to come over and punch Holly's lights out with one of her large diamond rings.

"You remind me of me when I was young!" Honey added.

Holly looked alarmed at this, but smiled at Honey, and said, "Let's have some more champagne."

"I gotta hit the loo," said Honey, rising from the table. "Get me a vodka, will you, Holly? I can't do champagne after 6 p.m. Hangover isn't worth it."

"Vodka coming right up!" said Holly, waving cheerfully at the waiter. "And Honey, I'm ordering you Grey Goose this time. That Smirnoff you're drinking is so 1974, and not in a good way. The Goose tastes so much better."

"Okay." Honey shrugged and ambled off toward the ladies' room.

"What's up with your outfit?" I asked Holly. "You look totally J. Crew meets L.L. Bean, but better."

"That's because I'm not wearing L.L. Bean," Holly told me and Bootsie.

"I love L.L. Bean," said Bootsie, affronted.

"L.L. Bean looks fantastic on you, Bootsie," Holly said, "because you're so tall." Bootsie looked less offended at this. "I decided to go with the Neiman Marcus version of L.L. Bean, which is Hermès."

I decided not to even try to guess how much Holly's outfit had cost. While my mind reeled at the quantity of poultry profits that Holly directed into the coffers of Neiman's, I suddenly heard a familiar noise: The clomping of horseshoes on pavement from the club driveway, punctuated by a loud whinny.

I looked up, horror-stricken. Mariellen had Norman's reins in hand and was walking him straight toward a massive, leafy oak tree near the porch. She must be moving her prized horse into the shade, I realized. Luckily, she was totally focused on murmuring sweet nothings into Norman's velvety brown ears, and hadn't seen us. I jumped up and almost knocked over George, who was just arriving at our table.

Without preamble, I handed over the signed contract. As Bootsie started to ask questions about the paperwork, I got up and grabbed my handbag.

"Have a wonderful night!" I said, zooming across the porch toward the back door before Mariellen could finish tethering Norman to his tree. Thank goodness the club building is so enormous: The left wing completely blocked me and my car from Mariellen and Norman. I was scrambling into my car when I heard a man's voice call out my name.

It was John, smiling, and carrying his tennis racket, a leather gym bag, and the giant men's championship silver tennis cup toward his SUV.

"Hey!" He held up the tennis trophy. "Just won the men's club championship. Want to help me celebrate?"

I DID, OF course, so when John suggested I follow him home to the condo he was renting in Haverford, I did just that. Ten minutes later, he opened the door, and four mutts rushed out at us wagging and making a beeline for a common yard space behind the condo building. "Sorry," said John apologetically. "This place is kind of a dump. It's not easy to find a landlord who will rent to you when you have four dogs."

The pack returned, he poured kibble into bowls, then popped the cork on a bottle of Taittinger with a satisfying thunk. Then he poured half the bottle into the club's silver tennis cup, held it up happily, and handed it to me, gesturing to me to chug the bubbly straight out of the trophy.

"Drink up!" he said, while all four dogs jumped up on the sofa. There were two small beige mixes who liked like they were mostly Chihuahua, one white fluffy giant dog of no discernible breed, and what I think was mostly bulldog. They seemed like one big happy dog family.

"Won't champagne tarnish the trophy?" I asked, looking inside the cup, which was about seventy-five years old and none too clean.

"Yeah, but it's tradition," John said happily. "I've tried to win this thing for fifteen years, and we're going to drink out of it if it kills me. To be honest, I only won this year because the club's two best players are both injured. I beat a seventy-two-year-old and a sixteen-year-old to win this cup, but it's still worth celebrating."

"Great!" I said, taking a quick gulp.

While John took a quick shower, I looked around

for glasses in which to pour the rest of the champagne. I found a couple of water glasses, so I made do with that. Had I been a snooper, I could have poked around a little, but I had a feeling there was really nothing to snoop through. Even Bootsie might have been defeated by this place, which felt totally unlived in, like a dorm room that's used only for sleeping and showering. John's condo was decorated with only the basics: a couch, a table, and presumably a bed, though I hadn't ventured into that part of the place. You could tell it was a guy's place, because the biggest things in it were the TV and the grill on his back patio. Lilly must have kept all the wedding gifts and monogrammed pillows when she and John had split up. The whole condo was beige, with nothing on the walls and nothing on the floor except for quite a bit of dog hair.

After some champagne outside on the patio, while the sun was setting and the dogs ventured out to surround our chairs happily, I realized that the freshly showered veterinarian smelled just as good as Mike Woodford. He might even smell *better*. I was shocked to realize John's forearms, which were currently on view with the rolled-up sleeves of a blue Oxford shirt, were even more amazing than I'd realized before. They were tan and had lots of sinewy muscle. I realized tipsily that I really wanted to check out the tennis muscles for myself. At that moment, John reached out and took my hand, and I could feel electricity between us. Or at least I felt it on my end. Who knew a country club tennis champ could be this sexy? And for the duration of the sunset, there was some fantastic kissing on the back porch as the sun disappeared and the dogs watched curiously.

After the kissing, John ordered a pizza.

"I have salad stuff in here, too," he said, rooting around in his fridge, while I sat at his kitchen table. "I try to be healthy and eat salad and grilled chicken, but I usually end up ordering pizza."

I was trying to project calmness and serenity, which was what I imagined Lilly's demeanor to be while she sipped champagne on summer evenings, but I was confused and doubtful about what John's situation vis-à-vis Lilly.

Against all Holly and Bootsie's advice, I blurted out a question. Actually, two questions. "I hate to ask you this," I said, "but why did you and Lilly split up? And do you think you two might get back together?"

John was pouring Pellegrino into coffee mugs, since we'd used his only water glasses for the champagne. He set a mug in front of me, sat down, and looked at me. He didn't look angry or upset, just thoughtful.

"It's not that I don't care about Lilly," he said. "But I realized within a few months after we got married that we weren't really in love with each other. She felt the same way, I'm pretty sure, though it took her longer to admit it. Neither of us wants to get back together. We're almost divorced. Should be final in a few weeks."

Yay, I cheered inwardly, at the same time feeling badly for him that he'd gone through the painful experience of getting married and finding out it was a dud. I also felt sympathy for Lilly. Honestly, though, since she's so beautiful, she wouldn't be single for long. "It was more that we seemed perfect for each other," John continued. "Everyone thought so, especially Mariellen, Lilly's mother. She's the one having the hardest time with our marriage ending."

While we waited for the pizza, John told me that Mariellen had been a major factor in their split due to her quietly controlling ways. He and Lilly had been planning to buy a house out in Chester County after they got married, but a few weeks before the wedding, Mariellen had given Lilly a roomy and charming cottage next door to Mariellen's property, which she'd bought, had fully renovated, and had furnished with a lot of chintz and pillows and paintings of horses and dogs. "It was really nice, but it looked exactly like Mariellen's house," he added. "Sometimes it seemed like I'd married Mariellen, too, and she's definitely not my type."

My eyebrows shot up when he said this. Had he not noticed that Lilly and Mariellen looked exactly alike, except that Lilly was thirty-five years younger? Men never notice things like that.

"So there we were," John went on, serving me some salad, "living a few hundred yards away from my mother-in-law, who was always inviting us for drinks, tennis, and Sunday dinners. And Tuesday dinners. And Wednesday dinners. I left in a cloud of Virginia Slim smoke every night. And then there were the horse events. I mean, Mariellen's obsession with Norman is bizarre. The horse comes to cocktails in the garden every night, and eats sliced carrots and apples off Mariellen's Limoges plates."

He shook his head. "Sometimes I think my ex-mother-in-law's kind of losing it."

Feeding a horse off fine china didn't seem all that strange to me, since I usually give Waffles half of whatever I'm eating for dinner, and honestly, he hates his dog bowl, so I usually serve him his meal in a vintage soup bowl. But then again, Norman's a horse, not a dog. I wondered how John would feel about sleeping with a seventy-five-pound basset hound every night. I looked at his motley pack of dogs, who were taking up the whole couch and drooling on the cushions. Probably he'd think it was fine, I decided hopefully.

The pizza guy arrived; John paid for it and put the box on the table, along with the salad.

The salad John had made looked fantastic. Actually, it had both carrots and apples in it, and we both thought of a certain horse and laughed. "Norman would love this salad," I said.

Chapter 20

THE NEXT MORNING, feeling upbeat after my impromptu date with John, I parked in back of The Striped Awning. When Waffles and I got inside and turned on the lights, I noticed the familiar form of Bootsie looming at the front door, waiting to chat, her tanned face flushed pink with excitement.

Not this again, I thought. My first guess was that she'd somehow learned I'd been at John's condo the night before. Given the breadth of Bootsie's network, she probably had at least one friend or relative living in John's rental complex, and who might have spied me entering the grounds, or even seen us kissing on his back patio. I steeled myself for an interrogation.

Truly, not all that much had happened between John and me the night before; I'd only stayed for dinner. We were still just in making-out mode. Even though he'd said he was one-hundred-percent not going work things out with Lilly, I wanted to be careful. What if he decided that having cocktails with his mother-in-law (and her horse) most nights wasn't all that bad, after all, and moved back in with Lilly? You never know with men.

"Update from Walt," Bootsie said breathlessly, after I unlocked the door, sat down at my desk, and turned on my computer.

Phew, I thought, realizing she was back in crime-fighting mode, and wasn't focused on my dating life. She took her customary seat in the in front of my desk, and tried to wave away Waffles, who was in his customary position of amiably licking her ankles.

"The acorn was definitely the weapon used to hit Barclay. The blood on it matches. Also, the chef is on bed rest for a few days, but he's home already. The bullet just grazed his foot, thanks to the cast," she informed me.

"The real news is that Channing doesn't have much of an alibi for yesterday morning when the chef was shot. He went to the gym at eight, and then left a little before nine, got a coffee from the Starbucks drive-through, and headed to work. He got to the restaurant fifteen minutes later, and you know the gym and Starbucks are less than five minutes away from Holly's. So he definitely could have swung into Holly's driveway, shot the chef, and then gone to work." Bootsie paused to take a breath and frowned. "Still, though, he just doesn't seem guilty to me. Why would Channing risk going to prison when he's busy having lots of inappropriate sex with Jessica?"

I nodded in agreement. Their hot affair had to be preferable to a stint at Graterford.

"Sophie and Gerda are still in the running as suspects, because they don't have much of an alibi for yesterday morning—only each other. If they have access to guns, they could have definitely done the shooting."

"I can't figure Sophie out," I said, shaking my head. "It doesn't seem possible that she could be as dumb as she seems, but then again, it seems more implausible that she's secretly smart."

"I agree," Bootsie said. "I'm starting to think Sophie's just what she seems to be. So I'm ruling her out, at least for now. Also, she has a motive against Barclay, but none that we know of for shooting Gianni."

"Great," I told her. "I like Sophie, at least when she's not talking about her and Barclay's sex life."

"Walt's pretty sure it wasn't Honey Potts who took the shot at the chef yesterday, but he can't completely clear her yet," Bootsie told me as I made a quick trip to the back room for my favorite Swiffer, some paper towels, and a bottle of Windex, and started to spruce up the store in hopes of foot traffic. I was listening to Bootsie, but also thinking that I really need to get customers in again, since Sophie's windfall won't last forever. Maybe I could go ahead with my mojito happy hour, or I could serve hors d'oeuvres on Friday afternoons at the store to lure in buyers, I thought hopefully.

"What do you think about me offering wine and cheese on Fridays here at the store?" I asked Bootsie.

"Kristin, focus!" she said impatiently. "This is important. As I was saying, the chef was shot at 9 a.m. yesterday. Or a few minutes before nine, since you and

Holly didn't note the exact time." She shot me an accusatory glance.

"A shot was fired six feet from us," I told her. "It was distracting."

"Honey's alibi is a little shaky, too. She had a 9 a.m. tee time at the club yesterday, where she was meeting Mariellen Merriwether," Bootsie continued. "The caddies said they're pretty sure that Honey picked up a golf cart right around nine, and they saw her and Mariellen teeing off not long after. Of course, those caddies are always stoned, so they have no concept of time."

"They get stoned that early?" I asked, surprised.

"They're college guys who just got home on summer break," Bootsie told me. "Anyway, I'm *sure* Honey isn't involved in the shooting"—her tone implied that Bootsie was actually thinking there was a big chance Honey was involved—"but there's one other thing I got out of Walt: They sent the bullet they pried out of the chef down to a lab in Philly, and it was fired from an old pistol that dates back to the 1930s or 1940s, and the bullet was also from that era.

"And here's the interesting part: Honey admits that there are old guns stored at Sanderson," Bootsie continued. "Her father used to host foxhunts at Sanderson, and they had quite a few weapons, including shotguns and pistols. They kept hounds, served sherry, played bugles, the whole bit. And the guns are still there, stored in the barn!"

Mike Woodford flashed into my mind when Bootsie mentioned the Sanderson barn. I'd been positive that he wasn't involved with any of the crimes, but he did *work* in the barn. The barn with the guns.

But I dismissed the thought of Mike shooting Gianni as unlikely—for one thing, I was pretty sure he didn't know where Holly lived, and possibly didn't even know who she was. And how would Mike know the chef was going to be at Holly's?

Plus I'd tried and failed to think of a reason why he would want to go after Barclay or Chef Gianni. Of course, if the guns were sitting around the barn, Channing would have seen them, too, when he worked at Sanderson. Maybe Channing *had* borrowed a gun from Sanderson to mow down the chef?

"Honey used to foxhunt, too, back in the sixties, before people gave up hunting around here!" Bootsie finished. "She's said to be a crack shot!"

We looked at each other, both of us thinking: That did make Honey sound guilty.

"Anyway, I do think you should have wine and cheese here on Friday afternoons," Bootsie told me, gathering up her stuff to leave. "I'll come. And if there's free food, you might even get Barclay as a regular customer, once he gets sprung from the hospital, which I hear is going to be very soon." I was about to remind Bootsie about Barclay's attitude toward antiques when I noticed a petite figure had just entered the store.

"Barclay *is* out of the hospital!" the customer squeaked. "Has been since yesterday morning!"

It was Sophie, of course, who'd just parked her Escalade illegally in front of the fire hydrant outside, and swung into The Striped Awning in a yellow silk top, miniskirt, and strappy sandals. With her blond hair and the yellow outfit, she reminded one of a very tiny stick of butter. I got hold of Waffles's collar, since he had a frisky look in his brown eyes that foretold tackling Sophie again.

"You gals might think it was Honey Potts who shot the chef," Sophie shrieked, "but I know it wasn't. It was Barclay!"

"Barclay got out yesterday morning?" asked Bootsie excitedly, sitting back down in her chair. "I have a great source at the hospital, and she didn't say a word. What time was he checked out?"

"Early. Like eight!" said Sophie. She whipped off a pair of enormous sunglasses that made her face look even smaller than usual. Underneath them, she was as well-groomed as ever, her blond hair perfectly blown out, full makeup and manicure in place, but she also had a slightly wild-eyed look this morning. "So he could have totally driven over to get a gun at his condo, and then gone to Holly's place to shoot the chef by nine!

"Barclay didn't actually get formally released," Sophie added. "He just ripped out his tubes and left, so the hospital tried to keep it quiet till this morning, but his doctor called me looking for him! And don't worry, I already called that Officer Walt guy to tell him that Barclay's out and about," she informed us.

"Does Barclay have a gun?" I asked her.

"You bet he does!" Sophie shrieked. "He has a bunch of 'em!"

"Does he have any old guns?" asked Bootsie.

"I don't know what-all he has," stormed Sophie with a toss of her head, "since he has so many. But he usually won't buy anything old, so I doubt he has an antique gun. Guns are like flat-screen TVs if you're from Jersey—everybody wants the newest and biggest. And by the way," Sophie added, "Barclay stopped by last night to tell me he wants *me* to move out of the house, so that *he* can move back in. The house Joe and I are redecorating. Can you believe that?"

"Are you going to move out?" Bootsie asked her.

Sophie stomped her foot. "No fucking way! I just turned a guest room into a shoe room. I got storage in there for two hundred seventy-five pairs, and we got 'em organized by designer and heel height. I just hope Barclay did shoot Gianni. I asked him about it when he came over last night, but he just laughed, and said Gianni got what he deserved."

Bootsie and I looked at each other again and shrugged. There seemed to be little chance that Barclay, fresh out of Bryn Mawr Hospital, would have been able to track Gianni down at Holly's house, but who knew?

"What's up with Barclay's angioplasty?" asked Bootsie.

"I don't know, and I don't care! We're getting the divorce agreement hammered out next week, if he doesn't have a heart attack by then," said Sophie triumphantly. "I think whoever's trying to whack him should just wait it out. He's one cheesesteak away from the grave!"

THE REST OF the day at the store was blissfully uneventful, other than three phone calls. The first was from Hugh

Best, who reported that Jimmy had safely returned home. I could hear music in the background and the tinkle of ice cubes into glass, and Hugh sounded very upbeat.

I could only imagine the rejoicing and general celebration going on in the kitchen and staff lounge at the club, the hallelujahs chorusing from the waiters and bartenders now that Jimmy was gone.

The next call was from George, who told me that he'd delivered the brothers' ring to a specialist at Sotheby's Upper East Side offices in New York.

George said that the woman was immediately able to identify its elegantly tattered black leather and velvet box as vintage Garrard (which, he told me, is Britain's crown jeweler). If the ring box was original, then the jewel was by Garrard—this remained to be verified, George said, but his colleague, a brilliant French woman in her forties, was locked in her office with her reference books, her computer, a jeweler's loupe, and the ring, doing a ridiculously thorough job of researching the provenance of the bauble. If it was Garrard, he told me, it definitely had value, much more than a few hundred dollars.

Honestly, I was impressed. Even if it sold for as much as, say, five or ten thousand dollars, it would be a nice windfall for Jimmy and Hugh. They could crank up the heat next winter and dial back on the casseroles. "I wouldn't say anything to the old guys yet, though," George suggested. "A lot of times, these things don't work out the way we hope. I'd hate to get their hopes up."

At five, the phone rang again.

"Doll!" said a voice speaking in a loud whisper. "Tim

Colkett here. Since we already spilled so much info to you, here's a little more news. We were at Gianni's restaurant today doing the flowers for the bar, and not that we were eavesdropping or anything like that, but we couldn't help listening to Jessica and Channing, who weren't being very careful about keeping their conversation on the QT.

"And I happened to hear Jessica and Channing talking over secret plans to move to Palm Beach."

"Palm Beach, *Florida*?" I asked.

"They're relocating there ASAP," said Tim. "Opening their own restaurant. Fresh pasta and grilled meats, sidewalk tables, very summer in Amalfi. Jessica's planning a late-sixties vibe, with glossy orange walls and white leather banquettes and mosaic tiled floors."

"Interesting," I murmured, wondering if this was a false lead to take attention away from Tim himself. I still didn't think Channing was the one who shot Gianni, but if he had, it shouldn't be too hard for the police to find him in Florida. Palm Beach isn't all that big.

Actually, moving to Palm Beach sounded like a good idea for him and Jessica. She'd need to get as far away as possible from the chef when he found out about her fling with Channing.

"By the way, not to gossip, but we just had to make a quick stop at the club, and guess who's here having drinks right now," added Tim.

"Honey Potts and Holly Jones?" I ventured.

"How did you know that!" screamed Tim.

"Just a lucky guess," I said.

"Well, you're right, and what's more, Honey is wearing a *dress*," he said. "A white linen number from Talbots that Holly told us she helped pick out." Wonders never cease, we agreed, and we ended the call and hung up.

Leaving the shop an hour later, I realized I was ecstatic at the prospect of a night at home with Waffles. There was a light breeze, the sun hadn't yet started to set, and I rolled down the car windows so Waffles could stick his head out, foot-long ears flying in the breeze, sniffing the yards full of blooming peonies and daylilies as we drove home. Lawnmowers, that classic summer soundtrack, buzzed outside the car, and when I got home and went into the gate, I could smell cigar smoke wafting over the holly bushes from Jimmy's porch, and the faint sound of what I think was a Dean Martin record.

This was pure bliss, I thought, taking off my shoes to feel the lush grass (which actually needed cutting again), cool and cushiony under my toes. I fed Waffles, got a glass of water, and sat on the back steps with my eyes closed, listening to the birds, who were singing even more loudly than Jimmy's record, and the wind whooshing through the tall maples up and down Dark Hollow Road. I heard Waffles's tail thumping, but he wags whenever the black cat who belongs to the neighbors on the other side of Jimmy and Hugh walks by the fence. Then I realized that mingling with the good scents of the early evening—flowers, grass, cigar smoke, warm dog—there was the scent of soap. Masculine, unfancy soap. I looked up into the black-lashed brown eyes and beard-stubbled face of Mike Woodford.

Mike had just showered with his signature Irish

Spring. He was wearing faded jeans and a white button-down shirt with the sleeves rolled up.

As Mike looked down at me, petting Waffles, I remembered John Hall's fantastic soap smell, which I'd been bowled over by just last night. What kind of person is unable to focus on one great-smelling man for more than twenty-four hours? And John has sincere blue eyes, great arms, makes great salads, and, I'm ninety-nine-percent sure, is getting divorced from his beautiful wife.

Plus I'd sworn off Mike a few days before. Watching him stroll into the pub on his own during Gerda's bender had just cemented the fact that Mike's definitely the kind of guy who likes to go out to a bar solo, on the spur of the moment, and not have to answer to some whiny girl about what time he'll be home. He could never commit to anyone other than a cow. I instinctively knew—from years of dating men who seem perfectly normal at first, and then one day show up in a hand-knit poncho they bartered for in Oaxaca—that Mike was poncho material. I'd bet everything I own that Mike already had a route mapped out for camping along the Andes this summer.

"I thought you might want to come over for some . . . lemonade," Mike said, reaching out his hand to help me up.

"Okay," I said, surprising myself. I found myself unable to look away from his stubble and brown eyes. "I guess I could go for some . . . lemonade."

TEN MINUTES LATER, I blinked in the subtle light from two brass sconces in the entryway of the Mike's Sanderson cottage. Waffles and I followed him inside, in a mild state of shock. There was a beautiful old hall table to my right—was that *Biedermeier*?—and just past it was the door to a small library-style living room. There were two large chocolate-brown sofas, a comfy upholstered chair, and a low table piled with books. Things were arranged in English country-house style, with botanical prints on the walls, big comfortable furniture, and an air of age and good style. This place was totally charming!

No Mexican blankets or camping gear were visible. Also, the house smelled really good. There was the scent of lemon oil used to polish the furniture and that faint, smoky smell that lingers into the summer after you've burned logs in your fireplace all winter. I couldn't even smell the farm through the open window. Not a whiff of cow shit anywhere.

"Have a seat," said Mike, gesturing to one of the giant puffy sofas.

"Thanks!" I said, squooshing into the cushions. I've never been one for huge furniture, but for some reason, it really worked in this small room, making it seem incredibly cozy in a man cave–ish way. Had he hired a decorator? Whatever the case, it was such a relaxing space that if I wasn't being kept awake by the sexual tension in the room—at least I thought there was sexual tension—I'd have immediately taken a nap. Mike pushed the two window sashes higher to let in the early-evening breeze, while I surreptitiously checked out his forearms. (Okay, a hint of cow blew in along with the fresh air, but mostly it was all lemon oil and Irish Spring in here.)

"Did you decorate this place yourself?" I asked him.

"Honey lent me most of the furniture and a lot of prints and paintings," he told me. "She has so many antiques handed down over the years, she was happy to move some stuff out here to the cottage. I'll get the drinks," he added, and disappeared.

I watched him leave and wondered: Is it possible to have a relationship that's based entirely on someone's muscular arms? I think it is. I mean, Holly's marriage to Howard only came about because of her fabulous legs in a tennis skirt.

Waffles launched himself off his back legs and landed beside me on the giant couch. I tried to shove him over, but he lay there like a sunbathing manatee. This wasn't too romantic.

Actually, though, Waffles looked really good in this old-English, clubby setting. It was very basset-friendly, perfect for a portly brown and white dog with floppy ears. The room was a little masculine for my taste, but if I wasn't possessed of the knowledge that Mike had a predilection for exotic camping trips, I could see myself living here. And if people asked where I lived, I could answer airily: "Sanderson."

And they'd say, "You do? What's it like with the ballroom and the greenhouse and the fourteen bedrooms and the dining room that's hosted several presidents at the Regency dining table that seats twenty-four?"

That's when I'd have to admit that I lived in a cottage down by the cow barn, but that's still pretty good. And so was this cottage, which spoke of stability and comfort.

Questions were whizzing around in my head, and chief among them was the worry: Was I wrong about Mike? Was he really a guy who couldn't be counted on for more than sexy groping in a barn?

Maybe it was just Honey's heirlooms and antiques that were making that statement, but was it possible there was a more permanent side to Mike? Since I'd never really spent much time talking to him, it was possible I was selling him short.

We'd met under such strange circumstances, and given all the crimes around Bryn Mawr lately and my precarious financial situation—not to mention meeting John Hall—I'd really never spent more than an hour at a time with him, had a meal with him, gone for a walk with him that didn't end up with a crime scene.

"Lemonade, as promised," Mike said, returning with two glasses and some hastily folded up paper towels as coasters.

Well, Mike definitely wasn't gay. Only a straight guy would have no napkins. "Want some vodka in that?" He held up a bottle with some Russian lettering and a red label on it.

"Sure!" I said. Phew—for a minute there, I'd been afraid Mike was actually going to serve plain old lemonade. He glugged some vodka into our glasses, sat down next to me in the overstuffed chair, and kissed me. This went on for a few amazing minutes, with me telling myself that this was the last time I'd be doing this, so I might as well get as much of those muscular arms as I could. Come to think of it, his thigh muscles, pressed up against my legs, were pretty fantastic, too . . . the low lighting in this room was really very romantic . . . I liked his sunburned nose and dark brown eyes . . .

In a pleasant fog of vodka and pheromones, I was considering ripping off Mike's white shirt when I suddenly noticed Waffles had gotten up and was standing a few feet away in front of a door that led from Mike's living room out into his small backyard. He was wagging and giving me his I-gotta-go look.

"He's got to go out," I told Mike.

"I'll take him," said Mike.

"Thanks!" I said gratefully, smoothing down my hair.

"C'mon, Waffles," he said, leading the dog outside into the dark under the trees. "Be right back," he said.

While they contemplated some azalea bushes, I got up to look at the bookshelves the flanked the fireplace, which held a mix of old classics, books on cows and horses, and a few coffee-table tomes about Ireland and England. WASP classics, courtesy of Honey. Then I spied it, between the *Field Guide to Cattle* and a collected works of P.G. Wodehouse.

Mike owned *The Lonely Planet Guide to Thailand*!

Regret coursed through my veins, mingling with the vodka to make for a depressing cocktail of despair. What was I doing here, anyway? Muscular arms or not, I was done with Mike, I thought, furious with myself. As he and Waffles came back through the back door, I glared at Mike and grabbed the dog's leash, but neither one of them noticed my irked mood.

"More vodka?" asked Mike, in a friendly manner.

"No, thanks," I said frostily. "I'm—"

"Did someone say vodka?" boomed a voice through the open window next to the front door. "You home, Mikey?"

Honey Potts! I'd know her Charlton-Heston-meets-Kathleen-Turner intonation anywhere.

Mike uttered something under his breath and went to the front door, Waffles got up and ran happily out to the front hallway, and I frantically plumped up the rumpled couch cushions.

"Hi, Honey," I heard Mike say to his boss.

"Is that *Waffles*?" said a shocked, more feminine voice. I knew the voice: It went with tanned legs, long blond hair, blue eyes, and overpriced YSL caftans. It was a voice that had been expensively educated and had traveled the world, thanks to tons of chicken nuggets being eaten all around our great country. A voice that was music to the ears of salespeople at Saks, Neiman's, and Chanel boutiques around the globe . . .

"Do you know Holly Jones?" growled Honey to Mike in the foyer. "She's a new friend of mine. Holly, meet Mike Woodford." I could hear Waffles's tail thumping against the wood floor.

Holly! I was in complete shock. Not only was Holly about to catch me *in flagrante* make out with Mike, I was struggling to absorb the fact that she actually knew Waffles's name. I would've bet ten bucks that Holly had no idea what the dog was called.

I busied myself getting more glasses from the shelves while the three of them and Waffles came into the living room. "Kristin, our neighbor across the street, and I were just having drinks," explained Mike, while Honey gave me a suspicious look. For her part, Holly appeared to be semi-angry with me for never having told her I knew Mike, but she also looked like she was struggling not to giggle.

If I hadn't been so mad about the *Lonely Planet Guide*, I would have laughed, too. Holly clearly had taken in the whole situation, and raised her eyebrows at me while Mike handed around drinks. Holly understands make-out interruptus, having been involved in quite a few such sessions herself in her pre-Howard days.

Holly perched on a small chair by the window, crossed her elegant legs, sipped her drink, and said, "Guess what, Kristin? One of Mrs. Potts's cows, Blossom, is giving birth tonight." Holly was winking at me and raising her eyebrows in a significant manner. "So she just called her *veterinarian*."

Uh-oh.

"I called John Hall and he's meeting us at the barn in twenty minutes," Honey told Mike, settling herself into one of the sofas and sipping her drink. *Time to go home!* blinked like neon in my mind while Holly's cell phone began to vibrate.

"Oh boy," Holly said, eyeing her caller ID. "Sophie Shields."

She answered and listened for a minute. "Okay, hold on." Holly paused for a second and looked at Mike. "Is it okay if our friend Sophie comes over? She has something important to tell me, and she insists she needs to do it in person."

"Why not?" Mike said, looking defeated. "Invite anyone you want."

"Sophie, turn into the driveway at Sanderson. Yes, the place your ex got whacked. Go straight past the barn to the little stone house. You'll see my car parked right out front," Holly told her, and hung up.

"Actually, knowing Sophie, she might miss it," Holly added to the three of us, while checking her manicure.

"Why's that dingbat coming over?" growled Honey, who, I noted, really did look nice in her white linen Talbots dress. Was that lipstick I noticed on her sun-baked lips, too?

"She has something urgent to tell me. Actually, she's not that bad," said Holly. "She's trying to reinvent herself."

A car squealed into the gravel road outside, heels rat-a-tatted up the steps, and Waffles and Mike went to the door. Sophie clacked in and Holly made the necessary introductions. That done, Sophie greeted us all amiably, and plopped her small Cavalli-clad frame into a chair, while Honey stared at her, perplexed.

"Nice piece a property you got here!" Sophie said to Honey Potts. "I can see why my ex tried to buy it off you. Not that I think you should sell to him, because I don't!"

She looked at Mike, and recognition dawned in her Bambi eyes.

"Hey, I remember you," Sophie said to him. "You came with Honey to my symphony party. Anyway, do you have any champagne?" she asked as Mike poured her a vodka lemonade. "'Cause vodka and I don't get along,

if you know what I mean. And also, I have an announcement to make. Champagne would help."

"I'll check," said Mike heading to the kitchen. He returned with a bottle of sparkling wine, popped the cork,
and passed us all some wineglasses. We all waited to take
a sip while Sophie got to her feet, put her hands on her
narrow hips, and told us dramatically:

"Well, girls, and, um, you, the hot guy with the cute
scruff and the champagne, I'm in love. I'm in love with
a man who wants to paint my whole house beige. I'm in
love with Joe!"

My jaw dropped, Holly's eyes widened in shock, Mike
looked confused, and Honey asked, "Who the hell is Joe?"

"He's my decorator!" Sophie replied. "Holly and Kristin's friend. Incredibly handsome and I'm nuts about
him!"

"Is he straight?" asked Mike.

"Yup," said Sophie proudly. "I checked."

For the next five minutes, I had an out-of-body experience listening to Sophie tell us all about how she'd finally
realized her true feelings for Joe at the Benjamin Moore
paint store the day before. Anyone who cared that much
about her house, she reasoned, and was willing to stand
up to her preference for purple and gold, was a man she
could count on. And she knew that he would never treat
her with the callousness that Barclay had. There would be
no need to hire PIs to follow Joe around.

I wondered distractedly if Joe could possibly have
feelings for Sophie. She was pretty and sweet enough, but
she and Joe were as different as Chippendale and Ikea, as

diametrically opposed as Campari and Coors. They had absolutely nothing in common. Then again, who knows? Maybe it was time for Joe to move out of Holly's guest room and get on with his life.

"Listen, girl," said Honey to Sophie. "I don't know you. You don't seem all that smart. And you married Barclay Shields, so your judgment can't be all that great. But most of us marry a horse's ass at some point."

"I did," agreed Holly.

"I did, too," said Honey. "And I spent a lot of time being miserable about it. I should've picked myself up and gone on with my life, and married someone else. And that's what you should do, too, Sophie. Go tell this Joe that you love him. Maybe it will all work out." We all looked at Honey in surprise, but just then a cow bellowed from the barn.

"Blossom!" barked Honey, worriedly. She and Mike got up and zoomed out the front door toward the barn, leaving me, Holly, and Sophie with our cocktails. It seemed Blossom was now in full-on labor, and while I felt badly for the poor cow, it didn't make me any less sure that Mike was definitely not a potential long-term relationship prospect.

"Let's go, Holly," I said. She yawned and agreed.

"I better get going, too," Sophie piped up.

"I'm exhausted," Holly moaned. "Just getting Honey to try on clothes at Talbots was a huge ordeal. But I've made a lot of headway in our new friendship, and I'm eighty-seven-percent sure she didn't try to kill Barclay or the chef."

"I just need to excuse myself for a second, and then I'm ready," I told her and Sophie. "Be right back."

Mike's powder room was snazzy, in an English country house kind of way. The walls were painted a pretty dark red, and there was an old white porcelain sink and a Venetian mirror that was blurry with age. There was a print of a handsome cow on the wall opposite the door, and some books on a shelf above the commode. It was a very cute bathroom. Whatever—so Mike had good taste. As soon as I washed my hands, which were covered with dog hair, I was out of here, and I never wanted to see Mike or his *Lonely Planet Guide* again.

Then I froze.

At one end of the little bookshelf above the toilet was a silver acorn bookend.

Only one acorn bookend.

I knew this didn't necessarily implicate Mike, since Walt had told me there were any number of the acorn figurines floating around Bryn Mawr, but, still—one of the acorns? Right here, on the grounds of Sanderson, where a heavy, sharp, bloodied acorn bookend had been found just days before? I felt a shiver of fear run down my spine. Why did I always find myself in these situations lately?

I threw open the door into the small front hallway, noticing in the dim light from the sconces that directly opposite the powder room door, above a small oil painting of a constipated-looking old woman in a bonnet, a *gun* was mounted on the wall.

It was a glossy, attractive, antique gun made of gleaming wood and elegantly tarnished metal, unmistakably a vintage piece. I don't know the first thing about firearms, but unless I was very much mistaken, this one was old. Who keeps a *gun* in their front hallway?

People who go around shooting chefs with antique guns, *that's* who! Mike had to be the attacker of both Barclay Shields and Chef Gianni. Why he had gone after the two men, I wasn't sure, but maybe he was trying to keep Barclay from taking land away from his precious herd of cows. Who knows why he'd target Gianni, but if Mike was a hothead, possibly he just thought the chef, being your basic jackass, was worth shooting.

Mike had been at Sophie's Symphony party, too, so he could have been the one to push Gianni. When I thought back, I hadn't seen him among the crowd who'd immediately gathered around the fallen chef. Had he gone inside and pushed Gianni?

"Yikes," I whispered, petrified. I'd been making out with a murderer. Well, attempted murderer. This was a new low.

I wheeled around to leave the bathroom and went back to the living room to grab Holly and Sophie.

"Look!" I whispered, dragging them into the hallway and pointing toward the gun.

"What?" said Sophie, staring at the rendering of the woman in the bonnet. "Not to be negative, but that painting's ugly as sin. This lady looks like she hasn't taken a crap for a week. Did I tell you that always happens to Barclay when we travel? One time when we went to Atlantic City—"

"No, above the painting," I squeaked, pointing above

the small painting. "The old gun. And in here, in the powder room"—I threw open the door and gestured wildly—"the acorn bookend. He's got all the weapons that have been used over the past week in the attacks on Gianni and Barclay."

Sophie's jaw dropped, and Holly looked stunned. She stared at me with comprehension, then clutched my wrist and Sophie's, one in each hand. Sophie also appeared to put two and two together, and I was pretty sure I saw a light bulb pop on inside her head.

"I know what we'd do in Joisey if we thought we were inside the house of a guy who's probably a wannabe murderer," she shrieked.

"What?" asked Holly, looking slightly hysterical.

"Run!" said Sophie.

I grabbed Waffles's leash, and Sophie ran for her convertible, while Waffles and I got into Holly's car. I could see that John's SUV was already parked over at the barn, but there was no sign of him, Mike, or Honey, who all seemed to be inside the brightly lit barn. We sped out up the long driveway of Sanderson toward the road.

"I can't believe you've been kissing a murderer!" Holly said, shooting me a glance as she hit fifty, gravel flying. "Even I have never done that." She seemed a little envious. "You didn't have sex with him, did you?"

"Nope," I told her, truthfully.

"Oh well." She looked disappointed. "Where did you make out? Was it always at his house?" she asked, pulling into my driveway across the street from the Sanderson gates.

"No, not at all. Once out by my fence, and one other time in the Sanderson barn," I admitted.

"Against a fence and in a barn?" Holly breathed. She looked impressed. "That's so . . . so . . . Kenny Chesney, in a good way."

"That was before I knew about Mike's crazed-murderer secret," I explained.

"I'll call you in the morning and we'll talk about everything," I promised, getting out of the car and running into my house like a spooked rabbit, Waffles following me.

"Lock yourself in," Holly called after me. "You never know if he'll get that acorn bookend out tonight and smash it into your skull—right after he talks his way into your house and has his way with you on your kitchen floor! Which honestly sounds kind of hot. Except for the skull-smashing part."

Holly backed out of the driveway and I bolted all the doors, latched all the first-floor windows, and closed the kitchen curtains. Then I ran upstairs, brushed my teeth, and got into bed, frantically clutching the blanket and Waffles, who blew out a sigh and gave me a look that implied I needed to pull myself together—the equivalent of a dog eye roll—before he curled up and went to sleep.

As I calmed down, breathed, and began to think more logically, I started to doubt my freak-out. The bookend wasn't proof of anything. Walt had said that Bryn Mawr was full of the acorn bookends; lots of people had been given them by Bryn Mawr Prep School, and had passed them along to family members or given them away.

But the acorn *and* the gun, both within a few feet of each other at Mike's house, and on the grounds of Sanderson, scene of the acorn crime? It was just too coincidental. I pulled the covers up higher around my ears, retrieved my cell phone from my bedside table, and tucked it under my pillow, wondering if I should call Officer Walt. He struck me as the early-to-bed type, though, and Bootsie had tortured him so much the past week that I hesitated to bother him again. It popped into my mind just before I fell into an exhausted sleep that the bonneted woman in the painting at Mike's house bore a strong resemblance to Honey. It must be a Potts ancestor that Honey couldn't stand looking at, since it was basically an ominous predictor of exactly how she was going to look in a few years—it was like the opposite of *The Picture of Dorian Gray.*

THE NEXT MORNING in the light of day, my terror had turned into a confused headache. I wasn't feeling too perky when I got to the shop, despite the fact that I'd spent five extra minutes under the shower, and had loaded up my biggest insulated coffee to-go cup at home.

I knew I had to call Officer Walt, but it could wait until after I finished my coffee and dusted.

Or *did* I really need to tell Walt about the acorn and gun we'd seen last night at Mike's? Would I sound like a paranoid nut job? And truthfully, even though I now really liked John, I'd harbored a pretty serious crush on Mike (unless, of course, he was a deranged killer, then my crush would immediately and retroactively become null and void). I didn't want to think badly of Mike.

It seemed a little unfair to call Walt and blab about my suspicions about Mike. Or was it insane *not* to call Walt? This was awful.

I looked out at the blue skies over Lancaster Avenue in hopes of finding an answer. I considered calling Bootsie and asking her advice, but if I did that, I might as well open a Twitter account, tweet it to CNN, and try to get Anderson Cooper to weigh in. As I ran a dust cloth over some Royal Doulton serving dishes near the front of the store, I realized that the only people I could really talk to about this were Holly and Joe. I knew Holly would have already discussed the discoveries of the gun and bookend at length with Joe, and they'd give me sound advice about whether or not to call Walt.

What I wasn't sure about was how Joe would react to the news that Sophie Shields was desperately enamored with him. But while this was a major development, it would have to take a backseat to the potentially murderous cowhand.

"People are complicated, Waffles," I said to the dog, who was happily panting at passersby near the front door. He turned and wagged, his rawhide bone poking sideways out of his mouth in a ridiculous way. I noticed his barrel-shaped body was indeed turning into a round mound of hound. Gerda was right. I sighed. I'd been so distracted lately that we hadn't been going on our usual long walks.

As I straightened up the shop, I vowed to myself that starting today, I was going to get my life back on track.

It was officially Time to Get Motivated. I was going to end—well, severely limit—my time at the club drinking wine with Holly and Joe, sipping coffee and gossiping with Bootsie, and gulping aspirin and listening to Sophie Shields. I needed to hit the flea markets this weekend, because when the shop's not fully stocked, it's not an alluring prospect for shoppers. The shop should look full, bursting with adorable accessories and statement-making furniture, which it most definitely didn't at the moment. This Saturday I'd go on a buying run to Lancaster County, organize the shop, mow my lawn, weed the perennial beds, and clean the house. I'd book a trip to visit my parents in Winkelman. I might even go *jogging*.

"And I won't be spending the weekend obsessing over anyone, including Mike, who I'm thinking this morning isn't a crazed killer," I told Waffles.

As I was about to dial Holly, I noticed there was a message on my cell phone. I checked the call log and saw that John had been the message leaver; he must have called last night or early this morning, while my phone had been set on silent. I dialed voice mail and listened to John's message.

He said that he'd like to take me to dinner that night, maybe somewhere downtown.

"Or we can go to the club," he said, sounding happy, "because my divorce came through yesterday. It's official. And both Lilly and I are happy about it. She's in love with a guy she met in Connecticut at a tennis tournament last summer, and she's finally free to move up there, which she's been hoping to do."

The wind was knocked out of me, honestly. I put my cell phone down on my desk, sat down, and took a sip of coffee.

A moment later, belching clouds of smoke in front of the shop announced the arrival of Jimmy and Hugh Best. They clambered in the front door accompanied by the scent of cigars and Old Spice.

"Good news!" said Hugh, who was looking dapper today in a faded Nantucket-red sport coat. "Your friend from New York called us this morning to tell us that the Frenchwoman appraising the ring has ascertained it *is* a Garrard design." He beamed, and Jimmy cracked a smile.

"George tells us that this Frenchie has a theory about the ring," Jimmy added, plunking himself down on the deco bench, while Hugh took Bootsie's customary Queen Anne chair and petted Waffles. "It could be part of a set of what he calls 'important jewels.' Which means—ka-ching!" he said with devilish glee. "Bring on the twenty-five-year-old Macallan and illegally imported Cohibas. Out with the cheap shit, and in with the good stuff!"

"George said there's a *small chance* that it's a significant piece of jewelry," pointed out Hugh, "and not to expect much." Hugh clearly was steeling himself against disappointment, and I didn't blame him.

"That's wonderful," I told them happily. "You deserve all the good fortune in the world."

"Well, we're very grateful to you and your friend Holly for putting us in touch with Sotheby's," said Hugh, sweetly. "This could be our ticket to a comfortable old age."

"I'm even starting to think we *should* sell our decrepit old house," agreed Jimmy, surprising me. "Hugh's got me half convinced to give in to Barclay Shields; get some fast cash for the old place, and start over. Get a condo where the oven works, there's no mold in the basement, and the heat doesn't thump and ping all night."

"I don't think that sounds like a very good idea at all," said a frosty feminine voice from the front of the store.

We all swiveled toward the coolly elegant voice; the sleigh bells I keep on the door handle jingled as the door closed behind Mariellen Merriwether, who stood there in a tasteful pale green linen frock, a beige handbag, and beige low-heeled pumps, her right hand caressing her ever-present pearls.

"I've been waiting for the opportunity to find you alone," Mariellen said to me in a low tone that threatened me more than an out-and-out hissy fit would have. Her Caribbean-blue eyes flashed demonically, and I had a sudden vision of her in a coat made of sewn-together Dalmatian puppy hides.

"Er—you have?" I said nervously.

"Well, she ain't alone, Mariellen," offered Jimmy jocularly. "Obviously. May I say, that dress makes you look positively fetching. Reminds me of our old school dances back in the sixties when I was dating Honey and you were going steady with Martin."

"This young woman never seems to be without one of her drunken cronies during the day, or at night," Mariellen observed, ignoring him. "Too busy trying to sleep with all the men in this town."

"I haven't slept with any of the men!" I protested, shocked. "At least, not lately. If you mean your daughter's ex-husband, I've barely even kissed him."

"Husband," she corrected me. "Her *current* husband. They are still married."

I didn't think this was the appropriate time to tell her that this was no longer the case, so I kept my mouth shut.

"Mariellen, be reasonable," said Jimmy, who was twirling an unlit cigar in his left hand. "You're being a bit rude, my dear. From what I hear at the club, your daughter dumped her hubby more than a year ago for some Andre Agassi type in Connecticut. You can't expect the fellow she's divorcing to stay single forever."

"*I'm* being rude?" sniffed Mariellen, still standing in the front of the store like a statue while Waffles sniffed her ankles happily, perhaps catching a whiff of Norman. "I don't think so at all.

"I'm merely being direct, and unlike everyone else in this town, I'm disciplined, and focused on getting things done," Mariellen continued, using her beige pump to give Waffles a swift kick in the neck. Shocked, he whimpered and ran over to his dog bed.

Nothing like that has ever happened to Waffles before. I was aghast, but I was so stunned that I didn't say anything for fear of setting her off even more.

"For instance," she went on, "I am determined to halt the awful, hideous, destructive spread of tacky new houses all over this town, and so I took a stand against that Shields person.

"And I'm equally against our town becoming the sort

of glitzed-up, celebrity-chef-worshipping, restaurant-obsessed place where people blab on about rare taleggio cheeses and which pig in Parma their prosciutto came from!" she ranted furiously. "People like Mr. Shields and that hideous chef are ruining Bryn Mawr!"

What exactly was Mariellen saying?

"Uh, Mariellen, are you angry about cheese?" said Hugh, confused and astonished at this geyser of rage.

"She's angry that Bryn Mawr is changing, and that she can't stop change," said Jimmy simply. "And so she tried to kill Mr. Shields and the Italian chef to send a message."

Mariellen nodded. "This is a cheddar and Triscuits town, not some fancy Neiman Marcus place with frou-frou pastas and overpriced wine. I get my chardonnay at the Wine Stop for six dollars a bottle, and that's good enough for me." She seemed to calm down for second while talking about her bargain wine, but then dialed up her nutty-rage factor again as she turned on the Bests.

"And you two, letting go of a house that's been in your family for two centuries. The idea of selling out to Barclay Shields!" she yelled at Hugh and Jimmy, incensed.

"The heat doesn't work," Jimmy told her. "Freeze my tuchus off all winter, Mariellen. We don't all have the millions of dollars in a trust fund that you enjoy. But we haven't sold the house. You're misinformed."

"I don't have time for this pointless debate," she said, more calmly, striding toward us. That's when I saw she was holding a small, but nonetheless very scary, antique gun.

She had a firm grip on the gun, which was tarnished

with age, but clearly a finely made handgun from decades back. If I had to make a guess, I realized, this gun was the same vintage as the one used to shoot the chef.

Mariellen's spine was straight as a NASA laser as she held the gun with a practiced hand.

"I thought I saw a gun in your handbag when you pulled out your cigarettes the other day," Jimmy told her. "Was up in the attic at the club, and had some old binoculars out. Told myself my eyes were playing tricks on me. Something glinted in your handbag, and it looked the right shape, but I didn't want to believe it of you."

Mariellen ignored him.

"If you try to scream or run, I'll shoot your dog," she told me. My heart plummeted, and I felt nauseated and numb. Why hadn't I grabbed my cell phone from my desk when she'd first walked in?

"Out the door, all of you, and get into my car. Anyone have a cell phone?" she asked.

I pointed sadly toward mine, sitting uselessly on the desk, while Jimmy and Hugh explained they didn't believe in cell phones, and in addition, why would they pay forty dollars a month for such an unnecessary device.

"I hope you know what you're doing with that gun, Mariellen," Jimmy barked at her.

"Of course I know what I'm doing," she retorted. "I've been around guns my whole life, rode in all the hunts at Sanderson in the old days, and had target practice with Papa every Saturday. How else do you think I shot that Italian chef from two hundred yards away with Papa's old shotgun? Not this gun, of course," she said, waving her pistol. "The shotgun has a much longer range. I could have killed him, but I was fairly sure that another warning note combined with shooting him in the foot would convince him to close the old firehouse and go back to the city. I left the note for him today, warning him that next time I won't aim low."

Jimmy, Hugh, and I exchanged glances, with Hugh looking as shaky as I felt, and Jimmy wearing an expression of true surprise. Well, it was official. Mariellen had shot the chef, and now she was prepared to shoot the three of us. I could feel my bones turning to mayonnaise as we all marched toward the door.

Including Waffles, who'd forgotten about getting kicked in the neck and was now galloping happily after the four of us, thinking we were going somewhere fun—maybe on a walk!—and he'd be missing out.

"Lie down, Waffles," I told the dog shakily, shooing him back toward his bed. "Go play with your bone," I told him desperately, while he ignored me.

"Bring him," Mariellen told me flatly. She looped the handles of her purse over her arm, so that her right hand was free to keep a grip on the weapon, and jingled her car keys with her left hand. Waffles trotted even faster after us. He loves the jingle of keys.

"He's fine here," I said, trying for a lighthearted tone while I choked back a sob.

"I said, bring that fat mutt."

I let Waffles out the door, shakily closed and locked the door behind us, then led my trusting hound to her Range Rover. Waffles even wagged at Mariellen when I opened the backseat to the roomy truck, looking around desperately for anyone to flag down on the normally busy street. Of course, there wasn't a soul in sight.

Why, today of all days, couldn't Bootsie be out walking Lancaster Avenue, sticking her nose into the café, the hardware store, the post office, and the bakery, hoping to catch a cheating spouse or hear about a drunken escapade at a party, as per her custom? Why wasn't Holly heading back from Booty Camp, or Joe and Sophie at the paint store a few doors down, debating fifty shades of beige? But there was absolutely no one out on the street at the moment. Even the elderly lady who runs the liquor store, who's almost always outside puffing on a Parliament, had disappeared.

"You drive," Mariellen told me, handing me the keys to her large black Mercedes, her gun aimed firmly at Waffles. My hand trembled as I climbed into the driver's seat and inserted the key into the ignition. Mariellen gestured for Hugh to sit shotgun, and she, Jimmy, and Waffles got into the backseat. A tear rolled down my cheek.

"What in the name of Johnnie Walker are you up to, Mariellen?" complained Jimmy as he buckled his seat belt—an unnecessary precaution, probably, since we all seemed as good as dead. "If you've gotten yourself into trouble, we should go discuss it with the police. And maybe a good headshrinker."

"We'll discuss it at my house," she said. "Head toward Sanderson, then take a right on Camellia Lane."

Mariellen's estate was only minutes away, in the opposite direction of Sophie Shields's house. Shady Camellia Lane is one of the prettiest roads in Bryn Mawr, but I didn't notice its namesake flowers in bloom as I shakily steered the large car into her driveway per Mariellen's instructions. Her property had no gates, just a small black mailbox set in a bank of irises and lilies. The driveway was lined with oak trees, and the sense of privacy would have been idyllic under different circumstances.

The driveway wound back from Camellia Lane, and as we rounded a curve and the house came into view, even in my panic I couldn't help noticing that Mariellen's stone farmhouse oozed good taste. Dogwoods bloomed along the walkway to her dark green front door, and flower boxes filled with hot-pink petunias were mounted on each front window. I guess elegance and insanity aren't mutually exclusive.

Behind her house was a paddock, and then a barn, painted pristine white, with none of the mud and muck you normally see outside a horse barn. The grass was as lush as that of a golf course, and the pathways were beautifully raked and maintained. To its right was a large pond, covering at least three acres, upon which a pair of geese was swimming; in front of the pond, a gravel lane led off into the woods. "That lane leads over to Lilly's house," Mariellen informed us. "The house I bought for her and her husband." She shot me a significant look as I pulled up and parked to the right of her house.

Mariellen had it made. She lived in one of the most beautiful houses I'd ever seen, inherited along with a large trust fund, making her one extremely lucky woman. She had a devoted daughter, and a schedule filled with cocktail parties, golf, and a beloved horse. Her life appeared to be as flawless as her pearls. How could anyone who lived in such a gorgeous setting be so mean? Even if the rest of Philadelphia was being developed and modernized, she had carved out an island of farmland that seemed frozen in time. She was completely isolated in bucolic perfection.

A whinny pierced the birdsong humming all around us as we climbed out of the car at Mariellen's direction, the gun aimed steadily at me. I saw Norman's tall brown head sticking out of his stall, looking around to see what was up.

"Mummy will bring you your alfalfa soon, darling!" cried Mariellen to the horse, who neighed back at her. Waffles sniffed and spied Norman, started wagging, and whined excitedly.

"Inside, please," said Mariellen frostily.

MARIELLEN'S FOYER WAS painted lime green, and had ornate old woodwork that was exceptionally lovely. In orderly lines along the front hallway hung a dozen pretty framed floral prints by Pierre-Joseph Redouté. A graceful staircase was directly in front of us, and then the hallway led back to a sunroom painted pale yellow and filled with orchids in full bloom. For the house of a psychotic country clubber, this was all very beautiful.

Also, as Bootsie had reported, there was toile and monograms out the yin-yang. On the antique console table in the hall sat lime-green lamps with monogrammed M shades, a silver tray embossed with double Ms, and M-monogrammed cocktail napkins. Flanking the console were two side chairs covered with a riot of green toile, depicting French milkmaids, cows, horses, and birds; the dining room, visible to our right, featured monograms everywhere, including the seats of the dining chairs. I began to feel a twinge of migraine in my left eye. Everything was in perfect order, of course, but the mind boggled at the varying patterns.

"We'll sit in the library," Mariellen announced, opening a door off the lime hallway into a pink and white library in which the theme seemed to be horses. Straight ahead was a lovely fireplace, and on either side of it were old-fashioned Dutch doors. The top halves of the horizontally-divided doors were open, with banks of buoyant rosebushes visible beyond them, and then a fenced paddock filled with jade grass. At the right was a pink-toile-covered window seat, and on the walls were several large old English paintings of Norman look-alikes depicted standing in Cotswold meadows. There were silver-framed photos of Norman himself on the glossy antique tables, looking quite regal as he was awarded ribbons at local horse shows, and a few pictures of Lilly were scattered around, too (though she got less play than the horse, I noticed).

However, on the mantel was a wedding picture taken just outside this very house, and I didn't need to look twice to realize who the couple was. I gulped and vowed to not look at this picture of Lilly and John, turning my attention instead to the coffee table, which featured monogrammed items including coasters, decanters, and glass bowls. The sofas were, naturally, pink toile. My eye began to twitch.

The twitch got worse when I noticed that as Hugh sat nervously in a pink wing chair and Jimmy leaned against a farm door, Waffles was eyeing the plump sofas with a look I knew all too well: The expression in his eyes foretold a flying sofa leap at any second, which I thought might mean instant shooting with Mariellen's pistol. I grabbed his collar and held tight while I stroked his ears, and tried to keep him from drooling on the pink needlepoint rug embroidered with Norman-style horses.

"Let's get down to brass tacks, Mariellen," Jimmy said impatiently as he looked around the room for a bar. His eye landed on a table over by the window with more decanters on it, and he made a beeline for it and poured himself a stiff Scotch. Mariellen kept the gun trained on him, and seated herself, ramrod straight, on the chair that was a twin to Hugh's.

"You're the one who banged Shields in the head. Is that what you're saying?" Jimmy asked her, plunking himself down on the window seat as he swigged his drink.

"Of course I did," Mariellen said primly. "See the empty spots on my bookshelves?" She pointed to shelves at our left. "That's where my acorn bookends used to be. I had four of the bookends—two of my own, two from my good-for-nothing former husband, who also went to Bryn Mawr Prep, before he married me and then bolted for some dusty hill town in South America—and I gave them away to the church charity sale last fall. Eula Morris was working at the charity sale that day.

"I knew Eula would remember that I'd given four bookends, since she's such a busybody," Mariellen continued, pleased with herself. "If anyone ever suspects me—which they won't—I could simply tell them to check with Eula and she'd confirm that I'd given away all four acorns months before Mr. Shields was hit.

"But during the church sale, while Eula was inside trying to hit up Honey for money to restore the stage at the symphony," Mariellen told us, "I quietly put one bookend back in the trunk of my car. Then, while I was manning the lemonade stand, two horrible hippie women came by in a *van* that reeked of marijuana, and bought the other three."

Annie and Jenny, I thought to myself, who couldn't remember where they'd gotten the bookends. They must have been high, and forgotten attending the church sale where they'd bought the acorns. Not that it mattered now. It was ironic that I'd ended up with Mariellen's acorns, but I didn't think this was a good time to bring that up.

"I saved the fourth bookend just for Mr. Shields," Mariellen said, pleased. "A man like that needs to be literally hit in the head with something to understand it. And I thought the acorn was a fitting symbol of what this area used to be: tasteful and modest."

Honestly, her house with its vast paddocks, barn, and ornate decorating wasn't all that modest, but I kept this to myself.

"So I set up a fake meeting for Mr. Shields and Honey ten days ago," she continued, crossing her slim legs as a light breeze blew in through the picturesque farm doors. "I knew he'd be positively chomping at the bit to buy some of Sanderson's acreage. When Honey dropped me off here at home after that disgusting party at the old firehouse, I simply slipped the bookend in my saddlebag, jumped on Norman, and rode over to Sanderson to meet Mr. Shields. Takes me a matter of minutes to ride there, as you know; it's just through the woods. A beautiful trail runs over that way. I tied Norman to a tree just past the barn and out of sight of the house, and then walked over and hit the despicable man right on his head. He was knocking so hard on the front door and cursing a blue streak about no one answering, that he never heard me coming."

Jimmy, Hugh, and I exchanged glances, with Hugh approximating the terrified, bulging eyes I once saw on a Pomeranian that Waffles once tried to befriend at the pet store over in Haverford. Jimmy put up a better front of bravado, and honestly didn't seem scared.

"Did Honey help you hide Shields after he was knocked out?" he asked. "How the hell did you move that big fat man into the bushes?"

"I didn't," Mariellen informed him, lighting a Virginia Slim.

"As a matter of fact, I left him right there on Honey's front doorstep. I took the bookend and went out to the pasture, where I tossed the bookend into a briar patch. Naturally, since I wear riding gloves, there weren't any fingerprints on the bookend." She paused and took an elegant puff on her cigarette. "Then the oddest thing happened. I was at least a quarter of a mile away, and just getting ready to ride Norman home, when two men came walking down Honey's driveway. I could just see them in the light over Honey's front door; they wore horrible leather jackets and jeans, and they grabbed Barclay by the feet and dragged him away from the house." She shrugged. "I didn't wait to see what happened after that."

"What are the chances!" hooted Jimmy, leaning back on the window seat cushions. "It must have been those mafia guys who've been looking for Shields. You got the job started for them, Mariellen." For someone who might be killed at any second, Jimmy seemed totally at ease. The only logical conclusion I could make was that Mariellen was intent on permanently silencing all of us, because why else would she be telling us all this? Hugh, on the other hand, appeared to be catatonic with fear, which was closer to my own state of mind. Maybe Jimmy thought Mariellen wouldn't really shoot him.

Personally, I really did think she'd shoot me.

"And when the chef fell at the symphony party—you pushed him off Sophie Shields's balcony?" I asked.

"Easily," said Mariellen proudly, twisting her pearls. "When that dreadful Sophie was showing us around the house, which I knew she'd be dying to do, I lingered behind in the kitchen for a few minutes and saw that there was a large pantry closet I could easily conceal myself in. Later, when the cooks all took a cigarette break and Honey was in the powder room—she takes forever in the bathroom, honestly—I simply slipped into the pantry, waited till the chef was outside on the landing, and gave him a good hard shove."

I was kind of impressed by this. Mariellen didn't screw around.

"If people still had the gumption we had back in the 1960s, we'd all be a lot better off!" Mariellen added. "That was a time when this area was serene and unspoiled. It's all been downhill from there, and in my own small way, I've been trying to stem the tide."

Mariellen had taken nostalgia to a psychotic level, I realized. In a strange way, I could understand her longing for the past, if not the extreme measures she'd taken toward trying to preserve it. We all mourn for things that are lost, of course, but hopefully we can put the losses in perspective. I always felt sad when I'd see one of the quirky old shops along Lancaster Avenue close, like the place that only sold antique trains, and then the musty old Irish sweater place, because they reminded me of my childhood. But truthfully, I'd never set foot in either of the shops. It was indeed awful to see chainsaws cutting down Bryn Mawr's ancient towering trees to make room for house upon new house, but change is inevitable, and, on a more positive note, if nothing ever changed, no one would have invented Starbucks. In her quest to maintain a bygone way of life, Mariellen had, to put it in clinical terms, gone cuckoo.

"And by the way, John, my son-in-law, is going to be a member of this family till the day he dies," Mariellen said to me. "Now, hand me that dog's leash."

Another tear trickled down my cheek as Waffles wagged, confused, and I clutched his collar more tightly.

"What are you going to do with him?" I whispered.

"I'm going to march all four of you over to the pond, and I think you can figure out what comes next," she said, stubbing out her cigarette in an Hermès ashtray. "My pond is enormous, and very deep, and the koi fish and trout will gobble up your corpses in no time. I'm a member of one of the oldest families in Bryn Mawr, darling. The police would never dare question me, let alone even consider me as a suspect, or think to look anywhere on my property for your sad selves. If anyone saw us get into my car—which they didn't—I'll say I dropped you all at the club, and no one will doubt a word I say.

"So let's all get up and start walking, shall we?"

I've always had a strange antipathy toward koi fish, with their huge mouths and chubby fish bodies. I felt like I'd gone into a coma of fear, when we suddenly heard a familiar whinny outside, accompanied by the clip-clop of hooves on the slate pathway just outside the library.

Norman stuck his long, gleaming, brown neck in through the open top of the farm door and neighed at Mariellen inquisitively, while Waffles woofed at the horse.

"Norman, how did you get out of your stall?" Mariellen asked the horse, irritated.

"Who is this horse, Mr. Ed?" demanded Jimmy.

"I let Norman out, Mummy," we heard a girly voice call out from some twenty yards away, just behind Norman in the sunshine. "I came back from early from Greenwich, and thought I'd turn him out in the paddock and come say hi to you. Do you have friends over? And was that a *dog* I heard in there?"

Lilly!

Lilly's beautiful face appeared next to Norman's, and she peered into the pink library. Her eyes widened in shock as she took in the scene around her. "Mummy! And the Best brothers? Why do you all look so serious . . . and, Mummy, what are you doing holding that *gun*?"

Chapter 21

"I CAN'T BELIEVE I'm saying this, but thank goodness for Lilly Merriwether," I told Holly and Joe that night at Holly's house.

It was a warm night with candles lit on the patio and drinks flowing, but even with a sweater on and chubby, snuggly Waffles next to me on Holly's enormous chaise longue, I was still shivering. "If she hadn't shown up with Norman, Waffles and I and the Bests would be fish food right now," I told them.

"There'd probably be nothing left of you. Your bones would be picked as clean as a Thanksgiving turkey," agreed Joe. "I had a client once whose terrier fell into her koi pond, and *whoosh*—before she could grab the dog, it was a feeding frenzy! The fish gobbled the pooch alive in like fifteen seconds."

"That's disgusting!" Holly told him, frowning. "And very insensitive."

"Sorry," said Joe, looking apologetic. "I just could never get that image out of my mind. You and the dog would probably be the ones the fish would eat first," he added to me, reflecting on this with some interest, "since the Bests are really old and wouldn't taste all that good. Too stringy. The dog would probably the best meal of the four of you, to be honest." He eyed Waffles approvingly.

I was about to beg him to change the subject when my cell phone rang. Bootsie, for about the seventy-fifth time that night. I'd taken her first six calls, and then was too tired to talk to her anymore. I hit ignore, figuring that Bootsie would probably just show up at Holly's soon anyway.

The past five hours had been beyond exhausting. Thankfully, when Lilly Merriwether saw her mother pointing a gun at the four of us, she had calmly taken in the situation, then walked into her mother's library and convinced Mariellen to give her the weapon. Mariellen was so crazy (literally) about Lilly that it took her daughter less than a minute to convince Mariellen that what she was doing "wasn't a very good idea," as Lilly told her.

Mariellen was led upstairs to take an aspirin and lie down, and Lilly hadn't objected when Jimmy had immediately called the police. Within twenty minutes of Officer Walt's arrival, it had been decided that Mariellen needed to be hospitalized, rather than spend time in a jail cell while awaiting a hearing with a judge; Walt and Lilly had driven Mariellen over to the hospital, where she was currently under psychiatric care.

It turned out that Lilly had already had her suspicions

about her mother's mental health, but had been feeling helpless as to what to do about them.

I felt terrible about all of this, but was happy that Mariellen was getting help, rather than sitting in jail with no toilet seats, polyester jumpsuits, and instant mashed potatoes. That didn't seem right for her, even though she'd attempted to murder an innocent doggie (and me, and the Bests). I couldn't believe all this had happened today, and here we were back on Holly's patio as if it was a typical early-summer evening. I shivered again despite the warm night.

"It's George calling," said Holly, as her cell phone buzzed. "Uh-huh," she said to George. "Um-hmm. That's interesting. *Very* interesting. Wow!"

Holly hung up and stared at us, her sky-blue eyes huge. "It turns out that Hugh and Jimmy's ring is part of a set of diamond-and-ruby jewels that was made in London for someone named the Countess of Cascott in 1884.

"Their jewelry department just got the confirmation from Garrard this afternoon that the ring is part of the Countess of Cascott jewels, and"—Holly paused dramatically—"the rest of the Cascott rubies, a necklace and a pair of earrings, sold a couple of years ago for almost five million dollars. And the ring has the biggest, rarest ruby of the whole set!"

As we sat there trying to absorb this information, wheels crunched on the driveway, and Sophie Shields popped around the hedge, waving.

"Hiya Kristin!" she said. "I heard you almost got killed today. I can't believe it!"

"I can't, either," I told her. I was glad Sophie wasn't a wannabe killer, after all, though I didn't mention that to her.

"It turns out it was Barclay's fake cousins from Jersey had come to slap him around a little last Thursday, and followed him over to that Sanderson place."

"I heard," I told her.

"The Jersey guys said Barclay owed them fifty grand from some construction company they owned together back in the late nineties, and he was cheaping out on paying it. Barclay called and told me he settled up with them this week, so they're not after him anymore," Sophie added. "Not that it changes anything between me and him. I'm still getting divorced, I'm still fighting for my shoe closet, and I'm still crazy about that one right there." She pointed at Joe and winked at him, making "mwah" kissing noises in his direction.

Just as Sophie wriggled herself into the sofa next to an embarrassed-looking Joe, John appeared around the hedge of rosebushes. "I went to your house, but your neighbors said you were here," he said, walking over and sitting down next to me and gently taking my hand. "I'm so sorry about all this. Can I give you a ride home?"

I DECIDED TO take the next day off work to celebrate not being killed by Mariellen, and because I'd stayed up late the night before with John, who had been very reassuring. Even if his ex-mother-in-law hadn't tried to kill me, he told me, he was ready to start over, and he was happy that his divorce from Lilly had come through. He felt terrible about Mariellen's mental breakdown, which obviously wasn't his fault.

I spent most of the morning over at the Bests', where the three of us pored over stories about their mother's ring in local newspapers. Even the *New York Times* had a short piece about the amazing discovery of a rare seventeen-carat Burmese ruby once belonging to the Cascott family of Ackworth, England.

"We did have a great-aunt Prunella whose last name was Cascott," Hugh Best told me, looking dazed as he sat out on the back screened porch, sipping a cup of coffee, his hands shaking.

"Auntie Pru always loaded a lot of jewelry on," agreed Jimmy. "Most of it she sold over the years, but she was the one who left the ring to our mother. Guess she forgot to tell Mother that it was good stuff, not just the usual costume junk."

George was quoted in the *Times* as saying that Sotheby's was rushing the ring into its summer sale as a last-minute addition on the following Thursday. It was too late for the ring to be included in the catalog, but they were printing a special insert, and he was sure all the media attention would bring in the right buyer. Sotheby's was indeed publicizing the ring with impressive zeal, calling it a lost treasure of English jewels, found in a "dusty, moldering mansion outside Philadelphia," which irked Hugh a bit. On a plus note, he and Jimmy were going to be interviewed the following day for the *Today Show*, and even that bible of excellent news, *People*, had called them.

At noon, Holly, Joe, and I met outside on the patio at Gianni's, where Holly shocked me by ordering the Bolognese pasta.

"I'm eating carbs today," she said, crossing her perfectly tanned legs. "You almost getting killed made me realize that I should eat carbs at least once a week. Plus I need to keep up my strength to follow all the news with the Bests' ring, and this budding romance between Sophie and Joe, and whatever's going on with you and that vet. Not to mention Mike Woodford."

"It's a lot of information," I agreed. "But I'm done with Mike. I really like John."

"I think Mike is really cute," Holly told us. "And, there's something that makes him even cuter. I had coffee with Honey this morning, who's obviously devastated that her best friend is a homicidal maniac."

Holly paused for effect. "Honey told me that Mike is actually her nephew, which is why he lives in that cottage at Sanderson. And when Honey dies, Mike inherits Sanderson, all three hundred acres and the huge house."

I WOULDN'T GO so far as to say I actually fainted when Holly told me this, but my vision got blurry and I teetered on the edge of consciousness. Holly didn't seem to notice, but rattled on about Honey and Mike for a few minutes, while I recovered myself and Joe and I listened raptly to these nuggets of Potts family lore.

It seemed Honey had a younger sister who'd gone away to college in the sixties to Johns Hopkins in Baltimore, married her geology professor, an older man named Roger Woodford, and never came back to Sanderson, except for the occasional visit at Thanksgiving, when Honey's parents would first berate her for marrying an academic, and then for not moving back to the family compound. The sister had one son, Mike, who Honey had always had a soft spot for.

"Honey says that Mike always had the Potts passion for cows," Holly told me, sipping a frosty glass of wine. "So Honey got him to move up here last year, and she's grooming him to take over Sanderson one day. Actually, I was thinking of asking Honey if she'd fix me up with Mike," added Holly casually.

What? I thought my brain would rocket straight out of the top of my head. I'm usually never jealous of Holly, but I'm only human. If she took her closets brimming with Chanel and her Ellsworth Kelly paintings and her piles of jewelry and moved to Sanderson with Mike, this would be truly unfair. She already had a gorgeous house and nice husband. I liked John more than Mike—I was pretty sure—but this was going too far.

"But then I realized that Mike's more your type," Holly added serenely to me, twirling her pasta on a silver fork. "He's got that burly carpenter look you always go for. And he's kind of hairy. Plus I'm getting back together with Howard. He convinced me that he didn't have an affair. He took a lie detector test in my lawyer's office yesterday about whether he slept with that bartender, and he passed."

My brain unswelled. I felt really happy for Holly, and

not just because I didn't want her to have barn sex with Mike, or marry him and move into Sanderson.

"That's great!" I told her sincerely. "I'm really happy for you and Howard."

"Finally!" said Joe, looking relieved. "Howard can move out of the city and in with you. I'm starting to feel like a surly teenager living in your guest room. I'm going back to my own apartment." He blushed. "At least until I figure out what's happening with me and Sophie."

"So are you going to keep making out with Mike, or go for the veterinarian?" Holly asked me. "Mike would be perfect for you. He's even been to Thailand. Honey told me he loves to travel and has been all over the world. All the guys you date love Thailand."

"It's funny you should mention that," I said, "because I don't want to date guys who backpack through Thailand anymore, and I think that rules out Mike."

"Maybe he's done with his Thai beach fantasy," Joe said. "People change. Look at me. If you told me a month ago that I'd be interested in the ex-wife of a Mafia guy, I'd have laughed my head off. Truth is, I kind of like Sophie."

I was happy for Joe, but was feeling more confused than ever. John was so handsome, kind, and reliable that he was doing a great job of making me forget—almost—about Mike's amazingly good soap smell and great arms. I sighed, and tried to enjoy the great lunch and the pretty patio setting at Gianni's. I didn't need to figure this out today. I was just happy to be alive, and nowhere near a koi pond.

Chapter 22

ON THE MORNING of Holly's housewarming—which was also Holly and Howard's Getting-Back-Together Party—my cell phone rang as Waffles and I were finishing up with some customers. It was the Thursday after Mariellen had tried to kill me and the Bests, and in the interim, I'd finally had a chance to go to the antiques markets and restock the store with some pretty new chairs, tables, silver, and framed prints. It was almost lunchtime now, and I'd been waiting for this call all morning: It was George, who was with the Bests at the jewelry auction in New York.

"We're all done here," he said in a jaunty, triumphant tone. "I just stepped outside with the Bests to call you. They wanted you to be the first to know that the ring sold to an anonymous buyer." I could hear car horns honking, bus gears crashing, and other New York City ambient noise around him.

"And I'm bringing the Bests home now," George continued. "With their check for $2.8 million."

WHEN JOHN, THE Bests, and I got to Holly's house that night at seven-thirty, a reggae band was playing over by the pool, delicious Italian aromas were wafting from several catering trucks parked behind her garage, and as soon as we rounded the corner, it was apparent that the Colketts had gone absolutely nuts with roses, hydrangeas, and ranunculus, all in varying shades of pink, and had set up about a thousand votive candles along the pool. Flowers floated on the pool's surface, and the Colketts had brought in dozens of pink cotton embroidered pillows, which covered every available lounge chair and chaise. There were Indian-print pink tablecloths thrown over cocktail tables, and a candlelit bar at the side of the pool, and a buffet of crusty bread, cheeses, olives, and—my stomach leaped with joy—shrimp! The food, of course, was catered by Gianni.

"What a spread!" said Jimmy admiringly. "Now that we're rich, we should throw a shindig like this."

"We aren't rich," said Hugh admonishingly. "We have to pay a percentage to Sotheby's, and the house is going to need a ton of repairs, and then there are taxes—"

"Can't you enjoy one fucking thing in life?" shouted Jimmy. "I told you, go ahead and get the condo in Florida! Now leave me alone. I'm getting a drink."

"You two are so cute," Holly said, floating over in a white silk minidress. "Still bickering. It's like me and Howard. We fight, but we adore each other."

"I don't think it's the same kind of relationship," Jimmy informed her grumpily, heading for the bar.

I looked around but didn't see Howard anywhere. In the week since Howard and Holly had reconciled, Joe had taken his former guest room and swiftly turned it into a specially vented, cigar lounge/media center for Howard. It was now painted a glossy dark grey and held leather furniture, carved bookcases, and a massive flat-screen TV. Holly and Joe hated the room, obviously, but Howard liked it.

"Where's Howard?" I asked Holly.

"He's in his cave," said Holly, with an airy wave of her hand. "Don't worry, he'll be out once the steak and personally-handmade-by-Gianni gnocchi are served." In the candlelight, something flashed on her right hand. It was large but delicate, intricately made, and looked familiar.

"Is that the *Bests' ring*?" I asked her.

She nodded in a blasé way.

"Howard was the silent bidder at the auction. He got it to celebrate our not getting divorced," she said. "Plus he thought it would be nice for the Bests if it stayed close to home, so he had it picked up and driven down here this afternoon. You can borrow it anytime. It's insured!"

"That's amazing. I'd love to borrow it," I told her, though honestly, I don't think I'd really want the responsibility of wearing that ring again. George is right. My house and my store have flimsy locks.

"I'll go say hi to Howard," John told me. "He's beaten me three times in the club tennis tournament, but since I won this year, I'm ready to be friends with the guy."

As John disappeared inside, Holly told me that she and Howard were heading down for an off-season trip to Palm Beach the following week. "We're going to meet up with Channing and Jessica about their new restaurant. We might want to become investors," she said.

"Palm Beach?" shrieked a shrill, small voice behind me. "I love Palm Beach!"

Sophie and Joe stood there, holding hands, while Bootsie brought up the rear. I saw Bootsie's husband Will veer off to the house, doubtless headed for the man-room.

"We should go to Palm Beach, too, honey bunny," Sophie said to Joe.

"Er, that might be fun." Joe hesitated. "Let's go get some cheese," he said, steering Sophie, in a dark purple floor-length gown that could only have been designed by Donatella Versace, over to the food. I guess he hadn't purged all the purple from Sophie just yet.

"I need more information on the ring for a story in the paper," Bootsie said to Holly, whipping out a notepad. "In fact, I should probably wear it tonight, just so I can write about it authoritatively."

"Okay," said Holly cheerfully, sliding the bauble off her right ring finger and handing it over to Bootsie. "I need to go tell the Colketts to move the candles, because I think Sophie's dress just caught on fire. Joe threw his drink on it, though, so she's fine. Plus I just saw Honey Potts arrive.

"Oh, look, Kristin," added Holly, as she waved to Mrs. Potts. "Mike's here, too."

"How are you?" said Mike, handing me a glass of wine. Since everyone else was either inside in the cigar lounge, or helping Sophie pluck pieces of burnt hem from her dress, we were alone by the bar.

I gulped. Mike had on a blue shirt tonight, sleeves rolled up, and looked even more tanned and scruffed than he had when I'd last seen him at his cottage.

"I heard you had a rough time with Mrs. Merriwether," he added. I looked at him thoughtfully. I guess I could picture him living in the manor house at Sanderson, though he really seemed more the cottage type.

"I'm doing great," I said, truthfully. "Everything's good at the store, and I think it's going to be a quiet summer. How are you?"

"I'm going away for a couple of months," Mike told me, leaning against a pillar on Holly's patio. "You should think about visiting me. I'll be in T—"

My ears went numb, and I stopped listening. I knew it!

I knew he'd go back to Thailand. The *Lonely Planet Guide* flashed in my mind, and I silently thanked the stars that I'd met John. Mike might be secretly rich and smell good, but this was too much. I recovered myself, and answered Mike.

"Thanks," I said, "but I won't have time to fly to Thailand this summer. Have a great time, though."

"No, I'm not going to Thailand," said Mike patiently. "I'm going to *Tuscany*. For two months. Meeting with some Italian bovine breeders, and drinking some wine. I rented a farmhouse."

"A farmhouse in Italy?" said John, appearing at my elbow. "Hey, Mike, how's it going?" he said, shaking Mike's hand. "Tuscany sounds like a great place to spend the summer," he added. "Maybe Kristin and I can come visit you there. I was planning to ask her if she'd like to go Italy with me in August."

I looked at John, surprised and pleased. I would *love* to go to Tuscany with John. Then again, I wouldn't mind going with Mike, either.

"Toscana?" said Chef Gianni, who'd fled the sweltering food trucks, and was out in his chef whites, mingling with guests, leaning on a cane and limping along with support from the Olivia Munn girl from his restaurant. Apparently, he was getting over Jessica's departure to Palm Beach. "I too will be in Toscana this summer," said the chef.

"Me too!" said Sophie, whose dress had been extinguished, and who looked none the worse for wear. "I need a Versace fix. Joe and I are gonna make it over, for sure!"

"Then that's that," said Holly, who had appeared with Howard in tow. "Tuscany in August. It's the perfect place to wear my new ring. Howard and I will meet you all there."

**Stay tuned for the next installment of
the Killer WASPs Mysteries
On sale March 2015 from Witness Impulse!**

About the Author

AMY KORMAN is a former senior editor and staff writer for *Philadelphia Magazine*, and author of *Frommer's Philadelphia and the Amish Country*. She has written for *Town & Country*, *House Beautiful*, *Men's Health*, and *Cosmopolitan*. She lives in Pennsylvania with her family and their basset hound, Murphy. *Killer WASPs* is her first novel.

Visit *www.AuthorTracker.com* for exclusive information on your favorite HarperCollins authors.